AROUND HIM, PINNED TO THE MAHOGANY WALLS, WERE ARTICLES AND REPORTS FROM ALL THE NEWSPAPERS SPECIFICALLY REFERRING TO AFFAIRS AT NUMBER TEN ...

There were photos of the youngest Prime Minister of the century, several of them. In fact, the eyes seemed to follow him about ...

'And I've got my eye on you, too, fella,' Dillon said softly.

The things that intrigued him were the constant daily meetings of the British War Cabinet at Number Ten. All those bastards, all together in the same spot. What a target. Brighton all over again and that affair had come close to taking out the entire British Government. But Number Ten as a target? That didn't seem possible ... There were footsteps on the deck overhead. He opened a drawer in the table casually revealing a Smith & Wesson .38 revolver ...

JACK HIGGINS

EYE OF THE STORM

A SIGNET BOOK

SIGNET

Published by the Penguin Group
Penguin Books Ltd, 27 Wrights Lane, London W8 5TZ, England
Penguin Books USA Inc., 375 Hudson Street, New York, New York 10014, USA
Penguin Books Australia Ltd, Ringwood, Victoria, Australia
Penguin Books Canada Ltd, 10 Alcorn Avenue, Toronto, Ontario, Canada M4V 3B2
Penguin Books (NZ) Ltd, 182–190 Wairau Road, Auckland 10, New Zealand

Penguin Books Ltd, Registered Offices: Harmondsworth, Middlesex, England

First published by Chapmans 1992
Published in Signet 1993
5 7 9 10 8 6 4 ˙

Copyright © Jack Higgins, 1992
All rights reserved

The moral right of the author has been asserted

Printed in England by Clays Ltd, St Ives plc

In memory of my grandfather
Robert Bell, M M
Gallant Soldier

The winds of heaven are blowing.
Implement all that is on the table.
May God be with you.

Coded message, Iraq Radio, Baghdad
January 1991

The mortar attack on Number Ten Downing Street when the War Cabinet was meeting at 10.00 a.m. on Thursday, 7 February 1991, is now a matter of history. It has never been satisfactorily explained. Perhaps it went something like this . . .

ONE

It was just before dark as Dillon emerged from the alley and paused on the corner. Rain drifted across the Seine in a flurry of snow, sleet mixed with it, and it was cold, even for January in Paris. He wore a reefer coat, peaked cap, jeans and boots, just another sailor off one of the barges working the river, which he very definitely was not.

He lit a cigarette in cupped hands and stayed there for a moment in the shadows, looking across the cobbled square at the lights of the small café on the other side. After a while he dropped the cigarette, thrust his hands deep in his pockets and started across.

In the darkness of the entrance two men waited, watching his progress. One of them whispered, 'That must be him.'

He made a move. The other held him back. 'No, wait till he's inside.'

Dillon, his senses sharpened by years of entirely the wrong kind of living, was aware of them, but gave no sign. He paused at the entrance, slipped his left hand under the reefer coat to check that the Walther PPK was securely tucked into the waistband of his jeans against the small of his back, then he opened the door and went in.

It was typical of the sort of place to be found on that part of the river: half a dozen tables with chairs, a zinc-topped bar, bottles lined against a cracked mirror behind it. The entrance to the rear was masked by a bead curtain.

The barman, a very old man with a grey moustache, wore an alpaca coat, the sleeves frayed at the cuffs, and there was no collar to his shirt. He put down the magazine he was reading and got up from the stool.

'Monsieur?'

Dillon unbuttoned his reefer coat and put his cap on the bar, a small man, no more than five feet five, with fair hair and eyes that seemed to the barman to be of no particular colour at all except for the fact that they were the coldest the old man had ever looked into. He shivered, unaccountably afraid, and then Dillon smiled. The change was astonishing, suddenly nothing but warmth there and immense charm. His French, when he spoke, was perfect.

'Would there be such a thing as half a bottle of champagne in the house?'

The old man stared at him in astonishment. 'Champagne? You must be joking, monsieur. I have two kinds of wine only. One is red and the other white.'

He placed a bottle of each on the bar. It was stuff of such poor quality that the bottles had screw tops instead of corks.

'All right,' Dillon said. 'The white it is. Give me a glass.'

He put his cap back on, went and sat at a table against the wall from where he could see both the entrance and the curtained doorway. He got the bottle open, poured some of the wine into the glass and tried it.

He said to the barman, 'And what vintage would this be, last week's?'

'Monsieur?' The old man looked bewildered.

'Never mind.' Dillon lit another cigarette, sat back and waited.

2

The man who stood closest to the curtain, peering through, was in his mid-fifties, of medium height with a slightly decadent look to his face, the fur collar of his dark overcoat turned up against the cold. He looked like a prosperous businessman right down to the gold Rolex on his left wrist, which in a way he was as a senior commercial attaché at the Soviet Embassy in Paris. He was also a colonel in the KGB, one Josef Makeev.

The younger, dark-haired man in the expensive vicuna overcoat who peered over his shoulder was called Michael Aroun. He whispered in French, 'This is ridiculous. He can't be our man. He looks like nothing.'

'A serious mistake many people have made, Michael,' Makeev said. 'Now wait and see.'

The bell tinkled as the outer door swung open, rain blowing in and the two men entered who had been waiting in the doorway as Dillon crossed the square. One of them was over six feet tall, bearded, an ugly scar running into the right eye. The other was much smaller and they were dressed in reefer coats and denims. They looked exactly what they were, trouble.

They stood at the bar and the old man looked worried. 'No trouble,' the younger one said. 'We only want a drink.'

The big man turned and looked at Dillon. 'It seems as if we've got one right here.' He crossed to the table, picked up Dillon's glass and drank from it. 'Our friend doesn't mind, do you?'

Without getting out of his chair Dillon raised his left foot and stamped downwards against the bearded man's kneecap. The man went down with a choked cry, grabbing at the table and Dillon stood. The bearded man tried to pull himself up and sank into one of the chairs. His friend took a hand from his pocket, springing the blade of a gutting knife and Dillon's left hand came up holding the Walther PPK.

3

'On the bar. Christ, you never learn, people like you, do you? Now get this piece of dung on his feet and out of here while I'm still in a good mood. You'll need the casualty department of the nearest hospital, by the way. I seem to have dislodged his kneecap.'

The small man went to his friend and struggled to get him on his feet. They stood there for a moment, the bearded man's face twisted in agony. Dillon went and opened the door, the rain pouring relentlessly down outside.

As they lurched past him, he said, 'Have a good night,' and closed the door.

Still holding the Walther in his left hand, he lit a cigarette using a match from the stand on the bar and smiled at the old barman who looked terrified. 'Don't worry, Dad, not your problem.' Then he leaned against the bar and called in English, 'All right, Makeev, I know you're there so let's be having you.'

The curtain parted and Makeev and Aroun stepped through.

'My dear Sean, it's good to see you again.'

'And aren't you the wonder of the world?' Dillon said, just the trace of an Ulster accent in his voice. 'One minute trying to stitch me up, the next all sweetness and light.'

'It was necessary, Sean,' Makeev said. 'I needed to make a point to my friend here. Let me introduce you.'

'No need,' Dillon told him. 'I've seen his picture often enough. If it's not on the financial pages it's usually in the society magazines. Michael Aroun, isn't it? The man with all the money in the world.'

'Not quite all, Mr Dillon.' Aroun put a hand out.

Dillon ignored it. 'We'll skip the courtesies, my old son, while you tell whoever is standing on the other side of that curtain to come out.'

'Rashid, do as he says,' Aroun called, and said to Dillon, 'It's only my aide.'

4

The young man who stepped through had a dark, watchful face and wore a leather car coat. the collar turned up, his hands thrust deep in the pockets.

Dillon knew a professional when he saw one. 'Plain view.' He motioned with the Walther. Rashid actually smiled and took his hands from his pockets. 'Good,' Dillon said. 'I'll be on my way then.'

He turned and got the door open. Makeev said, 'Sean, be reasonable. We only want to talk. A job, Sean.'

'Sorry, Makeev, but I don't like the way you do business.'

'Not even for a million, Mr Dillon?' Michael Aroun said.

Dillon paused and turned to look at him calmly, then smiled, again with enormous charm. 'Would that be in pounds or dollars, Mr Aroun?' he asked and walked out into the rain.

As the door banged Aroun said, 'We've lost him.'

'Not at all,' Makeev said. 'A strange one this, believe me.' He turned to Rashid. 'You have your portable phone?'

'Yes, Colonel.'

'Good. Get after him. Stick to him like glue. When he settles, phone me. We'll be at the Avenue Victor Hugo.'

Rashid didn't say a word, simply went. Aroun took out his wallet and extracted a thousand-franc note which he placed on the bar. He said to the barman who was looking totally bewildered, 'We're very grateful,' then turned and followed Makeev out.

As he slid behind the wheel of the black Mercedes saloon, he said to the Russian, 'He never even hesitated back there.'

'A remarkable man, Sean Dillon,' Makeev said as they drove away. 'He first picked up a gun for the IRA in nineteen seventy-one. Twenty years, Michael, twenty years and he hasn't seen the inside of a cell once. He was involved in the Mountbatten business. Then he became too hot for his own people to handle so he moved to Europe. As I told you, he's worked for everyone. The PLO, the Red Brigade in Germany in the old days. The Basque national movement, ETA. He killed a Spanish general for them.'

'And the KGB?'

'But of course. He's worked for us on many occasions. We always use the best and Sean Dillon is exactly that. He speaks English and Irish, not that that bothers you, fluent French and German, reasonable Arabic, Italian and Russian.'

'And no one has ever caught him in twenty years. How could anyone be that lucky?'

'Because he has the most extraordinary gift for acting, my friend. A genius, you might say. As a young boy his father took him from Belfast to London to live, where he was awarded a scholarship to the Royal Academy of Dramatic Art. He even worked for the National Theatre when he was nineteen or twenty. I have never known anyone who can change personality and appearance so much just by body language. Make-up seldom enters into it, although I admit that it helps when he wants. He's a legend that the security services of most countries keep quiet about because they can't put a face to him so they don't know what they're looking for.'

'What about the British? After all, they must be the experts where the IRA are concerned.'

'No, not even the British. As I said, he's never been arrested, not once, and unlike many of his IRA friends, he never courted media publicity. I doubt if there's a photo of him anywhere except for the odd boyhood snap.'

'What about when he was an actor?'

'Perhaps, but that was twenty years ago, Michael.'

'And you think he might undertake this business if I offer him enough money?'

'No, money alone has never been enough for this man. It always has to be the job itself where Dillon is concerned. How can I put it? How interesting it is. This is a man to

6

whom acting was everything. What we are offering him is a new part. The theatre of the street perhaps, but still acting.' He smiled as the Mercedes joined the traffic moving around the Arc de Triomphe. 'Let's wait and see. Wait until we hear from Rashid.'

At that moment, Captain Ali Rashid was by the Seine at the end of a small pier jutting out into the river. The rain was falling very heavily, still plenty of sleet in it. The floodlights were on at Notre Dame and the effect was of something seen partially through a net curtain. He watched Dillon turn along the narrow pier to the building on stilts at the far end, waited until he went in and followed him.

The place was quite old and built of wood, barges and boats of various kinds moored all around. The sign over the door said *Le Chat Noir*. He peered through the window cautiously. There was a bar and several tables just like the other place. The only difference was that people were eating. There was even a man sitting on a stool against the wall playing an accordion. All very Parisian. Dillon was standing at the bar speaking to a young woman.

Rashid moved back, walked to the end of the pier, paused by the rail in the shelter of a small terrace and dialled the number of Aroun's house in the Avenue Victor Hugo on his portable phone.

There was a slight click as the Walther was cocked and Dillon rammed the muzzle rather painfully into his right ear. 'Now then, son, a few answers,' he demanded. 'Who are you?'

'My name is Rashid,' the young man said. 'Ali Rashid.'

'What are you then? PLO?'

'No, Mr Dillon. I'm a captain in the Iraqi Army, assigned to protect Mr Aroun.'

'And Makeev and the KGB?'

'Let's just say he's on our side.'

'The way things are going in the Gulf you need somebody on your side, my old son.' There was the faint sound of a voice from the portable phone. 'Go on, answer him.'

Makeev said, 'Rashid, where is he?'

'Right here, outside a café on the river near Notre Dame,' Rashid told him. 'With the muzzle of his Walther well into my ear.'

'Put him on,' Makeev ordered.

Rashid handed the phone to Dillon who said, 'Now then, you old sod.'

'A million, Sean. Pounds if you prefer that currency.'

'And what would I have to be doing for all that money?'

'The job of a lifetime. Let Rashid bring you round here and we'll discuss it.'

'I don't think so,' Dillon said. 'I think what I'd really like is for you to get your arse into gear and come and pick us up yourself.'

'Of course,' Makeev said. 'Where are you?'

'The Left Bank opposite Notre Dame. A little pub on a pier called *Le Chat Noir*. We'll be waiting.'

He slipped the Walther into his pocket and handed the phone to Rashid who said, 'He's coming then?'

'Of course he is.' Dillon smiled. 'Now let's you and me go inside and have ourselves a drink in comfort.'

In the sitting room on the first floor of the house in the Avenue Victor Hugo overlooking the Bois de Boulogne, Josef Makeev put down the phone and moved to the couch where his overcoat was.

'Was that Rashid?' Aroun demanded.

'Yes. He's with Dillon now at a place on the river. I'm going to get them.'

8

'I'll come with you.'

Makeev pulled on his coat. 'No need, Michael. You hold the fort. We won't be long.'

He went out. Aroun took a cigarette from a silver box and lit it, then he turned on the television. He was halfway into the news. There was direct coverage from Baghdad, Tornado fighter bombers of the British Royal Air Force attacking at low level. It made him bitterly angry. He switched off, poured himself a brandy and went and sat by the window.

Michael Aroun was forty years of age and a remarkable man by any standards. Born in Baghdad of a French mother and an Iraqi father who was an army officer, he'd had a maternal grandmother who was American. Through her, his mother had inherited ten million dollars and a number of oil leases in Texas.

She had died the year Aroun had graduated from Harvard Law School leaving everything to her son because his father, retired as a general from the Iraqi Army, was happy to spend his later years at the old family house in Baghdad with his books.

Like most great businessmen, Aroun had no academic training in the field. He knew nothing of financial planning or business administration. His favourite saying, one much quoted, was: When I need a new accountant, I buy a new accountant.

His friendship with Saddam Hussein had been a natural development from the fact that the Iraqi President had been greatly supported in his early days in politics by Aroun's father, who was also an important member of the Baath Party. It had placed Aroun in a privileged position as regards the development of his country's oilfields, brought him riches beyond calculation.

After the first billion you stopped counting, another favourite saying. And now he was faced with disaster. Not only the promised riches of the Kuwait oilfields snatched from him, but that portion of his wealth which stemmed from Iraq dried up, finished as a result of the Coalition's massive airstrikes which had devastated his country since 17 January.

He was no fool. He knew that the game was over; should probably have never started, and that Saddam Hussein's dream was already finished. As a businessman he played the percentages and that didn't offer Iraq too much of a chance in the ground war that must eventually come.

He was far from ruined in personal terms. He had oil interests still in the USA and the fact that he was a French as well as an Iraqi citizen gave Washington a problem. Then there was his shipping empire and vast quantities of real estate in various capital cities around the world. But that wasn't the point. He was angry when he switched on the television and saw what was happening in Baghdad each night for, surprising in one so self-centred, he was a patriot. There was also the fact, infinitely more important, that his father had been killed in a bombing raid on the third night of the air war.

And there was a great secret in his life, for in August, shortly after the invasion of Kuwait by Iraqi forces, Aroun had been sent for by Saddam Hussein himself. Sitting here by the French window, a glass of brandy in one hand, rain slanting across the terrace, he gazed out across the Bois de Boulogne in the evening light and remembered that meeting.

There was an air-raid practice in progress as he was driven in an army Land Rover through the streets of Baghdad, darkness everywhere. The driver was a young intelligence captain named Rashid who he had met before, one of the new breed, trained by the British at Sandhurst. Aroun gave him an English cigarette and took one himself.

10

'What do you think, will they make some sort of move?'

'The Americans and Brits?' Rashid was being careful. 'Who knows? They're certainly reacting. President Bush seems to be taking a hard line.'

'No, you're mistaken,' Aroun said. 'I've met the man face to face twice now at White House functions. He's what our American friends call a nice guy. There's no steel there at all.'

Rashid shrugged. 'I'm a simple man, Mr Aroun, a soldier, and perhaps I see things simply. Here is a man, a navy combat pilot at twenty, who saw a great deal of active service, who was shot down over the Sea of Japan and survived to be awarded the Distinguished Flying Cross. I would not underestimate such a man.'

Aroun frowned. 'Come on, my friend, the Americans aren't going to come halfway round the world with an army to protect one little Arab state.'

'Isn't that exactly what the British did in the Falklands War?' Rashid reminded him. 'They never expected such a reaction in Argentina. Of course they had Thatcher's determination behind them, the Brits, I mean.'

'Damned woman,' Aroun said and leaned back as they went in through the gate of the presidential palace, feeling suddenly depressed.

He followed Rashid along corridors of marble splendour, the young officer leading the way, a torch in one hand. It was a strange, rather eerie experience, following that small pool of light on the floor, their footfalls echoing. There was a sentry on each side of the ornate door they finally halted before. Rashid opened it and they went in.

11

Saddam Hussein was alone, sitting in uniform at a large desk, the only light a shaded lamp. He was writing, slowly and carefully, looked up and smiled, putting down his pen.

'Michael.' He came round the desk and embraced Aroun like a brother. 'Your father? He is well?'

'In excellent health, my President.'

'Give him my respects. You look well, Michael. Paris suits you.' He smiled again. 'Smoke if you want. I know you like to. The doctors have unfortunately had to tell me to cut it out or else.'

He sat down behind the desk again and Aroun sat opposite, aware of Rashid against the wall in the darkness. 'Paris was fine, but my place is here now in these difficult times.'

Saddam Hussein shook his head. 'Not true, Michael. I have soldiers in plenty, but few men such as you. You are rich, famous, accepted at the highest levels of society and government anywhere in the world. More than that, because of your beloved mother of blessed memory, you are not just an Iraqi, but also a French citizen. No, Michael, I want you in Paris.'

'But why, my President?' Aroun asked.

'Because one day I may require you to do a service for me and for your country that only you could perform.'

Aroun said, 'You can rely on me totally, you know that.'

Saddam Hussein got up and paced to the nearest window, opened the shutters and stepped onto the terrace. The all clear sounded mournfully across the city and lights began to appear here and there.

'I still hope our friends in America and Britain stay in their own backyard, but if not . . .' He shrugged. 'Then we may have to fight them in *their* own backyard. Remember, Michael, as the Prophet instructs us in the Koran, there is more truth in one sword than ten thousand words.' He paused and then carried on, still looking out across the city. 'One sniper in the darkness, Michael, British SAS or

12

Israeli, it doesn't really matter, but what a coup – the death of Saddam Hussein.'

'God forbid it,' Michael Aroun said.

Saddam turned to him. 'As God wills, Michael, in all things, but you see my point? The same would apply to Bush or the Thatcher woman. The proof that my arm reaches everywhere. The ultimate coup.' He turned. 'Would you be capable of arranging such a thing, if necessary?'

Aroun had never felt so excited in his life. 'I think so, my President. All things are possible, especially when sufficient money is involved. It would be my gift to you.'

'Good.' Saddam nodded. 'You will return to Paris immediately. Captain Rashid will accompany you. He will have details of certain codes we will be using in radio broadcasts, that sort of thing. The day may never come, Michael, but if it does . . .' He shrugged. 'We have friends in the right places.' He turned to Rashid. 'That KGB colonel at the Soviet Embassy in Paris?'

'Colonel Josef Makeev, my President.'

'Yes,' Saddam Hussein said to Aroun. 'Like many of his kind, not happy with the changes now taking place in Moscow. He will assist in any way he can. He's already expressed his willingness.' He embraced Aroun, again like a brother. 'Now go. I have work to do.'

The lights had still not come on in the palace and Aroun had stumbled out into the darkness of the corridor, following the beam of Rashid's torch.

Since his return to Paris he had got to know Makeev well, keeping their acquaintance, by design, purely on a social level, meeting mainly at various Embassy functions. And Saddam Hussein had been right. The Russian was very definitely on their side, only too willing to do anything that would cause problems for the United States or Great Britain.

The news from home, of course, had been bad. The build-up of such a gigantic army. Who could have expected it? And then in the early hours of 17 January the air war had begun. One bad thing after another and the ground attack still to come.

He poured himself another brandy, remembering his despairing rage at the news of his father's death. He'd never been religious by inclination, but he'd found a mosque in a Paris side street to pray in. Not that it had done any good. The feeling of impotence was like a living thing inside him and then came the morning when Ali Rashid had rushed into the great ornate sitting room, a notepad in one hand, his face pale and excited.

'It's come, Mr Aroun. The signal we've been waiting for. I just heard it on the radio transmitter from Baghdad.'

The winds of heaven are blowing. Implement all that is on the table. May God be with you.

Aroun had gazed at it in wonder, his hand trembling as he held the notepad, and his voice was hoarse when he said, 'The President was right. The day has come.'

'Exactly,' Rashid said. '*Implement all that is on the table.* We're in business. I'll get in touch with Makeev and arrange a meeting as soon as possible.'

Dillon stood at the French windows and peered out across the Avenue Victor Hugo to the Bois de Boulogne. He was whistling softly to himself, a strange eerie little tune.

'Now this must be what the house agents call a favoured location.'

'May I offer you a drink, Mr Dillon?'

'A glass of champagne wouldn't come amiss.'

'Have you a preference?' Aroun asked.

'Ah, the man who has everything,' Dillon said. 'All right, Krug would be fine, but non-vintage. I prefer the grape mix.'

'A man of taste, I see.' Aroun nodded to Rashid who opened a side door and went out.

Dillon, unbuttoning his reefer coat, took out a cigarette and lit it. 'So, you need my services this old fox tells me.' He nodded at Makeev who lounged against the fireplace warming himself. 'The job of a lifetime, he said and for a million pounds. Now what would I have to do for all that?'

Rashid entered quickly with the Krug in a bucket, three glasses on a tray. He put them on the table and started to open the bottle.

Aroun said, 'I'm not sure, but it would have to be something very special. Something to show the world that Saddam Hussein can strike anywhere.'

'He needs something, the poor old sod,' Dillon said cheerfully. 'Things aren't going too well.' As Rashid finished filling three glasses the Irishman added, 'And what's your trouble, son? Aren't you joining us?'

Rashid smiled and Aroun said, 'In spite of Winchester and Sandhurst, Mr Dillon, Captain Rashid remains a very Muslim Muslim. He does not touch alcohol.'

'Well, here's to you.' Dillon raised his glass. 'I respect a man with principles.'

'This would need to be big, Sean, no point in anything small. We're not talking blowing up five British Army paratroopers in Belfast,' Makeev said.

'Oh, it's Bush you want, is it?' Dillon smiled. 'The President of the United States flat on his back with a bullet in him?'

'Would that be so crazy?' Aroun demanded.

'It would be this time, son,' Dillon told him. 'George Bush has not just taken on Saddam Hussein, he's taken on the Arabs as a people. Oh, that's total rubbish of course, but it's the way a lot of Arab fanatics see it. Groups like Hizbollah, the PLO or the wild cards like the Wrath of Allah people. The sort who would happily strap a bomb to their waist and detonate it while the President reached out to shake just another hand in the crowd. I know these people. I know how their minds tick. I've helped train Hizbollah people in Beirut. I've worked for the PLO.'

'What you are saying is nobody can get near Bush at the moment?'

'Read your papers. Anybody who looks even slightly Arab is keeping off the streets these days in New York and Washington.'

'But you, Mr Dillon, do not look Arab to the slightest degree,' Aroun said. 'For one thing you have fair hair.'

'So did Lawrence of Arabia and he used to pass himself off as an Arab.' Dillon shook his head. 'President Bush has the finest security in the world, believe me. A ring of steel and in present circumstances he's going to stay home while this whole Gulf thing works through, mark my words.'

'What about their Secretary of State, James Baker?' Aroun said. 'He's been indulging in shuttle diplomacy throughout Europe.'

'Yes, but knowing when, that's the problem. You'll know he's been in London or Paris when he's already left and they show him on television. No, you can forget the Americans on this one.'

There was silence and Aroun looked glum. Makeev was the first to speak. 'Give me then the benefit of your professional expertise, Sean. Where does one find the weakest security, as regards national leaders?'

16

Dillon laughed out loud. 'Oh, I think your man here can answer that, Winchester and Sandhurst.'

Rashid smiled. 'He's right. The British are probably the best in the world at covert operations. The success of their Special Air Service Regiment speaks for itself, but in other areas . . .' He shook his head.

'Their first problem is bureaucracy,' Dillon told them. 'The British Security Service operates in two main sections. What most people still call MI5 and MI6. MI5, or DI5 to be pedantic, specialises in counter-espionage in Great Britain. The other lot operates abroad. Then you have Special Branch at Scotland Yard who have to be brought into the act to make any actual arrests. The Yard also has an anti-terrorist squad. Then there's army intelligence units galore. All life is there and they're all at each other's throats and that, gentlemen, is when mistakes begin to creep in.'

Rashid poured some more champagne into his glass. 'And you are saying that makes for bad security with their leaders? The Queen, for example?'

'Come on,' Dillon said. 'It's not all that many years ago that the Queen woke up in Buckingham Palace and found an intruder sitting on the bed. How long ago, six years, since the IRA almost got Margaret Thatcher and the entire British Cabinet at a Brighton hotel during the Tory Party Conference?' He put down his glass and lit another cigarette. 'The Brits are very old-fashioned. They like a policeman to wear a uniform so they know who he is and they don't like being told what to do and that applies to Cabinet Ministers who think nothing of strolling through the streets from their houses in Westminster to Parliament.'

'Fortunate for the rest of us,' Makeev said.

'Exactly,' Dillon said. 'They even have to go softly-softly on terrorists, up to a degree anyway, not like French intelligence. Jesus, if the lads in Action Service got their hands on me they'd have me spread out and my bollocks wired up for electricity before I knew what was happening. Mind you, even they are prone to the occasional error.'

'What do you mean?' Makeev demanded.

'Have you got a copy of the evening paper handy?'

'Certainly, I've been reading it,' Aroun said. 'Ali, on my desk.'

Rashid returned with a copy of *Paris Soir*. Dillon said, 'Page two. Read it out. You'll find it interesting.'

He helped himself to more champagne while Rashid read the item aloud. *'Mrs Margaret Thatcher, until recently Prime Minister of Britain, is staying overnight at Choisy as a guest of President Mitterrand. They are to have further talks in the morning. She leaves at two o'clock for an air force emergency field at Valenton where an RAF plane returns her to England.* Incredible, isn't it, that they could have allowed such a press release, but I guarantee the main London newspapers will carry that story also.'

There was a heavy silence and then Aroun said, 'You're not suggesting . . . ?'

Dillon said to Rashid, 'You must have some road maps handy. Get them.'

Rashid went out quickly. Makeev said, 'Good God, Sean, not even you . . .'

'Why not?' Dillon asked calmly and turned to Aroun. 'I mean, you want something big, a major coup? Would Margaret Thatcher do or are we just playing games here?'

Before Aroun could reply, Rashid came back with two or three road maps. He opened one out on the table and they looked at it, all except Makeev who stayed by the fire.

'There we are, Choisy,' Rashid said. 'Thirty miles from Paris and here is the air force field at Valenton only seven miles away.'

'Have you got a map of larger scale?'

'Yes.' Rashid unfolded one of the others.

'Good,' Dillon said. 'It's perfectly clear that only one country road links Choisy to Valenton and here, about three miles before the airfield, there's a railway crossing. Perfect.'

'For what?' Aroun demanded.

'An ambush. Look, I know how these things operate. There'll be one car, two at the most, and an escort. Maybe half a dozen CRS police on motorbikes.'

'My God!' Aroun whispered.

'Yes, well. He's got very little to do with it. It could work. Fast, very simple. What the Brits call a piece of cake.'

Aroun turned in appeal to Makeev who shrugged. 'He means it, Michael. You said this was what you wanted so make up your mind.'

Aroun took a deep breath and turned back to Dillon. 'All right.'

'Good,' Dillon said calmly. He reached for a pad and pencil on the table and wrote on it quickly. 'Those are the details of my numbered bank account in Zurich. You'll transfer one million pounds to it first thing in the morning.'

'In advance?' Rashid said. 'Isn't that expecting rather a lot?'

'No, my old son, it's you people who are expecting rather a lot and the rules have changed. On successful completion, I'll expect a further million.'

'Now look here,' Rashid started, but Aroun held up a hand.

'Fine, Mr Dillon, and cheap at the price. Now what can we do for you?'

'I need operating money. I presume a man like you keeps large supplies of the filthy stuff around the house?'

'Very large,' Aroun smiled. 'How much?'

'Can you manage dollars? Say twenty thousand?'

'Of course.' Aroun nodded to Rashid who went to the

far end of the room, swung a large oil painting to one side disclosing a wall safe which he started to open.

Makeev said, 'And what can I do?'

'The old warehouse in rue de Helier, the one we've used before. You've still got a key?'

'Of course.'

'Good. I've got most things I need stored there, but for this job I'd like a light machine gun. A tripod job. A Heckler & Koch or an M60. Anything like that will do.' He looked at his watch. 'Eight o'clock. I'd like it there by ten. All right?'

'Of course,' Makeev said again.

Rashid came back with a small briefcase. 'Twenty thousand. Hundred-dollar bills, I'm afraid.'

'Is there any way they could be traced?' Dillon asked.

'Impossible,' Aroun told him.

'Good. And I'll take the maps.'

He walked to the door, opened it and started down the curving staircase to the hall. Aroun, Rashid and Makeev followed him.

'But is this all, Mr Dillon?' Aroun said. 'Is there nothing more we can do for you? Won't you need help?'

'When I do, it comes from the criminal classes,' Dillon said. 'Honest crooks who do things for cash are usually more reliable than politically motivated zealots. Not always, but most of the time. Don't worry, you'll hear from me, one way or another. I'll be on my way then.'

Rashid got the door open. Rain and sleet drifted in and Dillon pulled on his cap. 'A dirty old night for it.'

'One thing, Mr Dillon,' Rashid said. 'What happens if things go wrong? I mean, you'll have your million in advance and we'll –'

'Have nothing? Don't give it a thought, me old son. I'll provide an alternative target. There's always the new British Prime Minister, this John Major. I presume his head on a plate would serve your boss back in Baghdad just as well.'

He smiled once, then stepped out into the rain and pulled the door shut behind him.

TWO

Dillon paused outside *Le Chat Noir* on the end of the small pier for the second time that night. It was almost deserted, a young man and woman at a corner table holding hands, a bottle of wine between them. The accordion was playing softly and the musician talked to the man behind the bar at the same time. They were the Jobert brothers, gangsters of the second rank in the Paris underworld. Their activities had been severely curtailed since Pierre, the one behind the bar, had lost his left leg in a car crash after an armed robbery three years previously.

As the door opened and Dillon entered, the other brother, Gaston, stopped playing. 'Ah, Monsieur Rocard, back already.'

'Gaston.' Dillon shook hands and turned to the barman. 'Pierre.'

'See, I still remember that little tune of yours, the Irish one.' Gaston played a few notes on the accordion.

'Good,' Dillon said. 'A true artist.'

Behind them the young couple got up and left. Pierre produced half a bottle of champagne from the bar fridge. 'Champagne as usual I presume, my friend? Nothing special, but we are poor men here.'

'You'll have me crying all over the bar,' Dillon said.

'And what may we do for you?' Pierre enquired.

'Oh, I just want to put a little business your way.' Dillon nodded at the door. 'It might be an idea if you closed.'

Gaston put his accordion on the bar, went and bolted the door and pulled down the blind. He returned and sat on his stool. 'Well, my friend?'

'This could be a big pay day for you boys.' Dillon opened the briefcase, took out one of the road maps and disclosed the stacks of hundred-dollar bills. 'Twenty thousand American. Ten now and ten on successful completion.'

'My God!' Gaston said in awe, but Pierre looked grim. 'And what would be expected for all this money?'

Dillon had always found it paid to stick as close to the truth as possible and he spread the road map out across the bar.

'I've been hired by the Union Corse,' he said, naming the most feared criminal organisation in France, 'to take care of a little problem. A matter of what you might term business rivalry.'

'Ah, I see,' Pierre said. 'And you are to eliminate the problem?'

'Exactly. The men concerned will be passing along this road here towards Valenton shortly after two o'clock tomorrow. I intend to take them out here at the railway crossing.'

'And how will this be accomplished?' Gaston asked.

'A very simple ambush. You two are still in the transport business, aren't you? Stolen cars, trucks?'

'You should know. You've bought from us on enough occasions,' Pierre told him.

'A couple of vans, that's not too much to expect, is it?'

'And then what?'

'We'll take a drive down to this place tonight.' He

23

glanced at his watch. 'Eleven o'clock from here. It'll only take an hour.'

Pierre shook his head. 'Look, this could be heavy. I'm getting too old for gunplay.'

'Wonderful,' Dillon said. 'How many did you kill when you were with the OAS?'

'I was younger then.'

'Well, it comes to us all, I suppose. No gunplay. You two will be in and out so quickly you won't know what's happening. A piece of cake.' He took several stacks of hundred-dollar bills from the briefcase and put them on the bar counter. 'Ten thousand. Do we deal?'

And greed, as usual, won the day as Pierre ran his hands over the money. 'Yes, my friend, I think we do.'

'Good. I'll be back at eleven then.' Dillon closed his briefcase, Gaston went and unlocked the door for him and the Irishman left.

Gaston closed the door and turned. 'What do you think?'

Pierre poured two cognacs. 'I think our friend Rocard is a very big liar.'

'But also a very dangerous man,' Gaston said. 'So what do we do?'

'Wait and see.' Pierre raised his glass. '*Salut.*'

Dillon walked all the way to the warehouse in rue de Helier, twisting from one street to another, melting into the darkness occasionally to check that he wasn't being followed. He had learned a long time ago that the problem with all revolutionary political groups was that they were riddled with factions and informers, a great truth where the IRA was concerned. Because of that, as he had indicated to Aroun, he preferred to use professional criminals whenever possible when help was needed. Honest crooks who did things for cash, that was the phrase he'd used. Unfortunately it didn't always hold true and there had been something in big Pierre's manner.

There was a small Judas gate set in the larger double doors of the warehouse. He unlocked it and stepped inside. There were two cars, a Renault saloon and a Ford Escort, and a police BMW motorcycle covered with a sheet. He checked that it was all right, then moved up the wooden stairs to the flat in the loft above. It was not his only home. He also had a barge on the river, but it was useful on occasions.

On the table in the small living room there was a canvas holdall with a note on top that simply said, *As ordered*. He smiled and unzipped it. Inside was a Kalashnikov PK machine gun, the latest model. Its tripod was folded, the barrel off for easy handling and there was a large box of belt cartridges, a similar box beside it. He opened a drawer in the sideboard, took out a folded sheet and put it in the holdall. He zipped it up again, checked the Walther in his waistband and went down the stairs, the holdall in one hand.

He locked the Judas and went along the street, excitement taking control as it always did. It was the best feeling in the world when the game was in play. He turned into the main street and a few minutes later, hailed a cab and told the driver to take him to *Le Chat Noir*.

They drove out of Paris in Renault vans, exactly the same except for the fact that one was black and the other white. Gaston led the way, Dillon beside him in the passenger seat, and Pierre followed. It was very cold, snow still mixed with the rain, although it wasn't lying. They talked very little, Dillon lying back in the seat eyes closed so that the Frenchman thought he was asleep.

25

Not far from Choisy, the van skidded and Gaston said, 'Christ almighty,' and wrestled with the wheel.

Dillon said, 'Easy, the wrong time to go in a ditch. Where are we?'

'Just past the turning to Choisy. Not long now.' Dillon sat up. The snow was covering the hedgerows but not the road. Gaston said, 'It's a pig of a night. Just look at it.'

'Think of all those lovely dollar bills,' Dillon told him. 'That should get you through.'

It stopped snowing, the sky cleared showing a half-moon, and below them at the bottom of the hill was the red light of the railway crossing. There was an old disused building of some sort at one side, its windows boarded up, a stretch of cobbles in front of it lightly powdered with snow.

'Pull in here,' Dillon said.

Gaston did as he was told and braked to a halt switching off the motor. Pierre came up in the white Renault, got down from behind the wheel awkwardly because of the false leg and joined them.

Dillon stood looking at the crossing a few yards away and nodded. 'Perfect. Give me the keys.'

Gaston did as he was told. The Irishman unlocked the rear door, disclosing the holdall. He unzipped it as they watched, took out the Kalashnikov, put the barrel in place expertly, then positioned it so that it pointed to the rear. He filled the ammunition box, threading the cartridge belt in place.

'That looks a real bastard,' Pierre said.

'Seven point two millimetre cartridges mixed with tracer and armour piercing,' Dillon said. 'It's a killer all right. Kalashnikov. I've seen one of these take a Land Rover full of British paratroopers to pieces.'

'Really,' Pierre said and as Gaston was about to speak, he put a warning hand on his arm. 'What's in the other box?'

'More ammunition.'

Dillon took out the sheet from the holdall, covered the machine gun, then locked the door. He got behind the driving wheel, started the engine and moved the van a few yards, positioned it so that the tail pointed at an angle towards the crossing. He got out and locked the door and clouds scudded across the moon and the rain started again, more snow in it now.

'So, you leave this here?' Pierre said. 'What if someone checks it?'

'What if they do?' Dillon knelt down at the offside rear tyre, took a knife from his pocket, sprang the blade and poked at the rim of the wheel. There was a hiss of air and the tyre went down rapidly.

Gaston nodded. 'Clever. Anyone gets curious, they'll just think a breakdown.'

'But what about us?' Pierre demanded. 'What do you expect?'

'Simple. Gaston turns up with the white Renault just after two this afternoon. You block the road at the crossing, not the railway track, just the road, get out, lock the door and leave it. Then get the hell out of there.' He turned to Pierre. 'You follow in a car, pick him up and straight back to Paris.'

'But what about you?' the big man demanded.

'I'll be already here, waiting in the van. I'll make my own way. Back to Paris now. You can drop me at *Le Chat Noir* and that's an end of it. You won't see me again.'

'And the rest of the money?' Pierre demanded as he got behind the Renault's wheel and Gaston and Dillon joined him.

'You'll get it, don't worry,' Dillon said. 'I always keep my word just as I expect others to keep theirs. A matter of honour, my friend. Now let's get moving.'

He closed his eyes again, leaned back. Pierre glanced at his brother, switched on the engine and drove away.

It was just on half-past one when they reached *Le Chat Noir*. There was a lock-up garage opposite the pub. Gaston opened the doors and Pierre drove in.

'I'll be off then,' Dillon said.

'You're not coming in?' the big man asked. 'Then Gaston can run you home.'

Dillon smiled. 'No one's ever taken me home in my life.'

He walked away, turning into a side street and Pierre said to his brother, 'After him and don't lose him.'

'But why?' Gaston demanded.

'Because I want to know where he's staying, that's why. It stinks, this thing, Gaston, like bad fish stinks, so get moving.'

Dillon moved rapidly from street to street, following his usual pattern, but Gaston, a thief since childhood and an expert in such matters, managed to stay on his trail, never too close. Dillon had intended returning to the warehouse in rue de Helier, but pausing on the corner of an alley to light a cigarette, he glanced back and could have sworn he saw a movement. He was right, for it was Gaston ducking into a doorway out of sight.

For Dillon, even the suspicion was enough. He'd had a feeling about Pierre all night, a bad feeling. He turned left, worked his way back to the river and walked along the pavement and past a row of trucks, their windscreens covered with snow. He came to a small hotel, the cheapest sort of place, the kind used by prostitutes or truckers stopping overnight, and went in.

The desk clerk was very old and wore an overcoat and

28

scarf against the cold. His eyes were wet. He put down his book and rubbed them. 'Monsieur?'

'I brought a load in from Dijon a couple of hours ago. Intended to drive back tonight, but the damn truck's giving trouble. I need a bed.'

'Thirty francs, monsieur.'

'You're kidding,' Dillon said. 'I'll be out of here at the crack of dawn.'

The old man shrugged. 'All right, you can have number eighteen on the second landing for twenty, but the bed hasn't been changed.'

'When does that happen, once a month?' Dillon took the key, gave him his twenty francs and went upstairs.

The room was as disgusting as he expected even in the diffused light from the landing. He closed the door, moved carefully through the darkness and looked out cautiously. There was a movement under a tree on the river side of the road. Gaston Jobert stepped out and hurried away along the pavement.

'Oh dear,' Dillon whispered, then lit a cigarette and went and lay on the bed and thought about it, staring up at the ceiling.

Pierre, sitting at the bar of *Le Chat Noir* waiting for his brother's return, was leafing through *Paris Soir* for want of something better to do when he noticed the item on Margaret Thatcher's meeting with Mitterrand. His stomach churned and he read the item again with horror. It was at that moment the door opened and Gaston hurried in.

'What a night. I'm frozen to the bone. Give me a cognac.'

'Here.' Pierre poured some into a glass. 'And you can read this interesting titbit in *Paris Soir* while you're drinking.'

29

Gaston did as he was told and suddenly choked on the cognac. 'My God, she's staying at Choisy.'

'And leaves from that old air force field at Valenton. Leaves Choisy at two o'clock. How long to get to that railway crossing? Ten minutes?'

'Oh, God, no,' Gaston said. 'We're done for. This is out of our league, Pierre. If this takes place, we'll have every cop in France on the streets.'

'But it isn't going to. I knew that bastard was bad news. Always something funny about him. You managed to follow him?'

'Yes, he doubled around the streets for a while, then ended up at that fleapit old François runs just along the river. I saw him through the window booking in.' He shivered. 'But what are we going to do?' He was almost sobbing. 'This is the end, Pierre. They'll lock us up and throw away the key.'

'No they won't,' Pierre told him. 'Not if we shop him, they won't. They'll be too grateful. Who knows, there might even be a reward in it. Now what's Inspector Savary's home number?'

'He'll be in bed.'

'Of course he will, you idiot, nicely tucked up with his old lady where all good detectives should be. We'll just have to wake him up.'

Inspector Jules Savary came awake cursing as the phone rang at his bedside. He was on his own, for his wife was spending a week in Lyon at her mother's. He'd had a long night. Two armed robberies and a sexual assault on a woman. He'd only just managed to get to sleep.

He picked up the phone. 'Savary here.'

'It's me, Inspector, Pierre Jobert.'

30

Savary glanced at the bedside clock. 'For Christ's sake, Jobert, it's two-thirty in the morning.'

'I know, Inspector, but I've got something special for you.'

'You always have, so it can wait till the morning.'

'I don't think so, Inspector. I'm offering to make you the most famous cop in France. The pinch of a lifetime.'

'Pull the other one,' Savary said.

'Margaret Thatcher. She's staying at Choisy tonight, leaves for Valenton at two? I can tell you all about the man who's going to see she never gets there.'

Jules Savary had never come awake so fast. 'Where are you, *Le Chat Noir*?'

'Yes,' Jobert told him.

'Half an hour.' Savary slammed down the phone, leapt out of bed and started to dress.

It was at exactly the same moment that Dillon decided to move on. The fact that Gaston had followed him didn't necessarily mean anything more than the fact that the brothers were anxious to know more about him. On the other hand . . .

He left, locking the door, found the backstairs and descended cautiously. There was a door at the bottom which opened easily enough and gave access to a yard at the rear. An alley brought him to the main road. He crossed, walked along a line of parked trucks, chose one about fifty yards from the hotel, but giving him a good view. He got his knife out, worked away at the top of the passenger window. After a while it gave so that he could get his fingers in and exert pressure. A minute later he was inside. Better not to smoke so he sat back, collar up, hands in pockets and waited. It was half-past three when the four unmarked cars eased up to the

31

hotel. Eight men got out, none in uniform, which was interesting.

'Action Service, or I miss my guess,' Dillon said softly.

Gaston Jobert got out of the rear car and stood talking to them for a moment then they all moved into the hotel. Dillon wasn't angry, just pleased that he'd got it right. He left the truck, crossed the road to the shelter of the nearest alley and started to walk to the warehouse in rue de Helier.

The French secret service, notorious for years as the SDECE has had its name changed to Direction Générale de la Sécurité Extérieure, DGSE, under the Mitterrand government in an attempt to improve the image of a shady and ruthless organisation with a reputation for stopping at nothing. Having said that, measured by results, few intelligence organisations in the world are so efficient.

The service, as in the old days, was still divided into five sections and many departments, the most famous, or infamous depending on your point of view, being Section Five, more commonly known as Action Service, the department responsible for the smashing of the OAS.

Colonel Max Hernu had been involved in all that, had hunted the OAS down as ruthlessly as anyone in spite of having served as a paratrooper in both Indo-China and Algeria. He was sixty-one years of age, an elegant, white-haired man who now sat at his desk in the office on the first floor of DGSE's headquarters on the Boulevard Mortier. It was just before five o'clock and Hernu, wearing horn-rimmed reading glasses, studied the report in front of him. He had been staying the night at his country cottage forty miles out of Paris and had only just arrived. Inspector Savary watched respectfully.

Hernu removed his glasses. 'I loathe this time of the

morning. Takes me back to Dien Bien Phu and the waiting for the end. Pour me another coffee, will you?'

Savary took his cup, went to the electric pot on the stand and poured the coffee, strong and black. 'What do you think, sir?'

'These Jobert brothers, you believe they're telling us everything?'

'Absolutely, sir, I've known them for years. Big Pierre was OAS which he thinks gives him class, but they're second-rate hoods really. They do well in stolen cars.'

'So this would be out of their league?'

'Very definitely. They've admitted to me that they've sold this man Rocard cars in the past.'

'Of the hot variety?'

'Yes, sir.'

'Of course they are telling the truth. The ten thousand dollars speak for them there. But this man Rocard, you're an experienced copper, Inspector. How many years on the street?'

'Fifteen, sir.'

'Give me your opinion.'

'His physical description is interesting because according to the Jobert boys, there isn't one. He's small, no more than one sixty-five. No discernible colour to the eyes, fair hair. Gaston says the first time they met him he thought he was a nothing and then he apparently half-killed some guy twice his size in the bar in about five seconds flat.'

'Go on.' Hernu lit a cigarette.

'Pierre says his French is too perfect.'

'What does he mean by that?'

'He doesn't know. It's just that he always felt that there was something wrong.'

'That he wasn't French?'

'Exactly. Two facts of interest there. He's always whistling a funny little tune. Gaston picked it up because he plays accordion. He says Rocard told him once that it was Irish.'

'Now that is interesting.'

'A further point. When he was assembling the machine gun in the back of the Renault at Valenton he told the boys it was a Kalashnikov. Not just bullets. Tracer, armour piercing, the lot. He said he'd seen one take out a Land Rover full of British paratroopers. Pierre didn't like to ask him where.'

'So, you smell IRA here, Inspector? And what have you done about it?'

'Got your people to get the picture books out, Colonel. The Joberts are looking through them right now.'

'Excellent.' Hernu got up and this time refilled his coffee cup himself. 'What do you make of the hotel business? Do you think he's been alerted?'

'Perhaps, but not necessarily,' Savary said. 'I mean what have we got here, sir? A real pro out to make the hit of a lifetime. Maybe he was just being extra careful, just to make sure he wasn't followed to his real destination. I mean, I wouldn't trust the Joberts an inch, so why should he?'

He shrugged and Max Hernu said shrewdly, 'There's more. Spit it out.'

'I got a bad feeling about this guy, Colonel. I think he's special. I think he may have used the hotel thing because he suspected that Gaston might follow him, but then he'd want to know why. Was it the Joberts just being curious or was there more to it?'

'So you think he could have been up the street watching our people arrive?'

'Very possibly. On the other hand, maybe he didn't know Gaston was tailing him. Maybe the hotel thing was a usual precaution. An old Resistance trick from the war.'

34

Hernu nodded. 'Right, let's see if they've finished. Have them in.'

Savary went out and returned with the Jobert brothers. They stood there looking worried and Hernu said, 'Well?'

'No luck, Colonel. He wasn't in any of the books.'

'All right,' Hernu said. 'Wait downstairs. You'll be taken home. We'll collect you again later.'

'But what for, Colonel?' Pierre asked.

'So that your brother can go to Valenton in the Renault and you can follow in the car just like Rocard told you. Now get out.' They hurriedly left and Hernu said to Savary, 'We'll see Mrs Thatcher is spirited to safety by another route, but a pity to disappoint our friend Rocard.'

'If he turns up, Colonel.'

'You never know, he just might. You've done well, Inspector. I think I'll have to requisition you for Section Five. Would you mind?'

Would he mind? Savary almost choked with emotion. 'An honour, sir.'

'Good. Go and get a shower then and some breakfast. I'll see you later.'

'And you, Colonel.'

'Me, Inspector.' Hernu laughed and looked at his watch. 'Five-fifteen. I'm going to ring British intelligence in London. Disturb the sleep of a very old friend of mine. If anyone can help us with our mystery man it should be he.'

The Directorate General of the British Security Service occupies a large white and red brick building not far from the Hilton Hotel in Park Lane, although many of its departments are housed in various locations throughout London. The special number that Max Hernu rang was of a section known as Group Four, located on the third floor of the Ministry of Defence. It had been set up in 1972 to handle matters concerning terrorism and subversion in the British Isles. It was responsible only to the Prime Minister. It had been administered by only one man since its inception, Brigadier Charles Ferguson. He was asleep in his flat in Cavendish Square when the telephone beside his bed awakened him.

'Ferguson,' he said, immediately wide awake, knowing it had to be important.

'Paris, Brigadier,' an anonymous voice said. 'Priority one. Colonel Hernu.'

'Put him through and scramble.'

Ferguson sat up, a large, untidy man of sixty-five with rumpled grey hair and a double chin.

'Charles?' Hernu said in English.

'My dear Max. What brings you on the line at such a disgusting hour? You're lucky I'm still on the phone. The powers that be are trying to make me redundant along with Group Four.'

'What nonsense.'

'I know, but the Director General was never happy with my freebooter status all these years. What can I do for you?'

'Mrs Thatcher overnighting at Choisy. We've details of a plot to hit her on the way to the airfield at Valenton tomorrow.'

'Good God!'

'All taken care of. The lady will now take a different route home. We're still hoping the man concerned will show up, though I doubt it. We'll be waiting though, this afternoon.'

'Who is it? Anyone we know?'

'From what our informants say, we suspect he's Irish though his French is good enough to pass as a native. The thing is, the people involved have looked through all our IRA pictures with no success.'

36

'Have you a description?'

Hernu gave it to him. 'Not much to go on, I'm afraid.'

'I'll have a computer check done and get back to you. Tell me the story.' Which Hernu did. When he was finished Ferguson said, 'You've lost him, old chap. I'll bet you dinner on it at the Savoy Grill next time you're over.'

'I've a feeling about this one. I think he's special,' Hernu said.

'And yet not on your books and we always keep you up to date.'

'I know,' Hernu said. 'And you're the expert on the IRA, so what do we do?'

'You're wrong there,' Ferguson said. 'The greatest expert on the IRA is right there in Paris, Martin Brosnan, our Irish-American friend. After all, he carried a gun for them till nineteen seventy-five. I heard he was a Professor of Political Philosophy at the Sorbonne.'

'You're right,' Hernu said. 'I'd forgotten about him.'

'Very respectable these days. Writes books and lives rather well on all that money his mother left him when she died in Boston five years ago. If you've a mystery on your hands he might be the man to solve it.'

'Thanks for the suggestion,' Hernu said. 'But first we'll see what happens at Valenton. I'll be in touch.'

Ferguson put down the phone, pressed a button on the wall and got out of bed. A moment later the door opened and his manservant, an ex-Gurkha came in, putting a dressing-gown over his pyjamas.

'Emergency, Kim. I'll ring Captain Tanner and tell her to get round here, then I'll have a bath. Breakfast when she arrives.'

The Gurkha withdrew. Ferguson picked up the phone and dialled a number. 'Mary? Ferguson here. Something big. I want you at Cavendish Square within the hour. Oh, better wear your uniform. We've got that thing at the

Ministry of Defence at eleven. You always impress them in full war paint.'

He put the phone down and went into the bathroom feeling wide awake and extremely cheerful.

It was six-thirty when the taxi picked up Mary Tanner on the steps of her Lowndes Square flat. The driver was impressed, but then most people were. She wore the uniform of a captain in the Women's Royal Army Corps, the wings of an Army Air Corps pilot on her left breast. Below them the ribbon of the George Medal, a gallantry award of considerable distinction and campaign ribbons for Ireland and for service with the United Nations peacekeeping force in Cyprus.

She was a small girl, black hair cropped short, twenty-nine years of age and a lot of service under the belt. A doctor's daughter who'd taken an English degree at London University, tried teaching and hated it. After that came the army. A great deal of her service had been with the Military Police. Cyprus for a while, but three tours of duty in Ulster. It had been the affair in Derry that had earned her the George Medal and left her with the scar on her left cheek which had brought her to Ferguson's attention. She'd been his aide for two years now.

She paid off the taxi, hurried up the stairs to the flat on the first floor and let herself in with her own key. Ferguson was sitting on the sofa beside the fireplace in the elegant drawing room, a napkin under his chin while Kim served his poached eggs.

'Just in time,' he said. 'What would you like?'

'Tea, please. Earl Grey, Kim, and toast and honey.'

'Got to watch our figure.'

'Rather early in the day for sexist cracks, even for you, Brigadier. Now what have we got?'

He told her while he ate and Kim brought her tea and toast and she sat opposite, listening.

When he finished she said, 'This Brosnan, I've never heard of him.'

'Before your time, my love. He must be about forty-five now. You'll find a file on him in my study. He was born in Boston. One of those filthy rich American families. Very high society. His mother was a Dubliner. He did all the right things, went to Princeton, took his degree then went and spoiled it all by volunteering for Viet Nam and as an enlisted man. I believe that was nineteen sixty-six. Airborne Rangers. He was discharged a sergeant and heavily decorated.'

'So what makes him so special?'

'He could have avoided Viet Nam by staying at university, but he didn't. He also enlisted in the ranks. Quite something for someone with his social standing.'

'You're just an old snob. What happened to him after that?'

'He went to Trinity College, Dublin, to work on a doctorate. He's a Protestant, by the way, but his mother was a devout Catholic. In August sixty-nine, he was visiting an uncle on his mother's side, a priest in Belfast. Remember what happened? How it all started?'

'Orange mobs burning Catholics out?' she said.

'And the police not doing too much about it. The mob burned down Brosnan's uncle's church and started on the Falls Road. A handful of old IRA hands with a few rifles and handguns held them off and when one of them was shot, Brosnan picked up his rifle. Instinctive, I suppose. I mean Viet Nam and all that.'

'And from then on he was committed?'

'Very much so. You've got to remember that in those early days, there were plenty of men like him in the movement. Believers in Irish freedom and all that sort of thing.'

'Sorry, sir, I've seen too much blood on the streets of Derry to go for that one.'

'Yes, well I'm not trying to whitewash him. He's killed a few in his time, but always up front, I'll say that for him. He became quite famous. There was a French war photographer called Anne-Marie Audin. He saved her life in Viet Nam after a helicopter crash. Quite a romantic story. She turned up in Belfast and Brosnan took her underground for a week. She got a series out of it for *Life* magazine. The gallant Irish struggle. You know the sort of thing.'

'What happened after that?'

'In nineteen seventy-five he went to France to negotiate an arms deal. As it turned out it was a set-up and the police were waiting. Unfortunately he shot one of them dead. They gave him life. He escaped from prison in seventy-nine, at my instigation, I might add.'

'But why?'

'Someone else before your time, a terrorist called Frank Barry. Started off in Ulster with a splinter group called the Sons of Erin, then joined the European terrorist circuit, an evil genius if ever there was one. Tried to get Lord Carrington on a trip to France when he was Foreign Secretary. The French hushed it up, but the Prime Minister was furious. Gave me direct orders to hunt Barry down whatever the cost.'

'Oh, I see now. You needed Brosnan to do that?'

'Set a thief to catch a thief and so forth, and he got him for us.'

'And afterwards?'

'He went back to Ireland and took that doctorate.'

'And this Anne-Marie Audin, did they marry?'

'Not to my knowledge, but she did him a bigger favour than that. Her family is one of the oldest in France and enormously powerful politically and he had been awarded the Legion of Honour for saving her in Viet Nam. Anyway, her pressure behind the scenes bore fruit five years ago. President Mitterrand granted him a pardon. Wiped the slate clean.'

'Which is how he's at the Sorbonne now? He must be the only professor they've had who shot a policeman dead.'

'Actually one or two after the war had done just that when serving with the Resistance.'

'Does the leopard ever change its spots?' she asked.

'Oh, ye of little faith. As I say, you'll find his file in the study if you want to know more.' He passed her a piece of paper. 'That's the description of the mystery man. Not much to go on, but run it through the computer anyway.'

She went out.

Kim entered with a copy of *The Times*. Ferguson read the headlines briefly then turned to page two where his attention was immediately caught by the same item concerning Mrs Thatcher's visit to France as had appeared in *Paris Soir*.

'Well, Max,' he said softly, 'I wish you luck,' and he poured himself another cup of coffee.

THREE

It was much warmer in Paris later that morning, most of the snow clearing by lunchtime. It was clear in the countryside too, only a bit here and there on the hedgerows as Dillon moved towards Valenton keeping to the back roads. He was riding the BMW motorcycle from the garage and was dressed as a CRS policeman, helmet, goggles, a MAT49 machine gun slung across the front of the dark uniform raincoat.

Madness to have come, of course, but he couldn't resist the free show. He pulled off a narrow country lane by a farm gate after consulting his map, followed a track through a small wood on foot and came to a low stone wall on a hill. Way below, some two hundred yards on, was the railway crossing, the black Renault still parked where he had left it. There wasn't a soul about. Perhaps fifteen minutes later, a train passed through.

He checked his watch. Two-fifteen. He focused his Zeiss glasses on the scene below again and then the white Renault came down the road half-turning to block the crossing. There was a Peugeot behind it, Pierre at the wheel and he was already reversing, turning the car as Gaston ran towards him. It was an old model, painted scarlet and cream.

'Very pretty,' Dillon said softly as the Peugeot disappeared up the road.

'Now for the cavalry,' he said and lit a cigarette.

It was perhaps ten minutes later that a large truck came down the road and braked to a halt unable to progress further. It had high canvas sides on which was emblazoned 'Steiner Electronics'.

'Electronics my arse,' Dillon said.

A heavy machine gun opened up from inside the truck firing through the side, raking the Renault. As the firing stopped Dillon took a black plastic electronic detonator from his pocket, switched on and pulled out the aerial.

A dozen men in black overalls and riot helmets, all clutching machine carbines, jumped out. As they approached the Renault, Dillon pressed the detonator. The self-destruct charge in the second black box, the one he had told Pierre contained extra ammunition, exploded instantly, the vehicle disintegrating, parts of the panelling lifting into the air in slow motion. There were several men on the ground, others running for cover.

'There you are, chew on that, gentlemen,' Dillon said.

He walked back through the wood, pushed the BMW off its stand, swung a leg over and rode away.

He opened the door of the warehouse on rue de Helier, got back on the BMW, rode inside and parked it. As he turned to close the door, Makeev called from above, 'It went wrong, I presume?'

Dillon took off his helmet. 'I'm afraid so. The Jobert brothers turned me in.'

As he went up the stairs Makeev said, 'The disguise, I

like that. A policeman is just a policeman to people. Nothing to describe.'

'Exactly. I worked for a great Irishman called Frank Barry for a while years ago. Ever heard of him?'

'Certainly. A veritable Carlos.'

'He was better than Carlos. Got knocked off in seventy-nine. I don't know who by. He used the CRS copper on a motorcycle a lot. Postmen are good too. No one ever notices a postman.'

He followed the Russian into the sitting room. 'Tell me,' Makeev said.

Dillon brought him up to date. 'It was a chance using those two and it went wrong, that's all there is to it.'

'Now what?'

'As I said last night, I'll provide an alternative target. I mean, all that lovely money. I've got to think of my old age.'

'Nonsense, Sean, you don't give a damn about your old age. It's the game that excites you.'

'You could be right.' Dillon lit a cigarette. 'I know one thing. I don't like to be beaten. I'll think of something for you and I'll pay my debts.'

'The Joberts? Are they worth it?'

'Oh, yes,' Dillon said. 'A matter of honour, Josef.'

Makeev sighed. 'I'll go and see Aroun, give him the bad news. I'll be in touch.'

'Here or at the barge.' Dillon smiled. 'Don't worry, Josef. I've never failed yet, not when I set my mind to a thing.'

Makeev went down the stairs. His footsteps echoed across the warehouse, the Judas gate banged behind him. Dillon turned and went back into the long room, whistling softly.

44

'But I don't understand,' Aroun said. 'There hasn't been a word on television.'

'And there won't be.' Makeev turned from the French windows overlooking the Avenue Victor Hugo. 'The affair never happened, that is the way the French will handle it. The idea that Mrs Thatcher could have in any way been at risk on French soil would be considered a national affront.'

Aroun was pale with anger. 'He failed, this man of yours. A great deal of talk, Makeev, but nothing at the end of it. A good thing I didn't transfer that million to his Zurich account this morning.'

'But you agreed,' Makeev said. 'In any case, he may ring at any time to check the money has been deposited.'

'My dear Makeev, I have five hundred million dollars on deposit at that bank. Faced with the possibility of me transferring my business, the managing director was more than willing to agree to a small deception when Rashid spoke to him this morning. When Dillon phones to check on the situation, the deposit will be confirmed.'

'This is a highly dangerous man you are dealing with,' Makeev said. 'If he found out . . .'

'Who's going to tell him? Certainly not you and he'll get paid in the end, but only if he produces a result.'

Rashid poured him a cup of coffee and said to Makeev, 'He promised an alternative target, mentioned the British Prime Minister. What does he intend?'

'He'll be in touch when he's decided,' Makeev said.

'Talk,' Aroun walked to the window and stood sipping his coffee. 'All talk.'

'No, Michael,' Josef Makeev told him. 'You could not be more mistaken.'

Martin Brosnan's apartment was by the river on the Quai de Montebello opposite the Île de la Cité and had one of the finest views of Notre Dame in Paris. It was within decent walking distance of the Sorbonne which suited him perfectly.

It was just after four as he walked towards it, a tall man with broad shoulders in an old-fashioned trenchcoat, dark hair that still had no grey in it in spite of his forty-five years and was far too long, giving him the look of some sixteenth-century bravo. Martin Aodh Brosnan. The Aodh was Gaelic for Hugh and his Irishness showed in the high cheekbones and grey eyes.

It was getting colder again and he shivered as he turned the corner into the Quai de Montebello and hurried along to the apartment block. He owned it all, as it happened, which gave him the apartment on the corner of the first floor, the most favoured location. Scaffolding ran up the corner of the building to the fourth floor where some sort of building work was taking place.

As he was about to go up the steps to the ornate entrance, a voice called, 'Martin?'

He glanced up and saw Anne-Marie Audin leaning over the balustrade of the terrace. 'Where in the hell did you spring from?' he asked in astonishment.

'Cuba. I just got in.'

He went up the stairs two at a time and she had the door open as he got there. He lifted her up in his arms in an enormous hug and carried her back into the hall. 'How marvellous to see you. Why Cuba?'

She kissed him and helped him off with the trenchcoat. 'Oh, I had a rather juicy assignment for *Time* magazine. Come in the kitchen. I'll make your tea.'

A standing joke for years, the tea. Surprising in an American, but he couldn't stand coffee. He lit a cigarette and sat at the table and watched her move around the kitchen, her short hair as dark as his own, this supremely elegant woman who was the same age as himself and looked twelve years younger.

'You look marvellous,' he told her as she brought the tea. He sampled it and nodded in approval. 'That's grand. Just the way you learned to make it back in South Armagh in nineteen seventy-one with me and Liam Devlin showing you the hard way how the IRA worked.'

'How is the old rogue?'

'Still living in Kilrea outside Dublin. Gives the odd lecture at Trinity College. Claims to be seventy, but that's a wicked lie.'

'He'll never grow old, that one.'

'Yes, you really do look marvellous,' Brosnan said. 'Why didn't we get married?'

It was a ritual question he had asked for years, a joke now. There was a time when they had been lovers, but for some years now, just friends. Not that it was by any means the usual relationship. He would have died for her, almost had in a Viet Nam swamp the first time they had met.

'Now that we've got that over, tell me about the new book,' she said.

'A philosophy of terrorism,' he told her. 'Very boring. Not many people will buy a copy.'

'A pity,' she said, 'coming from such an expert in the field.'

'Doesn't really matter,' he said. 'Knowing the reasons still won't make people act any differently.'

'Cynic. Come on, let's have a real drink.' She opened the fridge and took out a bottle of Krug.

'Non-vintage?'

'What else?'

They went into the magnificent long drawing room. There was an ornate gold mirror over the marble fireplace, plants everywhere, a grand piano, comfortable, untidy sofas and a great many books. She had left the French windows to the balcony standing ajar. Brosnan went to close them as she opened the Krug at the sideboard and got two glasses. At the same moment, the bell sounded outside.

When Brosnan opened the door he found Max Hernu and Jules Savary standing there, the Jobert brothers behind them.

'Professor Brosnan?' Hernu said. 'I am Colonel Max Hernu.'

'I know very well who you are,' Brosnan said. 'Action Service, isn't it? What's all this? My wicked past catching up with me?'

'Not quite, but we do need your assistance. This is Inspector Savary and these two are Gaston and Pierre Jobert.'

'You'd better come in then,' Brosnan said, interested in spite of himself.

The Jobert brothers stayed in the hall, on Hernu's orders when he and Savary followed Brosnan into the drawing room. Anne-Marie turned, frowning slightly and Brosnan made the introductions.

'A great pleasure.' Hernu kissed her hand. 'I'm a long-time admirer.'

'Martin?' She looked worried now. 'You're not getting involved in anything?'

'Of course not,' he assured her. 'Now what can I do for you, Colonel?'

'A matter of national security, Professor. I hesitate to mention the fact, but Mademoiselle Audin is a photojournalist of some distinction.'

She smiled. 'Total discretion, you have my word, Colonel.'

'We're here because Brigadier Charles Ferguson in London suggested it.'

'That old Devil? And why should he suggest you see me?'

'Because you are an expert in matters relating to the IRA, Professor. Let me explain.'

Which he did, covering the whole affair as rapidly as possible. 'You see, Professor,' he said as he concluded, 'the Jobert brothers have combed our IRA picture books without finding him and Ferguson has had no success with the brief description we were able to give.'

'You've got a real problem.'

'My friend, this man is not just anybody. He must be special to attempt such a thing, but we know nothing more than that we think he's Irish and he speaks fluent French.'

'So what do you want me to do?'

'Speak to the Joberts.'

Brosnan glanced at Anne-Marie, then shrugged. 'All right, wheel them in.'

He sat on the edge of the table drinking champagne while they stood before him, awkward in such circumstances. 'How old is he?'

'Difficult, monsieur,' Pierre said. 'He changes from one minute to the next. It's like he's more than one person. I'd say late thirties.'

'And description?'

'Small with fair hair.'

'He looks like nothing,' Gaston put in. 'We thought he was a no-no and then he half-killed some big ape in our café one night.'

'All right. He's small, fair-haired, late thirties and he can handle himself. What makes you think he's Irish?'

'When he was assembling the Kalashnikov he made a crack about seeing one take out a Land Rover full of English paratroopers.'

'Is that all?'

Pierre frowned. Brosnan took the bottle of Krug from the bucket and Gaston said, 'No, there's something else. He's

49

always whistling a funny sort of tune. A bit eerie. I managed to follow it on my accordion. He said it was Irish.'

Brosnan's face had gone quite still. He stood there, holding the bottle in one hand, a glass in the other.

'And he likes that stuff, monsieur,' Pierre said.

'Champagne?' Brosnan asked.

'Well, yes, any champagne is better than nothing, but Krug is his favourite.'

'Like this, non-vintage?'

'Yes, monsieur. He told us he preferred the grape mix,' Pierre said.

'The bastard always did.'

Anne-Marie put a hand on Brosnan's arm. 'You know him, Martin?'

'Almost certainly. Could you pick that tune out on the piano?' he asked Gaston.

'I'll try, monsieur.'

He lifted the lid, tried the keyboard gently, then played the beginning of the tune with one finger.

'That's enough.' Brosnan turned to Hernu and Savary. 'An old Irish folk song, "The Lark in the Clear Air", and you've got trouble, gentlemen, because the man you're looking for is Sean Dillon.'

'Dillon?' Hernu said. 'Of course. The man of a thousand faces someone once called him.'

'A slight exaggeration,' Brosnan said, 'but it will do.'

They sent the Jobert brothers home and Brosnan and Anne-Marie sat on a sofa opposite Hernu and Savary. The inspector made notes as the American talked.

'His mother died in childbirth. I think that was nineteen fifty-two. His father was an electrician. Went to work in London so Dillon went to school there. He had an incredible talent for acting, a genius really. He can change before

50

your eyes, hunch his shoulders, put on fifteen years. It's astonishing.'

'So you knew him well?' Hernu asked.

'In Belfast in the bad old days, but before that he won a scholarship to the Royal Academy of Dramatic Art. Only stayed a year. They couldn't teach him anything. He did one or two things at the National Theatre. Nothing much. He was very young remember. Then in nineteen seventy-one his father, who'd returned home to Belfast, was killed by a British Army patrol. Caught in crossfire. An accident.'

'And Dillon took it hard?'

'You could say that. He offered himself to the Provisional IRA. They liked him. He had brains, an aptitude for languages. They sent him to Libya to one of those terrorist training camps for a couple of months. A fast course in weaponry. That's all it took. He never looked back. God knows how many he's killed.'

'So, he still operates for the IRA?'

Brosnan shook his head. 'Not for years. Oh, he still counts himself as a soldier, but he thinks the leadership are a bunch of old women and they couldn't handle him. He'd have killed the Pope if he'd thought it was needed. He was too happy to do things that were counter-productive. The word is that he was involved in the Mountbatten affair.'

'And since those days?' Hernu asked.

'Beirut, Palestine. He's done a lot for the PLO. Most terrorist groups have used his services.' Brosnan shook his head. 'You're going to have trouble here.'

'Why exactly?'

'The fact that he used a couple of crooks like the Joberts. He always does that. All right, it didn't work this time, but he knows the weakness of all revolutionary movements. That they're ridden with either hotheads or informers. You called him the faceless man, and that's right because I doubt if you'll find a photo of him on any file, and frankly it wouldn't matter if you did.'

'Why does he do it?' Anne-Marie asked. 'Not for any political ends?'

'Because he likes it,' Brosnan said. 'Because he's hooked. He's an actor, remember. This is for real and he's good at it.'

'I get the impression that you don't care for him very much,' Hernu said. 'In personal terms, I mean.'

'Well, he tried to kill me and a good friend of mine a long time ago,' Brosnan told him. 'Does that answer your question?'

'It's certainly reason enough.' Hernu got up and Savary joined him. 'We must be going. I want to get all this to Brigadier Ferguson as soon as possible.'

'Fine,' Brosnan said.

'We may count on your help in this thing, I hope, Professor?'

Brosnan glanced at Anne-Marie whose face was set. 'Look,' he said, 'I don't mind talking to you again if that will help, but I don't want to be personally involved. You know what I was, Colonel. Whatever happens I won't go back to anything like that. I made someone a promise a long time ago.'

'I understand perfectly, Professor.' Hernu turned to Anne-Marie. 'Mademoiselle, a distinct pleasure.'

'I'll see you out,' she said and led the way.

When she returned Brosnan had the French windows open and was standing looking across the river smoking a cigarette. He put an arm around her. 'All right?'

'Oh, yes,' she said. 'Perfect,' and laid her head against his chest.

At that precise moment Ferguson was sitting by the fire in the Cavendish Square flat when the phone rang. Mary Tanner answered it in the study. After a while she came out. 'That was Downing Street. The Prime Minister wants to see you.'

'When?'

'Now, sir.'

Ferguson got up and removed his reading glasses. 'Call the car. You come with me and wait.'

She picked up the phone, spoke briefly, then put it down. 'What do you think it's about, Brigadier?'

'I'm not sure. My imminent retirement or your return to more mundane duties. Or this business in France. He'll have been told all about it by now. Anyway, let's go and see,' and he led the way out.

They were checked through the security gates at the end of Downing Street. Mary Tanner stayed in the car while Ferguson was admitted through the most famous door in the world. It was rather quiet compared to the last time he'd been there, a Christmas party given by Mrs Thatcher for the staff in the Pillared Room. Cleaners, typists, office workers. Typical of her, that. The other side of the Iron Lady.

He regretted her departure, that was a fact, and sighed as he followed a young aide up the main staircase lined with replicas of portraits of all those great men of history. Peel, Wellington, Disraeli and many more. They reached the corridor, the young man knocked on the door and opened it.

'Brigadier Ferguson, Prime Minister.'

The last time Ferguson had been in that study it had been a woman's room, the feminine touches unmistakably there, but things were different now, a little more austere

53

in a subtle way, he was aware of that. Darkness was falling fast outside and John Major was checking some sort of report, the pen in his hand moving with considerable speed.

'Sorry about this. It will only take a moment,' he said.

It was the courtesy that astounded Ferguson, the sheer basic good manners that one didn't experience too often from heads of state. Major signed the report, put it on one side and sat back, a pleasant, grey-haired man in horn-rimmed glasses, the youngest Prime Minister of the twentieth century. Almost unknown to the general public on his succession to Margaret Thatcher and yet his handling of the crisis in the Gulf had already marked him out as a leader of genuine stature.

'Please sit down, Brigadier. I'm on a tight schedule, so I'll get right to the point. The business affecting Mrs Thatcher in France. Obviously very disturbing.'

'Indeed so, Prime Minister. Thank God it all turned out as it did.'

'Yes, but that seems to have been a matter of luck more than anything else. I've spoken to President Mitterrand and he's agreed that in all our interests and especially with the present situation in the Gulf there will be a total security clampdown.'

'What about the press, Prime Minister?'

'Nothing will reach the press, Brigadier,' John Major told him. 'I understand the French failed to catch the individual concerned?'

'I'm afraid that is so according to my latest information, but Colonel Hernu of Action Service is keeping in close touch.'

'I've spoken to Mrs Thatcher and it was she who alerted me to your presence, Brigadier. As I understand it, the intelligence section known as Group Four was set up in nineteen seventy-two, responsible only to the Prime Minister, its purpose to handle specific cases of terrorism and subversion?'

'That is correct.'

'Which means you will have served five prime ministers if we include myself.'

'Actually, Prime Minister, that's not quite accurate,' Ferguson said. 'We do have a problem at the moment.'

'Oh, I know all about that. The usual security people have never liked your existence, Brigadier, too much like the Prime Minister's private army. That's why they thought a changeover at Number Ten was a good time to get rid of you.'

'I'm afraid so, Prime Minister.'

'Well, it wasn't and it isn't. I've spoken to the Director General of Security Services. It's taken care of.'

'I couldn't be more delighted.'

'Good. Your first task quite obviously is to run down whoever was behind this French affair. If he's IRA, then he's our business, wouldn't you agree?'

'Absolutely.'

'Good. I'll let you go and get on with it then. Keep me informed of every significant development on an eyes only basis.'

'Of course, Prime Minister.'

The door behind opened as if by magic, the aide appeared to usher Ferguson out, the Prime Minister was already working over another sheaf of papers as the door closed and Ferguson was led downstairs.

As the limousine drove away, Mary Tanner reached forward to close the screen. 'What happened? What was it about?'

'Oh, the French business.' Ferguson sounded curiously remote. 'You know, he's really got something about him this one.'

'Oh, come off it, sir,' Mary said. 'I mean, don't you

honestly think we could do with a change, after all these years of Tory government?'

'Wonderful spokesperson for the workers you make,' he said. 'Your dear old Dad, God rest him, was a Professor of Surgery at Oxford, your mother owns half of Herefordshire. That flat of yours in Lowndes Square, a million, would you say? Why is it the children of the rich are always so depressingly left-wing while still insisting on dining at the Savoy?'

'A gross exaggeration.'

'Seriously, my dear, I've worked for Labour as well as Conservative prime ministers. The colour of the politician doesn't matter. The Marquess of Salisbury when he was Prime Minister, Gladstone, Disraeli, had very similar problems to those we have today. Fenians, anarchists, bombs in London, only dynamite instead of Semtex and how many attempts were there on Queen Victoria's life?' He gazed out at the Whitehall traffic as they moved towards the Ministry of Defence. 'Nothing changes.'

'All right, end of lecture, but what happened?' she demanded.

'Oh, we're back in business, that's what happened,' he said. 'I'm afraid we'll have to cancel your transfer back to the Military Police.'

'Damn you!' she cried and flung her arms around his neck.

Ferguson's office on the third floor of the Ministry of Defence was on a corner at the rear overlooking Horse Guards Avenue with a view of the Victoria Embankment and the river at the far end. He had hardly got settled behind his desk when Mary hurried in.

'Coded fax from Hernu. I've put it through the machine. You're not going to like it one little bit.'

It contained the gist of Hernu's meeting with Martin Brosnan, the facts on Sean Dillon – everything.

'Dear God,' Ferguson said. 'Couldn't be worse. He's like a ghost, this Dillon chap. Does he exist or doesn't he? As bad as Carlos in international terrorist terms, but totally unknown to the media or the general public and nothing to go on.'

'But we do have one thing, sir.'

'What's that?'

'Brosnan.'

'True, but will he help?' Ferguson got up and moved to the window. 'I tried to get Martin to do something for me the other year. He wouldn't touch it with a bargepole.' He turned and smiled. 'It's the girlfriend, you see, Anne-Marie Audin. She has a horror of him becoming what he once was.'

'Yes, I can understand that.'

'But never mind. We'd better get a report on their latest developments to the Prime Minister. Let's keep it brief.'

She produced a pen and took notes as he dictated. 'Anything else, sir?' she asked when he had finished.

'I don't think so. Get it typed. One copy for the file, the other for the PM. Send it straight round to Number Ten by messenger. Eyes only.'

Mary did a rough type of the report herself then went along the corridor to the typing and copying room. There was one on each floor and the clerks all had full security clearance. The copier was clattering as she went in. The man standing in front of it was in his mid-fifties, white hair, steel-rimmed army glasses, his shirt sleeves rolled up.

'Hello, Gordon,' she said. 'A priority one here. Your very best typing. One copy for the personal file. You'll do it straight away?'

'Of course, Captain Tanner.' He glanced at it briefly. 'Fifteen minutes. I'll bring it along.'

She went out and he sat down at his typewriter, taking a deep breath to steady himself as he read the words. *For the eyes of the Prime Minister only.* Gordon Brown had served in the Intelligence Corps for twenty-five years, reaching the rank of warrant officer. A worthy, if unspectacular career, culminating in the award of an MBE and the offer of employment at the Ministry of Defence on his retirement from the army. And everything had been fine until the death of his wife from cancer the previous year. They were childless, which left him alone in a cold world at fifty-five years of age, and then something miraculous happened.

There were invitation cards flying around at the Ministry all the time to receptions at the various embassies in London. He often helped himself to one. It was just something to do and at an art display at the German Embassy he'd met Tania Novikova, a secretary-typist at the Soviet Embassy.

They'd got on so well together. She was thirty and not particularly pretty, but when she'd taken him to bed on their second meeting at his flat in Camden it was like a revelation. Brown had never known sex like it, was hooked instantly. And then it had started. The questions about his job, anything and everything about what went on at the Ministry of Defence. Then there was a cooling off. He didn't see her and was distracted, almost out of his mind. He'd phoned her at her flat. She was cold at first, distant and then she'd asked him if he'd been doing anything interesting.

He knew then what was happening, but didn't care. There was a series of reports passing through on British Army changes in view of political changes in Russia. It was easy to run off spare copies. When he took them round to her flat, it was just as it had been and she took him to heights of pleasure such as he had never known.

From then on he would do anything, providing copies of everything that might interest her. *For the eyes of the Prime Minister only.* How grateful would she be for that? He finished typing, ran off two extra copies, one for himself. He had a file of them now in one of his bedroom drawers. The other was for Tania Novikova, who was, of course, not a secretary-typist at the Soviet Embassy as she had informed Brown, but a captain in the KGB.

Gaston opened the door of the lock-up garage opposite *Le Chat Noir* and Pierre got behind the wheel of the old cream and red Peugeot. His brother got in the rear seat and they drove away.

'I've been thinking,' Gaston said. 'I mean, what if they don't get him? He could come looking for us, Pierre.'

'Nonsense,' Pierre told him. 'He's long gone, Gaston. What kind of fool would hang around after what's happened? No, light me a cigarette and shut up. We'll have a nice dinner and go on to the *Zanzibar* afterwards. They've still got those Swedish sisters stripping.'

It was just before eight, the streets at that place quiet and deserted, people inside because of the extreme cold. They came to a small square and as they started to cross it a CRS man on his motorcycle came up behind them, flashing his lights.

'There's a cop on our tail,' Gaston said.

The policeman pulled up alongside, anonymous in his helmet and goggles and waved them down.

'A message from Savary, I suppose,' Pierre said, and pulled over to the pavement.

'Maybe they've got him,' Gaston said excitedly.

The CRS man halted behind them, pushed his bike up

on its stand and approached. Gaston got the rear door open and leaned out. 'Have they caught the bastard?'

Dillon took a Walther with a Carswell silencer from inside the flap of his raincoat and shot him twice in the heart. He pushed up his goggles and turned. Pierre crossed himself. 'It's you.'

'Yes, Pierre. A matter of honour.'

The Walther coughed twice more, Dillon pushed it back inside his raincoat, got on the BMW and rode away. It started to snow a little, the square very quiet. It was perhaps half an hour later that a policeman on foot patrol, caped against the cold, found them.

Tania Novikova's flat was just off the Bayswater Road not far from the Soviet Embassy. She'd had a hard day, had intended an early night. It was just before ten-thirty when her doorbell rang. She was towelling herself down after a nice relaxing bath. She pulled on a robe, and went downstairs.

Gordon Brown's evening shift had finished at ten. He couldn't wait to get to her and had had the usual difficulty parking his Ford Escort. He stood at the door, ringing the bell impatiently, hugely excited. When she opened the door and saw who it was she was immediately angry and drew him inside.

'I told you never to come here, Gordon, under any circumstances.'

'But this is special,' he pleaded. 'Look what I've brought you.'

In the living room she took the large envelope from him, opened it and slipped out the report. *For the eyes of the Prime Minister only.* Her excitement was intense as she read through it. Incredible that this fool could have delivered her such a coup. His arms were around her waist, sliding

60

up to her breasts and she was aware of his excitement.

'It's good stuff, isn't it?' he demanded.

'Excellent, Gordon. You *have* been a good boy.'

'Really?' His grip tightened. 'I can stay over then?'

'Oh, Gordon, it's such a pity. I'm on the night shift.'

'Please, darling.' He was shaking like a leaf. 'Just a few minutes then.'

She had to keep him happy, she knew that, put the report on the table and took him by the hand. 'Quarter of an hour, Gordon, that's all and then you'll have to go,' and she led him into the bedroom.

After she'd got rid of him, she dressed hurriedly, debating what to do. She was a hard, committed Communist. That was how she had been raised and how she would die. More than that, she served the KGB with total loyalty. It had nurtured her, educated her, given her whatever status she had in their world. For a young woman, she was surprisingly old-fashioned. Had no time for Gorbachev or the Glasnost fools who surrounded him. Unfortunately, many in the KGB did support him and one of those was her boss at the London Embassy, Colonel Yuri Gatov.

What would his attitude be to such a report, she wondered as she let herself out into the street and started to walk. What would Gorbachev's attitude be to the failed attempt to assassinate Mrs Thatcher? Probably the same outrage the British Prime Minister must feel and if Gorbachev felt that way, so would Colonel Gatov. So, what to do?

It came to her then as she walked along the frosty pavement of the Bayswater Road, that there was someone who might very well be interested and not only because he thought as she did, but because he was himself right in the centre of all the action – Paris. Her old boss, Colonel Josef

Makeev. That was it. Makeev would know how best to use such information. She turned into Kensington Palace Gardens and went into the Soviet Embassy.

By chance, Makeev was working late in his office that night when his secretary looked in and said, 'A call from London on the scrambler. Captain Novikova.'

Makeev picked up the red phone. 'Tania,' he said, a certain affection in his voice for they had been lovers during the three years she'd worked for him in Paris. 'What can I do for you?'

'I understand there was an incident affecting Empire over there earlier today?' she said.

It was an old KGB coded phrase, current for years, always used when referring to assassination attempts of any kind at high government level where Britain was concerned.

Makeev was immediately alert. 'That's correct. The usual kind of it-didn't-happen affair.'

'Have you an interest?'

'Very much so.'

'There's a coded fax on the way. I'll stand by in my office if you want to talk.'

Tania Novikova put down the phone. She had her own fax coding machine at a second desk. She went to it, tapping the required details out quickly, checking on the screen to see that she had got it right. She added Makeev's personal number, inserted the report and waited. A few moments later, she got a message received okay signal. She got up, lit a cigarette and went and stood by the window, waiting.

The jumbled message was received in the radio and coding room at the Paris Embassy. Makeev stood waiting impatiently for it to come through. The operator handed it to him and the Colonel inserted it into the decoder and tapped in his personal key. He couldn't wait to see the contents, was reading it as he went along the corridor, as excited as Tania Novikova when he saw the line *For the eyes of the Prime Minister only*. He sat behind his desk and read it through again. He thought about it for a while, then reached for the red phone.

'You've done well, Tania. This one was my baby.'
  'I'm so pleased.'
  'Does Gatov know about this?'
  'No, Colonel.'
  'Good, let's keep it that way.'
  'Is there anything else I can do?'
  'Very much so. Cultivate your contact. Let me have anything else on the instant. There could be more for you. I have a friend coming to London. The particular friend you've been reading about.'
  'I'll wait to hear.'
  She put down the phone, totally elated, and went along to the canteen.

In Paris, Makeev sat there for a moment, frowning, then he picked up the phone and rang Dillon. There was a slight delay before the Irishman answered.
  'Who is it?'
  'Josef, Sean, I'm on my way there. Utmost importance.'
  Makeev put down the phone, got his overcoat and went out.

FOUR

Brosnan had taken Anne-Marie to the cinema that evening and afterwards to a small restaurant in Montmartre called *La Place Anglaise*. It was an old favourite because, and in spite of the name, one of the specialities of the house was Irish stew. It wasn't particularly busy and they had just finished the main course when Max Hernu appeared, Savary standing behind him.

'Snow in London, snow in Brussels and snow in Paris.' Hernu brushed it from his sleeve and opened his coat.

'Do I deduce from your appearance here that you've had me followed?' Brosnan asked.

'Not at all, Professor. We called at your apartment where the porter told us you had gone to the cinema. He was also kind enough to mention three or four restaurants he thought you might be at. This is the second.'

'Then you'd better sit down and have a cognac and some coffee,' Anne-Marie told him. 'You both look frozen.'

They took off their coats and Brosnan nodded to the head waiter who hurried over and took the order.

'I'm sorry, mademoiselle, to spoil your evening, but this is most important,' Hernu said. 'An unfortunate development.'

Brosnan lit a cigarette. 'Tell us the worst.'

It was Savary who answered. 'About two hours ago the bodies of the Jobert brothers were found by a beat policeman in their car in a small square not far from *Le Chat Noir*.'

'Murdered, is that what you are saying?' Anne-Marie put in.

'Oh, yes, mademoiselle,' he said. 'Shot to death.'

'Two each in the heart?' Brosnan said.

'Why, yes, Professor, the pathologist was able to tell us that at the start of his examination. We didn't stay for the rest. How did you know?'

'Dillon, without a doubt. It's a real pro's trick, Colonel, you should know that. Never one shot, always two in case the other man manages to get one off at you as a reflex.'

Hernu stirred his coffee. 'Did you expect this, Professor?'

'Oh, yes. He'd have come looking for them sooner or later. A strange man. He always keeps his word, never goes back on a contract and he expects the same from those he deals with. What he calls a matter of honour. At least he did in the old days.'

'Can I ask you something?' Savary said. 'I've been on the street fifteen years. I've known killers in plenty and not just the gangsters who see it as part of the job, but the poor sod who's killed his wife because she's been unfaithful. Dillon seems something else. I mean, his father was killed by British soldiers so he joined the IRA. I can see that, but everything that's happened since. Twenty years of it. All those hits and not even in his own country. Why?'

'I'm not a psychiatrist,' Brosnan said. 'They'd give you all the fancy names starting with psychopath and working down. I knew men like him in the army in Viet Nam in Special Forces and good men, some of them, but once they started, the killing, I mean, it seemed to take over like a drug. They became driven men. The next stage was always to kill when it wasn't necessary. To do it without emotion. Back there in Nam it was as if people had become, how can I put it, just things.'

'And this, you think, happened to Dillon?' Hernu asked.

'It happened to me, Colonel,' Martin Brosnan said bleakly.

There was silence. Finally, Hernu said, 'We must catch him, Professor.'

'I know.'

'Then you'll join us in hunting him down?'

Anne-Marie put a hand on his arm, dismay on her face and she turned to the two men, a kind of desperate anger there. 'That's your job, not Martin's.'

'It's all right,' Martin soothed her. 'Don't worry.' He said to Hernu, 'Any advice I can give, any information that might help, but no personal involvement. I'm sorry, Colonel, that's the way it has to be.'

Savary said, 'You told us he tried to kill you once. You and a friend.'

'That was in seventy-four. He and I both worked for this friend of mine, a man named Devlin, Liam Devlin. He was what you might call an old-fashioned revolutionary. Thought you could still fight it out like the old days, an undercover army against the troops. A bit like the Resistance in France during the war. He didn't like bombs, soft target bits, that kind of stuff.'

'What happened?' the Inspector asked.

'Dillon disobeyed orders and the bomb that was meant for the police patrol killed half a dozen children. Devlin and I went after him. He tried to take us out.'

'Without success, obviously?'

'Well, we weren't exactly kids off the street.' His voice had changed in a subtle way. Harder, more cynical. 'Left

66

me with a groove in one shoulder and I gave him one in the arm himself. That was when he first dropped out of sight into Europe.'

'And you didn't see him again?'

'I was in prison for over four years from nineteen seventy-five, Inspector. Belle Isle. You're forgetting your history. He worked with a man called Frank Barry for a while, another refugee from the IRA who turned up on the European scene. A really bad one, Barry. Do you remember him?'

'I do, indeed, Professor,' Hernu said. 'As I recall, he tried to assassinate Lord Carrington, the British Foreign Secretary, on a visit to France in nineteen seventy-nine in very similar circumstances to this recent affair.'

'Dillon was probably doing a copy-cat of that operation. He worshipped Barry.'

'Who you killed, on behalf of British intelligence, I understand?'

Anne-Marie said, 'Excuse me.'

She got up and walked down to the powder room. Hernu said, 'We've upset her.'

'She worries about me, Colonel, worries that some circumstances might put a gun in my hand again and send me sliding all the way back.'

'Yes, I can see that, my friend.' Hernu got up and buttoned his coat. 'We've taken up enough of your time. My apologies to Mademoiselle Audin.'

Savary said, 'Your lectures at the Sorbonne, Professor, the students must love you. I bet you get a full house.'

'Always,' Brosnan said.

He watched them go and Anne-Marie returned. 'Sorry about that, my love,' he told her.

'Not your fault.' She looked tired. 'I think I'll go home.'

'You're not coming back to my place?'

'Not tonight. Tomorrow perhaps.'

The head waiter brought the bill which Brosnan signed, then helped them into their coats and ushered them to the door. Outside, snow sprinkled the cobbles. She shivered and turned to Brosnan. 'You changed, Martin, back there when you were talking to them. You started to become the other man again.'

'Really?' he said and knew that it was true.

'I'll get a taxi.'

'Let me come with you.'

'No, I'd rather not.'

He watched her go down the street, then turned and went the other way. Wondering about Dillon, where he was and what he was doing.

Dillon's barge was moored in a small basin on the Quai St Bernard. There were mainly motor cruisers there, pleasure craft with canvas hoods over them for the winter. The interior was surprisingly luxurious, a stateroom lined with mahogany, two comfortable sofas, a television. His sleeping quarters were in a cabin beyond with a divan bed and a small shower-room adjacent. The kitchen was on the other side of the passageway, small, but very modern. Everything a good cook could want. He was in there now, waiting for the kettle to boil when he heard the footfalls on deck. He opened a drawer, took out a Walther, cocked it and slipped it into his waistband at the rear. Then he went out.

Makeev came down the companionway and entered the stateroom. He shook snow from his overcoat and took it off. 'What a night. Filthy weather.'

'Worse in Moscow,' Dillon told him. 'Coffee?'

'Why not.'

Makeev helped himself to a cognac from a bottle on the

sideboard and the Irishman came back with a china mug in each hand. 'Well, what's happened?'

'First of all, my sources tell me the Jobert brothers have turned up very dead indeed. Was that wise?'

'To use an immortal phrase from one of those old James Cagney movies, they had it coming. Now what else has happened?'

'Oh, an old friend from your dim past has surfaced. One Martin Brosnan.'

'Holy Mother of God!' Dillon seemed transfixed for a moment. 'Martin? Martin Brosnan? Where in the hell did he turn up from?'

'He's living right here in Paris, just up the river from you on the Quai de Montebello, the block on the corner opposite Notre Dame. Very ornate entrance. Within walking distance of here. You can't miss it. Has scaffolding on the front. Some sort of building work going on.'

'All very detailed.' Dillon took a bottle of Bushmills from the cupboard and poured one. 'Why?'

'I've had a look on my way here.'

'What's all this got to do with me?'

So Makeev told him, Max Hernu, Savary, Tania Novikova in London, everything. 'So,' he said as he finished. 'At least we know what our friends are up to.'

'This Novikova girl could be very useful to me,' Dillon said. 'Will she play things our way?'

'No question. She worked for me for some years. A very clever young woman. Like me, she isn't happy with present changes back home. Her boss is a different matter. Colonel Yuri Gatov. All for change. One of those.'

'Yes, she could be important,' Dillon said.

'Do I take it this means you want to go to London?'

'When I know, I'll let you know.'

'And Brosnan?'

69

'I could pass him on the street and he wouldn't recognise me.'

'You're sure?'

'Josef, I could pass you and you wouldn't recognise me. You've never really seen me change, have you? Have you come in your car?'

'Of course not. Taxi. I hope I can get one back.'

'I'll get my coat and walk some of the way with you.'

He went out and Makeev buttoned his coat and poured another brandy. There was a slight sound behind him and when he turned, Dillon stood there in cap and reefer coat, hunched over in some strange way. Even the shape of his face seemed different. He looked fifteen years older. The change in body language was incredible.

'My God, it's amazing,' Makeev said.

Dillon straightened up and grinned, 'Josef, my old son, if I'd stuck to the stage I'd have been a theatrical knight by now. Come on, let's get going.'

The snow was only a light powdering on the ground, barges passed on the river and Notre Dame, floodlit, floated in the night. They reached the Quai de Montebello without seeing a taxi.

Makeev said, 'Here we are, Brosnan's place. He owns the block. It seems his mother left him rather well off.'

'Is that a fact?'

Dillon looked across at the scaffolding and Makeev said, 'Apartment Four, the one on the corner on the first floor.'

'Does he live alone?'

'Not married. Has a woman friend, Anne-Marie Audin . . .'

'The war photographer? I saw her once back in seventy-one in Belfast. Brosnan and Liam Devlin, my boss at the time, were giving her a privileged look at the IRA.'

'Did you meet her?'

'Not personally. Do they live together?'

'Apparently not.' A taxi came out of a side turning and moved towards them and Makeev raised an arm. 'We'll speak tomorrow.'

The taxi drove off and Dillon was about to turn away when Brosnan came round the corner. Dillon recognised him instantly.

'Now then, Martin, you old bastard,' he said softly.

Brosnan went up the steps and inside. Dillon turned, smiling, and walked away, whistling to himself softly.

At his flat in Cavendish Square, Ferguson was just getting ready to go to bed when the phone rang. Hernu said, 'Bad news. He's knocked off the Jobert brothers.'

'Dear me,' Ferguson said. 'He doesn't mess about, does he?'

'I've been to see Brosnan to ask him to come in with us on this. I'm afraid he's refused. Offered to give us his advice and so on, but he won't become actively involved.'

'Nonsense,' Ferguson said. 'We can't have that. When the ship is sinking it's all hands to the pumps and this ship is sinking very fast indeed.'

'What do you suggest?'

'I think it might be an idea if I came over to see him. I'm not sure of the time. I've things to arrange. Possibly this afternoon. We'll let you know.'

'Excellent. I couldn't be more pleased.'

Ferguson sat there thinking about it for a while and then he phoned Mary Tanner at her flat. 'I suppose like me, you'd hoped for a relatively quiet night after your early rise this morning?' he said.

'It had crossed my mind. Has something happened?'

He brought her up to date. 'I think it might be an idea

71

to go over tomorrow, have a chat with Hernu then speak to Brosnan. He must be made to realise how serious this is.'

'Do you want me to come?'

'Naturally. I can't even make sense of a menu over there whereas we all know that one of the benefits of your rather expensive education is fluency in the French language. Get in touch with the transport officer at the Ministry and tell him I want the Lear jet standing by tomorrow.'

'I'll handle it. Anything else?'

'No, I'll see you at the office in the morning and don't forget your passport.'

Ferguson put down the phone, got into bed and switched off the light.

Back on the barge, Dillon boiled the kettle, then poured a little Bushmills whiskey into a mug, added some lemon juice, sugar and the boiling water and went back into the stateroom, sipping the hot toddy. *My God, Martin Brosnan after all these years.* His mind went back to the old days with the American and Liam Devlin, his old commander. Devlin, the living legend of the IRA. Wild, exciting days, taking on the might of the British Army, face to face. Nothing would ever be the same as that.

There was a stack of London newspapers on the table. He'd bought them all at the Gare de Lyon newsstand earlier. There was the *Daily Mail*, the *Express*, *The Times*, and the *Telegraph*. It was the political sections that interested him most and all the stories were similar. The Gulf crisis, the air strikes on Baghdad, speculation on when the land war would start. And photos, of course. Prime Minister John Major outside Number Ten Downing Street. The British press was wonderful. There were discussions about security, speculation as to possible Arab terrorist attacks

72

and articles that even included maps and street plans of the immediate area around Downing Street. And more photos of the Prime Minister and cabinet ministers arriving for the daily meetings of the War Cabinet. London, that was where the action was, no doubt about it. He put the papers away neatly, finished his toddy and went to bed.

One of the first things Ferguson did on reaching his office was to dictate a further brief report to the Prime Minister bringing him up to date and informing him of the Paris trip. Mary took the draft along to the copy room. The duty clerk just coming to the end of the night shift was a woman, a Mrs Alice Johnson, a war widow whose husband had been killed in the Falklands. She got on with the typing of the report instantly, had just finished putting it through the copier when Gordon Brown entered. He was on a split shift. Three hours from ten until one and six until ten in the evening. He put his briefcase down and took off his jacket.

'You go whenever you like, Alice. Anything special?'

'Just this report for Captain Tanner. It's a Number Ten job. I said I'd take it along.'

'I'll take it for you,' Brown said. 'You get going.'

She passed him both copies of the report and started to clear her desk. No chance to make an extra copy, but at least he could read it which he did as he went along the corridor to Mary Tanner's office. She was sitting at her desk when he went in.

'That report you wanted, Captain Tanner. Shall I arrange a messenger?'

'No thanks, Gordon. I'll see to it.'

'Anything else, Captain?'

'No, I'm just clearing the desk. Brigadier Ferguson and I are going to Paris.' She glanced at her watch. 'I'll

73

have to get moving. We're due out of Gatwick at eleven.'

'Well, I hope you enjoy yourself.'

When he went back to the copy room Alice Johnson was still there. 'I say, Alice,' he said, 'would you mind hanging on for a little while? Only something's come up. I'll make it up to you.'

'That's all right,' she said. 'You get off.'

He put on his coat, hurried downstairs to the canteen and went into one of the public telephone booths. Tania Novikova was only at the flat because of the lateness of the hour when she had left the Embassy the previous night.

'I've told you not to ring me here. I'll ring you,' she told him.

'I must see you. I'm free at one.'

'Impossible.'

'I've seen another report. The same business.'

'I see. Have you got a copy?'

'No, that wasn't possible, but I've read it.'

'What did it say?'

'I'll tell you at lunchtime.'

She realised then that control on her part, severe control, was necessary. Her voice was cold and hard when she said, 'Don't waste my time, Gordon, I'm busy. I think I'd better bring this conversation to an end. I may give you a ring sometime, but then I may not.'

He panicked instantly. 'No, let me tell you. There wasn't much. Just that the two French criminals involved had been murdered, they presumed by the man Dillon. Oh, and Brigadier Ferguson and Captain Tanner are flying over to Paris in the Lear jet at noon.'

'Why?'

'They're hoping to persuade this man Martin Brosnan to help them.'

'Good,' she said. 'You've done well, Gordon. I'll see you

74

tonight at your flat. Six o'clock and bring your work sched-ule for the next couple of weeks.' She rang off.

Brown went upstairs, full of elation.

Ferguson and Mary Tanner had an excellent flight and touched down at Charles de Gaulle Airport just after one. By two o'clock they were being ushered into Hernu's office at DGSE headquarters in Boulevard Mortier.

He embraced Ferguson briefly. 'Charles, you old rogue, it's far too long.'

'Now then, none of your funny French ways,' Ferguson told him. 'You'll be kissing me on both cheeks next. Mary Tanner, my aide.'

She was wearing a rather nice Armani trouser suit of dark brown and a pair of exquisite ankle boots by Manolo Blahnik, diamond stud earrings and a small gold Rolex divers' watch completed the picture. For a girl who was not supposed to be particularly pretty, she looked stunning. Hernu, who knew class when he saw it, kissed her hand. 'Captain Tanner, your reputation precedes you.'

'Only in the nicest way, I hope,' she replied in fluent French.

'Good,' Ferguson said. 'So now we've got all that stuff over, let's get down to brass tacks. What about Brosnan?'

'I have spoken to him this morning and he's agreed to see us at his apartment at three. Time for a late lunch. We have excellent canteen facilities here. Everyone mixes in from the Director downwards.' He opened the door. 'Just follow me. It may not be quite the best food in Paris, but it's certainly the cheapest.'

In the stateroom at the barge, Dillon was pouring a glass of Krug and studying a large-scale map of London. Around

75

him, pinned to the mahogany walls, were articles and reports from all the newspapers specifically referring to affairs at Number Ten, the Gulf War and how well John Major was doing. There were photos of the youngest Prime Minister of the century, several of them. In fact, the eyes seemed to follow him about. It was as if Major was watching him.

'And I've got my eye on you, too, fella,' Dillon said softly.

The things that intrigued him were the constant daily meetings of the British War Cabinet at Number Ten. All those bastards, all together in the same spot. What a target. Brighton all over again and that affair had come close to taking out the entire British Government. But Number Ten as a target? That didn't seem possible. Fortress Thatcher it had been dubbed by some after that redoubtable lady's security improvements. There were footsteps on the deck overhead. He opened a drawer in the table casually revealing a Smith & Wesson .38 revolver, closed it again as Makeev came in.

'I could have telephoned, but I thought I'd speak to you personally,' the Russian said.

'What now?'

'I've brought you some photos we've had taken of Brosnan as he is now. Oh, and that's the girlfriend, Anne-Marie Audin.'

'Good. Anything else?'

'I've heard from Tania Novikova again. It seems Brigadier Ferguson and his aide, a Captain Mary Tanner, have flown over. They were due out of Gatwick at eleven.' He glanced at his watch. 'I'd say they'll be with Hernu right now.'

'To what end?'

'The real purpose of the trip is to see Brosnan. Try and persuade him to help actively in the search for you.'

'Really?' Dillon smiled coldly. 'Martin's becoming a serious inconvenience. I might have to do something about that.'

Makeev nodded at the clippings on the walls. 'Your own private gallery?'

'I'm just getting to know the man,' Dillon said. 'Do you want a drink?'

'No thanks.' Suddenly Makeev felt uncomfortable. 'I've things to do. I'll be in touch.'

He went up the companionway. Dillon poured himself a little more champagne, sipped a little then stopped, walked into the kitchen and poured the whole bottle down the sink. Conspicuous waste, but he felt like it. He went back into the stateroom, lit a cigarette and looked at the clippings again, but all he could think about was Martin Brosnan. He picked up the photos Makeev had brought and pinned them up beside the clippings.

Anne-Marie was in the kitchen at the Quai de Montebello, Brosnan going over a lecture at the table, when the doorbell rang. She hurried out, wiping her hands on a cloth.

'That will be them,' she said. 'I'll get it. Now don't forget your promise.'

She touched the back of his neck briefly and went out. There was a sound of voices in the hall and she returned with Ferguson, Hernu and Mary Tanner.

'I'll make some coffee,' Anne-Marie said and went into the kitchen.

'My dear Martin.' Ferguson held out his hand. 'It's been too long.'

'Amazing,' Brosnan said. 'We only ever meet when you want something.'

'Someone you haven't met, my aide, Captain Mary Tanner.'

Brosnan looked her over quickly, the small, dark girl

with the scar on the left cheek, and liked what he saw. 'Couldn't you find a better class of work than what this old sod has to offer?' he demanded.

Odd that she should feel slightly breathless faced with this forty-five-year-old man with the ridiculously long hair and the face that had seen rather too much of the worst of life.

'There's a recession on. You have to take what's going these days,' she said, her hand light in his.

'Right. We've had the cabaret act so let's get down to business,' Ferguson said. Hernu went to the window, Ferguson and Mary took the sofa opposite Brosnan.

'Max tells me he spoke to you last night after the murder of the Jobert brothers?'

Anne-Marie came in with coffee on a tray. Brosnan said, 'That's right.'

'He tells me you've refused to help us?'

'That's putting it a bit strongly. What I said was that I'd do anything I could except become actively involved myself and if you've come to attempt to change my mind, you're wasting your time.'

Anne-Marie poured coffee. Ferguson said, 'You agree with him, Miss Audin?'

'Martin slipped out of that life a long time ago, Brigadier,' she said carefully. 'I would not care to see him step back in for whatever reason.'

'But surely you can see that a man like Dillon must be stopped?'

'Then others must do the stopping. Why Martin, for God's sake?' She was distressed now and angry. 'It's your job, people like you. This sort of thing is how you make your living.'

Max Hernu came across and picked up a cup of coffee. 'But Professor Brosnan is in a special position as regards this business, you must see that, mademoiselle. He knew

Dillon intimately, worked with him for years. He could be of great help to us.'

'I don't want to see him with a gun in his hand,' she said, 'and that's what it would come to. Once his foot is on that road again, there can only be one end.'

She was very distressed, turned and went through into the kitchen. Mary Tanner went after her and closed the door. Anne-Marie was leaning against the sink, arms folded as if holding herself in, agony on her face.

'They don't see, do they? They don't understand what I mean.'

'I do,' Mary said simply. 'I understand exactly what you mean,' and as Anne-Marie started to sob quietly, went and put her arms around her.

Brosnan opened the French windows and stood on the terrace by the scaffolding taking in lungsful of cold air. Ferguson joined him. 'I'm sorry for the distress we've caused her.'

'No you're not, you only see the end in view. You always did.'

'He's a bad one, Martin.'

'I know,' Brosnan nodded. 'A real can of worms the little bastard has opened this time. I must get a smoke.'

He went inside. Hernu was sitting by the fire. Brosnan found a packet of cigarettes, hesitated, then opened the kitchen door. Anne-Marie and Mary were sitting opposite each other, holding hands across the table.

Mary turned. 'She'll be fine. Just leave us for a while.'

Brosnan went back to the terrace. He lit a cigarette and leaned against the balustrade. 'She seems quite a lady, that aide of yours. That scar on her left cheek. Shrapnel. What's her story?'

'She was doing a tour of duty as a lieutenant with the

Military Police in Londonderry. Some IRA chap was delivering a car bomb when the engine failed. He left it at the kerb and did a runner. Unfortunately it was outside an old folks' home. Mary was driving past in a Land Rover when a civilian alerted her. She got in the car, released the brake and managed to freewheel down the hill on to some waste land. It exploded as she made a run for it.'

'Good God!'

'Yes, I'd agree on that occasion. When she came out of hospital she received a severe reprimand for breaking standing orders and the George Medal for the gallantry of her action. I took her on after that.'

'A lot of still waters there.' Brosnan sighed and tossed his cigarette out into space as Mary Tanner joined them.

'She's gone to lie down in the bedroom.'

'All right,' Brosnan said. 'Let's go back in.' They went and sat down again and he lit another cigarette. 'Let's get this over with. What did you want to say?'

Ferguson turned to Mary. 'Your turn, my dear.'

'I've been through the files, checked out everything the computer can tell us.' She opened her brown hand-bag and took out a photo. 'The only likeness of Dillon we can find. It's from a group photo taken at RADA twenty years ago. We had an expert in the department blow it up.'

There was a lack of definition, the texture grainy and the face was totally anonymous. Just another young boy.

Brosnan gave it back. 'Useless. I didn't even recognise him myself.'

'Oh, it's him all right. The man on his right became quite successful on television. He's dead now.'

'Not through Dillon?'

'Oh, no, stomach cancer, but he was approached by one of our people back in nineteen eighty-one and confirmed that it was Dillon standing next to him in the photo.'

'The only likeness we have,' Ferguson said. 'And no bloody use at all.'

'Did you know that he took a pilot's licence and a commercial one at that?' Mary said.

'No, I never knew that,' Brosnan said.

'According to one of our informants, he did it in the Lebanon some years ago.'

'Why were your people on his case in eighty-one?' Brosnan asked.

'Yes, well that's interesting,' she told him. 'You told Colonel Hernu that he'd quarrelled with the IRA, had dropped out and joined the international terrorist circuit.'

'That's right.'

'It seems they took him back in nineteen eighty-one. They were having trouble with their active service units in England. Too many arrests, that kind of thing. Through an informer in Ulster we heard that he was operating in London for a time. There were at least three or four incidents attributed to him. Two car bombs and the murder of a police informant in Ulster who'd been relocated with his family in Maida Vale.'

'And we didn't come within spitting distance of catching him,' Ferguson said.

'Well, you wouldn't,' Brosnan told him. 'Let me go over it again. He's an actor of genius. He really can change before your eyes, just by use of body language. You'd have to see it to believe it. Imagine what he can do with make-up, hair colouring changes. He's only five feet five, remember. I've seen him dress as a woman and fool soldiers on foot patrol in Belfast.'

Mary Tanner was leaning forward intently. 'Go on,' she said softly.

'You want to know another reason why you've never caught him? He works out a series of aliases. Changes hair colour, uses whatever tricks of make-up are necessary, then

81

takes his photo. That's what goes on his false passport or identity papers. He keeps a collection, then when he needs to move, makes himself into the man on the photo.'

'Ingenious,' Hernu said.

'Exactly, so no hope of any help from television or newspaper publicity of the have-you-seen-this-man type. Wherever he goes, he slips under the surface. If he was working in London and needed anything at all, help, weapons, whatever, he'd simply pretend to be an ordinary criminal and use the underworld.'

'You mean he wouldn't go near any kind of IRA contact at all?' Mary said.

'I doubt it. Maybe someone who'd been in very deep cover for years, someone he could really trust and people like that are thin on the ground.'

'There is a point in all this which no one has touched on,' Hernu said. 'Who is he working for?'

'Well it certainly isn't the IRA,' Mary said. 'We did an instant computer check and we have links with both the RUC computer and British Army intelligence at Lisburn. Not a smell from anyone about the attempt on Mrs Thatcher.'

'Oh, I believe that,' Brosnan said, 'although you can never be sure.'

'There are the Iraqis, of course,' Ferguson said. 'Saddam would dearly love to blow everyone up at the moment.'

'True, but don't forget Hizbollah, PLO, Wrath of Allah and a few others in between. He's worked for them all,' Brosnan reminded him.

'Yes,' Ferguson said, 'and checking our sources through that lot would take time and I don't think we've got it.'

'You think he'll try again?' Mary asked.

'Nothing concrete, my dear, but I've been in this business a lifetime. I always go by my instincts and this time my instincts tell me there's more to it.'

'Well, I can't help you there. I've done all I can.' Brosnan stood up.

'All you're prepared to, you mean?' Ferguson said.

They moved into the hall and Brosnan opened the door. 'I suppose you'll be going back to London?'

'Oh, I don't know. I thought we might stay over and sample the delights of Paris. I haven't stayed at the Ritz since the refurbishment.'

Mary Tanner said, 'That will give the expenses a bashing.' She held out her hand. 'Goodbye, Professor Brosnan, it was nice to be able to put a face to the name.'

'And you,' he said. 'Colonel,' he nodded to Hernu and closed the door.

When he went into the drawing room, Anne-Marie came in from the bedroom. Her face was drawn and pale. 'Did you come to any decision?' she asked.

'I gave you my word. I've helped them all I can. Now they've gone and that's an end to it.'

She opened the table drawer. Inside there was an assortment of pens, envelopes, writing paper, stamps. There was also a Browning High Power 9-mm pistol, one of the most deadly handguns in the world, preferred by the SAS above all others.

She didn't say a word, simply closed the drawer and looked at him calmly. 'I'll make some coffee,' she said and went into the kitchen.

In the limousine Hernu said, 'You've lost him. He won't do any more.'

'I wouldn't be too sure of that. We'll discuss it over dinner at the Ritz later. You'll join us, I hope? Eight o'clock all right?'

'Delighted,' Hernu said. 'Group Four must be rather more generous with its expenses than my own poor department.'

'Oh, it's all on dear Mary here,' Ferguson said. 'Flashed this wonderful piece of plastic at me the other day which American Express had sent her. The Platinum Card. Can you believe that, Colonel?'

'Damn you!' Mary said.

Hernu lay back and laughed helplessly.

Tania Novikova came out of the bathroom of Gordon Brown's Camden flat combing her hair. He pulled on a dressing-gown.

'You've got to go?' he said.

'I must. Come into the living room.' She pulled on her coat and turned to face him. 'No more coming to the Bayswater flat, no more telephones. The work schedule you showed me. All split shifts for the next month. Why?'

'They're not popular, especially for people with families. That isn't a problem for me, so I agreed to do it for the moment. And it pays more.'

'So, you usually finish at one o'clock and start again at six in the evening?'

'Yes.'

'You have an answering machine, the kind where you can phone home and get your messages?'

'Yes.'

'Good. We can keep in touch that way.'

She started for the door and he caught her arm. 'But when will I see you?'

'Difficult at the moment, Gordon, we must be careful. If you've nothing better to do, always come home between shifts. I'll do what I can.'

He kissed her hungrily. 'Darling.'

She pushed him away. 'I must go now, Gordon.'

She opened the door, went downstairs and let herself out of the street entrance. It was still very cold and she pulled up her collar.

'My God, the things I do for Mother Russia,' she said, went down to the corner and hailed a cab.

FIVE

It was colder than ever in the evening, a front from Siberia sweeping across Europe, too cold for snow even. In the apartment, just before seven, Brosnan put some more logs on the fire.

Anne-Marie, lying full length on the sofa, stirred and sat up. 'So we stay in to eat?'

'I think so,' he said. 'A vile night.'

'Good. I'll see what I can do in the kitchen.'

He put on the television news programme. More air strikes against Baghdad, but still no sign of a land war. He switched the set off and Anne-Marie emerged from the kitchen and picked up her coat from the chair where she had left it.

'Your fridge, as usual, is almost empty. Unless you wish me to concoct a meal based on some rather stale cheese, one egg, and half a carton of milk, I'll have to go round the corner to the delicatessen.'

'I'll come with you.'

'Nonsense,' she said. 'Why should we both suffer? I'll see you soon.'

She blew him a kiss and went out. Brosnan went and opened the French windows. He stood on the terrace, shivering and lit a cigarette, watching for her. A moment later, she emerged from the front door and started along the pavement.

'Goodbye, my love,' he called dramatically. 'Parting is such sweet sorrow.'

'Idiot!' she called back. 'Go back in before you catch pneumonia.' She moved away, careful on the frozen pavement, and disappeared round the corner.

At that moment, the phone rang. Brosnan turned and hurried in, leaving the French windows open.

Dillon had an early meal at a small café he often frequented. He was on foot and his route back to the barge took him past Brosnan's apartment block. He paused on the other side of the road, cold in spite of the reefer coat and the knitted cap pulled down over his ears. He stood there, swinging his arms vigorously, looking up at the lighted windows of the apartment.

When Anne-Marie came out of the entrance, he recognised her instantly and stepped back into the shadows. The street was silent, no traffic movement at all and when Brosnan leaned over the balustrade and called down to her, Dillon heard every word he said. It gave him a totally false impression. That she was leaving for the evening. As she disappeared round the corner, he crossed the road quickly. He checked the Walther in his waistband at the rear, had a quick glance each way to see that no one was about, then started to climb the scaffolding.

It was Mary Tanner on the phone. 'Brigadier Ferguson wondered whether we could see you again in the morning before going back?'

'It won't do you any good,' Brosnan told her.

'Is that a yes or a no?'

'All right,' he said reluctantly. 'If you must.'

'I understand,' she said, 'I really do. Has Anne-Marie recovered?'

'A tough lady, that one,' he said. 'She's covered more wars than we've had hot dinners. That's why I've always found her attitude about such things where I'm concerned strange.'

'Oh, dear,' she said. 'You men can really be incredibly stupid on occasions. She loves you, Professor, it's as simple as that. I'll see you in the morning.'

Brosnan put the phone down. There was a draught of cold air, the fire flared up. He turned and found Sean Dillon standing in the open French windows, the Walther in his left hand.

'God bless all here,' he said.

The delicatessen in the side street, as with so many such places these days, was run by an Indian, a Mr Patel. He was most assiduous where Anne-Marie was concerned, carried the basket for her as they went round the shelves. Delicious French bread sticks, milk, eggs, Brie cheese, a beautiful quiche.

'Baked by my wife with her own hands,' Mr Patel assured her. 'Two minutes in the microwave and a perfect meal.'

She laughed. 'Then all we need is a very large tin of caviar and some smoked salmon to complement it.'

He packed the things carefully for her. 'I'll put them on Professor Brosnan's account as usual.'

'Thank you,' she said.

He opened the door for her. 'A pleasure, mademoiselle.'

She started back along the frosty pavement feeling suddenly unaccountably cheerful.

'Jesus, Martin, and the years have been good to you,' Dillon pulled the glove off his right hand with his teeth and found a pack of cigarettes in his pocket. Brosnan, a yard from the table drawer and the Browning High Power, made a cautious move. 'Naughty.' Dillon gestured with the Walther. 'Sit on the arm of the sofa and put your hands behind your head.'

Brosnan did as he was told. 'You're enjoying yourself, Sean.'

'I am so. How's that old sod Liam Devlin these days?'

'Alive and well. Still in Kilrea outside Dublin, but then you know that.'

'And that's a fact.'

'The job at Valenton, Mrs Thatcher,' Brosnan said. 'Very sloppy, Sean. I mean, to go with a couple of bums like the Joberts. You really must be losing your touch.'

'You think so?'

'Presumably it was a big pay day?'

'Very big,' Dillon said.

'I hope you got your money in advance.'

'Very funny.' Dillon was beginning to get annoyed.

'One thing does intrigue me,' Brosnan said. 'What you want with me after all these years?'

'Oh, I know all about you,' Dillon said. 'How they're pumping you for information about me. Hernu, the Action Service colonel, that old bastard Ferguson and this girl sidekick of his, this Captain Tanner. Nothing I don't know. I've got the right friends, you see, Martin, the kind of people who can access anything.'

'Really, and were they happy when you failed with Mrs Thatcher?'

'Just a try-out, that, just a perhaps. I've promised them an alternative target. You know how this game works.'

'I certainly do and one thing I do know is that the IRA don't pay for hits. Never have.'

'Who said I was working for the IRA?' Dillon grinned. 'Plenty of other people with enough reason to hit the Brits these days.'

Brosnan saw it then, or thought he did. 'Baghdad?'

'Sorry, Martin, you can go to your maker puzzling over that one for all eternity.'

Brosnan said, 'Just indulge me. A big hit for Saddam. I mean, the war stinks. He needs something badly.'

'Christ, you always did run on.'

'President Bush stays back in Washington so that leaves the Brits. You fail on the best-known woman in the world, so what's next? The Prime Minister?'

'Where you're going it doesn't matter, son.'

'But I'm right, aren't I?'

'Damn you, Brosnan, you always were the clever bastard!' Dillon exploded angrily.

'You'll never get away with it,' Brosnan said.

'You think so? I'll just have to prove you wrong then.'

'As I said, you must be losing your touch, Sean. This bungled attempt to get Mrs Thatcher. Reminds me of a job dear old Frank Barry pulled back in seventy-nine when he tried to hit the British Foreign Secretary, Lord Carrington, when he was passing through St Etienne. I'm rather surprised you used the same ground plan, but then you always did think Barry was special, didn't you?'

'He was the best.'

'And at the end of things, very dead,' Brosnan said.

'Yes, well whoever got him must have given it to him in the back,' Dillon said.

'Not true,' Brosnan told him. 'We were face to face as I recall.'

'You killed Frank Barry?' Dillon whispered.

'Well somebody had to,' Brosnan said. 'It's what usually happens to mad dogs. I was working for Ferguson, by the way.'

'You bastard.' Dillon raised the Walther, took careful aim and the door opened and Anne-Marie walked in with the shopping bags.

Dillon swung towards her. Brosnan called, 'Look out!' and went down and Dillon fired twice at the sofa.

Anne-Marie screamed, not in terror, but in fury, dropped her bags and rushed at him. Dillon tried to fend her off, staggered back through the French windows. Inside, Brosnan crawled towards the table and reached for the drawer. Anne-Marie scratched at Dillon's face. He cursed, pushing her away from him. She fell against the balustrade and went over backwards.

Brosnan had the drawer open now, knocked the lamp on the table sideways, plunging the room into darkness and reached for the Browning. Dillon fired three times very fast and ducked for the door. Brosnan fired twice, too late. The door banged. He got to his feet, ran to the terrace and looked over. Anne-Marie lay on the pavement below. He turned and ran through the drawing room into the hall, got the door open and went downstairs two at a time. It was snowing when he went out on the steps. Of Dillon there was no sign, but the night porter was kneeling beside Anne-Marie.

He looked up. 'There was a man, Professor, with a gun. He ran across the road.'

'Never mind.' Brosnan sat down and cradled her in his arms. 'An ambulance and hurry.'

The snow was falling quite fast now. He held her close and waited.

Ferguson, Mary and Max Hernu were having a thoroughly enjoyable time in the magnificent dining room at the Ritz. They were already on their second bottle of Louis Roederer Crystal champagne and the Brigadier was in excellent form.

'Who was it who said that when a man tires of champagne he's tired of life?' he demanded.

'He must certainly have been a Frenchman,' Hernu told him.

'Very probably, but I think the time has come when we should toast the provider of this feast.' He raised his glass. 'To you, Mary, my love.'

She was about to respond when she saw in the mirror on the wall Inspector Savary at the entrance speaking to the head waiter. 'I think you're being paged, Colonel,' she told Hernu.

He glanced round. 'What's happened now?' He got up, threaded his way through the tables and approached Savary. They talked for a few moments, glancing towards the table.

Mary said, 'I don't know about you, sir, but I get a bad feeling.'

Before he could reply, Hernu came back to them, his face grave. 'I'm afraid I've got some rather ugly news.'

'Dillon?' Ferguson asked.

'He paid a call on Brosnan a short while ago.'

'What happened?' Ferguson demanded. 'Is Brosnan all right?'

'Oh, yes. There was some gunplay. Dillon got away.' He sighed heavily. 'But Mademoiselle Audin is at the Hôpital St-Louis. From what Savary tells me, it doesn't look good.'

Brosnan was in the waiting room on the second floor when they arrived, pacing up and down smoking a cigarette. His eyes were wild, such a rage there as Mary Tanner had never seen.

She was the first to reach him. 'I'm so sorry.'

Ferguson said, 'What happened?'

Briefly, coldly, Brosnan told them. As he finished, a tall,

greying man in surgeon's robes came in. Brosnan turned to him quickly. 'How is she, Henri?' He said to the others, 'Professor Henri Dubois, a colleague of mine at the Sorbonne.'

'Not good, my friend,' Dubois told him. 'The injuries to the left leg and spine are bad enough, but even more worrying is the skull fracture. They're just preparing her for surgery now. I'll operate straight away.'

He went out. Hernu put an arm around Brosnan's shoulders. 'Let's go and get some coffee, my friend. I think it's going to be a long night.'

'But I only drink tea,' Brosnan said, his face bone white, his eyes dark. 'Never could stomach coffee. Isn't that the funniest thing you ever heard?'

There was a small café for visitors on the ground floor. Not many customers at that time of night. Savary had gone off to handle the police side of the business, the others sat at a table in the corner.

Ferguson said, 'I know you've got other things on your mind, but is there anything you can tell us? Anything he said to you?'

'Oh yes – plenty. He's working for somebody and definitely not the IRA. He's being paid for this one and from the way he boasted, it's big money.'

'Any idea who?'

'When I suggested Saddam Hussein he got angry. My guess is you wouldn't have to look much further. An interesting point. He knew about all of you.'

'All of us?' Hernu said. 'You're sure?'

'Oh, yes, he boasted about that.' He turned to Ferguson. 'Even knew about you and Captain Tanner being in town to pump me for information, that's how he put it. He said he had the right friends.' He frowned, trying to remember the phrase exactly. 'The kind of people who can access anything.'

'Did he indeed?' Ferguson glanced at Hernu. 'Rather worrying, that.'

'And you've got another problem. He spoke of the Thatcher affair as being just a try-out, that he had an alternative target.'

'Go on,' Ferguson said.

'I managed to get him to lose his temper by needling him about what a botch-up the Valenton thing was. I think you'll find he intends to have a crack at the British Prime Minister.'

Mary said, 'Are you certain?'

'Oh, yes.' He nodded. 'I baited him about that, told him he'd never get away with it. He lost his temper. Said he'd just have to prove me wrong.'

Ferguson looked at Hernu and sighed. 'So now we know. I'd better go along to the Embassy and alert all our people in London.'

'I'll do the same here,' Hernu said. 'After all, he has to leave the country sometime. We'll alert all airports and ferries. The usual thing, but discreetly, of course.'

They got up and Brosnan said, 'You're wasting your time. You won't get him, not in any usual way. You don't even know what you're looking for.'

'Perhaps, Martin,' Ferguson said. 'But we'll just have to do our best, won't we?'

Mary Tanner followed them to the door. 'Look, if you don't need me, Brigadier, I'd like to stay.'

'Of course, my dear. I'll see you later.'

She went to the counter and got two cups of tea. 'The French are wonderful,' she said. 'They always think we're crazy to want milk in our tea.'

'Takes all sorts,' he said and offered her a cigarette. 'Ferguson told me how you got that scar.'

'Souvenir of old Ireland,' she shrugged.

He was desperately trying to think of something to say. 'What about your family? Do they live in London?'

'My father was a Professor of Surgery at Oxford. He died some time ago. Cancer. My mother's still alive. Has an estate in Herefordshire.'

'Brothers and sisters?'

'I had one brother. Ten years older than me. He was shot dead in Belfast in nineteen-eighty. Sniper got him from the Divis Flats. He was a Marine Commando captain.'

'I'm sorry.'

'A long time ago.'

'It can't make you particularly well disposed towards a man like me.'

'Ferguson explained to me how you became involved with the IRA after Viet Nam.'

'Just another bloody Yank sticking his nose in, is that what you think?' he sighed. 'It seemed the right thing to do at the time, it really did and don't let's pretend. I was up to my neck in it for five long and bloody years.'

'And how do you see it now?'

'Ireland?' he laughed harshly. 'The way I feel I'd see it sink into the sea with pleasure.' He got up. 'Come on, let's stretch our legs,' and he led the way out.

Dillon was in the kitchen in the barge heating the kettle when the phone rang. Makeev said, 'She's in the Hôpital St-Louis. We've had to be discreet in our enquiries, but from what my informant can ascertain, she's on the critical list.'

'Sod it,' Dillon said. 'If only she'd kept her hands to herself.'

'This could cause a devil of a fuss. I'd better come and see you.'

'I'll be here.'

Dillon poured hot water into a basin then he went into the bathroom. First he took off his shirt, then he got a briefcase from the cupboard under the sink. It was exactly as Brosnan had forecast. Inside he had a range of passports, all of himself suitably disguised. There was also a first-class make-up kit.

Over the years he had travelled backwards and forwards to England many times, frequently through Jersey in the Channel Islands. Jersey was British soil. Once there, a British citizen didn't need a passport for the flight to the English mainland. So, a French tourist holidaying in Jersey. He selected a passport in the name of Henri Jacaud, a car salesman from Rennes.

To go with it, he found a Jersey driving licence in the name of Peter Hilton with an address in the Island's main town of St Helier. Jersey driving licences, unlike the usual British mainland variety, carry a photo. It was always useful to have positive identification on you, he'd learned that years ago. Nothing better than for people to be able to check the face with a photo and the photos on the driving licence and on the French passport were identical. That was the whole point.

He dissolved some black hair dye into the warm water and started to brush it into his fair hair. Amazing what a difference it made, just changing the hair colour. He blow-dried it and brilliantined it back in place, then he selected from a range in his case, a pair of horn-rimmed spectacles, slightly tinted. He closed his eyes, thinking about the role and when he opened them again, Henri Jacaud stared out of the mirror. It was quite extraordinary. He closed the case, put it back in the cupboard, pulled on his shirt and went into the stateroom carrying the passport and the driving licence.

At that precise moment Makeev came down the

companionway. 'Good God!' he said. 'For a moment I thought it was someone else.'

'But it is,' Dillon said. 'Henri Jacaud, car salesman from Rennes on his way to Jersey for a winter break. Hydrofoil from St Malo.' He held up the driving licence. 'Who is also Jersey resident Peter Hilton, accountant in St Helier.'

'You don't need a passport to get to London?'

'Not if you're a Jersey resident, it's British territory. The driving licence just puts a face to me. Always makes people feel happier. Makes them feel they know who you are, even the police.'

'What happened tonight, Sean? What really happened?'

'I decided the time had come to take care of Brosnan. Come on, Josef, he knows me too damned well. Knows me in a way no one else does and that could be dangerous.'

'I can see that. A clever one, the Professor.'

'There's more to it than that, Josef. He understands how I make my moves, how I think. He's the same kind of animal as I am. We inhabited the same world and people don't change. No matter how much he thinks he has he's still the same underneath, the same man who was the most feared enforcer the IRA had in the old days.'

'So you decided to eliminate him?'

'It was an impulse. I was passing his place, saw the woman leaving. He called to her. The way it sounded I thought she was gone for the night so I took a chance and went up the scaffolding.'

'What happened?'

'Oh, I had the drop on him.'

'But didn't kill him?'

Dillon laughed, went out to the kitchen and returned with a bottle of Krug and two glasses. As he uncorked it he said, 'Come on, Josef, face to face after all those years. There were things to be said.'

'You didn't tell him who you were working for?'

97

'Of course not,' Dillon lied cheerfully and poured the champagne. 'What do you take me for?'

He toasted Makeev who said, 'I mean, if he knew you had an alternative target, that you intended to go for Major . . .' He shrugged. 'That would mean that Ferguson would know. It would render your task in London impossible. Aroun, I'm sure, would want to abort the whole business.'

'Well he doesn't know.' Dillon drank some more champagne. 'So Aroun can rest easy. After all, I want that second million. I checked with Zurich, by the way. The first million has been deposited.'

Makeev shifted uncomfortably. 'Of course. So, when do you intend to leave?'

'Tomorrow or the next day. I'll see. Meanwhile something you can organise for me. This Tania Novikova in London. I'll need her help.'

'No problem.'

'First, my father had a second cousin, a Belfast man living in London called Danny Fahy.'

'IRA?'

'Yes, but not active. A deep-cover man. Brilliant with his hands. Worked in light engineering. Could turn his hand to anything. I used him in nineteen eighty-one when I was doing a few jobs for the organisation in London. In those days he lived at number ten Tithe Street in Kilburn. I want Novikova to trace him.'

'Anything else?'

'Yes, I'll need somewhere to stay. She can organise that for me too. She doesn't live in the Embassy, I suppose?'

'No, she has a flat off the Bayswater Road.'

'I wouldn't want to stay there, not on a regular basis. She could be under surveillance. Special Branch at Scotland Yard have a habit of doing that with employees of the Soviet Embassy, isn't that so?'

'Oh, it's not like the old days,' Makeev smiled. 'Thanks to that fool Gorbachev, we're all supposed to be friends these days.'

'I'd still prefer to stay somewhere else. I'll contact her at her flat, no more than that.'

'There is one problem,' Makeev said. 'As regards hardware, explosives, weapons, anything like that you might need, I'm afraid she won't be able to help you there. A handgun perhaps, but no more. As I mentioned when I first told you about her, her boss, Colonel Yuri Gatov, the commander of KGB station in London, is a Gorbachev man, and very well disposed to our British friends.'

'That's all right,' Dillon said, 'I have my own contacts for that kind of thing, but I will need more working capital. If I am checked going through customs on the Jersey to London flight, I couldn't afford to be caught with large sums of money in my briefcase.'

'I'm sure Aroun can fix that for you.'

'That's all right then. I'd like to see him again before I go. Tomorrow morning, I think. Arrange that, will you?'

'All right.' Makeev fastened his coat. 'I'll keep you posted on the situation at the hospital.' He reached the bottom of the companionway and turned. 'There is one thing. Say you managed to pull this thing off. It would lead to the most ferocious manhunt. How would you intend to get out of England?'

Dillon smiled. 'That's exactly what I'm going to give some thought to now. I'll see you in the morning.'

Makeev went up the companionway. Dillon poured another glass of Krug, lit a cigarette and sat at the table, looking at the clippings on the walls. He reached for the pile of newspapers and sorted through them and finally found what he wanted. An old copy of the magazine *Paris Match* from the previous year. Michael Aroun was featured on the front cover. Inside was a seven-page feature about his lifestyle and habits. Dillon lit a cigarette and started going through it.

It was one o'clock in the morning and Mary Tanner was sitting alone in the waiting room when Professor Henri Dubois came in. He was very tired, shoulders bowed, sank wearily into a chair and lit a cigarette.

'Where is Martin?' he asked her.

'It seems Anne-Marie's only close relative is her grandfather. Martin is trying to contact him. Do you know him?'

'Who doesn't, mademoiselle? One of the richest and most powerful industrialists in France. Very old. Eighty-eight, I believe. He was once a patient of mine. He had a stroke last year. I don't think Martin will get very far there. He lives on the family estate, Château Vercors. It's about twenty miles outside Paris.'

Brosnan came in, looking incredibly weary, but when he saw Dubois he said eagerly, 'How is she?'

'I won't pretend, my friend. She's not good. Not good at all. I've done everything that I possibly can. Now we wait.'

'Can I see her?'

'Leave it for a while. I'll let you know.'

'You'll stay?'

'Oh, yes. I'll grab a couple of hours' sleep on my office couch. How did you get on with Pierre Audin?'

'I didn't. Had to deal with his secretary, Fournier. The old man's confined to a wheelchair now. Doesn't know the time of day.'

Dubois sighed. 'I suspected as much. I'll see you later.'

When he'd gone, Mary said, 'You could do with some sleep yourself.'

He managed a dark smile. 'The way I feel now, I don't think I could ever sleep again. All my fault, in a way.' There was despair on his face.

100

'How can you say that?'

'Who I am or to put it another way, what I was. If it hadn't been for that, none of this would have happened.'

'You can't talk like that,' she said. 'Life doesn't work like that.'

The phone on the table rang and she answered it, spoke for a few brief moments, then put it down. 'Just Ferguson checking.' She put a hand on his shoulder. 'Come on, lie down on the couch. Just close your eyes. I'll be here. I'll wake you the moment there's word.'

Reluctantly, he lay back and did as he was told and surprisingly did fall into a dark dreamless sleep. Mary Tanner sat there, brooding, listening to his quiet breathing.

It was just after three when Dubois came in. As if sensing his presence, Brosnan came awake with a start and sat up. 'What is it?'

'She's regained consciousness.'

'Can I see her?' Brosnan got up.

'Yes, of course.' As Brosnan made for the door, Dubois put a hand on his arm. 'Martin, it's not good. I think you should prepare for the worst.'

'No,' Brosnan almost choked. 'It's not possible.'

He ran along the corridor, opened the door of her room and went in. There was a young nurse sitting beside her. Anne-Marie was very pale, her head so swathed in bandages that she looked like a young nun.

'I'll wait outside, monsieur,' the nurse said and left.

Brosnan sat down. He reached for her hand and Anne-Marie opened her eyes. She stared vacantly at him and then recognition dawned and she smiled.

'Martin, is that you?'

'Who else?' He kissed her hand.

Behind them, the door clicked open slightly as Dubois peered in.

'Your hair. Too long. Ridiculously too long.' She put up a hand to touch it. 'In Viet Nam, in the swamp, when the Viet Cong were going to shoot me. You came out of the reeds like some medieval warrior. Your hair was too long then and you wore a headband.'

She closed her eyes and Brosnan said, 'Rest now, don't try to talk.'

'But I must.' She opened them again. 'Let him go, Martin. Give me your promise. It's not worth it. I don't want you going back to what you were.' She grabbed at his hand with surprising strength. 'Promise me.'

'My word on it,' he said.

She lay back, staring up at the ceiling. 'My lovely wild Irish boy. Always loved you, Martin, no one else.'

Her eyes closed gently, the monitoring machine beside the bed changed its tone. Henri Dubois was in the room in a second. 'Outside, Martin – wait.'

He pushed Brosnan out and closed the door. Mary was standing in the corridor. 'Martin?' she said.

He stared at her vacantly and then the door opened and Dubois appeared. 'I'm so sorry, my friend. I'm afraid she's gone.'

On the barge, Dillon came awake instantly when the phone rang. Makeev said, 'She's dead, I'm afraid.'

'That's a shame,' Dillon said. 'It was never intended.'

'What now?' Makeev asked.

'I think I'll leave this afternoon. A good idea in the circumstances. What about Aroun?'

'He'll see us at eleven o'clock.'

'Good. Does he know what's happened?'

'No.'

'Let's keep it that way. I'll meet you outside the place just before eleven.'

He replaced the phone, propped himself up against the pillows. Anne-Marie Audin. A pity about that. He'd never gone in for killing women. An informer once in Derry, but she deserved it. An accident this time, but it smacked of bad luck and that made him feel uneasy. He stubbed out his cigarette and tried to go to sleep again.

It was just after ten when Mary Tanner admitted Ferguson and Hernu to Brosnan's apartment. 'How is he?' Ferguson asked.

'He's kept himself busy. Anne-Marie's grandfather is not well so Martin's been making all the necessary funeral arrangements with his secretary.'

'So soon?' Ferguson said.

'Tomorrow, in the family plot at Vercors.'

She led the way in. Brosnan was standing at the window staring out. He turned to meet them, hands in pockets, his face pale and drawn. 'Well?' he demanded.

'Nothing to report,' Hernu told him. 'We've notified all ports and airports, discreetly, of course.' He hesitated. 'We feel it would be better not to go public on this, Professor, Mademoiselle Audin's unfortunate death, I mean.'

Brosnan seemed curiously indifferent. 'You won't get him. London's the place to look and sooner rather than later. Probably on his way now and for London you'll need me.'

'You mean you'll help us? You'll come in on this thing?' Ferguson said.

'Yes.'

Brosnan lit a cigarette, opened the French windows and stood on the terrace. Mary joined him. 'But you can't, Martin, you promised Anne-Marie.'

'I lied,' he said calmly, 'just to make her going easier. There's nothing out there. Only darkness.'

His face was rock hard, the eyes bleak. It was the face of a stranger. 'Oh, my God,' she whispered.

'I'll have him,' Brosnan said. 'If it's the last thing I do on this earth I'll see him dead.'

SIX

It was just before eleven when Makeev drew up before Michael Aroun's apartment in the Avenue Victor Hugo. His chauffeur drew in beside the kerb and as he switched off the engine, the door opened and Dillon climbed into the rear seat.

'You'd better not be wearing designer shoes,' he said. 'Slush everywhere.'

He smiled and Makeev reached over to close the partition. 'You seem in good form considering the situation.'

'And why shouldn't I be? I just wanted to make sure you hadn't told Aroun about the Audin woman.'

'No, of course not.'

'Good.' Dillon smiled. 'I wouldn't like anything to spoil things. Now let's go and see him.'

Rashid opened the door to them. A maid took their coats. Aroun was waiting in the magnificent drawing room.

'Valenton, Mr Dillon. A considerable disappointment.'

Dillon said, 'Nothing's ever perfect in this life, you should know that. I promised you an alternative target and I intend to go for it.'

'The British Prime Minister?' Rashid asked.

'That's right.' Dillon nodded. 'I'm leaving for London later today. I thought we'd have a chat before I go.'

Rashid glanced at Aroun who said, 'Of course, Mr Dillon. Now how can we help you?'

'First, I'm going to need operating money again. Thirty thousand dollars. I want you to arrange that from someone in London. Cash, naturally. Colonel Makeev can finalise details.'

'No problem,' Aroun said.

'Secondly, there's the question of how I get the hell out of England after the successful conclusion of the venture.'

'You sound full of confidence, Mr Dillon,' Rashid told him.

'Well, you have to travel hopefully, son,' Dillon said. 'The thing with any major hit, as I've discovered during the years, is not so much achieving it as moving on with a whole skin afterwards. I mean, if I get the British Prime Minister for you, the major problem for me is getting out of England and that's where you come in, Mr Aroun.'

The maid entered with coffee on a tray. Aroun waited while she laid the cups out on a table and poured. As she withdrew he said, 'Please explain.'

'One of my minor talents is flying. I share that with you, I understand. According to an old *Paris Match* article I was reading, you bought an estate in Normandy called Château St Denis about twenty miles south of Cherbourg on the coast?'

'That's correct.'

'The article mentioned how much you loved the place, how remote and unspoiled it was. A time capsule from the eighteenth century.'

'Exactly what are we getting at here, Mr Dillon?' Rashid demanded.

'It also said it had its own landing strip and that it wasn't unknown for Mr Aroun to fly down there from Paris when he feels like it, piloting his own plane.'

'Quite true,' Aroun said.

'Good. This is how it will go then. When I'm close to, how shall we put it, the final end of things, I'll let you know. You'll fly down to this St Denis place. I'll fly out from England and join you there after the job is done. You can arrange my onwards transportation.'

'But how?' Rashid demanded. 'Where will you find a plane?'

'Plenty of flying clubs, old son, and planes to hire. I'll simply fly off the map. Disappear, put it any way you like. As a pilot yourself you must know that one of the biggest headaches the authorities have is the vast amount of uncontrolled air space. Once I land at St Denis, you can torch the bloody thing up.' He looked from Rashid to Aroun. 'Are we agreed?'

It was Aroun who said, 'Absolutely, and if there is anything else we can do.'

'Makeev will let you know. I'll be going now.' Dillon turned to the door.

Outside, he stood on the pavement beside Makeev's car, the snow falling lightly. 'That's it then. We shan't be seeing each other, not for a while anyway.'

Makeev passed him an envelope. 'Tania's home address and telephone number.' He glanced at his watch. 'I couldn't get her earlier this morning. I left a message to say I wanted to speak to her at noon.'

'Fine,' Dillon said. 'I'll speak to you from St Malo before I get the hydrofoil for Jersey, just to make sure everything is all right.'

'I'll drop you off,' Makeev told him.

'No thanks. I feel like the exercise.' Dillon held out his hand. 'To our next merry meeting.'

'Good luck, Sean.'

Dillon smiled. 'Oh, you always need that as well,' and he turned and walked away.

Makeev spoke to Tania on the scrambler at noon. 'I have a friend calling to see you,' he said. 'Possibly late this evening. The one we've spoken of.'

'I'll take care of him, Colonel.'

'You've never handled a more important business transaction,' he said, 'believe me. He'll need alternative accommodation, by the way. Make it convenient to your own place.'

'Of course.'

'And I want you to put a trace out on this man.'

He gave her Danny Fahy's details. When he was finished, she said, 'There should be no problem. Anything else?'

'Yes, he likes Walthers. Take care, my dear, I'll be in touch.'

When Mary Tanner went into the suite at the Ritz, Ferguson was having afternoon tea by the window.

'Ah, there you are,' he said. 'Wondered what was keeping you. We've got to get moving.'

'To where?' she demanded.

'Back to London.'

She took a deep breath. 'Not me, Brigadier, I'm staying.'

'Staying?' he said.

'For the funeral at Château Vercors at eleven o'clock tomorrow morning. After all, he's going to do what you want him to. Don't we owe him some support?'

Ferguson put up a hand defensively. 'All right, you've made your point. However, I need to go back to London now. You can stay if you want and follow tomorrow afternoon. I'll arrange for the Lear jet to pick you up, both of you. Will that suffice?'

'I don't see why not.' She smiled brightly and reached for the teapot. 'Another cup, Brigadier?'

Sean Dillon caught the express to Rennes and changed trains for St Malo at three o'clock. There wasn't much tourist traffic, the wrong time of the year for that and the atrocious weather all over Europe had killed whatever there was. There couldn't have been more than twenty passengers on the hydrofoil to Jersey. He disembarked in St Helier just before six o'clock on the Albert Quay and caught a cab to the airport.

He knew he was in trouble before he arrived, for the closer they got, the thicker the fog was. It was an old story in Jersey, but not the end of the world. He confirmed that both evening flights to London were cancelled, went out of the airport building, caught another taxi and told the driver to take him to a convenient hotel.

It was thirty minutes later that he phoned Makeev in Paris. 'Sorry I didn't have a chance to phone from St Malo. The train was late. I might have missed the hydrofoil. Did you contact Novikova?'

'Oh, yes,' Makeev told him. 'Everything is in order. Looking forward to meeting you. Where are you?'

'A place called Hotel L'Horizon in Jersey. There was fog at the airport. I'm hoping to get out in the morning.'

'I'm sure you will. Stay in touch.'

'I'll do that.'

Dillon put down the phone, then he put on his jacket and went downstairs to the bar. He'd heard somewhere that the hotel's grill was a quite exceptional restaurant. After a while he was approached by a handsome, energetic

109

Italian who introduced himself as the head waiter, Augusto. Dillon took a menu from him gratefully, ordered a bottle of Krug and relaxed.

It was at roughly the same time that the doorbell sounded at Brosnan's apartment on the Quai de Montebello. When he opened the door, a large glass of Scotch in one hand, Mary Tanner stood there.

'Hello,' he said. 'This is unexpected.'

She took the glass of Scotch and emptied it into the potted plant that stood by the door. 'That won't do you any good at all.'

'If you say so. What do you want?'

'I thought you'd be alone. I didn't think that was a good idea. Ferguson spoke to you before he left?'

'Yes, he said you were staying over. Suggested we followed him tomorrow afternoon.'

'Yes, well that doesn't take care of tonight. I expect you haven't eaten a thing all day so I suggest we go out for a meal and don't start saying no.'

'I wouldn't dream of it, Captain.' He saluted.

'Don't fool around. There must be somewhere close by that you like.'

'There is indeed. Let me get a coat and I'll be right with you.'

It was a typical little side-street bistro, simple and unpretentious, booths to give privacy and cooking smells from the kitchen that were out of this world. Brosnan ordered champagne.

'Krug?' she said when the bottle came.

'They know me here.'

'Always champagne with you?'

'I was shot in the stomach years ago. It gave me problems. The doctors said no spirits under any circumstances, no red wine. Champagne was okay. Did you notice the name of this place?'

'*La Belle Aurore.*'

'Same as the café in Casablanca. Humphrey Bogart? Ingrid Bergman?' He raised his glass. 'Here's looking at you, kid.'

They sat there in companionable silence for a while and then she said, 'Can we talk business?'

'Why not? What do you have in mind?'

'What happens next? I mean, Dillon just fades into the woodwork, you said that yourself. How on earth do you hope to find him?'

'One weakness,' Brosnan said. 'He won't go near any IRA contacts for fear of betrayal. That leaves him with only one choice. The usual one he makes. The underworld. Anything he needs, weaponry, explosives, even physical help, he'll go to the obvious place and you know where that is?'

'The East End of London?'

'Yes, just about as romantic as Little Italy in New York or the Bronx. The Kray brothers, the nearest thing England ever had to cinema gangsters, the Richardson gang. Do you know much about the East End?'

'I thought all that was history.'

'Not at all. A lot of the big men, the governors as they call them, have gone legitimate to a certain degree, but all the old-fashioned crimes, hold-ups, banks, security vans, are committed by roughly the same group. All family men, who just look upon it as business, but they'll shoot you if you get in the way.'

'How nice.'

'Everyone knows who they are, including the police. It's in that fraternity Dillon will look for help.'

'Forgive me,' she said. 'But that must be rather a close-knit community.'

'You're absolutely right, but as it happens, I've got what you might call the entrée.'

'And how on earth do you have that?'

He poured her another glass of champagne. 'Back in Viet Nam in nineteen sixty-eight, during my wild and foolish youth, I was a paratrooper, Airborne Rangers. I formed part of a Special Forces detachment to operate in Cambodia, entirely illegally, I might add. It was recruited from all branches of the services. People with specialist qualifications. We even had a few Marines and that's how I met Harry Flood.'

'Harry Flood?' she said and frowned. 'For some reason, that name's familiar.'

'Could be. I'll explain. Harry's the same age as me. Born in Brooklyn. His mother died when he was born. He grew up with his father who died when Harry was eighteen. He joined the Marines for something to do, went to Nam which is where I met him.' He laughed. 'I'll never forget the first time. Up to our necks in a stinking swamp in the Mekong Delta.'

'He sounds quite interesting.'

'Oh, that and more. Silver Star, Navy Cross. In sixty-nine when I was getting out, Harry still had a year of his enlistment to do. They posted him to London. Embassy Guard duty. He was a sergeant then and that's when it happened.'

'What did?'

'He met a girl at the old Lyceum Ballroom one night, a girl called Jean Dark. Just a nice, pretty twenty-year-old in a cotton frock only there was one difference. The Dark family were gangsters, what they call in the East End real villains. Her old man had his own little empire down by the river, was in his own way as famous as the Kray brothers. He died later that year.'

'What happened?' She was totally fascinated.

'Jean's mother tried to take over. Ma Dark everyone called her. There were differences. Rival gangs. That sort of thing. Harry and Jean got married, he took his papers in London, stayed on and just got sucked in. Sorted the rivals out and so on.'

'You mean he became a gangster?'

'Not to put too fine a point on it, yes, but more than that, much more. He became one of the biggest governors in the East End of London.'

'My God, now I remember. He has all those casinos. He's the man doing all that riverside development on the Thames.'

'That's right. Jean died of cancer about five or six years ago. Her mother died ages before that. He just carried on.'

'Is he British now?'

'No, never gave up his American nationality. The authorities could never toss him out because he has no criminal record. Never served a single day in gaol.'

'And he's still a gangster?'

'That depends on your definition of the term. There's plenty he got away with, or his people did, in the old days. What you might call old-fashioned crime.'

'Oh, you mean nothing nasty like drugs or prostitution? Just armed robbery, protection, that sort of thing?'

'Don't be bitter. He has the casinos, business interests in electronics and property development. He owns half of Wapping. Nearly all the river frontage. He's extremely legitimate.'

'And still a gangster?'

'Let's say, he's still the governor to a lot of East Enders. The Yank, that's what they call him. You'll like him.'

'Will I?' She looked surprised. 'And when are we going to meet?'

'As soon as I can arrange it. Anything that moves in the

East End and Harry or his people know about it. If anyone can help me catch Sean Dillon, he can.' The waiter appeared and placed bowls of French onion soup before them. 'Good,' he said. 'Now let's eat, I'm starving.'

Harry Flood crouched in one corner of the pit, arms folded to conserve his body heat. He was naked to the waist, barefooted, clad only in a pair of camouflage pants. The pit was only a few feet square and rain poured down relentlessly through the bamboo grid high above his head. Sometimes the Viet Cong would peer down at him, visitors being shown the Yankee dog who squatted in his own foulness although he'd long since grown used to the stench.

It seemed as if he'd been there for ever and time no longer had any meaning. He had never felt such total despair. It was raining faster now, pouring over the edge of the pit in a kind of waterfall, the water rising rapidly. He was on his feet and yet suddenly it was up to his chest and he was struggling. It poured over his head relentlessly and he no longer had a footing and struggled and kicked to keep afloat, fighting for breath, clawing at the side of the pit. Suddenly a hand grabbed his, a strong hand, and it pulled him up through the water and he started to breathe again.

He came awake with a start and sat upright. He'd had that dream for years on and off, ever since Viet Nam and that was a hell of a long time ago. It usually ended with him drowning. The hand pulling him out was something new.

He reached for his watch. It was almost ten. He always had a nap early evening before visiting one of the clubs later, but this time he'd overslept. He put his watch on, hurried into the bathroom, and had a quick shower. There was grey in his black hair now, he noticed that as he shaved.

'Comes to us all, Harry,' he said softly and smiled.

In fact he smiled most of the time, although anyone who

observed closely would have noticed a certain world-weariness to it. The smile of a man who had found life on the whole, disappointing. He was handsome enough in a rather hard way, muscular with good shoulders. In fact not bad for forty-six which he usually told himself at least once a day if only for encouragement. He dressed in a black silk shirt buttoned at the neck without a tie and a loose-fitting Armani suit in dark brown raw silk. He checked his appearance in the mirror.

'Here we go again, baby,' he said and went out.

His apartment was enormous, part of a warehouse development on Cable Wharf. The brick walls of the sitting room were painted white, the wooden floor lacquered, Indian rugs scattered everywhere. Comfortable sofas, a bar, bottles of every conceivable kind ranged behind. Only for guests. He never drank alcohol. There was a large desk in front of the rear wall and the wall itself was lined with books.

He opened French windows and went onto the balcony overlooking the river. It was very cold. Tower Bridge was to his right, the Tower of London just beyond it, floodlit. A ship passed down from the Pool of London in front of him, its lights clear in the darkness so that he could see crew members working on deck. It always gave him a lift and he took a great lungful of that cold air.

The door opened at the far end of the sitting room and Mordecai Fletcher came in. He was six feet tall with iron-grey hair and a clipped moustache and wore a well-cut, double-breasted blazer and a Guards tie. The edge was rather taken off his conventional appearance by the scar tissue round the eyes and the flattened nose that had been broken more than once.

'You're up,' he said flatly.

'Isn't that what it looks like?' Flood asked.

Mordecai had been his strong right arm for the best part

of fifteen years, a useful heavy-weight boxer who'd had the sense to get out of the ring before his brains were scrambled. He went behind the bar, poured a Perrier water, added ice and lemon and brought it over.

Flood took it without thanking him. 'God, how I love this old river. Anything come up?'

'Your accountant called. Some papers to sign on that market development. I told him to leave them till the morning.'

'Was that all?'

'Maurice was on the phone from the *Embassy*. He says Jack Harvey was in for a bite to eat with that bitch of a niece of his.'

'Myra?' Flood nodded. 'Anything happen?'

'Maurice said Harvey asked if you'd be in later. Said he'd come back and have a go at the tables.' He hesitated. 'You know what the bastard's after, Harry, and you've been avoiding him.'

'We aren't selling, Mordecai, and we certainly aren't going into partnership. Jack Harvey's the worst hood in the East End. He makes the Kray brothers look like kindergarten stuff.'

'I thought that was you, Harry.'

'I never did drugs, Mordecai, didn't run girls, you know that. Okay, I was a right villain for a few years, we both were.' He walked into the sitting room to the desk and picked up the photo in its silver frame that always stood there. 'When Jean was dying, for all those lousy months.' He shook his head. 'Nothing seemed important and you know the promise she made me give her towards the end. To get out.'

Mordecai closed the window. 'I know, Harry. She was a woman and a half, Jean.'

'That's why I made us legitimate, and wasn't I right? You know what the firm's net worth is? Nearly fifty

116

million. Fifty million.' He grinned. 'So let Jack Harvey and others like him keep dirtying their hands if they want.'

'Yes, but to most people in the East End you're still the governor, Harry, you're still the Yank.'

'I'm not complaining.' Flood opened a cupboard and took out a dark overcoat. 'There's times when it helps a deal along, I know that. Now let's get moving. Who's driving tonight?'

'Charlie Salter.'

'Good.'

Mordecai hesitated. 'Shall I carry a shooter, Harry?'

'For God's sake, Mordecai, we're legit now, I keep telling you.'

'But Jack Harvey isn't, that's the trouble.'

'Leave Jack Harvey to me.'

They went down in the old original freight elevator to the warehouse where the black Mercedes saloon waited, Charlie Salter leaning against it reading a paper, a small, wiry man in a grey chauffeur's uniform. He folded the paper quickly and got the rear door open.

'Where to, Harry?'

'The *Embassy* and drive carefully. A lot of frost around tonight and I'll have the paper.'

Salter got behind the wheel and Mordecai got in beside him and reached for the electronic door control. The warehouse doors opened and they turned on to the wharf. Flood opened the paper, leaned back and started catching up on how the Gulf War was progressing.

The *Embassy* club was only half a mile away, just off Wapping High Street. It had only been open six months, another of Harry Flood's developments of old warehouse property. The car park was up a side street at the rear and was already quite full. There was an old negro in charge who sat in a small hut.

'Kept your place free, Mr Flood,' he said, coming out.

Flood got out of the car with Mordecai and took out his wallet as Salter went off to park. He extracted a five-pound note and gave it to the old man. 'Don't go crazy, Freddy.'

'With this?' The old man smiled. 'Wouldn't even buy me a woman at the back of the pub these days. Inflation's a terrible thing, Mr Flood.'

Flood and Mordecai were laughing as they went up the side street and Salter caught up with them as they turned the corner and reached the entrance. Inside it was warm and luxurious, black and white tiles on the floor, oak panelling, oil paintings. As the cloakroom girl took their coats, a small man in evening dress hurried to meet them. His accent was unmistakably French.

'Ah, Mr Flood, a great pleasure. Will you be dining?'

'I should think so, Maurice. We'll just have a look round first. Any sign of Harvey?'

'Not yet.'

They went down the steps into the main dining room. The club atmosphere continued, panelled walls, paintings, table booths with leather seats. The place was almost full, waiters working busily. A trio played on a small dais in one corner and there was a dance floor, though not large.

Maurice threaded his way through the tables by the floor and opened a door in quilted leather that led to the casino part of the premises. It was just as crowded in there people jostling each other at the roulette wheel, the chairs occupied at most of the tables.

'We losing much?' Flood asked Maurice.

'Swings and roundabouts, Mr Flood. It all balances out as usual.'

'Plenty of punters, anyway.'

'And not an Arab in sight,' Mordecai said.

'They're keeping their heads down,' Maurice told him, 'what with the Gulf business.'

'Wouldn't you?' Flood grinned. 'Come on, let's go and eat.'

He had his own booth in a corner to one side of the band overlooking the floor. He ordered smoked salmon and scrambled eggs and more Perrier water. He took a Camel cigarette from an old silver case. English cigarettes were something he'd never been able to come to terms with. Mordecai gave him a light and leant against the wall. Flood sat there, brooding, surveying the scene, experiencing one of those dark moments when you wondered what life was all about, and Charlie Salter came down the steps from the entrance and hurried through the tables.

'Jack Harvey and Myra – just in,' he said.

Harvey was fifty years of age, of medium height and over-weight, a fact that the navy-blue barathea suit failed to hide in spite of having been cut in Savile Row. He was balding, hardly any hair there at all, and he had the fleshy decadent face of the wrong sort of Roman emperor.

His niece, Myra, was thirty and looked younger, her jet-black hair caught up in a bun and held in place by a diamond comb. There was little make-up on her face except for the lips and they were blood red. She wore a sequinned jacket and black mini-skirt by Gianni Versace and very high-heeled black shoes for she was only a little over five feet tall. She looked immensely attractive, men turning to stare at her. She was also her uncle's right hand, had a degree in business studies from London University and was just as ruthless and unscrupulous as he was.

Flood didn't get up, just sat there waiting. 'Harry, my old son,' Harvey said and sat down. 'Don't mind if we join you, do you?'

119

Myra leaned down and kissed Flood on the cheek. 'Like my new perfume, Harry? Cost a fortune, but Jack says it's like an aphrodisiac, the smell's so good.'

'That's a big word for you, isn't it?' Flood said.

She sat on his other side and Harvey took out a cigar. He clipped it and looked up at Mordecai. 'Come on, where's your bleeding lighter then?'

Mordecai took out his lighter and flicked it without a change of expression and Myra said, 'Any chance of a drink? We know you don't, Harry, but think about the rest of us poor sods.'

Her voice had a slight cockney accent, not too much and it had its own attraction. She put a hand on his knee and Flood said, 'Champagne cocktail, isn't that what you like?'

'It'll do to be going on with.'

'Not me, can't drink that kind of piss,' Harvey said. 'Scotch and water. A big one.'

Maurice, who had been hovering, spoke to a waiter, then whispered in Flood's ear, 'Your scrambled eggs, Mr Flood.'

'I'll have them now,' Flood told him.

Maurice turned away and a moment later, a waiter appeared with a silver salver. He removed the dome and put the plate in front of Flood who got to work straight away.

Harvey said, 'I've never seen you eat a decent meal yet, Harry. What's wrong with you?'

'Nothing really,' Flood told him. 'Food doesn't mean much to me, Jack. When I was a kid in Viet Nam, the Viet Cong had me prisoner for a while. I learnt you could get by on very little. Later on I was shot in the gut. Lost eighteen inches of my intestines.'

'You'll have to show me your scar sometime,' Myra said.

'There's always a silver lining. If I hadn't been shot, the Marine Corps wouldn't have posted me to that nice soft job as a guard at the London Embassy.'

'And you wouldn't have met Jean,' Harvey said. 'I remember the year you married her, Harry, the year her old Dad died. Sam Dark.' He shook his head. 'He was like an uncrowned king in the East End after the Krays got put inside. And Jean.' He shook his head again. 'What a goer. The boys were queuing for her. There was even a Guards officer, a lord.' He turned to Myra. 'Straight up.'

'And instead she married me,' Flood said.

'Could have done worse, Harry. I mean, you helped her keep things going a treat, especially after her Mum died, we all know that.'

Flood pushed his plate away and wiped his mouth with a napkin. 'Compliments night is it, Jack? Now what have you really come for?'

'You know what I want, Harry, I want in. The casinos, four of them now and how many clubs, Myra?'

'Six,' she said.

'And all this development on the river,' Harvey went on. 'You've got to share the cake.'

'There's only one trouble with that, Jack,' Flood told him. 'I'm a legitimate businessman, have been for a long time, whereas you . . .' He shook his head. 'Once a crook, always a crook.'

'You Yank bastard,' Harvey said. 'You can't talk to me like that.'

'I just did, Jack.'

'We're in, Harry, whether you like it or not.'

'Try me,' Flood said.

Salter had drifted across the room and leaned against the wall beside Mordecai. The big man whispered to him and Salter moved away.

Myra said, 'He means it, Harry, so be reasonable. All we're asking for is a piece of the action.'

'You come in with me you're into computers, building development, clubs and gambling,' Flood told her. 'Which

121

means I'm in with you into pimps, whores, drugs and protection. I shower three times a day, sweetness, and it still wouldn't make me feel clean.'

'You Yank bastard!' She raised her hand and he grabbed her wrist.

Harvey stood up. 'Let it go, Myra, let it go. Come on. I'll be seeing you, Harry.'

'I hope not,' Flood told him.

They went out and Mordecai leaned down. 'He's a disgusting piece of slime. Always turned my stomach, him and his boyfriends.'

'Takes all sorts,' Flood said. 'Don't let your prejudices show, Mordecai, and get me a cup of coffee.'

'The swine,' Jack Harvey said as he and Myra walked along the pavement towards the car park. 'I'll see him in hell, talking to me that way.'

'I told you we were wasting our time,' she said.

'Right.' He eased his gloves over his big hands. 'Have to show him we mean business then, won't we?'

A dark van was parked at the end of the street. As they approached, the sidelights were turned on. The young man who leaned out from behind the wheel was about twenty-five, hard and dangerous-looking in a black leather bomber jacket and flat cap.

'Mr Harvey,' he said.

'Good boy, Billy, right on time.' Harvey turned to his niece. 'I don't think you've met Billy Watson, Myra.'

'No, I don't think I have,' she said, looking him over.

'How many have you got in the back?' Harvey demanded.

'Four, Mr Harvey. I heard this Mordecai Fletcher was a bit of an animal.' He picked up a baseball bat. 'This should cool him.'

'No shooters, like I told you?'

'Yes, Mr Harvey.'

'Flesh on flesh, that's all it needs and maybe a couple of broken legs. Get on with it. He'll have to come out sooner or later.'

Harvey and Myra continued along the pavement. 'Five?' she said. 'You think that's enough?'

'Enough?' he laughed harshly. 'Who does he think he is, Sam Dark? Now he was a man, but this bloody Yank . . . They'll cripple him. Put him on sticks for six months. They're hard boys, Myra.'

'Really?' she said.

'Now come on and let's get out of this bleeding cold,' and he turned into the car park.

It was an hour later that Harry Flood got ready to leave. As the cloakroom girl helped him on with his coat, he said to Mordecai, 'Where's Charlie?'

'Oh, I gave him the nod a couple of minutes ago. He went ahead to get the car warmed up. I mean it's spawn of the north time out there, Harry, we'll have the bleeding Thames freezing over next.'

Flood laughed and they went down the steps and started along the pavement. When it happened, it was very quick, the rear doors of the van parked on the other side of the road swinging open, the men inside rushing out and crossing the road on the run. They all carried baseball bats. The first to reach them swung hard, Mordecai ducked inside, blocked the blow and pitched him over his hip down the steps of the basement area behind.

The other four paused and circled, bats ready. 'That won't do you any good,' Billy Watson said. 'It's leg-breaking time.'

There was a shot behind them, loud in the frosty air

and then another. As they turned Charlie Salter moved out of the darkness reloading a sawn-off shotgun. 'Now drop 'em,' he said. 'Unless you want to be jam all over the pavement.'

They did as they were told and stood there waiting for what was to come. Mordecai moved close and looked them over then he grabbed the nearest one by the hair. 'Who are you working for, sonny?'

'I don't know, mister.'

Mordecai turned him and ran him up against the railings, holding his face just above the spikes. 'I said who are you working for?'

The youth cracked instantly, 'Jack Harvey. It was just a wages job. It was Billy who pulled us in.'

Billy said, 'You bastard. I'll get you for that.'

Mordecai glanced at Flood who nodded. The big man said to Billy, 'You stay. The rest of you, piss off.'

They turned and ran for it. Billy Watson stood looking at them, his face wild. Salter said, 'He needs a good slapping this one.'

Billy suddenly picked up one of the baseball bats and raised it defensively. 'All right, let's be having you. Harry Flood – big man. No bloody good on your own are you, mate?'

Mordecai took a step forward and Flood said, 'No,' and moved in himself. 'All right, son.'

Billy swung, Flood swayed to one side, found the right wrist, twisting. Billy cried out and dropped the baseball bat and in the same moment, the American half-turned, striking him hard across the face with his elbow, sending him down on one knee.

Mordecai picked up the baseball bat. 'No, he's got the point, let's get going,' Flood said.

He lit a cigarette as they went along the street. Mordecai said, 'What about Harvey? You going to stitch him up?'

'I'll think about it,' Flood said and they moved across to the car park

Billy Watson got himself together, held on to the railings for a while. It was snowing a little as he turned and limped across the road to the van. As he went round to the driver's side, Myra Harvey stepped out of the entrance of a narrow alley, holding the collar of her fur coat up around her neck.

'Well that didn't go too well, did it?'

'Miss Harvey,' he croaked. 'I thought you'd gone.'

'After my uncle dropped me off, I got a taxi back. I wanted to see the fun.'

'Here,' he said, 'are you telling me you expected it to go like it did?'

'I'm afraid so, sunshine. My uncle gets it wrong sometimes. Lets his emotions get the better of him. You really think five young punks like you could walk all over Harry Flood?' She opened the driver's door and pushed him in. 'Go on, get over. I'll drive.'

She climbed behind the wheel, the fur coat opened and the mini-skirt went about as high as it could.

Billy said, 'But where are we going?'

'Back to my place. What you need is a nice hot bath, sunshine.' Her left hand squeezed his thigh hard and she switched on and drove away.

SEVEN

The flight from Jersey got into Heathrow Terminal One just after eleven the following morning. It took half an hour for Dillon's case to come through and he sat smoking and reading the paper while he waited. The war news was good for the coalition forces. A few pilots down in Iraq, but the airstrikes were having a terrible effect.

His case came and he walked through. There was a rush of customers as several planes had come in at around the same time. Customs didn't seem to be stopping anyone that morning, not that they'd have found anything on him. His suitcase contained a change of clothes and toilet articles, no more, and there were only a couple of newspapers in the briefcase. He also had two thousand dollars in his wallet which was in twenty hundred-dollar bills. Nothing wrong with that. He'd destroyed the French passport at the hotel in Jersey. No turning back now. When he went back to France it would be very definitely a different route and until then the Jersey driving licence in the name of Peter Hilton was all the identification he needed.

He took the escalator to the upper concourse and joined the queue at one of the bank counters, changing five hundred dollars for sterling. He repeated the exercise at three other banks, then went downstairs to get a taxi, whistling softly to himself.

He told the driver to drop him at Paddington Station where he left the suitcase in a locker. He phoned Tania Novikova on the number Makeev had given him, just on the chance she was at home, and got her answering machine. He didn't bother to leave a message, but went out and hailed a cab and told the driver to take him to Covent Garden.

In his tinted glasses, striped tie and navy-blue Burberry trenchcoat he looked thoroughly respectable.

The driver said, 'Terrible weather, guv. I reckon we're going to see some real heavy snow soon.'

'I shouldn't be surprised.' Dillon's accent was impeccable public school English.

'You live in London, guv?'

'No, just in town for a few days on business. I've been abroad for some time,' Dillon said glibly. 'New York. Haven't been in London for years.'

'A lot of changes. Not like it used to be.'

'So I believe. I was reading the other day that you can't take a walk up Downing Street any more.'

'That's right, guv. Mrs Thatcher had a new security system installed, gates at the end of the street.'

'Really?' Dillon said. 'I'd like to see that.'

'We'll go that way if you like. I can take you down to Whitehall then cut back to Covent Garden.'

'Suits me.'

Dillon sat back, lit a cigarette and watched. They moved down Whitehall from Trafalgar Square past Horse Guards with the two Household Cavalrymen on mounted duty, wearing greatcoats against the cold, sabres drawn.

'Must be bleeding cold for the horses,' the cabby said

and then added, 'Here we are, guv, Downing Street.' He slowed a little. 'Can't stop. If you do, the coppers come up and ask you what you're doing.'

Dillon looked across at the end of the street. 'So those are the famous gates?'

'Thatcher's folly, some twerps call it, but if you ask me, she was usually right. The bloody IRA have pulled off enough stunts in London during the past few years. I'd shoot the lot of them, I would. If I drop you in Long Acre, will that do, guv?'

'Fine,' Dillon told him and sat back, thinking about those rather magnificent gates at the end of Downing Street.

The taxi pulled into the kerb and Dillon gave him a ten-pound note. 'Keep it,' he said, turned and walked briskly away along Langley Street. The whole Covent Garden area was as busy as usual, people dressed for the extreme cold, more like Moscow than London. Dillon went with the throng and finally found what he wanted in an alley near Neal's Yard, a small theatrical shop, the window full of old costume masks and make-up. A bell tinkled when he went in. The man who appeared through a curtain at the rear was about seventy with snow-white hair and a round fleshy face.

'And what can I do for you?' he asked.

'Some make-up, I think. What have you got in boxes?'

'Some very good kits here,' the old boy said. He took one down and opened it on the counter. 'They use these at the National Theatre. In the business, are you?'

'Amateur, that's all, I'm afraid, church players.' Dillon checked the contents of the box. 'Excellent. I'll take an extra lipstick, bright red, some black hair dye and also some solvent.'

'You *are* going to town. Clayton's my name, by the way. I'll give you my card in case you ever need anything else.' He got the required items and put them inside the make-up box and closed it. 'Thirty quid for cash and don't forget, anything you need . . .'

'I won't,' Dillon said and went out whistling.

In the village of Vercors it was snowing as the cortège drove down from the château. In spite of the weather, villagers lined the street, men with their caps off, as Anne-Marie Audin went to her final rest. There were only three cars behind the hearse, old Pierre Audin and his secretary in the first, a number of servants in the other. Brosnan and Mary Tanner with Max Hernu following, walked up through the tombstones and paused as the old man was lifted from the car into his wheelchair. He was pushed inside, the rest followed.

It was very old, a typical village church, whitewashed walls, the stations of the Cross and it was cold, very cold. In fact Brosnan had never felt so cold and sat there, shaking slightly, hardly aware of what was being said, rising and kneeling obediently with everyone else. It was only when the service ended and they stood as the pallbearers carried the coffin down the aisle that he realised that Mary Tanner was holding his hand.

They walked through the graveyard to the family mausoleum. It was the size of a small chapel built in grey granite and marble with a steep Gothic roof. The oaken doors stood open. The priest paused to give the final benediction, the coffin was taken inside. The secretary turned the wheelchair and pushed it down the path past them, the old man huddled over, a rug across his knees.

'I feel so sorry for him,' Mary said.

'No need, he doesn't know what time of day it is,' Brosnan told her.

'That's not always true.'

She walked to the car, and put a hand on the old man's

129

shoulder as he sat there in his wheelchair. Then she returned.

'So, my friends, back to Paris,' Hernu said.

'And then London,' Brosnan said.

Mary took his arm as they walked towards the car. 'Tomorrow, Martin, tomorrow morning will be soon enough and I won't take no for an answer.'

'All right,' he said, 'tomorrow it is,' and he got in the rear of the car and leaned back, suddenly drained and closed his eyes, Mary sitting beside him as Hernu drove away.

It was just after six when Tania Novikova heard the door-bell. She went downstairs and opened the door. Dillon stood there, suitcase in one hand, briefcase in the other. 'Josef sends his regards.'

She was amazed. Since Makeev had spoken to her she had accessed KGB files in London to discover as much about Dillon as she could and had been astonished at his record. She had expected some kind of dark hero. Instead she had a small man in a trenchcoat with tinted glasses and a college tie.

'You are Sean Dillon?' she said.

'As ever was.'

'You'd better come in.'

Women had never been of great importance to Dillon. They were there to satisfy a need on occasions, but he had never felt the slightest emotional involvement with one. Following Tania Novikova up the stairs, he was aware that she had a good figure and that the black trouser suit became her. Her hair was caught up at the nape of the neck in a velvet bow, but, when she turned to him in the full light of her sitting room, he realised that she was really rather plain.

'You had a good trip?' she asked.

'All right. I was delayed in Jersey last night because of fog.'

'Would you like a drink?'

'Tea would be fine.'

She opened a drawer, produced a Walther, two spare clips and a Carswell silencer. 'Your preferred weapon according to Josef.'

'Definitely.'

'Also I thought this might come in useful.' She handed him a small bundle. 'They say it can stop a .45 bullet at point-blank range. Nylon and titanium.'

Dillon unfolded it. Nothing like as bulky as a flak jacket, it was designed like a small waistcoat and fastened with Velcro tabs.

'Excellent,' he said and put it in his briefcase together with the Walther and the silencer. He unbuttoned his trenchcoat, lit a cigarette and stood in the kitchen door and watched her make the tea. 'You're very convenient for the Soviet Embassy here?'

'Oh, yes, walking distance.' She brought the tea out on a tray. 'I've fixed you up with a room in a small hotel just round the corner in the Bayswater Road. It's the sort of place commercial travellers overnight at.'

'Fine.' He sipped his tea. 'To business. What about Fahy?'

'No luck so far. He moved from Kilburn a few years ago to a house in Finchley. Only stayed there a year and moved again. That's where I've drawn a blank. But I'll find him, I've got someone on his case.'

'You must. It's essential. Does KGB's London station still have a forgery department?'

'Of course.'

'Good.' He took out his Jersey driving licence. 'I want a private pilot's licence in the same name and address. You'll

131

need a photo.' He slipped a finger inside the plastic cover of the licence and pulled out a couple of identical prints. 'Always useful to have a few of these.'

She took one of them. 'Peter Hilton, Jersey. Can I ask why this is necessary?'

'Because when the right time comes, time to get the hell out of it, I want to fly and they won't hire a plane to you unless you have a licence issued by the Civil Aviation Authority.' He helped himself to some more tea. 'Tell your expert I want full instrument rating and twin-engine.'

'I'll write that down.' She opened her handbag, took out an envelope, slipped the photo inside and made a note on the cover. 'Is there anything else?'

'Yes, I'd like full details of the present security system at Number Ten Downing Street.'

She caught her breath. 'Am I to take it that is your target?'

'Not as such. The man inside, but that's a different thing. The Prime Minister's daily schedule, how easy is it to access that?'

'It depends what you want. There are always fixed points in the day. Question time in the House of Commons, for example. Of course, things are different because of the Gulf. The War Cabinet meets every morning at ten o'clock.'

'At Downing Street?'

'Oh, yes, in the Cabinet Room. But he has other appointments during the day. Only yesterday he did a broadcast on British Forces Network to the troops in the Gulf.'

'Was that from the BBC?'

'No, they have their own headquarters at Bridge House. That's near Paddington Station and not too far from here.'

'Interesting. I wonder what his security was like?'

'Not much, believe me. A few detectives, no more than that. The British are crazy.'

'A damn good job they are. This informant of yours, the

one who got you all the information on Ferguson. Tell me about him.' Which she did and when she was finished he nodded. 'You've got him well and truly by the cobblers then?'

'I think you could say that.'

'Let's keep it that way.' He got up and buttoned his coat. 'I'd better go and book in at this hotel.'

'Have you eaten?' she asked.

'No.'

'I have a suggestion. Just along from the hotel is an excellent Italian restaurant, Luigi's. One of those little family-owned places. You get settled in at the hotel and I'll walk along to the Embassy. I'll check on what we have on the Downing Street defences and see if anything's turned up on Fahy.'

'And the flying licence?'

'I'll put that in hand.'

'Twenty-four hours.'

'All right.'

She got a coat and scarf, went downstairs with him and they left together. The pavements were frosty and she carried his briefcase for him and held on to his arm until they reached the hotel.

'I'll see you in an hour,' she said and moved on.

It was the sort of place which had been a thriving pub and hotel in late Victorian times. The present owners had done their best with it and that wasn't very much. The dining room to the left of the foyer was totally uninviting, no more than half a dozen people eating there. The desk clerk was an old man with a face like a skull who wore a faded brown uniform. He moved with infinite slowness, booking Dillon in and gave him his key. Guests were obviously expected to carry their own cases.

The room was exactly what he'd expected. Twin beds, cheap coverings, a shower room, a television with a slot for coins and a kettle, a little basket beside it containing sachets of coffee, teabags and powdered milk. Still, it wouldn't be for long and he opened his suitcase and unpacked.

Among Jack Harvey's interests was a funeral business in Whitechapel. It was a sizeable establishment and did well for, as he liked to joke, the dead were always with us. It was an imposing three-storeyed Victorian building which he'd had renovated. Myra had the top floor as a penthouse and took an interest in the running of the place. Harvey had an office on the first floor.

Harvey told his driver to wait, went up the steps and rang the bell. The night porter answered.

'My niece in?' Harvey demanded.

'I believe so, Mr Harvey.'

Harvey moved through the main shop with coffins on display and along the passage with the little chapels of rest on each side where relatives could view the bodies. He went up two flights of stairs and rang the bell on Myra's door.

She was ready for him, alerted by a discreet call from the porter, let him wait for a moment, then opened the door. 'Uncle Jack.'

He brushed past her. She was wearing a gold sequinned mini-dress, black stockings and shoes. 'You going out or something?' he demanded.

'A disco, actually.'

'Well, never mind that now. You saw the accountants? Is there any way I can get at Flood legally? Any problems with leases? Anything?'

'Not a chance,' Myra said. 'We've gone through the lot with a fine-tooth comb. There's nothing.'

'Right, then I'll just have to get him the hard way.'

'That didn't exactly work last night, did it?'

'I used rubbish, that's why, a bunch of young jerks who didn't deserve the time of day.'

'So what do you intend?'

'I'll think of something.' As he turned to the door, he heard a movement in the bedroom. 'Here, who's in there?' He flung the door open and revealed Billy Watson standing there, looking hunted. 'Jesus!' Harvey said to Myra. 'Disgusting. All you can ever think of is a bit of the other.'

'At least we do it the right way,' she told him.

'Screw you!' he said.

'No, he'll do that.'

Harvey stormed downstairs. Billy said, 'You don't give a monkey's for anyone, do you?'

'Billy love, this is the house of the dead,' she said and picked up her fur coat and handbag. 'They're lying in their coffins downstairs and we're alive. Simple as that, so make the most of it. Now let's get going.'

Dillon was sitting in a small booth in the corner at Luigi's drinking the only champagne available, a very reasonable Bollinger non-vintage, when Tania came in. Old Luigi greeted her personally and as a favoured customer and she sat down.

'Champagne?' Dillon asked.

'Why not?' She looked up at Luigi. 'We'll order later.'

'One thing that hasn't been mentioned is my operating money. Thirty thousand dollars. Aroun was to arrange that,' Dillon said.

'It's taken care of. The man in question will be in touch with me tomorrow. Some accountant of Aroun's in London.'

'Okay, so what have you got for me?' he asked.

'Nothing on Fahy yet. I've set the wheels in motion as regards the flying licence.'

'And Number Ten?'

'I've had a look at the file. The public always had a right of way along Downing Street. The IRA coming so close to blowing up the whole cabinet at the Tory Party Conference in Brighton the other year made for a change in thinking about security. The bombing campaign in London and attacks on individuals accelerated things.'

'So?'

'Well, the public used to be able to stand at the opposite side of the road from Number Ten watching the great and the good arrive and depart, but no longer. In December eighty-nine Mrs Thatcher ordered new security measures. In effect the place is now a fortress. The steel railings are ten feet high. The gates, by the way, are neo-Victorian, a nice touch that, from the Iron Lady.'

'Yes, I saw them today.'

Luigi hovered anxiously and they broke off and ordered minestrone, veal chops, sauté potatoes and a green salad.

Tania carried on, 'There were accusations in some quarters that she's become the victim of paranoid delusions. Nonsense, of course. That lady has never been deluded about anything in her life. Anyway, on the other side of the gates there's a steel screen designed to come up fast if an unauthorised vehicle tries to get through.'

'And the building itself?'

'The windows have specially strengthened glass and that includes the Georgian windows. Oh, and the net curtains are definitely a miracle of modern science. They're blast-proof.'

'You certainly have the facts.'

'Incredibly, everything I've told you has been reported in either a British newspaper or magazine. The British press puts its own right to publish above every other consideration. They just refuse to face up to security implications. On file at the clippings library of any major British newspaper you'll find details of the interior of Number Ten or the Prime Minister's country home, Chequers, or even Buckingham Palace.'

'What about getting in as ancillary staff?'

'That used to be a real loophole. Most catering for functions is done by outside firms and some of the cleaning, but they're very tough about security clearance for these people. There are always slip-ups, of course. There was a plumber working on the Chancellor of the Exchequer's home at Number Eleven who opened a door and found himself wandering about Number Ten trying to get out.'

'It sounds like a French farce.'

'Only recently staff from one of the outside firms employed to offer cleaning services of one kind or another, staff who had security clearance, were found to be operating under false identities. Some of them had clearance for the Home Office and other ministries.'

'Yes, but all you're saying is mistakes occur.'

'That's right.' She hesitated. 'Have you anything particular in mind?'

'You mean potshots with a sniper's rifle from a rooftop two hundred yards away as he comes out of the door? I don't think so. No, I really have no firm idea at the moment, but I'll come up with something. I always do.' The waiter brought their soup. Dillon said, 'Now that smells good enough to eat. Let's do just that.'

Afterwards, he walked her round to her door. It was snowing just a little and very cold. He said, 'Must remind you of home, this weather?'

'Home?' She looked blank for a moment then laughed. 'Moscow, you mean?' She shrugged. 'It's been a long time. Would you like to come up?'

'No thanks. It's late and I could do with the sleep. I'll stay at the hotel tomorrow morning. Let's say till noon. From what I saw I don't think I could stand the thought of lunch there. I'll be back after two so you'll know where I'll be.'

'Fine,' she said.

'I'll say goodnight then.'

She closed the door, Dillon turned and walked away. It was only after he rounded the corner into the Bayswater Road that Gordon Brown moved out of the shadows of a doorway opposite and looked up at Tania's window. The light came on. He stayed there for a while longer then turned and walked away.

In Paris the following morning the temperature went up three or four degrees and it started to thaw. Mary and Hernu in the Colonel's black Citroën picked Brosnan up just before noon. He was waiting for them in the entrance of the Quai de Montebello apartment block. He wore his trenchcoat, a tweed cap and carried a suitcase. The driver put the case in the boot and Brosnan got in the rear with the other two.

'Any news?' he asked.

'Not a thing,' the Colonel told him.

'Like I said, he's probably there already. What about Ferguson?'

Mary glanced at her watch. 'He's due to see the Prime Minister now, to alert him as to the seriousness of this whole business.'

'About all he can do,' Brosnan said. 'That and spread the word to the other branches of the security services.'

'And how would you handle it, my friend?' Hernu asked.

'We know he worked in London for the IRA in nineteen eighty-one. As I told Mary, he must have used underworld contacts to supply his needs. He always does and it will be the same this time. That's why I must see my old friend Harry Flood.'

'Ah, yes, the redoubtable Mr Flood. Captain Tanner was telling me about him, but what if he can't help?'

'There's another way. I have a friend in Ireland just outside Dublin at Kilrea, Liam Devlin. There's nothing he doesn't know about IRA history in the last few years and who did what. It's a thought.' He lit a cigarette and leaned back. 'But I'll get the bastard, one way or another. I'll get him.'

The driver took them to the end of the Charles de Gaulle terminal where the private planes parked. The Lear was waiting on the tarmac. There was no formality. Everything had been arranged. The driver took their cases across to where the second pilot waited.

Hernu said, 'Captain, if I may presume.' He kissed Mary lightly on both cheeks. 'And you, my friend.' He held out his hand. 'Always remember that when you set out on a journey with revenge at the end of it, it is necessary to first dig two graves.'

'Philosophy now?' Brosnan said. 'And at your time of life? Goodbye, Colonel.'

They strapped themselves into their seats, the second pilot pulled up the stairs, locked the door and went and joined his companion in the cockpit.

'Hernu is right, you know,' Mary said.

'I know he is,' Brosnan answered. 'But there's nothing I can do about that.'

'I understand, believe me, I do,' she said as the plane rolled forward.

When Ferguson was shown into the study at Number Ten the Prime Minister was standing at the window drinking a cup of tea. He turned and smiled. 'The cup that refreshes, Brigadier.'

'They always say it was tea that got us through the war, Prime Minister.'

'Well as long as it gets me through my present schedule We've a meeting of the War Cabinet at ten every morning as you know, and all the other pressing matters to do with the Gulf.'

'And the day-to-day running of the country,' Ferguson said.

'Yes, well we do our best. No one ever said politics was easy, Brigadier.' He put down the cup. 'I've read your latest report. You think it likely the man Dillon is here somewhere in London?'

'From what he said to Brosnan, I think we must assume that, Prime Minister.'

'You've alerted all branches of the security services?'

'Of course, but we can't put a face to him, you see. Oh, there's the description. Small, fair-haired and so on, but as Brosnan says, he'll look entirely different by now.'

'It's been suggested to me that perhaps some press coverage might be useful.'

Ferguson said, 'Well, it's a thought, but I doubt it would achieve anything. What could they say? In furtherance of an enquiry the police would like to contact a man named Sean Dillon who isn't called that any more? As regards a description, we don't know what he looks like and if we did, he wouldn't look like that anyway.'

'My goodness, you carried that off beautifully, Brigadier.' The Prime Minister roared with laughter.

'Of course there could be more lurid headlines. IRA jackal stalks the Prime Minister.'

'No, I'm not having any of that nonsense,' the Prime Minister said firmly. 'By the way, as regards the suggestion that Saddam Hussein might be behind this affair, I must tell you your other colleagues in the intelligence services disagree. They are firmly of the opinion this is an IRA matter and I must tell you that is how they are pursuing it.'

'Well, if Special Branch think they'll find him by visiting Irish pubs in Kilburn, that's their privilege.'

There was a knock at the door, an aide came in. 'We're due at the Savoy in fifteen minutes, Prime Minister.'

John Major smiled with great charm. 'Another of those interminable luncheons, Brigadier. Prawn cocktail to start . . .'

'And chicken salad to follow,' Ferguson said.

'Find him, Brigadier,' the Prime Minister told him. 'Find him for me,' and the aide showed Ferguson out.

Tania, with good news for Dillon, knew there was no point in calling at the hotel before two so she went to her flat. As she was looking for her key in her handbag Gordon Brown crossed the road.

'I was hoping I might catch you,' he said.

'For God's sake, Gordon, you must be crazy.'

'And what happens when something important comes up and you need to know? Can't wait for you to get in touch. It might be too late, so I'd better come in, hadn't I?'

'You can't. I'm due back at the Embassy in thirty minutes. I'll have a drink with you, that's all.'

She turned and walked down to the pub on the corner before he could argue. They sat in a corner of the snug which was empty, aware of the noise from the main bar. Brown had a beer and Tania a vodka and lime.

'What have you got for me?' she asked.

'Shouldn't the question be the other way about?' She got

up at once and he put a hand on her arm. 'I'm sorry. Don't go.'

'Then behave yourself.' She sat down again. 'Now get on with it.'

'Ferguson had a meeting with the Prime Minister just before twelve. He was back in the office at twelve-thirty before I finished the first half of my shift. He dictated a report to Alice Johnson, she's one of the confidential typists who works with me. The report was for the file.'

'Did you get a copy?'

'No, but I did the same as last time. Took it along to his office for her and read it on the way. Captain Tanner stayed in Paris with Brosnan for the funeral of a French woman.'

'Anne-Marie Audin?' she prompted him.

'They're flying in today. Brosnan has promised full co-operation. Oh, all the other branches of the intelligence services have been notified about Dillon. No newspaper coverage on the PM's instructions. The impression I got was he's told Ferguson to get on with it.'

'Good,' she said. 'Very good, but you must stay on the case, Gordon. I have to go.'

She started to get up and he caught her wrist. 'I saw you last night, about eleven it was, coming back to your flat with a man.'

'You were watching my flat?'

'I often do on my way home.'

Her anger was very real, but she restrained it. 'Then if you were there you'll know that the gentleman in question, a colleague from the Embassy, didn't come in. He simply escorted me home. Now let me go, Gordon.'

She pulled free and walked out and Brown, thoroughly depressed, went to the bar and ordered another beer.

When she knocked on the door of Dillon's room just after two he opened it at once. She brushed past him and went inside.

'You look pleased with yourself,' he said.

'I should do.'

Dillon lit a cigarette. 'Go on, tell me.'

'First, I've had words with my mole at Group Four. Ferguson's just been to see the Prime Minister. They believe you're here and all branches of intelligence have been notified. Brosnan and the Tanner woman are coming in from Paris. Brosnan's offered full co-operation.'

'And Ferguson?'

'The Prime Minister said no press publicity. Just told him to go all out to get you.'

'It's nice to be wanted.'

'Second.' She opened her handbag and took out a passport-style booklet. 'One pilot's licence as issued by the Civil Aviation Authority to one Peter Hilton.'

'That's bloody marvellous,' Dillon said and took it from her.

'Yes, the man who does this kind of thing pulled out all the stops. I told him all your requirements. He said he'd give you a commercial licence. Apparently you're also an instructor.'

Dillon checked his photo and riffled through the pages. 'Excellent. Couldn't be better.'

'And that's not the end,' she said. 'You wanted to know the whereabouts of one Daniel Maurice Fahy?'

'You've found him?'

'That's right, but he doesn't live in London. I've brought you a road map.' She unfolded it. 'He has a farm here at a place called Cadge End in Sussex. It's twenty-five to thirty miles from London. You take the road through Dorking towards Horsham then head into the wilds.'

'How do you know all this?'

'The operative I put on the job managed to trace him late yesterday afternoon. By the time he'd looked the place over, then dropped into the pub in the local village to make a few enquiries, it was very late. He didn't get back to London until after midnight. I got his report this morning.'

'And?'

'He says the farm is very out of the way near a river called the Arun. Marsh country. The village is called Doxley. The farm is a mile south of it. There's a signpost.'

'He is efficient, your man.'

'Well he's young and trying to prove himself. From what he heard in the pub, Fahy runs a few sheep and dabbles in agricultural machinery.'

Dillon nodded. 'That makes sense.'

'One thing that might come as a surprise. He has a girl staying with him, his grandniece, it seems. My man saw her.'

'And what did he say?'

'That she came into the pub for some bottles of beer. About twenty. Angel, they called her, Angel Fahy. He said she looked like a peasant.'

'Wonderful.' He got up and reached for his jacket. 'I must get down there right away. Do you have a car?'

'Yes, but it's only a Mini. Easier parking in London.'

'No problem. As you said, thirty miles at the most. I can borrow it then?'

'Of course. It's in the garage at the end of my street. I'll show you.'

He put on his trenchcoat, opened the briefcase, took out the Walther, rammed a clip in the bolt and put it in his left-hand pocket. The silencer he put in the right. 'Just in case,' he said and they went out.

The car was in fact a Mini Cooper which meant performance, jet black with a gold trim. 'Excellent,' he said, 'I'll get moving.'

144

He got behind the wheel and she said, 'What's so important about Fahy?'

'He's an engineer who can turn his hand to anything, a bomb maker of genius and he's been in deep cover for years. He helped me when I last operated here in eighty-one, helped me a lot. It also helps that he was my father's second cousin. I knew him when I was a kid over here. You haven't mentioned the cash from Aroun, by the way.'

'I've to pick it up this evening at six. All very dramatic. A Mercedes stops at the corner of Brancaster Street and Town Drive. That's not far from here. I say, "It's cold, even for this time of the year," and the driver hands me a briefcase.'

'God help us, he must have been seeing too much television,' Dillon said. 'I'll be in touch,' and he drove away.

Ferguson had stopped off at his office at the Ministry of Defence after Downing Street to bring the report on the Dillon affair file up to date and clear his desk generally. As always, he preferred to work at the flat so he returned to Cavendish Square, had Kim prepare him a late lunch of scrambled eggs and bacon and was browsing through his *Times* when the doorbell rang. A moment later Kim showed in Mary Tanner and Brosnan

'My dear Martin,' Ferguson got up and shook hands. 'So here we are again.'

'So it would seem,' Brosnan said.

'Everything go off all right at the funeral?' Ferguson asked.

'As funerals go, it went,' Brosnan said harshly and lit a cigarette. 'So where are we? What's happening?'

'I've seen the Prime Minister again. There's to be no press publicity.'

145

'I agree with him there,' Brosnan said. 'It would be pointless.'

'All relevant intelligence agencies, plus Special Branch, of course, have been notified. They'll do what they can.'

'Which isn't very much,' Brosnan said.

'Another point,' Mary put in. 'I know he's threatened the Prime Minister but we don't have a clue what he intends or when. He could be up to something this very evening for all we know.'

Brosnan shook his head. 'No, I think there'll be more to it than that. These things take time. I should know.'

'So where will you start?' Ferguson asked.

'With my old friend Harry Flood. When Dillon was here in eighty-one he probably used underworld contacts to supply his needs. Harry may be able to dig something out.'

'And if not?'

'Then I'll borrow that Lear jet of yours again, fly to Dublin and have words with Liam Devlin.'

'Ah, yes,' Ferguson said, 'who better?'

'When Dillon went to London in nineteen eighty-one he must have been under someone's orders. If Devlin could find out who, that could be a lead to all sorts.'

'Sounds logical to me. So you'll see Flood tonight?'

'I think so.'

'Where are you staying?'

'With me,' Mary said.

'At Lowndes Square?' Ferguson's eyebrows went up. 'Really?'

'Come on, Brigadier, don't be an old fuddy-duddy. I've got four bedrooms remember, each with its own bathroom and Professor Brosnan can have one with a lock on the inside of his door.'

Brosnan laughed. 'Come on, let's get out of here. See you later, Brigadier.'

They used Ferguson's car. She closed the sliding window

between them and the driver and said, 'Don't you think you'd better ring your friend, let him know you'd like to see him?'

'I suppose so. I'll need to check his number.'

She took a notebook from her handbag. 'I have it here. It's ex-directory. There you go. Cable Wharf. That's in Wapping.'

'Very efficient.'

'And here's a phone.'

She handed him the car phone. 'You do like to be in charge,' he said and dialled the number.

It was Mordecai Fletcher who answered. Brosnan said, 'Harry Flood, please.'

'Who wants him?'

'Martin Brosnan.'

'The Professor? This is Mordecai. We haven't heard from you for what – three or four years? Christ, but he's going to be pleased.'

A moment later a voice said, 'Martin?'

'Harry?'

'I don't believe it. You've come back to haunt me, you bastard.'

EIGHT

For Dillon in the Mini Cooper, the run from London went easily enough. Although there was a light covering of snow on the fields and hedgerows the roads were perfectly clear and not particularly busy. He was in Dorking within half an hour. He passed straight through and continued towards Horsham, finally pulling into a petrol station about five miles outside.

As the attendant was topping up the tank Dillon got his road map out. 'Place called Doxley, you know it?'

'Half a mile up the road on your right a signpost says Grimethorpe. That's the airfield, but before you get there you'll see a sign to Doxley.'

'So it's not far from here?'

'Three miles maybe, but it might as well be the end of the world.' The attendant chuckled as he took the notes Dillon gave him. 'Not much there, mister.'

'Thought I'd take a look. Friend told me there might be a weekend cottage going.'

'If there is, I haven't heard of it.'

Dillon drove away, came to the Grimethorpe sign within a few minutes, followed the narrow road and found the Doxley sign as the garage man had indicated. The road was even narrower, high banks blocking the view until he came to the brow of a small hill and looked across a desolate landscape, powdered with snow. There was the occasional small wood, a scattering of hedged fields and then flat marshland drifting towards a river which had to be the Arun. Beside it, perhaps a mile away, he saw houses, twelve or fifteen, with red pantiled roofs and there was a small church, obviously Doxley. He started down the hill to the wooded valley below and as he came to it, saw a five-barred gate standing open and a decaying wooden sign with the legend 'Cadge End Farm'.

The track led through the wood and brought him almost at once to a farm complex. There were a few chickens running here and there, a house and two large barns linked to it so that the whole enclosed a courtyard. It looked incredibly run-down as if nothing had been done to it for years, but then, as Dillon knew, many country people preferred to live like that. He got out of the Mini and crossed to the front door, knocked and tried to open it. It was locked. He turned and went to the first barn. Its old wooden doors stood open. There was a Morris van in there and a Ford car jacked up on bricks, no wheels, agricultural implements all over the place.

Dillon took out a cigarette. As he lit it in cupped hands, a voice behind said, 'Who are you? What do you want?'

He turned and found a girl in the doorway. She wore baggy trousers tucked into a pair of rubber boots, a heavy roll-neck sweater under an old anorak and a knitted beret like a tam-o'-shanter, the kind of thing you found in fishing villages on the west coast of Ireland. She was holding a double-barrelled shotgun threateningly. As he took a step towards her, she thumbed back the hammer.

'You stay there.' The Irish accent was very pronounced.

'You'll be the one they call Angel Fahy?' he said.

'Angela if it's any of your business.'

Tania's man had been right. She did look like a little peasant. Broad cheekbone, upturned nose and a kind of fierceness there. 'Would you really shoot with that thing?'

'If I had to.'

'A pity that and me only wanting to meet my father's cousin, once removed, Danny Fahy.'

She frowned. "And who in the hell might you be, mister?"

'Dillon's the name. Sean Dillon.'

She laughed harshly. 'That's a damn lie. You're not even Irish and Sean Dillon is dead, everyone knows that.'

Dillon dropped into the hard distinctive accent of Belfast. 'To steal a great man's line, girl dear, all I can say is reports of my death have been greatly exaggerated.'

The gun went slack in her hands. 'Mother Mary, are you Sean Dillon?'

'As ever was. Appearances can be deceiving.'

'Oh, God,' she said. 'Uncle Danny talks about you all the time, but it was always like stories, nothing real to it at all and here you are.'

'Where is he?'

'He did a repair on a car for the landlord of the local pub, took it down there an hour ago. Said he'd walk back, but he'll be there a while yet drinking, I shouldn't wonder.'

'At this time? Isn't the pub closed until evening?'

'That might be the law, Mr Dillon, but not in Doxley. They never close.'

'Let's go and get him then.'

She left the shotgun on a bench and got into the Mini beside him. As they drove away, he said, 'What's your story then?'

'I was raised on a farm in Galway. My Da was Danny's nephew, Michael. He died six years ago when I was fourteen. After a year, my mother married again.'

'Let me guess,' Dillon said. 'You didn't like your stepfather and he didn't like you?'

150

'Something like that. Uncle Danny came over for my father's funeral so I'd met him and liked him. When things got too heavy, I left home and came here. He was great about it. Wrote to my mother and she agreed I could stay. Glad to get rid of me.'

There was no self-pity at all and Dillon warmed to her. 'They always say some good comes out of everything.'

'I've been working it out,' she said. 'If you're Danny's second cousin and I'm his great-niece, then you and I are blood related, isn't that a fact?'

Dillon laughed. 'In a manner of speaking.'

She looked ecstatic as she leaned back. 'Me, Angel Fahy, related to the greatest gunman the Provisional IRA ever had.'

'Well, now, there would be some who would argue about that,' he said as they reached the village and pulled up outside the pub.

It was a small, desolate sort of place, no more than fifteen rather dilapidated cottages and a Norman church with a tower and an overgrown graveyard. The pub was called the Green Man and even Dillon had to duck to enter the door. The ceiling was very low and beamed. The floor was constructed of heavy stone flags worn with the years, the walls were whitewashed. The man behind the bar in his shirt sleeves was at least eighty.

He glanced up and Angel said, 'Is he here, Mr Dalton?'

'By the fire, having a beer,' the old man said.

A fire burned in a wide stone hearth and there was a wooden bench and a table in front of it. Danny Fahy sat there reading the paper, a glass in front of him. He was sixty-five with an untidy grizzled beard and wore a cloth cap and an old Harris Tweed suit.

Angel said, 'I've brought someone to see you, Uncle Danny.'

He looked up at her and then at Dillon, puzzlement on his face. 'And what can I do for you, sir?'

Dillon removed his glasses. 'God bless all here!' he said in his Belfast accent, 'and particularly you, you old bastard.'

Fahy turned very pale, the shock was so intense. 'God save us, is that you, Sean, and me thinking you were in your box long ago?'

'Well, I'm not and I'm here.' Dillon took a five-pound note from his wallet and gave it to Angel. 'A couple of whiskeys, Irish for preference.'

She went back to the bar and Dillon turned. Danny Fahy actually had tears in his eyes and he flung his arms around him. 'Dear God, Sean, but I can't tell you how good it is to see you.'

The sitting room at the farm was untidy and cluttered, the furniture very old. Dillon sat on a sofa while Fahy built up the fire. Angel was in the kitchen cooking a meal. It was open to the sitting room and Dillon could see her moving around.

'And how's life been treating you, Sean?' Fahy stuffed a pipe and lit it. 'Ten years since you raised Cain in London town. By God, boy, you gave the Brits something to think about.'

'I couldn't have done it without you, Danny.'

'Great days. And what happened after?'

'Europe, the Middle East. I kept on the move. Did a lot for the PLO. Even learned to fly.'

'Is that a fact?'

Angel came and put plates of bacon and eggs on the table. 'Get it while it's hot.' She returned with a tray laden with teapot and milk, three mugs and a plate piled high with bread and butter. 'I'm sorry there's nothing fancier, but we weren't expecting company.'

'It looks good to me,' Dillon told her and tucked in.

'So now you're here Sean and dressed like an English gentleman,' Fahy turned to Angel. 'Didn't I tell you the actor this man was? They never could put a glove on him in all these years, not once.'

She nodded eagerly, smiling at Dillon and her personality had changed with the excitement. 'Are you on a job now, Mr Dillon, for the IRA, I mean?'

'It would be a cold day in hell before I put myself on the line for that bunch of old washerwomen,' Dillon said.

'But you are working on something, Sean?' Fahy said. 'I can tell. Come on, let's in on it.'

Dillon lit a cigarette. 'What if I told you I was working for the Arabs, Danny, for Saddam Hussein himself?'

'Jesus, Sean, and why not? And what is it he wants you to do?'

'He wants something now – a coup. Something big. America's too far away. That leaves the Brits.'

'What could be better?' Fahy's eyes were gleaming.

'Thatcher was in France the other day seeing Mitterrand. I had plans for her on the way to her plane. Perfect set-up, quiet country road and then someone I trusted let me down.'

'And isn't that always the way?' Fahy said. 'So you're looking for another target? Who, Sean?'

'I was thinking of John Major.'

'The new Prime Minister?' Angel said in awe. 'You wouldn't dare.'

'Sure and why wouldn't he? Didn't the boys nearly get the whole bloody British Government at Brighton?' Danny Fahy told her. 'Go on, Sean, what's your plan?'

'I haven't got one, Danny, that's the trouble, but there would be a pay day for this like you wouldn't believe.'

'And that's as good a reason to make it work as any. So you've come to Uncle Danny looking for help?' Fahy went to a cupboard, came back with a bottle of Bushmills and two glasses and filled them. 'Have you any ideas at all?'

'Not yet, Danny. Do you still work for the movement?'

'Stay in deep cover, that was the order from Belfast so many years ago I've forgotten. Since then not a word and me bored out of my socks, so I moved down here. It suits me. I like the countryside here, I like the people. They keep to themselves. I've built up a fair business repairing agricultural machinery and I run a few sheep. We're happy here, Angel and me.'

'And still bored out of your socks. Do you remember Martin Brosnan, by the way?'

'I do so. You were bad friends with that one.'

'I had a run-in with him in Paris recently. He'll probably turn up in London looking for me. He'll be working for Brit intelligence.'

'The bastard.' Fahy frowned as he refilled his pipe. 'Didn't I hear some fanciful talk of how Brosnan got into Ten Downing Street as a waiter years ago and didn't do anything about it?'

'I heard that story too. A flight of fancy and no one would get in these days as a waiter or anything else. You know they've blocked the street off? The place is a fortress. No way in there, Danny.'

'Oh, there's always a way, Sean. I was reading in a magazine the other day how a lot of French Resistance people in the Second World War were held at some Gestapo headquarters. Their cells were on the ground floor, the Gestapo on the first floor. The RAF had a fella in a Mosquito fly in at fifty feet and drop a bomb that bounced off the street and went in through the first-floor window, killing all the bloody Gestapo so the fellas downstairs got away.'

'What in the hell are you trying to say to me?' Dillon demanded.

'That I'm a great believer in the power of the bomb and

the science of ballistics. You can make a bomb go anywhere if you know what you're doing.'

'What is this?' Dillon demanded.

Angel said, 'Go on, show him, Uncle Danny.'

'Show me what?' Dillon said.

Danny Fahy got up, putting another match to his pipe. 'Come on, then,' and he turned and went to the door.

Fahy opened the door of the second barn and led the way in. It was enormous, oak beams rearing up to a steeply pitched roof. There was a loft stuffed with hay and reached by a ladder. There were various items of farm machinery including a tractor. There was also a fairly new Land Rover, an old BSA 500cc motorcycle in fine condition, up on its stand.

'This is a beauty,' Dillon said in genuine admiration.

'Bought it second-hand last year. Thought I'd renovate it to make a profit, but now I'm finished, I can't bear to let it go. It's as good as a BMW.' There was another vehicle in the shadows of the rear and Fahy switched on a light and a white Ford Transit van stood revealed.

'So?' Dillon said. 'What's so special?'

'You wait, Mr Dillon,' Angel told him. 'This is really something.'

Fahy said, 'Not what it seems.'

There was an excited look on his face, a kind of pride as he opened the sliding door. Inside there was a battery of metal pipes, three in all, bolted to the floor, pointing up to the roof at an angle.

'Mortars, Sean, just like the lads have been using in Ulster.'

Dillon said, 'You mean this thing works?'

'Hell, no, I've no explosives. It would work, that's all I can say.'

155

'Explain it to me.'

'I've welded a steel platform to the floor, that's to stand the recoil and I've also welded the tubing together. That's standard cast-iron stuff available anywhere. The electric timers are dead simple. Stuff you can buy at any do-it-yourself shop.'

'How would it work?'

'Once switched on it would give you a minute to get out of the van and run for it. The roof is cut out. That's just stretched polythene covering the hole. You can see I've sprayed it the same colour. It gives the mortars a clean exit. I've even worked out an extra little device linked to the timer that will self-destruct the van after it's fired the mortars.'

'And where would they be?'

'Over here.' Fahy walked to a work bench. 'Standard oxygen cylinders.' There were several stacked together, the bottom plates removed.

'And what would you need for those, Semtex?' Dillon asked, naming the Czechoslovakian explosive so popular with terrorists everywhere.

'I'd say about twelve pounds in each would do nicely, but that's not easily come by over here.'

Dillon lit a cigarette and walked around the van, his face blank. 'You're a bad boy, Danny. The movement told you to stay in deep cover.'

'Like I told you, how many years ago was that?' Fahy demanded. 'A man would go crazy.'

'So you found yourself something to do?'

'It was easy, Sean. You know I was in the light engineering for years.'

Dillon stood looking at it. Angel said, 'What do you think?'

'I think he's done a good job.'

'As good as anything they've done in Ulster,' Fahy said.

'Maybe, but whenever they've been used, they've never been too strong on accuracy.'

'They worked like a dream in that attack on Newry Police Station six years ago. Killed nine coppers.'

'What about all the other times they couldn't hit a barn door? Someone even blew himself up with one of these things in Portadown. A bit hit and miss.'

'Not the way I'd do it. I can plot the target on a large-scale map, have a look at the area on foot beforehand, line the van up and that's it. Mind you, I've been thinking that some sort of fin welded onto the oxygen cylinders would help steady them in flight. A nice big curve and then down and the whole world blows up. All the security in the world wouldn't help. I mean, what good are gates if you go over them?'

'You're talking Downing Street now?' Dillon said.

'And why not?'

'They meet at ten o'clock every morning in the Cabinet Room. What they call the War Cabinet. You'd not only get the Prime Minister, you'd get virtually the whole Government.'

Fahy crossed himself. 'Holy Mother of God, it would be the hit of a lifetime.'

'They'd make up songs about you, Danny,' Dillon told him. 'They'd be singing about Danny Fahy in bars all over Ireland fifty years from now.'

Fahy slammed a clenched fist into his palm. 'All hot air, Sean, no meaning to it without the Semtex and like I said, that stuff's impossible to get your hands on over here.'

'Don't be too sure, Danny,' Dillon said. 'There might be a source. Now let's go and have a Bushmills and sort this out.'

Fahy had a large-scale map of London spread across the table and examined it with a magnifying glass. 'Here would be the place,' he said. 'Horse Guards Avenue running up from the Victoria Embankment at the side of the Ministry of Defence.'

'Yes.' Dillon nodded.

'If we left the Ford on the corner with Whitehall then as long as I had a pre-determined sighting, to get my direction, I reckon the mortar bombs would go over those roofs in a bloody great curve and land smack on Ten Downing Street!' He put his pencil down beside the ruler. 'I'd like to have a look, mind you.'

'And so you will,' Dillon said.

'Would it work, Mr Dillon?' Angel demanded.

'Oh, yes,' he said. 'I think it really could. Ten o'clock in the morning, the whole bloody War Cabinet.' He started to laugh. 'It's beautiful, Danny, beautiful.' He grabbed the other man's arm. 'You'll come in with me on this?'

'Of course I will.'

'Good,' Dillon said. 'Big, big money, Danny. I'll set you up for your old age. Total luxury. Spain, Greece, anywhere you want to go.' Fahy rolled up the map and Dillon said, 'I'll stay overnight. We'll go up to London tomorrow and have a look.' He smiled and lit another cigarette. 'It's looking good, Danny. Really good. Now tell me about this airfield near here at Grimethorpe?'

'A real broken down sort of a place. It's only three miles from here. What would you want with Grimethorpe?'

'I told you I learned to fly in the Middle East. A good way of getting out of places fast. Now what's the situation at this Grimethorpe place?'

'It goes way back into the past. A flying club in the thirties. Then the RAF used it as a feeder station during the Battle of Britain so they built three hangars. Someone tried it as a flying club a few years ago. There's a tarmac

158

runway. Anyway, it failed. A fella called Bill Grant turned up three years ago. He has two planes there, that's all I know. His firm is called Grant's Air Taxis. I heard recently he was in trouble. His two mechanics had left. Business was bad.' He smiled. 'There's a recession on, Sean, and it even affects the rich.'

'Does he live on the premises?'

'Yes,' Angel said. 'He did have a girlfriend, but she moved on.'

'I think I'd like to meet him,' Dillon said. 'Maybe you could show me, Angel?'

'Of course.'

'Good, but first I'd like to make a phone call.'

He rang Tania Novikova at her flat. She answered at once. 'It's me,' he said.

'Has it gone well?'

'Unbelievable. I'll tell you tomorrow. Did you pick up the money?'

'Oh, yes, no problem.'

'Good. I'll be at the hotel at noon. I'm overnighting here. See you then,' and he rang off.

Brosnan and Mary Tanner went up in the freight elevator with Charlie Salter and found Mordecai waiting for them. He pumped Brosnan's hand up and down. 'It's great to see you, Professor. I can't tell you how great. Harry's been on hot bricks.'

'This is Mary Tanner,' Brosnan said. 'You'd better be nice. She's an army captain.'

'Well, this is a pleasure, miss.' Mordecai shook her hand. 'I did my National Service in the Grenadier Guards, but lance corporal was all I managed.'

He led them into the sitting room. Harry Flood was seated at the desk going over some accounts. He glanced up and jumped to his feet. 'Martin.' He rushed round the desk and embraced Brosnan, laughing in delight.

Brosnan said, 'Mary Tanner. She's army, Harry, a real hot-shot so watch your step. I'm working for Brigadier Charles Ferguson of British intelligence and she's his aide.'

'Then I'll behave.' Flood took her hand. 'Now come over here and let's have a drink and you tell me what all this is about, Martin.'

They sat in the sofa complex in the corner and Brosnan covered everything in finest detail. Mordecai leaned against the wall listening, no expression on his face.

When Brosnan was finished, Flood said, 'So what do you want from me, Martin?'

'He always works the underworld, Harry, that's where he gets everything he needs. Not only physical help, but explosives, weaponry. He'll work the same way now, I know he will.'

'So what you want to know is who he'd go to?'

'Exactly.'

Flood looked up at Mordecai. 'What do you think?'

'I don't know, Harry. I mean there are plenty of legit arms dealers, but what you need is someone who's willing to supply the IRA.'

'Any ideas?' Flood asked.

'Not really, guv. I mean, most of your real East End villains love Maggie Thatcher and wear Union Jack underpants. They don't go for Irish geezers letting off bombs at Harrods. We could make enquiries, of course.'

'Then do that,' Flood said. 'Put the word out now, but discreetly.'

Mordecai went out and Harry Flood reached for the champagne bottle. 'You're still not drinking?' Brosnan said.

'Not me, old buddy, but no reason you shouldn't. You can fill me in with the events of recent years and then we'll go along to the *Embassy*, one of my more respectable clubs, and have something to eat.'

At around the same time, Sean Dillon and Angel Fahy were driving along the dark country road from Cadge End to Grimethorpe. The lights of the car picked out light snow and frost on the hedgerows.

'It's beautiful, isn't it?' she said.

'I suppose so.'

'I like it here, the countryside and all that. I like Uncle Danny, too. He's been really good to me.'

'That makes sense. You were raised in the country back there in Galway.'

'It wasn't the same. It was poor land there. It was hard work to make any kind of living and it showed in the people, my mother, for instance. It was as if they'd been to war and lost and there was nothing to look forward to.'

'You've got a way with the words, girl,' he told her.

'My English teacher used to say that. She said if I worked hard and studied I could do anything.'

'Well that must have been a comfort.'

'It didn't do me any good. My stepfather just saw me as an unpaid farm labourer. That's why I left.'

The lights picked out a sign that said Grimethorpe Airfield, the paintwork peeling. Dillon turned into a narrow tarmac road that was badly potholed. A few moments later, they came to the airfield. There were three hangars, an old control tower, a couple of Nissen huts, a light at the windows of one of them. A Jeep was parked there and Dillon pulled in beside it. As they got out, the door of the Nissen hut opened and a man stood there.

'Who is it?'

'It's me, Mr Grant, Angel Fahy. I've brought someone to see you.'

Grant, like most pilots, was small and wiry. He looked to be in his mid-forties, wore jeans and an old flying jacket of the kind used by American aircrews in the Second World War. 'You'd better come in, then.'

The interior of the Nissen hut was warm, heated by a coke-burning stove, the pipe going up through the roof. Grant obviously used it as a living room. There was a table with the remains of a meal on it, an old easy chair by the stove facing a television set in the corner. Beneath the windows on the other side there was a long sloping desk with a few charts.

Angel said, 'This is a friend of my uncle's.'

'Hilton,' Dillon said, 'Peter Hilton.'

Grant put his hand out, looking wary. 'Bill Grant. I don't owe you money, do I?'

'Not to my knowledge.' Dillon was back in his public school role.

'Well that makes a nice change. What can I do for you?'

'I want a charter in the next few days. Just wanted to check if you might be able to do something before I tried anywhere else.'

'Well that depends.'

'On what? You do have a plane, I take it?'

'I've got two. The only problem is how long the bank lets me hang on to them. Do you want to have a look?'

'Why not?'

They went out, crossed the apron to the end hangar and he opened a Judas so they could step through. He reached to one side, found a switch and lights came on. There were two planes there, side by side, both twin-engines.

Dillon walked up to the nearest. 'I know this baby, a Cessna Conquest. What's the other?'

'Navajo Chieftain.'

'If things are as tricky as you say, what about fuel?'

'I always keep my planes juiced up, Mr Hilton, always full tanks. I'm too old a hand to do otherwise. You never know when a job might come up.' He smiled ruefully. 'Mind you, I'll be honest. What with the recession, there aren't too many people looking for charters these days. Where would you like me to take you?'

'Actually I was thinking of going for a spin myself one day,' Dillon said. 'I'm not sure when.'

'You're certified then?' Grant looked dubious.

'Oh, yes, fully.' Dillon took out his pilot's licence and passed it across.

Grant examined it quickly and handed it back. 'You could handle either of these two, but I'd rather come myself, just to make sure.'

'No problem,' Dillon said smoothly. 'It's the West Country I was thinking of. Cornwall. There's an airfield at Land's End.'

'I know it well. Grass runway.'

'I've got friends near there. I'd probably want to stay overnight.'

'That's fine by me.' Grant switched off the lights and they walked back to the Nissen hut. 'What line are you in, Mr Hilton?'

'Oh, finance, accountancy, that sort of thing,' Dillon said.

'Have you any idea when you might want to go? I should point out that kind of charter's going to be expensive. Around two thousand five hundred pounds. With half a dozen passengers that's not so bad, but on your own . . .'

'That's fine,' Dillon said.

'Then there would be my overnight expenses. A hotel and so on.'

'No problem.' Dillon took ten fifty-pound notes from his wallet and put them on the table. 'There's five hundred

163

down. It's a definite booking for sometime in the next four or five days. I'll phone you here to let you know when.'

Grant's face brightened as he picked up the bank notes. 'That's fine. Can I get you a coffee or something before you go?'

'Why not?' Dillon said.

Grant went into the kitchen at the far end of the Nissen hut. They heard him filling a kettle, Dillon put a finger to his lips, made a face at Angel and crossed to the charts on the desk. He went through them quickly, found the one for the general English Channel area and the French coast. Angel stood beside him watching as he traced his finger along the Normandy coast. He found Cherbourg and moved south. There it was, St Denis, with the landing strip clearly marked, and he pushed the charts back together. Grant in the kitchen had been watching through the half-open door. As the kettle boiled, he quickly made coffee in three mugs and took them in.

'Is this weather giving you much trouble?' Dillon said. 'The snow?'

'It will if it really starts to lay,' Grant said. 'It could make it difficult for that grass runway at Land's End.'

'We'll just have to keep our fingers crossed.' Dillon put down his mug. 'We'd better be getting back.'

Grant went to the door to see them off. They got in the Mini and drove away. He waved, closed the door and went to the desk and examined the charts. It was the third or fourth down, he was sure of that. *General English Channel area and the French coast.*

He frowned and said softly, 'And what's your game, mister, I wonder?'

As they drove back through the dark country lanes Angel said, 'Not Land's End at all, Mr Dillon, it's that St Denis 'place in Normandy, that's where you want to fly to.'

'Our secret,' he said and put his left hand on hers, still steering. 'Can I ask you to promise me one thing?'

'Anything, Mr Dillon.'

'Let's keep it to ourselves, just for now. I don't want Danny to know. You do drive, do you?'

'Drive? Of course I do. I take the sheep to market in the Morris van myself.'

'Tell me, how would you like a trip up to London tomorrow morning with me, you and Danny?'

'I'd like it fine.'

'Good, that's all right then.'

As they carried on through the night her eyes were shining.

NINE

It was a cold, crisp morning, winter on every hand, but the roads were clear as Dillon drove up to London, Angel and Danny Fahy following in the Morris van. Angel was driving and more than competently. He could see her in his rear-view mirror and she stayed right on his tail all the way into London until they came to the Bayswater Road. There was a plan already half-formed in his mind and he got out of the Mini Cooper, parked it at the kerb and opened the doors of Tania's garage.

As Angel and Danny drew up behind him he said, 'Put the Morris inside.' Angel did as she was told. When she and Danny Fahy came out, Dillon closed the doors and said, 'You'll remember the street and the garage, if you lose me, that is?'

'Don't be silly, Mr Dillon, of course I will,' Angel said.

'Good. It's important. Now get in the Mini. We're going for a little run round.'

Harry Flood was sitting at the desk in his apartment at Cable Wharf checking the casino accounts from the night before when Charlie Salter brought in coffee on a tray. The phone rang and the small man picked it up. He handed it to Flood.

'The Professor.'

'Martin, how goes it?' Flood said. 'I enjoyed last night. The Tanner lady is something special.'

'Is there any news? Have you managed to come up with anything?' Brosnan asked.

'Not yet, Martin, just a minute.' Flood put a hand over the receiver and said to Salter, 'Where's Mordecai?'

'Doing the rounds, Harry, just like you asked him, putting the word out discreetly.'

Flood returned to Brosnan. 'Sorry, old buddy, we're doing everything we can, but it's going to take time.'

'Which we don't really have,' Brosnan said. 'All right, Harry, I know you're doing your best. I'll stay in touch.'

He was standing at Mary Tanner's desk in the living room of her Lowndes Square flat. He put the phone down, walked to the window and lit a cigarette.

'Anything?' she asked and crossed the room to join him.

'I'm afraid not. As Harry has just said, it takes time. I was a fool to think anything else.'

'Just try and be patient, Martin.' She put a hand on his arm.

'But I can't,' he said. 'I've got this feeling and it's hard to explain. It's like being in a storm and waiting for that bloody great thunderclap you know is going to come. I know Dillon, Mary. He's moving fast on this. I'm certain of it.'

'So what would you like to do?'

'Will Ferguson be at Cavendish Square this morning?'

'Yes.'

'Then let's go to see him.'

Dillon parked the Mini Cooper near Covent Garden. An enquiry in a bookshop nearby led them to a shop not too far away specialising in maps and charts of every description. Dillon worked his way through the large-scale Ordnance Survey maps of Central London until he found the one covering the general area of Whitehall.

'Would you look at the detail in that thing?' Fahy whispered. 'You could measure the size of the garden at Number Ten to half an inch.'

Dillon purchased the map which the assistant rolled up tightly and inserted into a protective cardboard tube. He paid for it and they walked back to the car.

'Now what?' Danny asked.

'We'll take a run round. Have a look at the situation.'

'That suits me.'

Angel sat in the rear, her uncle beside Dillon as they drove down towards the river and turned into Horse Guards Avenue. Dillon paused slightly on the corner before turning into Whitehall and moving towards Downing Street.

'Plenty of coppers around,' Danny said.

'That's to make sure people don't park.' A car had drawn in to the kerb on their left and as they pulled out to pass, they saw that the driver was consulting a map.

'Tourist, I expect,' Angel said.

'And look what's happening,' Dillon told her.

She turned and saw two policemen converging on the car. A quiet word, it started up and moved away.

Angel said, 'They don't waste time.'

'Downing Street,' Dillon announced a moment later.

'Would you look at those gates?' Danny said in wonder. 'I like the Gothic touch. Sure and they've done a good job there.'

Dillon moved with the traffic round Parliament Square and went back up Whitehall towards Trafalgar Square.

'We're going back to Bayswater,' he said. 'Notice the route I've chosen.'

He moved out of the traffic of Trafalgar Square through Admiralty Arch along the Mall, round the Queen Victoria monument past Buckingham Palace and along Constitution Hill, eventually reaching Marble Arch by way of Park Lane and turning into the Bayswater Road.

'And that's simple enough,' Danny Fahy said.

'Good,' Dillon said. 'Then let's go and get a nice cup of tea at my truly awful hotel.'

Ferguson said, 'You're getting too restless, Martin.'

'It's the waiting,' Brosnan told him. 'Flood's doing his best, I know that, but I don't think time is on our side.'

Ferguson turned from the window and sipped a little of the cup of tea he was holding. 'So what would you like to do?'

Brosnan hesitated, glanced at Mary and said, 'I'd like to go and see Liam Devlin in Kilrea. He might have some ideas.'

'Something he was never short of.' Ferguson turned to Mary. 'What do you think?'

'I think it makes sense, sir. After all, a trip to Dublin's no big deal. An hour and a quarter from Heathrow on either Aer Lingus or BA.'

'And Liam's place at Kilrea is only half an hour from the city,' Brosnan said.

'All right,' Ferguson said, 'you've made your point, both of you, but make it Gatwick and the Lear jet, just in case anything comes up and you need to get back here in a hurry.'

'Thank you, sir,' Mary said.

As they reached the door, Ferguson added, 'I'll give the

169

old rogue a call, just to let him know you're on your way,' and he reached for the phone.

As they went downstairs Brosnan said, 'Thank God. At least I feel we're doing something.'

'And I get to meet the great Liam Devlin at long last,' Mary said and led the way out to the limousine.

In the small café at the hotel Dillon, Angel and Fahy sat at a corner table drinking tea. Fahy had the Ordnance Survey map partially open on his knee. 'It's extraordinary. The things they give away. Every detail.'

'Could it be done, Danny?'

'Oh, yes, no trouble. You remember that corner, Horse Guards Avenue and Whitehall? That would be the place, slightly on an angle. I can see it in my mind's eye. I can plot the distance from that corner to Number Ten exactly from this map.'

'You're sure you'd clear the buildings in between?'

'Oh, yes. I've said before, Sean, ballistics is a matter of science.'

'But you can't stop there,' Angel said. 'We saw what happened to that man in the car. The police were on him in seconds.'

Dillon turned to Fahy. 'Danny?'

'Well, that's all you need. Everything pre-timed, Angel. Press the right switch to activate the circuit, get out of the van and the mortars start firing within a minute. No policeman could act fast enough to stop it.'

'But what would happen to you?' she demanded.

It was Dillon who answered. 'Just listen to this. We drive up from Cadge End one morning early, you, Danny, in the Ford Transit and Angel and me in the Morris van. We'll have that BSA motorcycle in the back of that. Angel will park the Morris, like today, in the garage at the end of the

170

road. We'll have a duckboard in the back so I can run the BSA out.'

'And you'll follow me, is that it?'

'I'll be right up your tail. When we reach the corner of Horse Guards Avenue and Whitehall, you set your switch, get out and jump straight on my pillion and we'll be away. The War Cabinet meets every morning at ten. With luck we could get the lot.'

'Jesus, Sean, they'd never know what hit them.'

'Straight back to Bayswater to Angel waiting in the garage with the Morris, BSA in the back and away we go. We'll be in Cadge End while they're still trying to put the fires out.'

'It's brilliant, Mr Dillon,' Angel told him.

'Except for one thing,' Fahy said. 'Without the bloody explosives, we don't have any bloody bombs.'

'You leave that to me,' Dillon said. 'I'll get your explosives for you.' He stood up. 'But I've got things to do. You two go back to Cadge End and wait. I'll be in touch.'

'And when would that be, Sean?'

'Soon – very soon,' and Dillon smiled as they went out.

Tania was knocking at his door precisely at noon. He opened it and said, 'You've got it?'

She had a briefcase in her right hand, opened it on the table to reveal the thirty thousand dollars he'd asked for.

'Good,' he said. 'I'll just need ten thousand to be going on with.'

'What will you do with the rest?'

'I'll hand it in at the desk. They can keep your briefcase in the hotel safe.'

'You've worked something out, I can tell.' She looked excited. 'What happened at this Cadge End place?'

So he told her and in detail, the entire plan. 'What do you think?' he asked when he'd finished.

'Incredible. The coup of a lifetime. But what about the explosives? You'd need Semtex.'

'That's all right. When I was operating in London in eighty-one I used to deal with a man who had access to Semtex.' He laughed. 'In fact he had access to everything.'

'And who is this man? How can you be sure he's still around?'

'A crook named Jack Harvey and he's around all right. I looked him up.'

'But I don't understand?'

'Amongst other things he has a funeral business in Whitechapel. I looked it up in Yellow Pages and it's still there. By the way, your Mini, I can still use it?'

'Of course.'

'Good. I'll park it somewhere in the street. I want that garage free.'

He picked up his coat. 'Come on, we'll go and have a bite to eat and then I'll go and see him.'

'You've read the file on Devlin, I suppose?' Brosnan asked Mary Tanner as they drove through the centre of Dublin and crossed the River Liffey by St George's Quay and moved on out of the other side of the city, driven by a chauffeur in a limousine from the Embassy.

'Yes,' she said, 'but is it all true? The story about his involvement with the German attempt to get Churchill in the war?'

'Oh, yes.'

'The same man who helped you break out of that French prison in nineteen seventy-nine?'

'That's Devlin.'

'But Martin, you said he claimed to be seventy. He must be older than that.'

'A few years is a minor detail where Liam Devlin is concerned. Let's put it this way, you're about to meet the most extraordinary man you've ever met in your life. Scholar, poet and gunman for the IRA.'

'The last part is no recommendation to me,' she said.

'I know,' he told her. 'But never make the mistake of lumping Devlin in with the kind of rubbish the IRA employs these days.'

He retreated into himself, suddenly sombre, and the car continued out into the Irish countryside, leaving the city behind.

Kilrea Cottage, the place was called, on the outskirts of the village next to a convent. It was a period piece, single-storeyed with Gothic-looking gables and leaded windows on either side of the porch. They sheltered in there from the light rain while Brosnan tugged an old-fashioned bell pull. There was the sound of footsteps, the door opened.

'*Cead míle fáilte*,' Liam Devlin said in Irish. 'A hundred thousand welcomes,' and he flung his arms around Brosnan.

The interior of the house was very Victorian. Most of the furniture was mahogany, the wallpaper was a William Morris replica, but the paintings on the walls, all Atkinson Grimshaws, were real.

Liam Devlin came in from the kitchen with tea things on a tray. 'My housekeeper comes mornings only. One of the good sisters from the convent next door. They need the money.'

Mary Tanner was totally astonished. She'd expected an

old man and found herself faced with this ageless creature in black silk Italian shirt, black pullover, grey slacks in the latest fashionable cut. There was still considerable colour in hair that had once been black and the face was pale, but she sensed that had always been so. The blue eyes were extraordinary as was that perpetual ironic smile with which he seemed to laugh at himself as much as the world.

'So, you work for Ferguson, girl?' he said to Mary as he poured the tea.

'That's right.'

'That business in Derry the other year when you moved that car with the bomb. That was quite something.'

She felt herself flushing. 'No big deal, Mr Devlin, it just seemed like the right thing to do at the time.'

'Oh, we can all see that on occasions, it's the doing that counts.' He turned to Brosnan. 'Anne-Marie. A bad business, son.'

'I want him, Liam,' Brosnan said.

'For yourself or for the general cause?' Devlin shook his head. 'Push the personal thing to one side, Martin, or you'll make mistakes and that's something you can't afford to do with Sean Dillon.'

'Yes, I know,' Brosnan said. 'I know.'

'So, he intends to take a crack at this John Major fella, the new Prime Minister?' Devlin said.

'And how do you think he's likely to do that, Mr Devlin?' Mary asked.

'Well, from what I hear about security at Ten Downing Street these days, I wouldn't rate his changes of getting in very high.' He looked at Brosnan and grinned. 'Mind you, Mary, my love, I remember a young fella of my acquaintance called Martin Brosnan who got into Number Ten posing as a waiter at a party not ten years ago. Left a rose on the Prime Minister's desk. Of course, the office was held by a woman then.'

Brosnan said, 'All in the past, Liam, what about now?'

'Oh, he'll work as he always has using contacts in the underworld.'

'Not the IRA?'

'I doubt whether the IRA has any connection with this whatsoever.'

'But they did last time he worked in London ten years ago.'

'So?'

'I was wondering. If we knew who recruited him that time, it could help.'

'I see what you mean, give you some sort of lead as to who he worked with in London?'

'All right, not much of a chance, but the only one we've got, Brosnan.'

'There's still your friend Flood, in London.'

'I know and he'll pull out all the stops, but that takes time and we don't have much to spare.'

Devlin nodded. 'Right, son, you leave it with me and I'll see what I can do.' He glanced at his watch. 'One o'clock. We'll have a sandwich and perhaps a Bushmills together and I suggest you go to your Lear jet and hare back to London. I'll be in touch, believe me, the minute I have something.'

Dillon parked round the corner from Jack Harvey's funeral business in Whitechapel and walked, the briefcase in one hand. Everything was beautifully discreet down to the bell push that summoned the day porter to open the door.

'Mr Harvey,' Dillon lied cheerfully. 'He's expecting me.'

'Down the hall past the chapels of rest and up the stairs. His office is on the first floor. What was the name, sir?'

'Hilton.' Dillon looked around at the coffins on display, the flowers. 'Not much happening.'

175

'Trade you mean.' The porter shrugged. 'That all comes in the back way.'

'I see.'

Dillon moved down the hall, pausing to glance into one of the chapels of rest, taking in the banked flowers, the candles. He stepped in and looked down at the body of a middle-aged man neatly dressed in a dark suit, hands folded, the face touched with make-up.

'Poor sod,' Dillon said and went out.

At the reception desk, the porter picked up a phone. 'Miss Myra? A visitor. A Mr Hilton, says he has an appointment.'

Dillon opened the door to Harvey's outer office and moved in. There were no office furnishings, just a couple of potted plants and several easy chairs. The door to the inner office opened and Myra entered. She wore skin-tight black trews, black boots and a scarlet three-quarter-length kaftan. She looked very striking.

'Mr Hilton?'

'That's right.'

'I'm Myra Harvey. You said you had an appointment with my uncle.'

'Did I?'

She looked him over in a casual way and behind him the door opened and Billy Watson came in. The whole thing was obviously pre-arranged. He leaned against the door, suitably menacing in a black suit, arms folded.

'Now what's your game?' she said.

'That's for Mr Harvey.'

'Throw him out, Billy,' she said and turned to the door.

Billy put one rough hand on Dillon's shoulder. Dillon's foot went all the way down the right leg stamping on the instep, he pivoted and struck sideways with clenched fist, the knuckles on the back of the hand connecting with Billy's temple. Billy cried out in pain and fell back into one of the chairs.

'He's not very good, is he?' Dillon said.

He opened his briefcase and took out ten one-hundred-dollar bills with a rubber band round them and threw them at Myra. She missed the catch and had to bend to pick them up. 'Would you look at that,' she said. 'And brand new.'

'Yes, new money always smells so good,' Dillon said. 'Now tell Jack an old friend would like to see him with more of the same.'

She stood there looking at him for a moment, eyes narrowed, then she turned and opened the door to Harvey's office. Billy tried to get up and Dillon said, 'I wouldn't advise it.'

Billy subsided as the door opened and Myra appeared. 'All right, he'll see you.'

The room was surprisingly businesslike with walls panelled in oak, a green carpet in Georgian silk and a gas fire that almost looked real, burning in a steel basket on the hearth. Harvey sat behind a massive oak desk smoking a cigar.

He had the thousand dollars in front of him and looked Dillon over calmly. 'My time's limited so don't muck me about, son.' He picked up the bank notes. 'More of the same?'

'That's right.'

'I don't know you. You told Myra you were an old friend, but I've never seen you before.'

'A long time ago, Jack, ten years to be precise. I looked different then. I was over from Belfast on a job. We did business together, you and me. You did well out of it as I recall. All those lovely dollars raised by IRA sympathisers in America.'

Harvey said, 'Coogan. Michael Coogan.'

Dillon took off his glasses. 'As ever was, Jack.'

Harvey nodded slowly and said to his niece, 'Myra, an old friend, Mr Coogan from Belfast.'

'I see,' she said. 'One of those.'

Dillon lit a cigarette, sat down, the briefcase on the floor beside him and Harvey said, 'You went through London like bloody Attila the Hun last time. I should have charged you more for all that stuff.'

'You gave me a price, I paid it,' Dillon said. 'What could be fairer?'

'And what is it this time?'

'I need a little Semtex, Jack. I could manage with forty pounds, but that's the bottom line. Fifty would be better.'

'You don't want much, do you? That stuff's like gold. Very strict government controls.'

'Bollocks,' Dillon said. 'It passes from Czechoslovakia to Italy, Greece, onwards to Libya. It's everywhere, Jack, you know it and I know it so don't waste my time. Twenty thousand dollars.' He opened the briefcase on his knee and tossed the rest of the ten thousand packet by packet across the desk. 'Ten now and ten on delivery.'

The Walther with the Carswell silencer screwed on the end of the barrel lay ready in the briefcase. He waited, the lid up and then Harvey smiled. 'All right, but it'll cost you thirty.'

Dillon closed the briefcase. 'No can do, Jack. Twenty-five I can manage, but no more.'

Harvey nodded. 'All right. When do you want it?'

'Twenty-four hours.'

'I think I can manage that. Where can we reach you?'

'You've got it wrong way round, Jack, I contact you.'

Dillon stood up and Harvey said affably, 'Anything else we can do for you?'

'Actually there is,' Dillon said. 'Sign of goodwill, you might say. I could do with a spare handgun.'

'Be my guest, my old son.' Harvey pushed his chair back and opened the second drawer down on his right-hand side. 'Take your pick.'

There was a Smith & Wesson .38 revolver, a Czech Cesca and an Italian Beretta which was the one Dillon selected. He checked the clip and slipped the gun in his pocket. 'This will do nicely.'

'Lady's gun,' Harvey said, 'but that's your business. We'll be seeing you then tomorrow.'

Myra opened the door. Dillon said, 'A pleasure, Miss Harvey,' and he brushed past Billy and walked out.

Billy said, 'I'd like to break that little bastard's legs.'

Myra patted his cheek. 'Never mind, sunshine, on your two feet you're useless. It's in the horizontal position you come into your own. Now go and play with your motorbike or something,' and she went back in her uncle's office.

Dillon paused at the bottom of the stairs and slipped the Beretta inside the briefcase. The only thing better than one gun was two. It always gave you an ace in the hole and he walked back to the Mini Cooper briskly.

Myra said, 'I wouldn't trust him an inch, that one.'

'A hard little bastard,' Harvey said. 'When he was here for the IRA in nineteen eighty-one I supplied him with arms, explosives, everything. You were at college then, not in the business, so you probably don't remember.'

'Is Coogan his real name?'

'Course not.' He nodded. 'Yes, hell on wheels. I was having a lot of hassle in those days from George Montoya down in Bermondsey, the one they called Spanish George. Coogan knocked him off for me one night, him and his brother, outside a bar called the Flamenco. Did it for free.'

'Really?' Myra said. 'So where do we get him Semtex?'

He laughed, opened the top drawer and took out a bunch of keys. 'I'll show you.' He led the way out and along the corridor and unlocked a door. 'Something even you didn't know, darling.'

The room was lined with shelves of box files. He put his hand on the middle shelf of the rear wall and it swung open. He reached for a switch and turned on a light revealing a treasure house of weapons of every description.

'My God!' she said.

'Whatever you want, it's here,' he said. 'Handguns, AK assault rifles, M15s.' He chuckled. 'And Semtex.' There were three cardboard boxes on a table. 'Fifty pounds in each of those.'

'But why did you tell him it might take time?'

'Keep him dangling.' He led the way out and closed things up. 'Might screw a few more bob out of him.'

As they went back into his office she said, 'What do you think he's up to?'

'I couldn't care less. Anyway, why should you worry? You suddenly turned into a bleeding patriot or something?'

'It isn't that, I'm just curious.'

He clipped another cigar. 'Mind you, I have had a thought. Very convenient if I got the little bugger to knock off Harry Flood for me,' and he started to laugh.

It was just after six and Ferguson was just about to leave his office at the Ministry of Defence when his phone rang. It was Devlin. 'Now then, you old sod, I've news for you.'

'Get on with it then,' Ferguson said.

'Dillon's control in eighty-one in Belfast was a man called Tommy McGuire. Remember him?'

'I do indeed. Wasn't he shot a few years ago? Some sort of IRA feud?'

'That was the story, but he's still around up there using another identity.'

'And what would that be?'

'I've still to find that out. People to see in Belfast. I'm driving up there tonight. I take it, by the way, that involving myself in this way makes me an official agent of Group Four? I mean I wouldn't like to end up in prison, not at my age.'

'You'll be covered fully, you have my word on it. Now what do you want us to do?'

'I was thinking that if Brosnan and your Captain Tanner wanted to be in on the action, they could fly over in the morning in that Lear jet of yours, to Belfast, that is and wait for me at the Europa Hotel in the bar. Tell Brosnan to identify himself to the head porter. I'll be in touch probably around noon.'

'I'll see to it,' Ferguson said.

'Just one more thing. Don't you think you and I are getting just a little geriatric for this sort of game?'

'You speak for yourself,' Ferguson said and put the phone down.

He sat thinking about it, then phoned through for a secretary. He also called Mary Tanner at the Lowndes Square flat. As he was talking to her, Alice Johnson came in with her notepad and pencil. Ferguson waved her down and carried on speaking to Mary.

'So, early start in the morning. Gatwick again, I think. You'll be there in an hour in the Lear. Are you dining out tonight?'

'Harry Flood suggested the River Room at the Savoy, he likes the dance band.'

'Sounds like fun.'

'Would you like to join us, sir?'

'Actually, I would,' Ferguson said.

'We'll see you then. Eight o'clock.'

Ferguson put down the phone and turned to Alice Johnson. 'A brief note, eyes of the Prime Minister only, the special file.' He quickly dictated a report that brought everything up to date including his conversation with Devlin. 'One copy for the PM and alert a messenger. Usual copy for me and the file. Hurry it up and bring them along for my signature. I want to get away.'

She went down to the office quickly. Gordon Brown was standing at the copier as she sat behind the typewriter. 'I thought he'd gone?' he said.

'So did I, but he's just given me an extra. Another eyes of the Prime Minister only.'

'Really.'

She started to type furiously, was finished in two minutes. She stood up. 'He'll have to hang on. I need to go to the toilet.'

'I'll do the copying for you.'

'Thanks, Gordon.'

She went out and along the corridor, was opening the toilet door when she realised she'd left her handbag on the desk. She turned and hurried back to the office. The door was partially open and she could see Gordon standing at the copier reading a copy of the report. To her astonishment, he folded it, slipped it in his inside pocket and hurriedly did another.

Alice was totally thrown, had no idea what to do. She went back along the corridor to the toilet, went in and tried to pull herself together. After a while she went back.

The report and a file copy were on her desk. 'All done,' Gordon Brown said, 'and I've requested a messenger.'

She managed a light smile. 'I'll get them signed.'

'Right, I'm just going down to the canteen. I'll see you later.'

Alice went along the corridor, knocked on Ferguson's door and went in. He was at his desk writing and looked up. 'Oh, good. I'll sign those and you can get the PM's copy off to Downing Street straight away.' She was trembling now and he frowned. 'My dear Mrs Johnson, what is it?'

So she told him.

He sat there, grim-faced and as she finished, reached for the telephone. 'Special Branch, Detective Inspector Lane for Brigadier Ferguson, Group Four. Top Priority, no delay. My office now.'

He put the phone down. 'Now this is what you do. Go back to the office and behave as if nothing has happened.'

'But he isn't there, Brigadier, he went to the canteen.'

'Really?' Ferguson said. 'Now why would he do that?'

When Tania heard Gordon Brown's voice she was immediately angry. 'I've told you about this, Gordon.'

'Yes, but it's urgent.'

'Where are you?'

'In the canteen at the Ministry. I've got another report.'

'Is it important?'

'Very.'

'Read it to me.'

'No, I'll bring it round after I come off shift at ten.'

'I'll see you at your place, Gordon, I promise, but I want to know what you've got now and if you refuse, then don't bother to call again.'

'No, that's all right, I'll read it.'

Which he did and when he was finished she said, 'Good boy, Gordon, I'll see you later.'

He put the phone down and turned, folding the copy of the report. The door to the phone box was jerked open and Ferguson plucked the report from his fingers.

TEN

Dillon was in his room at the hotel when Tania called him. 'I've got rather hot news,' she said. 'The hunt for a lead on you is moving to Belfast.'

'Tell me,' he said.

Which she did. When she was finished, she said, 'Does any of this make any sense?'

'Yes,' he said. 'The McGuire fella was a big name with the Provos in those days.'

'And he's dead, is he, or is he still around?'

'Devlin's right about that. His death was reported, supposedly because of in-fighting in the movement, but it was just a ruse to help him drop out of sight.'

'If they found him, could it give you problems?'

'Maybe, but not if I found him first.'

'And how could you do that?'

'I know his half-brother, a fella called Macey. He would know where he is.'

'But that would mean a trip to Belfast yourself.'

'That would be no big deal. An hour and a quarter by British Airways. I don't know what time the last plane tonight gets in, I'd have to check.'

'Just a minute, I've got a BA Worldwide Timetable here.'

she said and opened her desk drawer. She found it and looked at the Belfast schedule. 'The last plane is eight-thirty. You'll never make it. It's quarter to seven now. It's murder getting out to Heathrow in the evening traffic and this weather will make it worse. Probably at least an hour or maybe an hour and a half.'

'I know,' Dillon said. 'What about the morning?'

'Same time, eight-thirty.'

'I'll just have to get up early.'

'Is it wise?'

'Is anything in this life? I'll handle it, don't worry. I'll be in touch.'

He put the phone down, thought about it for a while then called British Airways and booked a seat on the morning flight with an open return. He lit a cigarette and walked to the window. Was it wise, she'd said, and he tried to remember what Tommy McGuire had known about him in eighty-one. Nothing about Danny Fahy, that was certain because Fahy wasn't supposed to be involved that time. That had been personal. But Jack Harvey was another matter. After all, it had been McGuire who'd put him on to Harvey as an arms supplier in the first place.

He pulled on his jacket, got his trenchcoat from the wardrobe and went out. Five minutes later he was hailing a cab on the corner. He got in and told the driver to take him to Covent Garden.

Gordon Brown sat on the other side of Ferguson's desk in the half-light. He had never been so frightened in his life. 'I didn't mean any harm, Brigadier, I swear it.'

'Then why did you take a copy of the report?'

'It was just a whim. Stupid, I know, but I was so intrigued with it being for the Prime Minister.'

'You realise what you've done, Gordon, a man of your

service? All those years in the army? This could mean your pension.'

Detective Inspector Lane of Special Branch was in his late thirties and in his crumpled tweed suit and glasses looked like a schoolmaster. He said, 'I'm going to ask you again, Mr Brown.' He leaned on the end of the desk. 'Have you ever taken copies like this before?'

'Absolutely not, I swear it.'

'You've never been asked by another person to do such a thing?'

Gordon managed to look suitably shocked. 'Good heavens, Inspector, that would be treason. I was a sergeant major in the Intelligence Corps.'

'Yes, Mr Brown, we know all that,' Lane said.

The internal phone went and Ferguson lifted it. It was Lane's sergeant, Mackie. 'I'm outside, Brigadier, just back from the flat in Camden. I think you and the Inspector should come out.'

'Thank you.' Ferguson put the phone down. 'Right, I think we'll give you time to think things over, Gordon. Inspector?'

He nodded to Lane, got up and moved to the door and Lane followed him. Mackie was standing in the anteroom still in trilby and raincoat, a plastic bag in one hand.

'You found something, Sergeant?' Lane asked.

'You could call it that, sir.' Mackie took a cardboard file from his plastic bag and opened it. 'A rather interesting collection.'

The copies of the reports were neatly stacked in order, the latest ones for the Prime Minister's attention on top.

Lane said, 'Christ, Brigadier, he's been at it for a while.'

'So it would seem,' Ferguson said. 'But to what purpose?'

'You mean he's working for someone, sir?'

'Without a doubt. The present operation I'm engaged on is most delicate. There was an attack on a man working

186

for me in Paris. A woman died. We wondered how the villain of the piece knew about them, if you follow me. Now we know. Details of these reports were passed on to a third party. They must have been.'

Lane nodded. 'Then we'll have to work on him some more.'

'No, we don't have the time. Let's try another way. Let's just let him go. He's a simple man. I think he'd do the simple thing.'

'Right, sir.' Lane turned to Mackie. 'If you lose him, you'll be back pounding the pavement in Brixton, and so will I because I'm coming with you.'

They hurried out and Ferguson opened the door and went back in the office. He sat down behind the desk. 'A sad business, Gordon.'

'What's going to happen to me, Brigadier?'

'I'll have to think about it.' Ferguson picked up the copy of the report. 'Such an incredibly stupid thing to do.' He sighed. 'Go home, Gordon, go home. I'll see you in the morning.'

Gordon Brown couldn't believe his luck. He got the door open somehow and left, hurrying down the corridor to the staff cloakroom. The narrowest escape of his life. It could have meant the end of everything. Not only his career and pension, but prison. But that was it: no more and Tania would have to accept that. He went downstairs to the car park, pulling on his coat, found his car and was turning into Whitehall a few moments later, Mackie and Lane hard on his tail in the sergeant's unmarked Ford Capri.

Dillon knew that late-night shopping was the thing in the Covent Garden area. There were still plenty of people around in spite of the winter cold and he hurried along until he came to the theatrical shop, Clayton's, near Neal's

Yard. The lights were on in the window, the door opened to his touch, the bell tinkling.

Clayton came through the bead curtain and smiled. 'Oh, it's you. What can I do for you?'

'Wigs,' Dillon told him.

'A nice selection over here.' He was right. There was everything, short, long, permed, blonde, red-head. Dillon selected one that was shoulder length and grey.

'I see,' Clayton said. 'The granny look?'

'Something like that. What about costume? I don't mean anything fancy. Second-hand?'

'In here.'

Clayton went through the bead curtain and Dillon followed him. There was rack upon rack of clothes and a jumbled heap in the corner. He worked very quickly, sorting through, selected a long brown skirt with an elastic waist and a shabby raincoat that almost came down to his ankles.

Clayton said, 'What are you going to play, Old Mother Riley or a bag lady?'

'You'd be surprised.' Dillon had seen a pair of jeans on top of the jumble in the corner. He picked them up and searched through a pile of shoes beside them, selecting a pair of runners that had seen better days.

'These will do,' he said. 'Oh, and this,' and he picked an old headscarf from a stand. 'Stick 'em all in a couple of plastic bags. How much?'

Clayton started to pack them. 'By rights I should thank you for taking them away, but we've all got to live. Ten quid to you.'

Dillon paid him and picked up the bags. 'Thanks a lot.'

Clayton opened the door for him. 'Have a good show, luv, give 'em hell.'

'Oh, I will,' Dillon said and he hurried down to the

corner, hailed a cab and told the driver to take him back to the hotel.

When Tania Novikova went down to answer the bell and opened the door to find Gordon Brown there she knew, by instinct, that something was wrong.

'What's this, Gordon? I told you I'd come round to your place.'

'I must see you, Tania, it's essential. Something terrible has happened!'

'Calm down,' she said. 'Just take it easy. Come upstairs and tell me all about it.'

Lane and Mackie were parked at the end of the street and the Inspector was already on the car phone to Ferguson and gave him the address.

'Sergeant Mackie's done a quick check at the door, sir. The card says a Miss Tania Novikova.'

'Oh, dear,' Ferguson said.

'You know her, sir?'

'Supposedly a secretary at the Soviet Embassy, Inspector. In fact she's a captain in the KGB.'

'That means she's one of Colonel Yuri Gatov's people, sir, he runs London station.'

'I'm not so sure. Gatov is a Gorbachev man and very pro-West. On the other hand, I always understood the Novikova woman to be to the right of Genghis Khan. I'd be surprised if Gatov knew about this.'

'Are you going to notify him, sir?'

'Not yet. Let's see what she's got to say first. It's information we're after.'

'Shall we go in, sir?'

'No, wait for me. I'll be with you in twenty minutes.'

Tania peered cautiously through a chink in the curtains. She saw Mackie standing by his car at the end of the street and it was enough. She could smell policemen anywhere in the world, Moscow, Paris, London – it was always the same.

'Tell me again, Gordon, exactly what happened.'

Gordon Brown did as he was told and she sat there listening patiently. She nodded when he'd finished. 'We were lucky, Gordon, very lucky. Go and make us a cup of coffee in the kitchen. I've got a couple of phone calls to make.' She squeezed his hand. 'Afterwards we'll have a very special time together.'

'Really?' His face brightened and he went out.

She picked up the phone and called Makeev at his Paris apartment. It rang for quite a time and she was about to put it down when it was picked up at the other end.

'Josef, it's Tania.'

'I was in the shower,' he said. 'I'm dripping all over the carpet.'

'I've only got seconds, Josef. I just wanted to say goodbye. I'm blown. My mole was exposed. They'll be kicking in the door any minute.'

'My God!' he said. 'And Dillon?'

'He's safe. All systems go. What that man has planned will set the world on fire.'

'But you, Tania?'

'Don't worry, I won't let them take me. Goodbye, Josef.'

She put the phone down, lit a cigarette, then called the hotel and asked for Dillon's room. He answered at once.

'It's Tania,' she said. 'We've got trouble.'

He was quite calm. 'How bad?'

'They rumbled my mole, let him go and the poor idiot came straight here. I smell Special Branch at the end of the street.'

'I see. What are you going to do?'

'Don't worry, I won't be around to tell them anything. One thing. They'll know that Gordon gave me the contents of tonight's report. He was in the telephone booth in the Ministry canteen when Ferguson arrested him.'

'I see.'

'Promise me one thing,' she said.

'What's that?'

'Blow them away, all of them.' The doorbell rang. She said, 'I've got to go. Luck, Dillon.'

As she put down the phone, Gordon Brown came in with the coffee. 'Was that the door?'

'Yes, be an angel, Gordon, and see who it is.'

He opened the door and started downstairs. Tania took a deep breath. Dying wasn't difficult. The cause she believed in had always been the most important thing in her life. She stubbed out her cigarette, opened a drawer in the desk, took out a Makarov pistol and shot herself through the right temple.

Gordon Brown, halfway down the stairs, turned and bounded up, bursting into the room. At the sight of her lying there beside the desk, the pistol still in her right hand, he let out a terrible cry and fell on his knees.

'Tania, my darling,' he moaned.

And then he knew what he must do as he heard something heavy crash against the door below. He prised the Makarov from her hand and as he raised it, his own hand was trembling. He took a deep breath to steady himself and pulled the trigger in the same moment that the front door burst open and Lane and Mackie started upstairs, Ferguson behind them.

There was a small crowd at the end of the street exhibiting the usual public curiosity. Dillon joined in, his collar up, hands in pockets. It started to snow slightly as they opened the rear doors of the ambulance. He watched as the two blanket-covered stretchers were loaded. The ambulance drove away. Ferguson stood on the pavement for a few moments talking to Lane and Mackie. Dillon recognised the Brigadier straight away, had been shown his photo many years previously Lane and Mackie were obviously policemen.

After a while, Ferguson got in his car and was driven away, Mackie went into the flat and Lane also drove away. The stratagem was obvious. For Mackie to wait just in case someone turned up. One thing was certain. Tania Novikova was dead and so was the boyfriend and Dillon knew that thanks to her sacrifice, he was safe.

He went back to the hotel and phoned Makeev at his flat in Paris. 'I've got bad news, Josef.'

'Tania?'

'How did you know?'

'She phoned. What's happened?'

'She was blown or rather her mole was. She killed herself, Josef, rather than get taken. A dedicated lady.'

'And the mole? The boyfriend?'

'Did the same. I've just seen the bodies carted out to an ambulance. Ferguson was there.'

'How will this affect you?'

'In no way. I'm off to Belfast in the morning to cut off the only chance of a lead they might have.'

'And then?'

'I'll amaze you, Josef, and your Arab friend. How does the entire British War Cabinet sound to you?'

'Dear God, you can't be serious?'

'Oh, but I am. I'll be in touch very soon now.'

He replaced the phone, put on his jacket and went down to the bar, whistling.

Ferguson was sitting in a booth in the lounge bar of the pub opposite Kensington Park Gardens and the Soviet Embassy, waiting for Colonel Yuri Gatov. The Russian, when he appeared, looked agitated, a tall, white-haired man in a camel overcoat. He saw Ferguson and hurried over.

'Charles, I can't believe it. Tania Novikova dead. Why?'

'Yuri, you and I have known each other for better than twenty-five years, often as adversaries, but I'll take a chance on you now, a chance that you really do want to see change in our time and an end to East–West conflict.'

'But I do, you know that.'

'Unfortunately, not everyone in the KGB would agree with you, and Tania Novikova was one.'

'She was a hardliner, true, but what are you saying, Charles?'

So Ferguson told him, Dillon, the attempt on Mrs Thatcher, Gordon Brown, Brosnan, everything.

Gatov said, 'This IRA wild card intends to attempt the life of the Prime Minister, that's what you're telling me, and Tania was involved?'

'Oh, very directly.'

'But Charles, I knew nothing, I swear.'

'And I believe you, old chap, but she must have had a link with someone. I mean she managed to convey vital information to Dillon in Paris. That's how he knew about Brosnan and so on.'

'Paris,' Gatov said. 'That's a thought. Did you know she was in Paris for three years before transferring to London and you know who's head of Paris station for the KGB?'

'Of course, Josef Makeev,' Ferguson said.

'Anything but a Gorbachev man. Very much of the old guard.'

'It would explain a great deal,' Ferguson said. 'But we'll never prove it.'

'True,' Gatov nodded. 'But I'll give him a call anyway, just to worry him.'

Makeev had not strayed far from the phone and picked it up the moment it rang.

'Makeev here.'

'Josef? Yuri Gatov. I'm phoning from London.'

'Yuri. What a surprise,' Makeev said, immediately wary.

'I've got some distressing news, Josef. Tania, Tania Novikova.'

'What about her?'

'She committed suicide earlier this evening along with some boyfriend of hers, a clerk at the Ministry of Defence.'

'Good heavens.' Makeev tried to sound convincing.

'He was feeding her classified information. I've just had a session with Charles Ferguson of Group Four. You know Charles?'

'Of course.'

'I was quite shocked. I must tell you I had no knowledge of Tania's activities. She worked for you for three years, Josef, so you know her as well as anyone. Have you any thoughts on the matter?'

'None, I'm afraid.'

'Ah, well, if you can think of anything, let me know.'

Makeev poured himself a Scotch and went and looked out into the frostbound Paris street. For a wild moment he'd had an impulse to phone Michael Aroun, but what would be the point? And Tania had sounded so certain. Set the world on fire, that had been her phrase.

He raised his glass. 'To you, Dillon,' he said softly. 'Let's see if you can do it.'

It was almost eleven in the River Room at the Savoy, the band still playing and Harry Flood, Brosnan and Mary were thinking of breaking up the party when Ferguson appeared at last.

'If ever I've needed a drink I need one now. A Scotch and a very large one.'

Flood called a waiter and gave the order and Mary said, 'What on earth's happened?'

Ferguson gave them a quick résumé of the night's events. When he was finished, Brosnan said, 'It explains a great deal, but the infuriating thing is it gets us no closer to Dillon.'

'One point I must make,' Ferguson said. 'When I arrested Brown in the canteen at the Ministry he was on the phone and he had the report in his hand. I believe it likely he was speaking to the Novikova woman then.'

'I see what you're getting at,' Mary said. 'You think she, in her turn, may have transmitted the information to Dillon?'

'Possibly,' Ferguson said.

'So what are you suggesting?' Brosnan asked. 'That Dillon would go to Belfast too?'

'Perhaps,' Ferguson said. 'If it was important enough.'

'We'll just have to take our chances then.' Brosnan turned to Mary. 'Early start tomorrow. We'd better get moving.'

As they walked through the lounge to the entrance, Brosnan and Ferguson went ahead and stood talking. Mary said to Flood, 'You think a lot of him, don't you?'

'Martin?' He nodded. 'The Viet Cong had me in a pit for weeks. When the rains came, it used to fill up with water and I'd have to stand all night so I didn't drown. Leeches, worms, you name it, and then one day, when it was as bad as it could be, a hand reached down and pulled me out and it was Martin in a headband, hair to his shoulders and his

195

face painted like an Apache Indian. He's special people.'

Mary looked across at Brosnan. 'Yes,' she said. 'I suppose that just about sums him up.'

Dillon ordered a taxi to pick him up at six o'clock from the hotel. He was waiting for it on the steps, his case in one hand when it arrived, a briefcase in the other. He was wearing his trenchcoat, suit, striped tie and glasses to fit the Peter Hilton persona, carried the Jersey driving licence and the flying licence as proof of identity. In the case was a toilet bag and the items he had obtained from Clayton at Covent Garden, all neatly folded. He'd included a towel from the hotel, socks and underpants. It all looked terribly normal and the wig could be easily explained.

The run to Heathrow was fast at that time in the morning. He went and picked up his ticket at the booking desk, then put his case through and got his seat assignment. He wasn't carrying a gun. No possible way he could do that, not with the kind of maximum security that operated on the Belfast planes.

He got a selection of newspapers, went up to the gallery restaurant and ordered a full English breakfast, then he started to work his way through the papers, checking on how the war in the Gulf was doing.

At Gatwick, there was a light powdering of snow at the side of the runway as the Lear jet lifted off. As they levelled off, Mary said, 'How do you feel?'

'I'm not sure,' Brosnan said. 'It's been a long time since I was in Belfast. Liam Devlin, Anne-Marie. So long ago.'

'And Sean Dillon?'

'Don't worry, I wasn't forgetting him, I could never do that.'

196

He turned and stared far out into the distance as the Lear jet lifted up out of the clouds and turned north-west.

Although Dillon wasn't aware of it, Brosnan and Mary had already landed and were on their way to the Europa Hotel when his flight touched down at Aldergrove Airport outside Belfast. There was a half-hour wait for the baggage and when he got his case, he made for the green line and followed a stream of people through. Customs officers stopped some, but he wasn't one of them and within five minutes he was outside and into a taxi.

'English, are you?' the driver asked.

Dillon slipped straight into his Belfast accent. 'And what makes you think that?'

'Jesus, I'm sorry,' the driver said. 'Anywhere special?'

'I'd like a hotel in the Falls Road,' Dillon said. 'Somewhere near Craig Street.'

'You won't get much round there.'

'Scenes of my youth,' Dillon told him. 'I've been working in London for years. Just in town for business overnight. Thought I'd like to see the old haunts.'

'Suit yourself. There's the Deepdene, but it's not much, I'm telling you.'

A Saracen armoured car passed then and as they turned into a main road, they saw an army patrol. 'Nothing changes,' Dillon said.

'Sure and most of those lads weren't even born when the whole thing started,' the driver told him. 'I mean, what are we in for? Another hundred years war?'

'God knows,' Dillon said piously and opened his paper.

The driver was right. The Deepdene wasn't much. A tall Victorian building in a mean side street off the Falls Road.

He paid off the driver, went in and found himself in a shabby hall with a worn carpet. When he tapped the bell on the desk a stout, motherly woman emerged.

'Can I help you, dear?'

'A room,' he said. 'Just the one night.'

'That's fine.' She pushed a register at him and took a key down. 'Number nine on the first floor.'

'Shall I pay now?'

'Sure and there's no need for that. Don't I know a gentleman when I see one?'

He went up the stairs, found the door and unlocked it. The room was as shabby as he'd expected, a single brass bedstead, a wardrobe. He put his case on the table and went out again, locking the door, then went the other way along the corridor and found the backstairs. He opened the door at the bottom into an untidy backyard. The lane beyond backed on to incredibly derelict houses, but it didn't depress him in the slightest. This was an area he knew like the back of his hand, a place where he'd led the British Army one hell of a dance in his day. He moved along the alley, a smile on his face, remembering, and turned into the Falls Road.

ELEVEN

'I remember them opening this place in seventy-one,' Brosnan said to Mary. He was standing at the window of the sixth-floor room of the Europa Hotel in Great Victoria Street next to the railway station. 'For a while it was a prime target for IRA bombers, the kind who'd rather blow up anything rather than nothing.'

'Not you, of course.'

There was a slight, sarcastic edge which he ignored. 'Certainly not. Devlin and I appreciated the bar too much. We came in all the time.'

She laughed in astonishment. 'What nonsense. Are you seriously asking me to believe that with the British Army chasing you all over Belfast you and Devlin sat in the Europa's bar?'

'Also the restaurant on occasion. Come on, I'll show you. Better take our coats, just in case we get a message while we're down there.'

As they were descending in the lift, she said, 'You're not armed, are you?'

'No.'

'Good, I'd rather keep it that way.'

'How about you?'

'Yes,' she said calmly. 'But that's different. I'm a serving officer of Crown forces in an active service zone.'

'What are you carrying?'

She opened her handbag and gave him a brief glimpse of the weapon. It was not much larger than the inside of her hand, a small automatic.

'What is it?' he asked.

'Rather rare. An old Colt .25. I picked it up in Africa.'

'Hardly an elephant gun.'

'No, but it does the job.' She smiled bleakly. 'As long as you can shoot, that is.'

The lift doors parted and they went across the lounge.

Dillon walked briskly along the Falls Road. Nothing had changed, nothing at all. It was just like the old days. He twice saw RUC patrols backed up by soldiers and once, two armoured troop carriers went by, but no one paid any attention. He finally found what he wanted in Craig Street about a mile from the hotel. It was a small, double-fronted shop with steel shutters on the windows. The three brass balls of a pawnbroker hung over the entrance with the sign 'Patrick Macey'.

Dillon opened the door and walked into musty silence. The dimly lit shop was crammed with a variety of items. Television sets, video recorders, clocks. There was even a gas cooker and a stuffed bear in one corner.

There was a mesh screen running along the counter and the man who sat on a stool behind it was working on a watch, a jeweller's magnifying glass in one eye. He glanced up, a wasted-looking individual in his sixties, his face grey and pallid.

'And what can I do for you?'

Dillon said, 'Nothing ever changes, Patrick. This place still smells exactly the same.'

Macey took the magnifying glass from his eye and frowned. 'Do I know you?'

'And why wouldn't you, Patrick? Remember that hot night in June of seventy-two when we set fire to that Orangeman Stewart's warehouse and shot him and his two nephews as they ran out. Let me see, there were the three of us.' Dillon put a cigarette in his mouth and lit it carefully. 'There was you and your half-brother, Tommy McGuire, and me.'

'Holy Mother of God, Sean Dillon, is that you?' Macey said.

'As ever was, Patrick.'

'Jesus, Sean, I never thought to see you in Belfast City again. I thought you were . . .'

He paused and Dillon said, 'Thought I was where, Patrick?'

'London,' Patrick Macey said. 'Somewhere like that,' he added lamely.

'And where would you have got that idea from?' Dillon went to the door, locking it and pulled down the blind.

'What are you doing?' Macey demanded in alarm.

'I just want a nice private talk, Patrick, me old son.'

'No, Sean, none of that. I'm not involved with the IRA, not any more.'

'You know what they say, Patrick, once in never out. How is Tommy these days, by the way?'

'Ah, Sean, I'd have thought you'd know. Poor Tommy's been dead these five years. Shot by one of his own. A stupid row between the Provos and one of the splinter groups. INLA were suspected.'

'Is that a fact?' Dillon nodded. 'Do you see any of the other old hands these days? Liam Devlin for instance?'

And he had him there for Macey was unable to keep the look of alarm from his face. 'Liam? I haven't seen him since the seventies.'

'Really?' Dillon lifted the flap at the end of the counter and walked round. 'It's a terrible liar you are.' He slapped him across the face. 'Now get in there,' and pushed him through the curtain that led to the office at the rear.

Macey was terrified. 'I don't know a thing.'

'About what? I haven't asked you anything yet, but I'm going to tell you a few things. Tommy McGuire isn't dead. He's living somewhere else in this fair city under another name and you're going to tell me where. Secondly, Liam Devlin has been to see you. Now I'm right on both counts, aren't I?' Macey was frozen with fear, terrified and Dillon slapped him again. 'Aren't I?'

The other man broke then. 'Please, Sean, please. It's my heart. I could have an attack.'

'You will if you don't speak up, I promise you.'

'All right. Devlin was here a little earlier this morning enquiring about Tommy.'

'And shall I tell you what he said?'

'Please, Sean.' Macey was shaking. 'I'm ill.'

'He said that bad old Sean Dillon was on the loose in London Town and that he wanted to help run him down and who could be a better source of information than Dillon's old chum, Tommy McGuire. Am I right?'

Macey nodded. 'Yes.'

'Good, now we're getting somewhere.' Dillon lit another cigarette and nodded at the large old-fashioned safe in the corner. 'Is that where the guns are?'

'What guns, Sean?'

'Come on, don't muck me about. You're been dealing in handguns for years. Get it open.'

Macey took a key from his desk drawer, went and opened the safe. Dillon pulled him to one side. There were several weapons in there. An old Webley, a couple of Smith & Wesson revolvers. The one that really caught his eyes was an American Army Colt .45 automatic. He hefted it in his hand and checked the magazine.

'Wonderful, Patrick. I knew I could depend on you.' He put the gun on the desk and sat down opposite Macey. 'So what happened?'

Macey's face was very strange in colour now. 'I don't feel well.'

'You'll feel better when you've told me. Get on with it.'

'Tommy lives on his own about half a mile from here in Canal Street. He's done up the old warehouse at the end. Calls himself Kelly, George Kelly.'

'I know that area well, every stick and stone.'

'Devlin asked for Tommy's phone number and called him there and then. He said it was essential to see him. That it was to do with Sean Dillon. Tommy agreed to see him at two o'clock.'

'Fine,' Dillon said. 'See how easy it was? Now I can call on him myself before Devlin does and discuss old times only I won't bother to phone. I think I'll surprise him. Much more fun.'

'You'll never get in to see him,' Macey said. 'You can only get in at the front, all the other doors are welded. He's been paranoid for years. Terrified someone's going to knock him off. You'd never get in the front door. It's all TV security cameras and that kind of stuff.'

'There's always a way,' Dillon said.

'There always was for you.' Macey tore at his shirt collar, choking. 'Pills,' he moaned and got the drawer in front of him open. The bottle he took fell from his hands.

He lay back on the chair and Dillon got up and went round and picked up the bottle. 'Trouble is, Patrick, the moment I go out of the door you'll be on the phone to Tommy and that wouldn't do, would it?'

He walked across to the fireplace and dropped the pill bottle into the gleaming coals. There was a crash behind him and he turned to find Macey had tumbled from the chair to the floor. Dillon stood over him for a moment. Macey's face was very suffused with purple now and his legs were jerking. Suddenly, he gave a great gasp like air escaping, his head turned to one side and he went completely still.

Dillon put the Colt in his pocket, went through the shop and opened the door, locking it with the Yale, leaving the blind down. A moment later he turned the corner into the Falls Road and walked back towards the hotel as fast as he could.

He laid the contents of the case on the bed in the shabby hotel room, then he undressed. First of all he put on the jeans, the old runners and a heavy jumper. Then came the wig. He sat in front of the mirror at the small dressing-table, combing the grey hair until it looked wild and unkempt. He tied the headscarf over it and studied himself. Then he pulled on the skirt that reached his ankles. The old raincoat that was far too large completed the outfit.

He stood in front of the wardrobe examining himself in the mirror. He closed his eyes, thinking the role and when he opened them again it wasn't Dillon any more, it was a decrepit, broken, bag lady.

He hardly needed any make-up, just a foundation to give him the sallow look and the slash of scarlet lipstick for the mouth. All wrong, of course, but totally right for the character. He took a half-bottle of whiskey from a pouch in the briefcase and poured some into his cupped hands, slapping it over his face, then he splashed some more over the front of the raincoat. He put the Colt, a couple of newspapers and the whiskey bottle into a plastic bag and was ready to leave.

He glanced in the mirror at that strange, nightmarish

old woman. 'Showtime,' he whispered and let himself out.

All was quiet as he went down the backstairs and went out into the yard. He closed the door behind him carefully and crossed to the door which led to the alley. As he reached it, the hotel door opened behind him.

A voice called, 'Here, what do you think you're doing?'

Dillon turned and saw a kitchen porter in a soiled white apron putting a cardboard box in the dustbin.

'Go fuck yourself,' Dillon croaked.

'Go on, get out of it, you old bag!' the porter shouted.

Dillon closed the door behind him. 'Ten out of ten, Sean,' he said softly and went up the alley.

He turned into the Falls Road and started to shuffle along the pavement, acting so strangely that people stepped out of the way to avoid him.

It was almost one and Brosnan and Mary Tanner at the bar of the Europa were thinking about lunch when a young porter approached. 'Mr Brosnan?'

'That's right.'

'Your taxi is here, sir.'

'Taxi?' Mary said. 'But we didn't order one.'

'Yes we did,' Brosnan said.

He helped her on with her coat and they followed the young porter through the foyer, down the steps at the front entrance to the black cab waiting at the kerb. Brosnan gave the porter a pound and they got in. The driver on the other side of the glass wore a tweed cap and an old reefer coat. Mary Tanner pulled the sliding glass partition to one side.

'I presume you know where we're going?' she said.

'Oh, I certainly do, my love.' Liam Devlin smiled at her over his shoulder, moved into gear and drove away.

It was just after one-thirty when Devlin turned the taxi into Canal Street. 'That's the place at the end,' he said. 'We'll park in the yard at the side.' They got out and moved back into the street and approached the entrance. 'Be on your best behaviour, we're on television,' he said and reached to a bell push beside the massive ironbound door.

'Not very homelike,' Mary commented.

'Yes, well with Tommy McGuire's background he needs a fortress rather than a cosy semi-detached on some desirable estate.' Devlin turned to Brosnan. 'Are you carrying, son?'

'No,' Brosnan said. 'But she is. You are, I suppose?'

'Call it my innate caution or perhaps the wicked habits of a lifetime.'

A voice sounded through the box beside the door. 'Is that you, Devlin?'

'And who else, you stupid bugger. I've got Martin Brosnan with me and a lady-friend of his and we're freezing in this damn cold so get the door open.'

'You're early. You said two o'clock.'

They could hear steps on the other side and then the door opened to reveal a tall, cadaverous man in his mid-sixties. He wore a heavy Aran pullover and baggy jeans and carried a Sterling sub-machine gun.

Devlin brushed past him, leading the way in. 'What do you intend to do with that thing, start another war?'

McGuire closed the door and barred it. 'Only if I have to.' He looked them over suspiciously. 'Martin?' He held out a hand. 'It's been a long time. As for you, you old sod,' he said to Devlin, 'whatever's keeping you out of your grave you should bottle it. We'd make a fortune.' He looked Mary over. 'And who might you be?'

'A friend,' Devlin told him. 'So let's get on with it.'

'All right, this way.'

The interior of the warehouse was totally bare except for

206

a van parked to one side. A steel staircase led to a landing high above with what had once been glass-fronted offices. McGuire went first and turned into the first office on the landing. There was a desk and a bank of television equipment, one screen showing the street, another the entrance. He put the Sterling on the desk.

Devlin said, 'You live here?'

'Upstairs. I've turned what used to be the storage loft into a flat. Now let's get on with it, Devlin. What is it you want? You mentioned Sean Dillon.'

'He's on the loose again,' Brosnan said.

'I thought he must have come to a bad end. I mean, it's been so long.' McGuire lit a cigarette. 'Anyway, what's it to do with me?'

'He tried to knock off Martin here in Paris. Killed his girlfriend instead.'

'Jesus!' McGuire said.

'Now he's on the loose in London and I want him,' Brosnan told him.

McGuire looked at Mary again. 'And where does she fit in?'

'I'm a captain in the British Army,' she said crisply. 'Tanner's the name.'

'For God's sake, Devlin, what is this?' McGuire demanded.

'It's all right,' Devlin told him. 'She hasn't come to arrest you although we all know that if Tommy McGuire was still in the land of the living he'd draw about twenty-five years.'

'You bastard!' McGuire said.

'Be sensible,' Devlin told him. 'Just answer a few questions and you can go back to being George Kelly again.'

McGuire put a hand up defensively. 'All right, I get the point. What do you want to know?'

'Nineteen eighty-one, the London bombing campaign,' Brosnan said. 'You were Dillon's control.'

McGuire glanced at Mary. 'That's right.'

'We know Dillon would have experienced the usual problems as regards weapons and explosives, Mr McGuire,' Mary said. 'And I've been given to understand he always favours underworld contacts in that sort of situation. Is that so?'

'Yes, he usually worked in that way,' McGuire said reluctantly and sat down.

'Have you any idea who he used in London in nineteen eighty-one?' Mary persisted.

McGuire looked hunted. 'How would I know? It could have been anybody.'

Devlin said, 'You lying bastard, you know something, I can tell you do.' His right hand came out of the pocket of the reefer holding an old Luger pistol and he touched McGuire between the eyes. 'Quick now, tell us or I'll . . .'

McGuire pushed the gun to one side. 'All right, Devlin, you win.' He lit another cigarette. 'He dealt with a man in London called Jack Harvey, a big operator, a real gangster.'

'There, that wasn't so hard, was it?' Devlin said.

There was a thunderous knocking on the door below and they all looked at the television screen to see an old bag lady on the front step. Her voice came clearly through the speaker. 'The lovely man you are, Mr Kelly. Could you spare a poor soul a quid?'

McGuire said into the microphone, 'Piss off, you old bag.'

'Oh Jesus, Mr Kelly, I'll die here on your step in this terrible cold so I will for the whole world to see.'

McGuire got up. 'I'll go and get rid of her. I'll only be a minute.'

He hurried down the stairs and extracted a five-pound note from an old wallet as he approached the door. He got it open and held it out. 'Take this and clear off.'

Dillon's hand came up out of the plastic shopping bag

208

holding the Colt. 'A fiver, Tommy boy. You're getting generous in your old age. Inside.'

He pushed him through and closed the door. McGuire was terrified. 'Look, what is this?'

'Nemesis,' Dillon said. 'You pay for your sins in this life, Tommy, we all do. Remember that night in seventy-two, you, me and Patrick when we shot the Stewarts as they ran out of the fire?'

'Dillon?' McGuire whispered. 'It's you?' He started to turn and raised his voice. 'Devlin!' he called.

Dillon shot him twice in the back breaking his spine, driving him on his face. As he got the door open behind him, Devlin appeared on the landing, the Luger in his hand, already firing. Dillon fired three times rapidly, shattering the office window, then was outside, slamming the door behind him.

As he started up the street, two stripped-down Land Rovers, four soldiers in each, turned out of the main road, attracted by the sound of the firing and came towards him. The worst kind of luck, but Dillon didn't hesitate. As he came to a drain in the gutter, he pretended to slip and dropped the Colt through the bars.

As he got up someone called, 'Stay where you are.'

They were paratroopers in camouflage uniforms, flak jackets and red berets, each man with his rifle ready and Dillon gave them the performance of his life. He staggered forward, moaning and crying and clutching at the young lieutenant in charge.

'Jesus, sir, there's terrible things going on back there in that warehouse. There's me sheltering from the cold and these fellas come on and start shooting each other.'

The young officer smelt the whiskey and pushed him away. 'Check what's in the carrier, Sergeant.'

The sergeant riffled through. 'Bottle of hooch and some newspapers, sir.'

209

'Right, go and wait over there.' The officer pushed Dillon along the pavement behind the patrol and got a loud-hailer from one of the Land Rovers. 'You inside,' he called. 'Throw your weapons out through the door then follow them with your hands up. Two minutes or we'll come in to get you.'

All members of the patrol were in a readiness posture, intent only on the entrance. Dillon eased back into the courtyard, turned and hurried past Devlin's taxi, finding what he was seeking in seconds, a manhole cover. He got it up and went down a steel ladder, pulling the cover behind him. It had been a way in which he had evaded the British Army on many occasions in the old days and he knew the system in the Falls Road area perfectly.

The tunnel was small and very dark. He crawled along it, aware of the sound of rushing water and came out on the sloping side of a larger tunnel, the main sewer. There were outlets to the canal that ran down to Belfast Lough, he knew that. He pulled off the skirt, the wig and threw them in the water using the headscarf to wipe his lips and face vigorously, then he hurried along the side until he came to another steel ladder. He started up towards the rays of light beaming in through the holes in the cast iron, waited a moment, then eased it up. He was on a cobbled pathway beside the canal, the backs of decaying, boarded-up houses on the other side. He put the manhole cover back in place and made for the Falls Road as fast as possible.

In the warehouse, the young officer stood beside McGuire's body and examined Mary Tanner's ID card. 'It's perfectly genuine,' she said. 'You can check.'

'And these two?'

'They're with me. Look, Lieutenant, you'll get a full

210

explanation from my boss. That's Brigadier Charles Ferguson at the Ministry of Defence.'

'All right, Captain,' he said defensively. 'I'm only doing my job. It's not like the old days here, you know. We have the RUC on our backs. Every death has to be investigated fully otherwise there's the Devil to pay.'

The sergeant came in. 'The colonel's on the wire, boss.'

'Fine,' the young lieutenant said and went out.

Brosnan said to Devlin, 'Do you think it was Dillon?'

'A hell of a coincidence if it wasn't. A bag lady?' Devlin shook his head. 'Who'd have thought it?'

'Only Dillon would be capable.'

'Are you trying to say he came over from London specially?' Mary demanded.

'He knew what we were about thanks to Gordon Brown and how long is the scheduled flight from London to Belfast?' Brosnan asked. 'An hour and a quarter?'

'Which means he's got to go back,' she said.

'Perhaps,' Liam Devlin nodded. 'But nothing's absolute in this life, girl, you'll learn that and you're dealing with a man who's kept out of police hands for twenty years or more, all over Europe.'

'Well, it's time we got the bastard.' She looked down at McGuire. 'Not too nice, is it?'

'The violence, the killing. Drink with the Devil and this is what it comes down to,' Devlin told her.

Dillon went in through the back door of the hotel at exactly two-fifteen and hurried up to his room. He stripped off the jeans and jumper, put them in the case and shoved them up into a cupboard above the wardrobe. He washed his face quickly, then dressed in white shirt and tie, dark suit and blue Burberry. He was out of the room and descending the backstairs, briefcase in hand, within five minutes of having entered. He went up the alley, turned into the Falls Road and started to walk briskly. Within five minutes he managed to hail a taxi and told the driver to take him to the airport.

The officer in charge of Army Intelligence for the Belfast city area was a Colonel McLeod and he was not best pleased with the situation with which he was confronted.

'It really isn't good enough, Captain Tanner,' he said. 'We can't have you people coming in here like cowboys and acting on your own initiative.' He turned to look at Devlin and Brosnan. 'And with people of very dubious background into the bargain. There is a delicate situation here these days and we do have the Royal Ulster Constabulary to placate. They see this as their turf.'

'Yes, well, that's as may be,' Mary told him. 'But your sergeant outside was kind enough to check on flights to London for me. There's one at four-thirty and another at six-thirty. Don't you think it would be a good idea to check out the passengers rather thoroughly?'

'We're not entirely stupid, Captain. I've already put that in hand, but I'm sure I don't need to remind you that we are not an army of occupation. There is no such thing as martial law here. It's impossible for me to close down the airport, I don't have the authority. All I can do is notify the police and airport security in the usual way and as you've been at pains to explain, where this man Dillon is concerned, we don't have much to tell them.' His phone went. He picked it up and said, 'Brigadier Ferguson? Sorry to bother you, sir. Colonel McLeod, Belfast HQ. We appear to have a problem.'

But Dillon, at the airport, had no intention of returning on the London flight. Perhaps he could get away with it, but madness to try when there were other alternatives. It was just after three as he searched the departure board. He'd just missed the Manchester flight, but there was a flight to Glasgow due out at three-fifteen and it was delayed.

He crossed to the booking desk. 'I was hoping to catch the Glasgow flight,' he told the young woman booking clerk, 'but got here too late. Now I see it's delayed.'

She punched details up on her screen. 'Yes, half-hour delay, sir, and there's plenty of space. Would you like to try for it?'

'I certainly would,' he said gratefully and got the money from his wallet as she made out the ticket.

There was no trouble with security and the contents of his briefcase were innocuous enough. Passengers had already been called and he boarded the plane and sat in a seat at the rear. Very satisfactory. Only one thing had gone wrong. Devlin, Brosnan and the woman had got to McGuire first. A pity, that, because it raised the question of what he'd told them. Harvey, for example. He'd have to move fast there, just in case.

He smiled charmingly when the stewardess asked him if he'd like a drink. 'A cup of tea would be just fine,' he said and took a newspaper from his briefcase.

McLeod had Brosnan, Mary and Devlin taken up to the airport and they arrived just before the passengers were called for the four-thirty London flight. An RUC police inspector took them through to the departure lounge.

'Only thirty passengers as you can see and we've checked them all thoroughly.'

'I've an idea we're on a wild goose chase,' McLeod said.

The passengers were called and Brosnan and Devlin stood by the door and looked each person over as they went through. When they'd passed, Devlin said, 'The old nun, Martin, you didn't think of doing a strip search?'

McLeod said impatiently, 'Oh, for God's sake, let's get moving.'

'An angry man,' Devlin said as the colonel went ahead. 'They must have laid the cane on something fierce at his public school. It's back to London for you two then?'

'Yes, we'd better get on with it,' Brosnan said.

'And you, Mr Devlin?' Mary asked. 'Will you be all right?'

'Ah, Ferguson, to be fair, secured me a clean bill of health years ago for services rendered to Brit intelligence. I'll be fine.' He kissed her on the cheek. 'A real pleasure, my love.'

'And for me.'

'Watch out for the boy here. Dillon's the original tricky one.'

They had reached the concourse. He smiled and suddenly was gone, disappeared into the crowd.

Brosnan took a deep breath. 'Right, then, London. Let's get moving,' and he took her arm and moved through the throng.

The flight to Glasgow was only forty-five minutes. Dillon landed at four-thirty. There was a shuttle service plane to London at five-fifteen. He got a ticket at the desk, hurried through to the departure lounge where the first thing he did was phone Danny Fahy at Cadge End. It was Angel who answered.

'Put your Uncle Danny on, it's Dillon,' he told her.

Danny said, 'Is that you, Sean?'

'As ever was. I'm in Glasgow waiting for a plane. I'll be

arriving at Heathrow Terminal One at six-thirty. Can you come and meet me? You'll just have time.'

'No problem, Sean. I'll bring Angel for the company.'

'That's fine and, Danny, be prepared to work through the night. Tomorrow could be the big one.'

'Jesus, Sean,' but Dillon put the phone down before Fahy could say anything more.

Next, he phoned Harvey's office at the undertakers in Whitechapel. It was Myra who answered.

'This is Peter Hilton here, we met yesterday. I'd like a word with your uncle.'

'He isn't here. He's gone up to Manchester for a function. Won't be back until tomorrow morning.'

'That's no good to me,' Dillon said. 'He promised me my stuff in twenty-four hours.'

'Oh, it's here,' Myra said. 'But I'd expect cash on delivery.'

'You've got it.' He looked at his watch and allowed for the time it would take to drive from Heathrow to Bayswater to get the money. 'I'll be there about seven forty-five.'

'I'll be waiting.'

As Dillon put the phone down, the flight was called and he joined the crowd of passengers hurrying through.

Myra, standing by the fire in her uncle's office, came to a decision. She got the key of the secret room from his desk drawer and then went out to the head of the stairs.

'Billy, are you down there?'

He came up a moment later. 'Here I am.'

'Been in the coffin room again, have you? Come on, I need you.' She went along the corridor to the end door, opened it and pulled back the false wall. She indicated one of the boxes of Semtex. 'Take that to the office.'

When she rejoined him, he'd put the box on the desk. 'A right bloody weight. What is it?'

'It's money, Billy, that's all that concerns you. Now listen and listen good. That small guy, the one who roughed you up yesterday.'

'What about him?'

'He's turning up here at seven forty-five to pay me a lot of money for what's in that box.'

'So?'

'I want you waiting outside from seven-thirty in those nice black leathers of yours with your BMW handy. When he leaves, you follow him, Billy, to bloody Cardiff if necessary.' She patted his face, 'And if you lose him, sunshine, don't bother coming back.'

It was snowing lightly at Heathrow as Dillon came through at Terminal One. Angel was waiting for him and waved excitedly.

'Glasgow,' she said. 'What were you doing there?'

'Finding out what Scotsmen wear under their kilts.'

She laughed and hung on to his arm. 'Terrible, you are.'

They went out through the snow and joined Fahy in the Morris van. 'Good to see you, Sean. Where to?'

'My hotel in Bayswater,' Dillon said. 'I want to book out.'

'You're moving in with us?' Angel asked.

'Yes,' Dillon nodded, 'but I've a present to pick up for Danny first at an undertakers in Whitechapel.'

'And what would that be, Sean?' Fahy demanded.

'Oh, about fifty pounds of Semtex.'

The van swerved and skidded slightly, Fahy fighting to control it. 'Holy Mother of God!' he said.

216

At the undertakers, the night porter admitted Dillon at the front entrance.

'Mr Hilton, is it? Miss Myra's expecting you, sir.'

'I know where to go.'

Dillon went up the stairs, along the corridor and opened the door of the outer office. Myra was waiting for him. 'Come in,' she said.

She was wearing a black trouser suit and smoking a cigarette. She went and sat behind the desk and tapped the carton with one hand. 'There it is. Where's the money?'

Dillon put the briefcase on top of the carton and opened it. He took out fifteen thousand, packet by packet, and dropped it in front of her. That left five thousand dollars in the briefcase, the Walther with the Carswell silencer and the Beretta. He closed the case and smiled.

'Nice to do business with you.'

He placed the briefcase on top of the carton and picked it up and she went to open the door for him.

'What are you going to do with that, blow up the Houses of Parliament?'

'That was Guy Fawkes,' he said and moved along the passage and went downstairs.

The pavement was frosty as he walked along the street and turned the corner to the van. Billy, waiting anxiously in the shadows, manhandled his BMW up the street past the parked cars until he could see Dillon stop at the Morris van. Angel got the back door open and Dillon put the carton inside. She closed it and they went round and got in beside Fahy.

'Is that it, Sean?'

'That's it, Danny, a fifty-pound box of Semtex with the factory stamp on it all the way from Prague. Now let's get out of here, we've got a long night ahead of us.'

Fahy drove through a couple of side streets and turned onto the main road and as he joined the traffic stream, Billy went after him on the BMW.

TWELVE

For technical reasons the Lear jet had not been able to get a flight slot out of Aldergrove Airport until five-thirty. It was a quarter to seven when Brosnan and Mary landed at Gatwick and a Ministry limousine was waiting. Mary checked on the car phone and found Ferguson at the Cavendish Square flat. He was standing by the fire warming himself when Kim showed them in.

'Beastly weather and a lot more snow on the way, I fear.' He sipped some of his tea. 'Well, at least you're in one piece, my dear, it must have been an enlivening experience.'

'That's one way of describing it.'

'You're absolutely certain it was Dillon?'

'Well let's put it this way,' Brosnan said, 'if it wasn't it was one hell of a coincidence that someone decided to choose that moment to shoot Tommy McGuire. And then there's the bag lady act. Typical Dillon.'

'Yes, quite remarkable.'

'Admittedly he wasn't on the London plane, sir, coming back,' Mary said.

'You mean you *think* he wasn't on the plane,' Ferguson corrected her. 'For all I know the damned man might have passed himself off as the pilot. He seems capable of anything.'

'There is another plane due out to London at eight-thirty, sir Colonel McLeod said he'd have it thoroughly checked.'

'A waste of time.' Ferguson turned to Brosnan. 'I suspect you agree, Martin?'

'I'm afraid so.'

'Now let's go over the whole thing again. Tell me everything that happened.'

When Mary was finished, Ferguson said, 'I checked the flight schedules out of Aldergrove a little while ago. There were planes available to Manchester, Birmingham, Glasgow. There was even a flight to Paris at six-thirty. No big deal to fly back to London from there. He'd be here tomorrow.'

'And there's always the sea trip,' Brosnan reminded him. 'The ferry from Larne to Stranraer in Scotland and a fast train from there to London.'

'Plus the fact that he could have crossed the Irish border, gone to Dublin and proceeded from there in a dozen different ways,' Mary said, 'which doesn't get us anywhere.'

'The interesting thing is the reason behind his trip,' Ferguson said. 'He didn't know of your intention to seek out McGuire until last night when Brown revealed the contents of that report to Novikova and yet he went rushing off to Belfast at the earliest opportunity. Now why would that be?'

'To shut McGuire's mouth,' Mary said. 'It's an interesting point that our meeting with McGuire was arranged for two o'clock, but we were nearly half an hour early. If we hadn't been, Dillon would have got to him first.'

'Even so he still can't be certain what McGuire told you, if anything.'

'But the point was. sir, that Dillon *knew* McGuire had

something on him, that's why he went to such trouble to get to him and it was obviously the information that this man Jack Harvey was his arms supplier in the London campaign of eighty-one.'

'Yes, well when you spoke to me at Aldergrove before you left I ran a check. Detective Inspector Lane of Special Branch tells me that Harvey is a known gangster and on a big scale. Drugs, prostitution, the usual things. The police have been after him for years with little success. Unfortunately, he is now also a very established businessman. Property, clubs, betting shops and so forth.'

'What are you trying to say, sir?' Mary asked.

'That it isn't as easy as you might think. We can't just pull Harvey in for questioning because a dead man accused him of something that happened ten years ago. Be sensible, my dear. He'd sit still, keep his mouth shut and a team of the best lawyers in London would have him out on the pavement in record time.'

'In other words it would be laughed out of court?' Brosnan said.

'Exactly.' Ferguson sighed. 'I've always had a great deal of sympathy for the idea that where the criminal classes are concerned, the only way we're going to get any justice is to take all the lawyers out into the nearest square and shoot them.'

Brosnan peered out of the window at the lightly falling snow. 'There is another way.'

'I presume you're referring to your friend Flood?' Ferguson smiled tightly. 'Nothing at all to stop you seeking his advice, but I'm sure you'll stay within the bounds of legality.'

'Oh, we will, Brigadier, I promise you.' Brosnan picked up his coat. 'Come on, Mary, let's go and see Harry.'

Following the Morris wasn t too much of a problem for Billy on his BMW The snow was only lying on the sides of the road and the tarmac was wet. There was plenty of traffic all the way out of London and through Dorking. There wasn't quite as much on the Horsham road but still enough to give him cover.

He was lucky when the Morris turned at the Grimethorpe sign because it had stopped snowing and the sky had cleared exposing a half-moon. Billy switched off his headlamp and followed the lights of the Morris at a distance, anonymous in the darkness. When it turned at the Doxley sign, he followed cautiously, pausing on the brow of the hill, watching the lights move in through the farm gate.

He switched off his engine and coasted down the hill, pulling in by the gate and the wooden sign that said Cadge End Farm. He walked along the track through the trees and could see into the lighted interior of the barn across the yard. Dillon, Fahy and Angel were standing beside the Morris. Dillon turned, came out and crossed the yard.

Billy beat a hasty retreat, got back on the BMW and rolled on down the hill, only switching on again when he was some distance from the farm. Five minutes later he was on the main road and returning to London.

In the sitting room Dillon called Makeev at the Paris apartment. 'It's me,' he said.

'I've been worried,' Makeev told him, 'what with Tania . '

'Tania took her own way out,' Dillon said, 'I told you. It was her way of making sure they didn't get anything out of her.'

'And this business you mentioned, the Belfast trip?'

'Taken care of. It's all systems go, Josef.'

'When?'

'The War Cabinet meets at ten o'clock in the morning at Downing Street. That's when we'll hit.'

'But how?'

'You can read about it in the papers. The important thing now is for you to tell Michael Aroun to fly down to his St Denis place in the morning. I hope to be flying in sometime in the afternoon.'

'As quickly as that?'

'Well I won't be hanging about, will I? What about you, Josef?'

'I should think I might well make the flight from Paris to St Denis with Aroun and Rashid myself.'

'Good. Till our next merry meeting, then, and remind Aroun about that second million.'

Dillon put the phone down, lit a cigarette, then picked up the phone again and called Grimethorpe Airfield. After a while he got an answer.

'Bill Grant here.' He sounded slightly drunk.

'Peter Hilton, Mr Grant.'

'Oh, yes,' Grant said, 'and what can I do for you?'

'That trip I wanted to make to Land's End, tomorrow, I think.'

'What time?'

'If you could be ready from noon onwards. Is that all right?'

'As long as the snow holds off. Much more and we could be in trouble.'

Grant put the phone down slowly, reached for the bottle of Scotch whisky at his hand and poured a generous measure, then he opened the table drawer. There was an old Webley service revolver in there and a box of .38 cartridges. He loaded the weapon then put it back in the drawer.

'Right, Mr Hilton, we'll just have to see what you're about, won't we?' and he swallowed the whisky down.

'Do I know Jack Harvey?' Harry Flood started to laugh, sitting there behind his desk and looked up at Mordecai Fletcher. 'Do I know, Mordecai?'

The big man smiled at Brosnan and Mary who were standing there, still with their coats on. 'Yes, I think you could say we know Mr Harvey rather well.'

'Sit down, for God's sake, and tell me what happened in Belfast,' Flood said.

Which they did, Mary giving him a rapid account of the entire affair. When she was finished she said, 'Do you think it's possible that Harvey was Dillon's weapons supplier in eighty-one?'

'Nothing would surprise me about Jack Harvey. He and his niece, Myra, run a tight little empire that includes every kind of criminal activity. Women, drugs, protection, big-scale armed robbery, you name it, but arms for the IRA?' He looked up at Mordecai. 'What do you think?'

'He'd dig up his granny's corpse and sell it if he thought there was a profit in it,' the big man said.

'Very apt.' Flood turned to Mary. 'There's your answer.'

'Fine,' Brosnan said, 'and if Dillon used Harvey in eighty-one, the chances are he's using him again.'

Flood said, 'The police would never get anywhere with Harvey on the basis of your story, you must know that. He'd walk.'

'I should imagine the Professor was thinking of a more subtle approach like beating it out of the bastard,' Mordecai said and slammed a fist into his palm.

Mary turned to Brosnan who shrugged. 'What else would you suggest? Nobody's going to get anywhere with a man like Harvey by being nice.'

'I have an idea,' Harry Flood said. 'Harvey's been putting a lot of pressure on me lately to form a partnership. What if I tell him I'd like to have a meeting to discuss things?'

'Fine,' Brosnan said, 'but as soon as possible. We can't hang around on this, Harry.'

Myra was sitting at her uncle's desk going through club accounts when Flood called her.

'Harry,' she said, 'what a nice surprise.'

'I was hoping for a word with Jack.'

'Not possible, Harry, he's in Manchester at some sporting club function at the Midland.'

'When is he due back?'

'First thing. He's got some business later in the morning so he's getting up early and catching the seven-thirty breakfast shuttle from Manchester.'

'So he should be with you about nine?'

'More like nine-thirty with the morning traffic into London. Look, what is this, Harry?'

'I've been thinking, Myra, maybe I've been stupid. About a partnership, I mean. Jack might have a point. There's a lot we could do if we got together.'

'Well I'm sure he'll be pleased to hear that,' Myra said.

'I'll see you then, nine-thirty sharp in the morning with my accountant,' Flood told her and rang off.

Myra sat there looking at the phone for a while, then she picked it up, rang the Midland in Manchester and asked for her uncle. Jack Harvey, champagne and more than one brandy inside him, was in excellent humour when he picked up the phone at the hotel's front desk.

'Myra, my love, what's up? A fire or something or a sudden rush of bodies?'

'Even more interesting. Harry Flood's been on the phone.'

She told him what had happened and Harvey sobered up instantly. 'So he wants to meet at nine-thirty?'

'That's right. What do you think?'

'I think it's a load of cobblers. Why should he suddenly change his mind just like that? No, I don't like it.'

'Shall I phone him back and cancel?'

'No, not at all, I'll meet him. We'll just take precautions, that's all.'

'Listen,' she said, 'Hilton or whatever his bloody name is called and told me he wanted his stuff. He came round, paid cash and went on his way. Is that all right?'

'Good girl. Now as regards Flood, all I'm saying is be ready to give him the proper reception, just in case. Know what I mean?'

'I think so, Jack,' she said, 'I think so.'

Harry Flood said, 'We'll meet outside the Harvey Funeral Emporium just before half-nine in the morning then. I'll bring Mordecai and you can play my accountant,' he told Brosnan.

'What about me?' Mary demanded.

'We'll see.'

Brosnan got up and went and stood at the French windows looking at the river. 'I wish I knew what the bastard was doing right now,' he said.

'Tomorrow, Martin,' Flood told him. 'All things come to he who waits.'

It was around midnight when Billy parked the BMW in the yard at the rear of the Whitechapel premises and went in. He climbed the stairs wearily to Myra's apartment. She heard him coming, got her door open and stood there, light flowing through her short nightdress.

'Hello, sunshine, you made it,' she said to Billy.

'I'm bloody frozen,' Billy told her.

She got him inside, sat him down and started to unzip his leathers. 'Where did he go?'

He reached for a bottle of brandy, poured a large one and got it down. 'Only an hour out of London, Myra, but the back of bloody beyond.'

He told her everything, Dorking, the Horsham road, Grimethorpe, Doxley and Cadge End Farm.

'Brilliant, sunshine. What you need is a nice hot bath.'

She went into the bathroom and turned on the taps. When she went back into the living room Billy was asleep on the couch, legs sprawled. 'Oh, dear,' she said, got a blanket to cover him, then went to bed.

When Makeev knocked on the door at the Avenue Victor Hugo it was opened by Rashid. 'You've news for us?' the young Iraqi asked.

Makeev nodded. 'Where's Michael?'

'He's waiting for you.'

Rashid took him through to the drawing room where Aroun was standing beside the fire. He was wearing a black dinner jacket for he had been to the opera.

'What is it?' he demanded. 'Has something happened?'

'I've had Dillon on the phone from England. He wants you to fly down to St Denis in the morning. He intends to fly in himself sometime in the afternoon.'

Aroun was pale with excitement. 'What is it? What does he intend?'

227

He poured the Russian a cognac and Rashid passed it to him. 'He told me he intends some sort of attack on the British War Cabinet at Downing Street.'

There was total silence, only astonishment on Aroun's face. It was Rashid who spoke. 'The War Cabinet? All of them? That's impossible. How could he even attempt such a thing?'

'I've no idea,' Makeev said. 'I'm simply telling you what he told me, that the War Cabinet meets at ten in the morning and that is when he makes his move.'

'God is great,' Michael Aroun said. 'If he can do this thing, now, in the middle of the war, before the land offensive starts, the effect on the whole Arab world would be incredible.'

'I should imagine so.'

Aroun took a step forward and fastened his right hand in Makeev's lapel. 'Can he, Josef, can he do it?'

'He seems certain.' Makeev disengaged himself. 'I only tell you what he has told me.'

Aroun turned and stood looking down at the fire, then said to Rashid, 'We'll leave at nine from Charles de Gaulle in the Citation. We'll be there in not much more than an hour.'

'At your orders,' Rashid said.

'You can phone old Alphonse at the Château now. I want him out of there at breakfast time. He can take a few days off. I don't want him around.'

Rashid nodded and went out to the study. Makeev said, 'Alphonse?'

'The caretaker. At this time of the year he's on his own unless I tell him to bring the servants in from the local village. They're all on retainers.'

Makeev said, 'I'd like to come with you if that's all right.'

'Of course, Josef.' Aroun poured two more glasses of cognac. 'God forgive me, I know I drink when I should

228

not, but on this occasion.' He raised his glass. 'To Dillon and may all go as he intends.'

It was one o'clock in the morning and Fahy was working on one of the oxygen cylinders on the bench when Dillon entered the barn.

'How's it going?'

'Fine,' Fahy said. 'Nearly finished. This one and one to go. How's the weather?'

Dillon walked to the open door. 'It's stopped snowing, but more's expected. I checked on the teletext on your television.'

Fahy carried the cylinder to the Ford Transit, got inside and fitted it into one of the tubes with great care while Dillon watched. Angel came in with a jug and two mugs in one hand. 'Coffee?' she asked.

'Lovely.' Her uncle held a mug while she filled it and then did the same for Dillon.

Dillon said, 'I've been thinking. The garage where I wanted you to wait with the van, Angel, I'm not sure that's such a good idea now.'

Fahy paused, a spanner in his hand and looked up. 'Why not?'

'It was where the Russian woman, my contact, kept her car. The police will probably know that. If they're keeping an eye on her flat they may well be checking the garage too.'

'So what do you suggest?'

'Remember where I was staying, the hotel on the Bayswater Road? There's a supermarket next door with a big parking area at the rear. We'll use that. It won't make much of a difference,' he said to Angel. 'I'll show you when we get there.'

'Anything you say, Mr Dillon.' She stayed watching as

Fahy finished the fitting of his improvised mortar bomb and moved back to the bench. 'I was thinking, Mr Dillon, this place in France, this St Denis?'

'What about it?'

'You'll be flying straight off there afterwards?'

'That's right.'

She said carefully, 'Where does that leave us?'

Fahy paused to wipe his hands. 'She's got a point, Sean.'

'You'll be fine, the both of you,' Dillon said. 'This is a clean one, Danny, the cleanest I ever pulled. Not a link with you or this place. If it works tomorrow, and it will, we'll be back here by eleven-thirty at the outside and that will be the end of it.'

'If you say so,' Fahy said.

'But I do, Danny, and if it's the money you're worried about, don't. You'll get your share. The man I'm working for can arrange financial payments anywhere. You can have it here if you want or Europe if that's better.'

'Sure and the money was never the big thing, Sean,' Fahy said, 'you know that. It's just that if there's a chance of something going wrong, any kind of chance.' He shrugged. 'It's Angel I'm thinking about.'

'No need. If there was any risk I'd be the first to say come with me, but there won't be.' Dillon put his arm about the girl. 'You're excited, aren't you?'

'Me stomach's turning over something dreadful, Mr Dillon.'

'Go to bed.' He pushed her towards the door. 'We'll be leaving at eight.'

'I won't sleep a wink.'

'Try. Now go on, that's an order.'

She went out reluctantly. Dillon lit another cigarette and turned back to Fahy. 'Is there anything I can do?'

'Not a thing, another half-hour should do it. Go and put your head down yourself, Sean. As for me, I'm as bad as

Angel. I don't think I could. I've found some old biker's leathers for you, by the way,' Fahy added. 'They're over there by the BSA.'

There was a jacket and leather trousers and boots. They'd all seen considerable service and Dillon smiled. 'Takes me back to my youth. I'll go and try them on.'

Fahy paused and ran a hand over his eyes as if tired. 'Look, Sean, does it have to be tomorrow?'

'Is there a problem?'

'I told you I wanted to weld some fins onto the oxygen cylinders to give more stability in flight. I haven't time to do that now.' He threw his spanner down on the bench. 'It's all too rushed, Sean.'

'Blame Martin Brosnan and his friends, not me, Danny,' Dillon told him. 'They're breathing down my neck. Nearly had me in Belfast. God knows when they might turn up again. No, Danny, it's now or never.'

He turned and went out and Fahy picked up his spanner reluctantly and went back to work.

The leathers weren't bad at all and Dillon stood in front of the wardrobe mirror as he zipped up the jacket. 'Would you look at that?' he said softly. 'Eighteen years old again when the world was young and anything seemed possible.'

He unzipped the jacket again, took it off then opened his briefcase and unfolded the bulletproof waistcoat Tania had given him at their first meeting. He pulled it snugly into place, fastened the Velcro tabs, then put his jacket on again.

He sat on the edge of the bed, took the Walther out of the briefcase, examined it and screwed the Carswell silencer in place. Next he checked the Beretta and put it on the bedside locker close to hand. He put the briefcase in the wardrobe then switched off the light and lay on the bed, looking up at the ceiling through the darkness.

He never felt emotional, not about anything, and it was exactly the same now, on the eve of the greatest coup of his life. 'You're making history with this one, Sean,' he said softly. 'History.'

He closed his eyes and after a while, slept.

It snowed again during the night and just after seven, Fahy walked along the track to check the road. He walked back and found Dillon standing at the farmhouse door eating a bacon sandwich, a mug of tea in his hand.

'I don't know how you can,' Fahy told him. 'I couldn't eat a thing. I'd bring it straight up.'

'Are you scared, Danny?'

'To death.'

'That's good. It sharpens you up, gives you that edge that can make all the difference.'

They crossed to the barn and stood beside the Ford Transit. 'Well, she's as ready as she ever will be,' Fahy said.

Dillon put a hand on his shoulder. 'You've done wonders, Danny, wonders.'

Angel appeared behind them. She was dressed ready to go in her old trousers and boots, anorak and sweater and the tam-o'-shanter. 'Are we moving?'

'Soon,' Dillon said. 'We'll get the BSA into the Morris now.'

They opened the rear doors of the Morris, put the duckboard on the incline and ran the bike up inside. Dillon lifted it up on its stand and Fahy shoved the duckboard in. He passed a crash helmet through. 'That's for you. I'll have one for myself in the Ford.' He hesitated. 'Are you carrying, Sean?'

Dillon took the Beretta from inside his black leather jacket. 'What about you?'

'Jesus, Sean, I always hated guns, you know that.'

Dillon slipped the Beretta back in place and zipped up his jacket. He closed the van doors and turned. 'Everybody happy?'

'Are we ready for off then?' Angel asked.

Dillon checked his watch. 'Not yet. I said we'd leave at eight. We don't want to be too early. Time for another cup of tea.'

They went across to the farmhouse and Angel put the kettle on in the kitchen. Dillon lit a cigarette and leaned against the sink watching. 'Don't you have any nerves at all?' she asked him. 'I can feel my heart thumping.'

Fahy called, 'Come and see this, Sean.'

Dillon went in the living room. The television was on in the corner and the morning show was dealing with the snow which had fallen over London overnight. Trees in the city squares, statues, monuments, were all covered, and many of the pavements.

'Not good,' Fahy said.

'Stop worrying, the roads themselves are clear,' Dillon said as Angel came in with a tray. 'A nice cup of tea, Danny, with plenty of sugar for energy and we'll be on our way.'

At the Lowndes Square flat Brosnan was boiling eggs in the kitchen and watching the toast when the phone went. He heard Mary answer it. After a while she looked in. 'Harry's on the phone, he'd like a word.'

Brosnan took the phone. 'How goes it?'

'Okay, old buddy, just checking you were leaving soon.'

'How are we going to handle things?'

'We'll just have to play it by ear, but I also think we'll have to play rough.'

'I agree,' Brosnan said.

'I'm right in assuming that would give Mary a problem?'

'I'm afraid so.'

'Then she definitely can't go in. Leave it to me. I'll handle it when we get there. See you soon.'

Brosnan put the phone down and went back to the kitchen where Mary had put out the eggs and toast and was pouring tea. 'What did he have to say?' she asked.

'Nothing special. He was just wondering what the best approach would be.'

'And I suppose you think that would be to batter Harvey over the head with a very large club?'

'Something like that.'

'Why not thumbscrews, Martin?'

'Why not indeed?' He reached for the toast. 'If that's what it takes.'

The early morning traffic on the Horsham road to Dorking and onwards to London was slower than usual because of the weather. Angel and Dillon led the way in the Morris, Fahy close behind in the Ford Transit. The girl was obviously tense, her knuckles white as she gripped the wheel too tightly, but she drove extremely well. Epsom then Kingston and on towards the river, crossing the Thames at Putney Bridge. It was already nine-fifteen as they moved along the Bayswater Road towards the hotel.

'Over there,' Dillon said. 'There's the supermarket. The entrance to the car park is down the side.' She turned in, changing to the lowest gear, crawling along as she went into the car park which was already quite full. 'There at the far end,' Dillon said. 'Just the spot.'

There was a huge trailer parked there, protected by a plastic sheet that was itself covered by snow. She parked on the other side of it and Fahy stopped nearby. Dillon jumped out, pulling on his crash helmet, went round and opened the doors. He put the duckboard in the right position, got inside and eased the BSA out, Angel helping. As he threw a leg over the seat she shoved the duckboard back inside the van and closed the doors. Dillon switched on and the BSA responded sweetly, roaring into life. He glanced at his watch. It was nine-twenty. He pulled the machine up on its stand and went over to Fahy in the Ford.

'Remember, the timing is crucial and we can't go round and round in circles at Whitehall, somebody might get suspicious. If we're too early try and delay things on the Victoria Embankment. Pretend you've broken down and I'll stop as if I'm assisting, but from the Embankment up Horse Guards Avenue to the corner with Whitehall will only take a minute, remember that.'

'Jesus, Sean.' Fahy looked terrified.

'Easy, Danny, easy,' Dillon said. 'It'll be fine, you'll see. Now get moving.'

He swung a leg over the BSA again and Angel said, 'I prayed for you last night, Mr Dillon.'

'Well that's all right then. See you soon,' and he rode away and joined up behind the Ford.

THIRTEEN

Harry Flood and Mordecai were waiting in the Mercedes, Salter at the wheel, when a taxi drew up outside the undertakers in Whitechapel and Brosnan and Mary got out. They picked their way carefully through the snow on the pavement and Flood opened the door for them to get in.

He glanced at his watch. 'Just coming up to nine-thirty. We might as well go straight in.'

He took a Walther from his breast pocket and checked the slider. 'You want something, Martin?' he asked.

Brosnan nodded. 'It's a thought.'

Mordecai opened the glove compartment, took out a Browning and passed it over the seat. 'That suit you, Professor?'

Mary said, 'For God's sake, anybody would think you were trying to start the Third World War.'

'Or prevent it starting,' Brosnan said. 'Have you ever thought of that?'

'Let's move,' Flood said. Brosnan followed him out and Mordecai emerged from the other side. As Mary tried to follow, Flood said, 'Not this time, lover. I told Myra I'd be bringing my accountant which takes care of Martin, and

Mordecai goes everywhere with me. That's all they're expecting.'

'Now look here,' she said, 'I'm the case officer on this, the official representative of the Ministry.'

'Well bully for you. Take care of her, Charlie,' Flood told Salter and he turned to the entrance where Mordecai was already ringing the bell.

The porter who admitted them smiled obsequiously. 'Morning, Mr Flood, Mr Harvey presents his compliments and wonders whether you'd mind stepping into the waiting room for a few moments. He's only just arrived from Heathrow.'

'That's fine,' Flood said and followed him through.

The waiting room was suitably subdued with dark leather chairs, rust-coloured walls and carpet. The lighting was mainly provided by fake candles and music suitable to the establishment played softly over a speaker system.

'What do you think?' Brosnan asked.

'I think he's just in from Heathrow,' Flood said. 'Don't worry.'

Mordecai peered out through the entrance and across to one of the chapels of rest. 'Flowers, that's what I find funny about these places. I always associate death with flowers.'

'I'll remember that when your turn comes to go,' Flood said. 'No flowers by request.'

It was approximately nine-forty as the Ford Transit pulled into a lay-by on the Victoria Embankment and Fahy's hands were sweating. In the rear-view mirror, he saw Dillon pull the BSA up on its stand and walk towards him. He leaned in the window.

'Are you okay?'

'Fine, Sean.'

'We'll stay here for as long as we can get away with it.

Fifteen minutes would be ideal. If a traffic warden comes, just pull away and I'll follow you. We'll drive along the Embankment for half a mile, turn and come back.'

'Right, Sean.' Fahy's teeth were chattering.

Dillon took out a packet of cigarettes, put two in his mouth, lit them and passed one to Fahy. 'Just to show you what a romantic fool I am,' and he started to laugh.

When Harry Flood, Brosnan and Mordecai went into the outer office, Myra was waiting for them. She was wearing the black trouser suit and boots and carried a sheaf of documents in one hand.

'You look very businesslike, Myra,' Flood told her.

'So I should, Harry, the amount of work I do around here.' She kissed him on the cheek and nodded to Mordecai. 'Hello, muscles.' Then she looked Brosnan over. 'And this is?'

'My new accountant, Mr Smith.'

'Really?' She nodded. 'Jack's waiting.' She opened the door and led the way into the office.

The fire burned brightly in the grate, it was warm and comfortable. Harvey sat behind the desk smoking his usual cigar. Billy was over to the left sitting on the arm of the sofa, his raincoat casually draped across his knee.

'Jack,' Harry Flood said. 'Nice to see you.'

'Is that so?' Harvey looked Brosnan over. 'Who's this?'

'Harry's new accountant, Uncle Jack.' Myra moved round the desk and stood beside him. 'This is Mr Smith.'

Harvey shook his head. 'I've never seen an accountant that looked like Mr Smith, have you, Myra?' He turned back to Flood. 'My time's valuable, Harry, what do you want?'

'Dillon,' Harry Flood said. 'Sean Dillon.'

'Dillon?' Harvey looked totally mystified. 'And who the Christ is Dillon?'

'Small man,' Brosnan said, 'Irish, although he can pass as anything he wants. You sold him guns and explosives in nineteen eighty-one.'

'Very naughty of you that, Jack,' Harry Flood said. 'He blew up large parts of London and now we think he's at it again.'

'And where else would he go for his equipment except his old chum, Jack Harvey?' Brosnan said. 'I mean, that's logical, isn't it?'

Myra's grip tightened on her uncle's shoulder and Harvey, his face flushed said, 'Billy!'

Flood put up a hand. 'I'd just like to say that if that's a sawn-off he's got under the coat I hope it's cocked.'

Billy fired instantly through the raincoat, catching Mordecai in the left thigh as the big man drew his pistol. Flood's Walther came out of his pocket in one smooth motion and he hit Billy in the chest, sending him back over the sofa, the other barrel discharging, some of the shot catching Flood in the left arm.

Jack Harvey had the desk drawer open, his hand came up clutching a Smith & Wesson and Brosnan shot him very deliberately through the shoulder. There was chaos for a moment, the room full of smoke and the stench of cordite.

Myra leaned over her uncle who sank back into the chair, moaning. Her face was set and angry. 'You bastards!' she said.

Flood turned to Mordecai. 'You okay?'

'I will be when Dr Aziz has finished with me, Harry. The little bastard was quick.'

Flood, still holding the Walther, clutched his left arm, blood seeping between his fingers. He glanced at Brosnan. 'Okay, let's finish this.'

He took two paces to the desk and raised the Walther

directly at Harvey. 'I'll give it to you right between the eyes if you don't tell us what we want to know. What about Sean Dillon?'

'Screw you!' Jack Harvey said.

Flood lowered the Walther for a moment and then took deliberate aim and Myra screamed, 'No, for God's sake, leave him alone. The man you want calls himself Peter Hilton. He was the one Uncle Jack dealt with in eighty-one. He used another name then. Michael Coogan.'

'And more recently?'

'He bought fifty pounds of Semtex. Picked it up last night and paid cash. I had Billy follow him home on his BMW.'

'And where would that be?'

'Here.' She picked a sheet of paper up from the desk. 'I'd written it all down for Jack.'

Flood looked it over and passed it to Brosnan, managing a smile in spite of the pain. 'Cadge End Farm, Martin, sounds promising. Let's get out of here.'

He walked to the door and Mordecai limped out ahead of him, dripping blood. Myra had crossed to Billy who started to groan loudly. She turned and said harshly, 'I'll get you for this, the lot of you.'

'No you won't, Myra,' Harry Flood told her. 'If you're sensible you'll put it all down to experience and give your personal doctor a call,' and he turned and went out followed by Brosnan.

It was just before ten as they got into the Mercedes. Charlie Salter said, 'Jesus, Harry, we're getting blood all over the carpets.'

'Just drive, Charlie, you know where to go.'

Mary looked grim. 'What happened in there?'

'This happened.' Brosnan held up the sheet of paper with the directions to Cadge End Farm.

'My God,' Mary said as she read it. 'I'd better call the Brigadier.'

'No you don't,' Flood said. 'I figure this is our baby considering the trouble we've gone to and the wear and tear, wouldn't you agree, Martin?'

'Definitely.'

'So, the first thing we do is call at the quiet little nursing home in Wapping run by my good friend Dr Aziz so he can take care of Mordecai and see to my arm. After that, Cadge End.'

As Fahy turned out of the traffic on the Victoria Embankment into Horse Guards Avenue past the Ministry of Defence building, he was sweating in spite of the cold. The road itself was clear and wet from the constant traffic, but there was snow on the pavements and the trees and the buildings on either hand. He could see Dillon in his rear-view mirror, a sinister figure in his black leathers on the BSA and then it was the moment of truth and everything seemed to happen at once.

He pulled in at the junction of Horse Guards Avenue and Whitehall on the angle he'd worked out. On the other side of the road at Horse Guards Parade there were two troopers of the Household Cavalry, mounted as usual, with drawn sabres.

Some distance away, a policeman turned and saw the van. Fahy turned off the engine, switched on the timers and pulled on his crash helmet. As he got out and locked the door the policeman called to him and hurried forward. Dillon swerved in on the BSA, Fahy swung a leg over the pillion seat and they were away, sliding past the astonished policeman in a half-circle and moving fast up towards Trafalgar Square. As Dillon joined the traffic around the square, the first explosion sounded. There was another, perhaps two, and then it all seemed to become one with the greater explosion of the Ford Transit self-destructing.

Dillon kept on going, not too fast, through Admiralty Arch and along the Mall. He was at Marble Arch and turning along the Bayswater Road within ten minutes and rode into the car park of the supermarket soon after. As soon as she saw them, Angel was out of the van. She got the doors open and put the duckboard in place. Dillon and Fahy shoved the bike inside and slammed the doors.

'Did it work?' Angel demanded. 'Did everything go all right?'

'Just leave it for now. Get in and drive,' Dillon told her. She did as she was told and he and Fahy got in beside her. A minute later and they were turning into the Bayswater Road. 'Just go back the way we came and not too fast,' Dillon said.

Fahy switched on the radio, fiddling his way through the various BBC stations. 'Nothing,' he said. 'Bloody music and chat.'

'Leave it on,' Dillon told him, 'and just be patient. You'll hear all about it soon enough.'

He lit a cigarette and sat back, whistling softly.

In the small theatre at the nursing home just off Wapping High Street, Mordecai Fletcher lay on the operating table while Dr Aziz, a grey-haired Indian in round steel spectacles, examined his thigh.

'Harry, my friend, I thought you'd given this kind of thing up?' he said. 'But here we are again like a bad Saturday night in Bombay.'

Flood was sitting in a chair, jacket off, while a young Indian nurse attended to his arm. She had cut the shirt sleeve off and was swabbing the wound. Brosnan and Mary stood watching.

Flood said to Aziz, 'How is he?'

'He'll have to stay in for two or three days. I can only get some of this shot out under anaesthetic and an artery is severed. Now let's look at you.'

He held Flood's arm and probed gently with a pair of small pincers. The nurse held an enamel bowl. Aziz dropped one piece of shot in it then two. Flood winced with pain. The Indian found another. 'That could be it, Harry, but we'll need an X-ray.'

'Just bandage it up for now and give me a sling,' Flood said. 'I'll be back later.'

'If that's what you want.'

He bandaged the arm skilfully, assisted by the nurse, then opened a cupboard and found a pack of morphine ampoules. He jabbed one in Flood's arm.

'Just like Vietnam, Harry,' Brosnan said.

'It will help with the pain,' Aziz told Flood as the nurse eased him into his jacket. 'I'd advise you to be back no later than this evening though.'

The nurse fastened a sling behind Flood's neck. As she put his overcoat across his shoulders, the door burst open and Charlie Salter came in. 'All hell's broken loose, just heard it on the radio. Mortar attack on Ten Downing Street.'

'Oh, my God!' Mary Tanner said.

Flood showed her through the door and she turned to Brosnan. 'Come on, Martin, at least we know where the bastard's gone.'

The War Cabinet had been larger than usual that morning, fifteen including the Prime Minister. It had just begun its meeting in the Cabinet Room at the back of Number Ten Downing Street when the first mortar, curving in a great arc of some two hundred yards from the Ford Transit van at the corner of Horse Guards Avenue and Whitehall, landed. There was a huge explosion, so loud that it was clearly audible in the office of Brigadier Charles Ferguson at the Ministry of Defence overlooking Horse Guards Avenue.

'Christ!' Ferguson said and like most people in the Ministry, rushed to the nearest window.

At Downing Street in the Cabinet Room the specially strengthened windows cracked but most of the blast was absorbed by the special blast-proof net curtains. The first bomb left a crater in the garden, uprooting a cherry tree. The other two landed further off target in Mountbatten Green where some outside broadcast vehicles were parked. Only one of those exploded, but at the same moment, the van blew up as Fahy's self-destruct device went into action. There was surprisingly little panic in the Cabinet Room. Everyone crouched, some seeking the protection of the table. There was a draught of cold air from shattered windows, voices in the distance.

The Prime Minister stood up and actually managed a smile. With incredible calm he said, 'Gentlemen, I think we had better start again somewhere else,' and he led the way out of the room.

Mary and Brosnan were in the back of the Mercedes, Harry Flood in the passenger seat beside Charlie Salter who was making the best time he could through heavy traffic.

Mary said, 'Look, I need to speak to Brigadier Ferguson. It's essential.'

They were crossing Putney Bridge. Flood turned and looked at Brosnan who nodded. 'Okay,' Flood said. 'Do what you like.'

She used her car phone, ringing the Ministry of Defence, but Ferguson wasn't there. There was some confusion as to his whereabouts. She left the car phone number with the control room and put the phone down.

'He'll be running round half-demented like everyone else,' Brosnan said and lit a cigarette.

Flood said to Salter, 'Okay, Charlie, Epsom, then Dorking and the Horsham road beyond that and step on it.'

The BBC newsflash which came over the radio in the Morris van was delivered in the usual calm and unemotional way. There had been a bomb attack on Number Ten Downing Street at approximately 10.00 a.m. The building had sustained some damage, but the Prime Minister and members of the War Cabinet meeting together at that time were all safe.

The van swerved as Angel sobbed. 'Oh, God, no!'

Dillon put a hand on the wheel. 'Steady girl,' he said calmly. 'Just stick to your driving.'

Fahy looked as if he was going to be sick. 'If I'd had time to put those fins on the cylinders it would have made all the difference. You were in too much of a hurry, Sean. You let Brosnan rattle you and that was fatal.'

'Maybe it was,' Dillon said, 'but at the end of the day all that matters is we missed.'

He took out a cigarette, lit it and suddenly started to laugh helplessly.

Aroun had left Paris at nine-thirty, flying the Citation jet himself, Rashid having the rating qualifying him as the second pilot necessary under flight regulations. Makeev, in the cabin behind them, was reading the morning paper when Aroun called in to the control tower at Maupertus Airport at Cherbourg to clear for his landing on the private strip at St Denis.

The controller gave him his clearance and then said, 'We've just had a newsflash. Bomb attack on the British Cabinet at Downing Street in London.'

'What happened?' Aroun demanded.

'That's all they're saying at the moment.'

Aroun smiled excitedly at Rashid who'd also heard the message. 'Take over and handle the landing.' He scrambled back to the cabin and sat opposite Makeev. 'Newsflash just in. Bomb attack on Ten Downing Street.'

Makeev threw down his paper 'What happened?'

'That's all for the moment.' Aroun looked up to heaven, spreading his hands. 'Praise be to God.'

Ferguson was standing beside the outside broadcast vans at Mountbatten Green with Detective Inspector Lane and Sergeant Mackie. It was snowing slightly and a police forensic team were making a careful inspection of Fahy's third mortar bomb, the one which hadn't exploded.

'A bad business, sir,' Lane said. 'To use an old-fashioned phrase, right at the heart of Empire. I mean, how can they get away with this kind of thing?'

'Because we're a democracy, Inspector, because people have to get on with their lives and that means we can't turn London into some Eastern-European-style armed fortress.'

A young constable came across with a mobile phone and whispered to Mackie. The sergeant said, 'Excuse me, Brigadier, it's urgent. Your office has been trying to contact you. Captain Tanner's been on the line.'

'Give it to me.' Ferguson took the phone. 'Ferguson here. I see. Give me the number.' He gestured to Mackie who took out pad and pencil and wrote it down as Ferguson dictated it.

The Mercedes was passing through Dorking when the phone went. Mary picked it up at once. 'Brigadier?'

'What's going on?' he demanded.

'The mortar attack on Number Ten. It has to be Dillon. We found out he picked up fifty pounds of Semtex in London last night, supplied by Jack Harvey.'

'Where are you now?'

'Just leaving Dorking, sir, taking the Horsham road, Martin and me and Harry Flood. We've got an address for Dillon.'

'Give it to me.' He nodded to Mackie again and repeated it aloud so the sergeant could write it down.

Mary said, 'The road's not good, sir, with the snow, but we should be at this Cadge End place in half an hour.'

'Fine. Nothing rash, Mary, my love, but don't let the bastard get away. We'll get back-up to you as soon as possible. I'll be in my car, so you've got the phone number.'

'All right, sir.'

She put the phone down and Flood turned. 'Okay?'

'Back-up on the way, but we're not to let him get away.'

Brosnan took the Browning from his pocket and checked it. 'He won't,' he said grimly. 'Not this time.'

Ferguson quietly filled in Lane on what had happened. 'What do you think Harvey will be up to, Inspector?'

'Receiving treatment from some bent doctor in a nice little private nursing home somewhere, sir.'

'Right, have that checked out and if it's as you say, don't interfere. Just have them watched, but this Cadge End place is where we go and fast. Now go and organise the cars.'

Lane and Mackie hurried away and as Ferguson made to follow them the Prime Minister appeared round the corner of the building. He was wearing a dark overcoat, the Home Secretary and several aides with him. He saw Ferguson and came over.

'Dillon's work, Brigadier?'

'I believe so, Prime Minister.'

'Rather close.' He smiled. 'Too close for comfort. A remarkable man, this Dillon.'

'Not for much longer, Prime Minister. I've just had an address for him at last.'

'Then don't let me detain you, Brigadier. Carry on, by all means.'

Ferguson turned and hurried away.

The track through the trees at Cadge End was covered with more snow since they had left. Angel bumped along it to the farmyard and turned into the barn. She switched off and it seemed terribly quiet.

Fahy said, 'Now what?'

'A nice cup of tea, I think.' Dillon got out, went round and opened the van doors and pulled out the duckboard. 'Help me, Danny.' They got the BSA out and he lifted it up on its stand. 'Performed brilliantly. You did a good job there, Danny.'

Angel had gone ahead and as they followed her, Fahy said, 'You haven't a nerve in your body, have you, Sean?'

'I could never see the point.'

'Well I have, Sean, and what I need isn't bloody tea, it's whiskey.'

He went in the living room and Dillon went up to his bedroom. He found an old holdall and packed it quickly with his suit, trenchcoat, shirts, shoes and general bits and pieces. He checked his wallet. About four hundred pounds left in there. He opened his briefcase which held the five thousand dollars remaining from his expense money and the Walther with the Carswell silencer on the end. He cocked the gun, leaving it ready for action, put it back in the briefcase together with the Jersey driving licence and the pilot's licence. He unzipped his jacket, took out the Beretta and checked it, then he slipped it into the waistband of his leather trousers at the rear, tucking the butt under the jacket.

When he went downstairs carrying the holdall and brief-case Fahy was standing looking at the television set. There were shots of Whitehall in the snow, Downing Street and Mountbatten Green.

'They just had the Prime Minister on inspecting the damage. Looked as if he didn't have a worry in the world.'

'Yes, his luck is good,' Dillon said.

Angel came in and handed him a cup of tea. 'What happens now, Mr Dillon?'

'You know very well what happens, Angel, I fly off into the wild blue yonder.'

'To that St Denis place?'

'That's right.'

'Okay for you, Sean, and us left here to carry the can,' Fahy said.

'And what can would that be?'

'You know what I mean.'

'Nobody has any kind of a line on you, Danny. You're safe till domesday. I'm the one the buggers are after. Brosnan and his girlfriend, and Brigadier Ferguson, I'm the one they'll put this down to.'

Fahy turned away and Angel said, 'Can't we go with you, Mr Dillon?'

He put down his cup and put his hands on her shoulders. 'There's no need, Angel. I'm the one running, not you or Danny. They don't even know you exist.'

He went across to the phone, picked it up and rang Grimethorpe Airfield. Grant answered straight away. 'Yes, who is it?'

'Peter Hilton, old boy.' Dillon reverted to his public school persona. 'Okay for my flight? Not too much snow?'

'It's clear down at the other end in the West Country,' Grant said. 'Might be tricky taking off here though. When were you thinking of going?'

'I'll be round in half an hour. That all right?' Dillon asked.

'I'll expect you.'

As Dillon put the phone down, Angel cried, 'No, Uncle Danny.'

Dillon turned and found Fahy standing in the doorway with a shotgun in both hands. 'But it's not all right with me, Sean,' and he thumbed back the hammers.

'Danny boy,' Dillon spread his hands. 'Don't do this.'

'We're going with you, Sean and that's an end to it.'

'Is it your money you're worried about, Danny? Didn't I tell you the man I'm working for can arrange payments anywhere?'

Fahy was trembling now, the shotgun shaking in his hand. 'No, it's not the money.' He broke a little then. 'I'm frightened, Sean. Jesus, when I saw that on the television. If I'm caught, I'll spend the rest of my life in gaol. I'm too old, Sean.'

'Then why did you come in with me in the first place?'

'I wish I knew. Sitting here, all these years, bored out of my mind. The van, the mortars, it was just something to do, a fantasy and then you turned up and made it real.'

'I see,' Dillon said.

Fahy raised the shotgun. 'So that's it, Sean. If we don't go, you don't go.'

Dillon's hand at his back found the butt of the Beretta, his arm swung and he shot Fahy twice in the heart sending

250

him staggering out into the hall. He hit the wall on the other side and slid down.

Angel screamed, ran out and knelt beside him. She stood up slowly, staring at Dillon. 'You've killed him.'

'He didn't give me any choice.'

She turned, grabbed at the front door, and Dillon went after her. She dashed across the yard into one of the barns and disappeared. Dillon moved inside the entrance and stood there listening. There was a rustling somewhere in the loft and straw dust floated down.

'Angel, listen to me. I'll take you with me.'

'No you won't. You'll kill me like me Uncle Danny. You're a bloody murderer.' Her voice was muffled.

For a moment, he extended his left arm pointing the Beretta up to the loft. 'And what did you expect? What did you think it was all about?'

There was silence. He turned, hurried across to the house, stepped over Fahy's body. He put the Beretta back in his waistband at the rear, picked up his briefcase and the holdall containing his clothes, went back to the barn and put them on the passenger seat of the Morris.

He tried once more. 'Come with me, Angel. I'd never harm you, I swear it.' There was no reply. 'To hell with you then,' he said, got behind the wheel and drove away along the track.

It was some time later, when everything was very quiet, that Angel came down the ladder and crossed to the house. She sat beside her uncle's body, back against the wall, a vacant look on her face and didn't move, not even when she heard the sound of a car driving into the courtyard outside.

FOURTEEN

The runway at Grimethorpe was completely covered with snow. The hangar doors were closed and there was no sign of either of the planes. Smoke was drifting up from the iron stove pipe, the only sign of life as Dillon drove up to the huts and the old tower and braked to a halt. He got out with his holdall and briefcase and walked to the door. When he went in, Bill Grant was standing by the stove drinking coffee.

'Ah, there you are, old man. Place looked deserted,' Dillon said. 'I was beginning to worry.'

'No need.' Grant, who was wearing old black flying overalls and leather flying jacket reached for a bottle of Scotch and poured some into his mug of coffee.

Dillon put down his holdall, but still carried the briefcase in his right hand. 'I say, is that wise, old chap?' he asked in his most public school voice.

'I never was particularly wise, old chap.' Grant seemed to be mocking him now. 'That's how I ended up in a dump like this.'

He crossed to his desk and sat down behind it. Dillon saw that there was a chart on the desk, the English Channel area, the Normandy coast, the Cherbourg approaches, the chart Dillon had checked out with Angel that first night.

'Look, I'd really like to get going, old chap,' he said. 'If it's the rest of the fee you're worried about I can pay cash.' He held up the briefcase. 'I'm sure you've no objection to American dollars.'

'No, but I do have an objection to being taken for a fool.' Grant indicated the chart. 'Land's End my arse. I saw you checking this out the other night with the girl. English Channel and French coast. What I'd like to know is what you're trying to get me into?'

'You're really being very silly,' Dillon said.

Grant pulled open a drawer in the desk and took out his old Webley revolver. 'We'll see, shall we? Now just put the briefcase on the desk and stand back while I see what we've got.'

'Certainly, old chap, no need for violence.' Dillon stepped close and put the briefcase on the desk. At the same moment he pulled the Beretta from his waistband at the rear, reached across the table and shot Grant at point-blank range.

Grant went backwards over the chair. Dillon put the Beretta back in place, folded the chart, put it under his arm, picked up his holdall and briefcase and went out, trudging through the snow to the hangar. He went in through the Judas, unbolted the great sliding door inside so that the two aircraft stood revealed. He chose the Cessna Conquest for no better reason than that it was the nearest. The stairs to the door were down. He threw the holdall and the briefcase inside, went up, pulling the door behind him.

He settled in the left-hand pilot's seat and sat there studying the chart. Approximately a hundred and forty miles to the airstrip at St Denis. Unless he encountered problems with headwinds, in a plane like this he should do it in forty-five minutes. No flight plan filed, of course, so he would be a bogey on somebody's radar screen but that didn't matter. If he went straight out to sea over Brighton, he would be lost in mid-Channel before anyone knew what was going on. There was a question of the approach to St Denis, but if he hit the coast at six hundred feet, with any luck he would be below the radar screen operated at Maupertus Airport at Cherbourg.

He put the chart on the other seat where he could see it and switched on, firing first the port engine then the starboard. He took the Conquest out of the hangar and paused to make a thorough cockpit check. As Grant had boasted, the fuel tanks were full. Dillon strapped himself in and taxied across the apron and down to the end of the runway.

He turned into the wind and started forward. He was immediately aware of the drag from the snow, boosted power and gave it everything he could, easing back the column. The Conquest lifted and started to climb. He banked to turn towards his heading for Brighton and saw a black limousine down below moving out of the trees towards the hangars.

'Well, I don't know who the hell you are,' he said softly, 'but if it's me you're after you're too late,' and he turned the Conquest in a great curve and started for the coast.

Angel sat at the kitchen table, holding the mug of coffee Mary had given her. Brosnan and Harry Flood, his arm in the sling, stood listening and Charlie Salter leaned on the door.

'It was Dillon and your uncle at Downing Street, is that what you're saying?' Mary asked.

Angel nodded. 'I drove the Morris with Mr Dillon's motorbike in it. He followed Uncle Danny, he was in the Ford Transit.' She looked dazed. 'I drove them back from Bayswater and Uncle Danny was afraid, afraid of what might happen.'

'And Dillon?' Mary asked.

'He was flying away from the airfield up the road, Grimethorpe. He made arrangements with Mr Grant who runs the place. Said he wanted to go to Land's End, but he didn't.'

She sat clutching the mug, staring into space. Brosnan said gently, 'Where did he want to go, Angel, do you know?'

'He showed me on the chart. It was in France. It was down along the coast from Cherbourg. There was a landing strip marked. A place called St Denis.'

'You're sure?' Brosnan said.

'Oh, yes. Uncle Danny asked him to take us too, but he wouldn't, then Uncle Danny got upset. He came in with the shotgun and then . . .' She started to sob.

Mary put her arms around her. 'It's all right now, it's all right.'

Brosnan said, 'Was there anything else?'

'I don't think so.' Angel still looked dazed. 'He offered Uncle Danny money. He said the man he was working for could arrange payments anywhere in the world.'

'Did he say who the man was?' Brosnan asked.

'No, he never did.' She brightened. 'He did say something about working for the Arabs the first time he came.'

Mary glanced at Brosnan. 'Iraq?'

'I always did think that was a possibility.'

'Right, let's get going,' Flood said. 'Check out this Grimethorpe place. You stay here with the kid, Charlie,' he said to Salter, 'until the cavalry arrives. We'll take the Mercedes,' and he turned and led the way out.

In the Great Hall at St Denis, Rashid, Aroun and Makeev stood drinking champagne waiting for the television news.

'A day for rejoicing in Baghdad,' Aroun said. 'The people will know now how strong their President is.'

The screen filled with the announcer who spoke briefly, then the pictures followed. Whitehall in the snow, the Household Cavalry guards, the rear of Ten Downing Street, curtain hanging from smashed windows, Mountbatten Green and the Prime Minister inspecting the damage. The three men stood in shocked silence.

It was Aroun who spoke first. 'He has failed,' he whispered. 'All for nothing. A few broken windows, a hole in the garden.'

'The attempt was made,' Makeev protested. 'The most sensational attack on the British Government ever mounted and at the seat of power.'

'Who gives a damn?' Aroun tossed his champagne glass into the fireplace. 'We needed a result and he hasn't given us one. He failed with the Thatcher woman and he failed with the British Prime Minister. In spite of all your big talk, Josef, nothing but failure.'

He sat down in one of the high-backed chairs at the dining table and Rashid said, 'A good job we didn't pay him his million pounds.'

'True,' Aroun said. 'But the money is the least of it. It's my personal position with the President which is at stake.'

'So what are we going to do?' Makeev demanded.

'Do?' Aroun looked up at Rashid. 'We're going to give our friend Dillon a very warm reception on a cold day, isn't that so, Ali?'

'At your orders, Mr Aroun,' Rashid said.

'And you, Josef, you're with us in this?' Aroun demanded.

'Of course,' Makeev said because there was little else he could say. 'Of course.' When he poured another glass of champagne, his hands were shaking.

As the Mercedes came out of the trees at Grimethorpe, the Conquest banked and flew away. Brosnan was driving, Mary beside him, Harry Flood in the back.

Mary leaned out of the window. 'Do you think that's him?'

'Could be,' Brosnan said. 'We'll soon find out.'

They drove past the open hangar with the Navajo Chieftain inside and stopped at the huts. It was Brosnan, first through the door, who found Grant. 'Over here,' he said.

Mary and Flood joined him. 'So it *was* Dillon in that plane,' she commented.

'Obviously,' Brosnan said grimly.

'Which means the bastard's slipped the lot of us,' Flood said.

'Don't be too sure,' Mary told him. 'There was another plane in the hangar,' and she turned and ran out.

'What goes on?' Flood demanded as he followed Brosnan out.

'Amongst other things, the lady happens to be an Army Air Corps pilot,' Brosnan said.

When they reached the hangar, the Airstair door of the Navajo was open and Mary was inside in the cockpit. She got up and came out. 'Full tanks.'

'You want to follow him?' Brosnan demanded.

'Why not? With any luck we'll be right up his tail.' She looked fierce and determined, opened her handbag and took out her Cellnet phone. 'I'm not having this man get away with what he's done. He needs putting down once and for all.'

She moved outside, pulled up the aerial on her phone and dialled the number of Ferguson's car.

The limousine, leading a convoy of six unmarked Special Branch cars, was just entering Dorking when Ferguson received her call. Detective Inspector Lane was sitting beside him, Sergeant Mackie in front beside the driver.

Ferguson listened to what Mary had to say and made his decision. 'I totally agree. You must follow Dillon at your soonest to this St Denis place. What do you require from me?'

'Speak to Colonel Hernu at Service Five. Ask him to discover who owns the airstrip at St Denis so we know what we're getting into. He'll want to come himself obviously, but that will take time. Ask him to deal with the authorities at Maupertus Airport at Cherbourg. They can act as a link for us when I get close to the French coast.'

'I'll see to that at once and you take down this radio frequency.' He gave her the details quickly. 'That will link you directly to me at the Ministry of Defence. If I'm not back in London they'll patch you through.'

'Right, sir.'

'And Mary, my love,' he said, 'take care. Do take care.'

'I'll do my best, sir.' She closed her Cellnet phone, put it in her handbag and went back into the hangar.

'Are we on our way then?' Brosnan asked.

'He's going to talk to Max Hernu in Paris. He'll arrange a link for us with Maupertus Airport at Cherbourg to let us know what we're getting into.' She smiled tightly. 'So let's get going. It would be a shame to get there and find he'd moved on.'

She climbed up into the Navajo and moved into the cockpit. Harry Flood went next and settled himself into one of the cabin seats. Brosnan followed, pulled up the Airstair door, then went and settled in the co-pilot's seat beside her. Mary switched on first one engine then the other, completed her cockpit check then took the Navajo outside. It had started to snow, a slight wind whipping it across the runway in a curtain as she taxied to the far end and turned.

'Ready?' she asked.

Brosnan nodded. She boosted power, the Navajo roared along the runway and lifted up into the grey sky as she pulled back the control column.

Max Hernu was sitting at his desk in his office at DGSE headquarters going through some papers with Inspector Savary when Ferguson was put through to him. 'Charles, exciting times in London this morning.'

'Don't laugh, old friend, because the whole mess could well land in your lap,' Ferguson said. 'Number one, there's a private airstrip at a place called St Denis down the coast from Cherbourg. Who owns it?'

Hernu put a hand over the phone and said to Savary, 'Check the computer. Who owns a private airstrip at St Denis on the Normandy coast?' Savary rushed out and Hernu continued, 'Tell me what all this is about, Charles.'

Which Ferguson did. When he was finished, he said, 'We've got to get this bastard this time, Max, finish him off for good.'

'I agree, my friend.' Savary hurried in with a piece of paper and passed it to Hernu who read it and whistled. 'The airstrip in question is part of the Château St Denis estate which is owned by Michael Aroun.'

'The Iraqi billionaire?' Ferguson laughed harshly. 'All is explained. Will you arrange clearance for Mary Tanner with Cherbourg and also see that she has that information?'

'Of course, my friend. I'll also arrange a plane at once and get down there myself with a Service Five team.'

'Good hunting to all of us,' Charles Ferguson said and rang off.

There was a great deal of low cloud over the Normandy coast. Dillon, still a few miles out to sea, came out of it at about a thousand feet and went lower, approaching the coastline at about five hundred feet over a turbulent white-capped sea.

The trip had gone like a dream, no trouble at all. Navigation had always been his strong point and he came in off the sea and saw Château St Denis perched on the edge of the cliffs, the airstrip a few hundred yards beyond. There was some snow, but not as much as there had been in England. There was a small prefabricated hangar, the Citation jet parked outside. He made a single pass over the house, turned into the wind and dropped his flaps for a perfect landing.

Aroun and Makeev were sitting by the fire in the Great Hall when they heard the sound of a plane overhead. Rashid hurried in, went and opened the French windows. They joined him on the snow-covered terrace, Aroun holding a pair of binoculars. Three hundred yards away on the airstrip, the Cessna Conquest landed and taxied towards the hangar, turning to line itself up beside the Citation.

'So, he's here,' Aroun said.

He focused the binoculars on the plane, saw the door open and Dillon appear. He passed the binoculars to Rashid who had a look then handed them to Makeev.

'I'll go down and pick him up in the Land Rover,' Rashid said.

'No you won't.' Aroun shook his head. 'Let the bastard walk through the snow, a suitable welcome and when he gets here, we'll be waiting for him.'

Dillon left the holdall and the briefcase just inside the Conquest when he climbed down. He walked across to the Citation and lit a cigarette, looking the aircraft over. It was

'What do you want me to do, say I'm sorry?'

Rashid was sitting on the edge of the table, swinging a leg. He said to Aroun, 'In the circumstances, a wise decision not to pay this man.'

Dillon said, 'What's he talking about?'

'The million in advance that you instructed me to deposit in Zurich.'

'I spoke to the manager. He confirmed it had been placed in my account,' Dillon said.

'On my instructions, you fool. I have millions on deposit at that bank. I only had to threaten to transfer it elsewhere to bring him to heel.'

'You shouldn't have done that,' Dillon said calmly. 'I always keep my word, Mr Aroun, I expect others to keep theirs. A matter of honour.'

'Honour? You talk to me of honour.' Aroun laughed out loud. 'What do you think of that, Josef?'

Makeev, who had been standing behind the door, stepped out, the Makarov in his hand. Dillon half-turned and the Russian said, 'Easy, Sean, easy.'

'Aren't I always, Josef?' Dillon said.

'Hands on head, Mr Dillon,' Rashid told him. Dillon complied. Rashid unzipped the biker's jacket, checked for a weapon and found nothing. His hands went round Dillon's waist and discovered the Beretta. 'Very tricky,' he said and put it on the table.

'Can I have a cigarette?' Dillon put a hand in his pocket and Aroun threw the newspaper aside and picked up the Smith & Wesson. Dillon produced a cigarette pack. 'All right?' He put one in his mouth and Rashid gave him a light. The Irishman stood there, the cigarette dangling from the corner of his mouth. 'What happens now? Does Josef blow me away?'

'No, I reserve that pleasure for myself,' Aroun said.

'Mr Aroun, let's be reasonable.' Dillon flicked the

catches on his briefcase and started to open it. 'I'll give you back what's left of the operating money and we'll call it quits. How's that?'

'You think money can make this right?' Aroun asked.

'Not really,' Dillon said and took the Walther with the Carswell silencer from the briefcase and shot him between the eyes. Aroun went over, his chair toppling and Dillon, turning, dropped to one knee and hit Makeev twice as the Russian got off one wild shot.

Dillon was up and turning, the Walther extended and Rashid held his hands at shoulder height. 'No need for that, Mr Dillon, I could be useful.'

'You're damn right you could be,' Dillon said.

There was a sudden roaring of an aircraft passing overhead. Dillon grabbed Rashid by the shoulder and pushed him to the French windows. 'Open them,' he ordered.

'All right.' Rashid did as he was told and they went out on the terrace from where they could see the Navajo landing in spite of the mist rolling in.

'Now who might that be?' Dillon asked. 'Friends of yours?'

'We weren't expecting anyone, I swear it,' Rashid said.

Dillon shoved him back in and put the end of the Carswell silencer to the side of his neck. 'Aroun had a nice private safe hidden safely away in the apartment at the Avenue Victor Hugo in Paris. Don't tell me he didn't have the same here.'

Rashid didn't hesitate. 'It's in the study, I'll show you.'

'Of course you will,' Dillon said and shoved him towards the door.

Mary taxied the Navajo along the strip and lined it up to the Conquest and the Citation. She killed the engine. Brosnan was already into the cabin and had the door open. He went down quickly and turned to give Flood a hand. Mary followed. It was very quiet, wind lifting the snow in a flurry.

'The Citation?' Mary said. 'It can't be Hernu, there hasn't been enough time.'

'It must be Aroun's,' Brosnan told her.

Flood pointed to where Dillon's footsteps, clearly visible in the snow, led towards the track to the wood, the château standing proudly on the other side. 'That's our way,' he said and started forward, Brosnan and Mary following.

FIFTEEN

The study was surprisingly small and panelled in bleached oak, the usual oil paintings of past aristocrats on the walls. There was an antique desk with a chair, an empty fireplace, a television with a fax machine and shelves lined with books on one wall.

'Hurry it up,' Dillon said and he sat on the end of the desk and lit a cigarette.

Rashid went to the fireplace and put his hand to the panelling on the right-hand side. There was obviously a hidden spring. A panel opened outwards revealing a small safe. Rashid twirled the dial in the centre backwards and forwards, then tried the handle. The safe refused to open.

Dillon said, 'You'll have to do better.'

'Just give me time.' Rashid was sweating. 'I must have got the combination wrong. Let me try again.'

He tried, pausing only to wipe sweat from his eyes with his left hand and then there was a click that even Dillon heard.

'That's it,' Rashid said.

'Good,' Dillon told him. 'Let's get on with it.' He extended his left arm, the Walther pointing at Rashid's back.

Rashid opened the safe, reached inside and turned, a Browning in his hand. Dillon shot him in the shoulder spinning him around and shot him again in the back. The young Iraqi bounced off the wall, fell to the floor and rolled on his face.

Dillon stood over him for a moment. 'You never learn, you people,' he said softly.

He looked inside the safe. There were neat stacks of hundred-dollar bills, French francs, English fifty-pound notes. He went back to the Great Hall and got his briefcase. When he came back he opened it on the desk and filled it with as much money as he could from the safe, whistling softly to himself. When the briefcase could hold no more he snapped it shut. It was at that moment he heard the front door open.

Brosnan led the way up the snow-covered steps, the Browning Mordecai had given him in his right hand. He hesitated for a moment and then tried the front door. It opened to his touch.

'Careful,' Flood said.

Brosnan peered in cautiously, taking in the vast expanse of black and white tiles, the curving stairway. 'Quiet as the grave. I'm going in.'

As he started forward, Flood said to Mary, 'Stay here for the moment,' and went after him.

The double doors to the Great Hall stood fully open and Brosnan saw Makeev's body at once. He paused, then moved inside, the Browning ready. 'He's been here, all right. I wonder who this is?'

'Another on the far side of the table,' Flood told him.

They walked round and Brosnan dropped to one knee and turned the body over. 'Well, well,' Harry Flood said. 'Even I know who that is. It's Michael Aroun.'

Mary moved into the entrance hall, closing the door behind her and watched the two men go into the Great Hall. There was a slight eerie creaking on her left and she turned and saw the open door to the study. She took the Colt .25 from her handbag and went forward.

As she approached the door, the desk came into view and she also saw Rashid's body on the floor beside it. She took a quick step inside in a kind of reflex action and Dillon moved from behind the door, tore the Colt from her hand and slipped it into a pocket.

'Well, now,' he said, 'isn't this an unexpected pleasure?' and he rammed the Walther into her side.

'But why would he kill him?' Flood asked Brosnan. 'I don't understand that.'

'Because the bastard cheated me. Because he wouldn't pay his debts.'

They turned and found Mary at the door, Dillon behind her, the Walther in his left hand, the briefcase in the other. Brosnan raised the Browning. Dillon said, 'On the floor and kick it over, Martin, or she dies. You know I mean it.'

Brosnan put the Browning down carefully then kicked it across the parquet floor.

'Good,' Dillon said. 'That's much better.' He pushed Mary towards them and sent the Browning sliding into the outer hall with the toe of his boot.

'Aroun we recognise, but as a matter of interest, who was this one?' Brosnan indicated Makeev.

'Colonel Josef Makeev, KGB, Paris station. He was the fella that got me into this. A hardliner who didn't like Gorbachev or what he's been trying to do.'

'There's another body in the study,' Mary told Brosnan.

'An Iraqi intelligence captain named Ali Rashid, Aroun's minder,' Dillon said.

'Gun for sale, is that what it's come down to, Sean?' Brosnan nodded to Aroun. 'Why did you really kill him?'

'I told you, because he wouldn't pay his debts. A matter of honour, Martin, I always keep my word, you know that. He didn't. How in the hell did you find me?'

'A lady called Myra Harvey had you followed last night. That led us to Cadge End. You're getting careless, Sean.'

'So it would seem. If it's any consolation to you, the only reason we didn't blow the entire British War Cabinet to hell was because you and your friends got too close. That pushed me into doing things in a hurry, always fatal. Danny wanted to fit stabilising fins on those oxygen cylinders that we used as mortar bombs. It would have made all the difference as regards their accuracy, but there wasn't time, thanks to you.'

'I'm delighted to hear it,' Brosnan said.

'And how did you find me here?'

'That poor, wretched young woman told us,' Mary said.

'Angel? I'm sorry about her. A nice kid.'

'And Danny Fahy and Grant at the airfield? You're sorry about them too?' Brosnan demanded.

'They shouldn't have joined.'

'Belfast and the Tommy McGuire shooting, it was you?' Mary said.

'One of my better performances.'

'And you didn't come back on the London plane,' she added. 'Am I right?'

'I flew to Glasgow, then got the shuttle to London from there.'

'So what happens now?' Brosnan asked.

'To me?' Dillon held up the briefcase. 'I've got a rather large sum in cash that was in Aroun's safe in here and a choice of airplanes. The world's my oyster. Anywhere, but Iraq.'

'And us?' Harry Flood looked ill, his face drawn with pain and he eased his left arm in the sling.

'Yes, what about us?' Mary demanded. 'You've killed everyone else, what's three more?'

'But I don't have any choice,' Dillon said patiently.

'No, but I do, you bastard.'

Harry Flood's right hand slipped inside the sling, pulled out the Walther he had been concealing in there and shot him twice in the heart. Dillon staggered back against the panelling, dropping his briefcase and slid to the floor, turning over in a kind of convulsion. Suddenly he was still and lay there, face down, the Walther with the Carswell silencer still clutched in his left hand.

Ferguson was in his car and halfway back to London when Mary called him using the phone in Aroun's study.

'We got him, sir,' she said simply when he replied.

'Tell me about it.'

So she did, Michael Aroun, Makeev, Ali Rashid, everything. When she was finished, she said, 'So that's it, sir.'

'So it would appear. I'm on my way back to London, just passed through Epsom. I left Detective Inspector Lane to clear things up at Cadge End.'

'What now, Brigadier?'

'Get back on your plane and leave at once. French territory, remember. I'll speak to Hernu now. He'll take care of it. Now go and get your plane. Contact me in mid-flight and I'll give you landing arrangements.'

The moment she was off the line he phoned Hernu's office at DGSE headquarters. It was Savary who answered. 'Ferguson here, have you got an arrival time for Colonel Hernu at St Denis?'

'The weather isn't too good down there, Brigadier.

270

They're landing at Maupertus Airport at Cherbourg and will proceed onwards by road.'

'Well, what he's going to find there rivals the last act of *Macbeth*,' Ferguson said, 'so let me explain and you can forward the information.'

Visibility was no more than a hundred yards at the airstrip, mist drifting in from the sea as Mary Tanner taxied the Navajo to the end of the runway, Brosnan sitting beside her. Flood leaned over from his seat to peer into the cockpit.

'Are you sure we can make it?' he asked.

'It's landing in this stuff that's the problem, not taking off,' she said and took the Navajo forward into the grey wall. She pulled the column back and started to climb and gradually left the mist behind and turned out to sea, levelling at nine thousand feet. After a while she put on the automatic pilot and sat back.

'You all right?' Brosnan asked.

'Fine. Slightly drained, that's all. He was so – so elemental. I can't believe he's gone.'

'He's gone all right,' Flood said cheerfully, a half-bottle of Scotch in one hand, a plastic cup held awkwardly in the other, for he had discovered the Navajo's bar box.

'I thought you never drank?' Brosnan said.

'Special occasion.' Flood raised his cup. 'Here's to Dillon. May he roast in hell.'

Dillon was aware of voices, the front door closing. When he surfaced it was like coming back from death to life. The pain in his chest was excruciating, but that was hardly surprising. The shock effect of being hit at such close quarters was considerable. He examined the two ragged holes in his biker's jacket and unzipped it, putting the Walther on the floor. The bullets Flood had fired at him were embedded in the titanium and nylon vest Tania had given him that first night. He unfastened the Velcro tabs, pulled the vest away and threw it down, then he picked up the Walther and stood.

He'd been genuinely unconscious for a while, but that was a common experience when shot at close quarters and wearing any kind of body armour. He went to the drinks cabinet and poured a brandy, looking round the room at the bodies, his briefcase still on the floor where he had dropped it and when he heard the roar of the Navajo's engine starting up, he saw it all. Everything was being left to the French, which was logical. It was their patch after all and that probably meant Hernu and the boys from Action Service were on their way.

Time to go, but how? He poured another brandy and thought about it. There was Michael Aroun's Citation jet, but where could he fly without leaving some sort of trail? No, the best answer, as usual, was Paris. He'd always been able to fade into the woodwork there. There was the barge and the apartment over the warehouse at rue de Helier. Everything he would ever need.

He finished the brandy, picked up the briefcase and hesitated, looking down at the titanium waistcoat with the two rounds embedded in it. He smiled and said softly, 'You can chew on that, Martin.'

He pulled the French windows wide and stood on the terrace for a moment, breathing deeply on the cold air, then he went down the steps to the lawn and walked quickly across to the trees, whistling softly.

Mary tuned her radio to the frequency Ferguson had given her. She was picked up by the radio room at the Ministry of Defence immediately, a sophisticated scrambling device was brought into operation and then she was patched through to him.

'Well out over the Channel, sir, heading for home.'

'We'll make that Gatwick,' he said. 'They'll be expecting you. Hernu has just phoned me from his car on the way to St Denis. Exactly as I thought. The French don't want this kind of mess on their patch. Aroun, Rashid and Makeev died in a car crash, Dillon goes straight into a pauper's grave. No name, just a number. Similar sort of thing at our end over that chap Grant.'

'But how, sir?'

'One of our doctors has already been alerted to certify him as having died of a heart attack. We've had our own establishment to handle this sort of thing since the Second World War. Quiet Street in North London. Has its own crematorium. Grant will be five pounds of grey ash by tomorrow. No autopsy.'

'But Jack Harvey?'

'That's slightly different. He and young Billy Watson are still with us, in bed at a private nursing home in Hampstead. Special Branch are keeping an eye on them.'

'Do I get the impression that we're not going to do anything?'

'No need. Harvey doesn't want to do twenty years in prison for working with the IRA. He and his motley crew will keep their mouths shut. So, by the way, will the KGB.'

'And Angel?'

'I thought she might come and stay with you for a while. I'm sure you can handle her, my dear. The woman's touch and all that.' There was a pause and then he said, 'Don't you see, Mary, it never happened, not any of it.'

'That's it then, sir?'

'That's it, Mary, see you soon.'

Brosnan said, 'What did the old sod have to say?'

So she told them. When she was finished, Flood laughed out loud. 'So it never happened? That's marvellous.'

Mary said, 'What now, Martin?'

'God knows.' He leaned back and closed his eyes.

She turned to Harry Flood who toasted her and emptied his cup. 'Don't ask me,' he said.

She sighed, switched off the auto pilot, took control of the plane herself and flew onwards towards the English coast.

Ferguson, writing quickly, completed his report and closed the file. He got up and walked to the window. It was snowing again as he looked out to the left towards the junction of Horse Guards Avenue and Whitehall where it had all happened. He was tired, more tired than he had been in a long time, but there was still one thing to do. He turned back to his desk, was reaching for the scrambler phone when it rang.

Hernu said, 'Charles, I'm at St Denis and we've got trouble.'

'Tell me,' Ferguson said and already his stomach was hollow.

'Three bodies only. Makeev, Rashid and Michael Aroun.'

'And Dillon?'

'No sign, just a very fancy bulletproof vest on the floor with two Walther rounds embedded in it.'

'Oh, my God,' Ferguson said, 'the bastard's still out there.'

'I'm afraid so, Charles. I'll put the word out to the police, of course, and all the usual agencies, but I can't say I'm particularly hopeful.'

'Why would you be?' Ferguson asked. 'We haven't succeeded in putting a hand on Dillon in twenty years so why should it be any different now?' He took a deep breath. 'All right, Max, I'll be in touch.'

He went back to the window and stood looking out at the falling snow. No point in calling the Navajo. Mary, Brosnan and Flood would hear the bad news soon enough, but there was still one thing to be done. He turned reluctantly to his desk, picked up the scrambler, pausing for only a moment before phoning Downing Street and asking to speak to the Prime Minister.

It was towards evening, snow falling heavily as Pierre Savigny, a farmer from the village of St Just outside Bayeux drove carefully along the main road towards Caen in his old Citroën truck. He almost didn't see the man in biker's leathers who stepped into the road, an arm raised.

The Citroën skidded to a halt and Dillon opened the passenger door and smiled. 'Sorry about that,' he said in his impeccable French, 'but I've been walking for quite a while.'

'And where would you be going on a filthy evening like this?' Savigny asked as Dillon climbed into the passenger seat.

'Caen. I'm hoping to catch the night train to Paris. My motorbike broke down. I had to leave it in a garage in Bayeux.'

'Then you're in luck, my friend,' Savigny said. 'I'm on my way to Caen now. Potatoes for tomorrow's market.' He moved into gear and drove away.

'Excellent.' Dillon put a cigarette in his mouth, flicked his lighter and sat there, the briefcase on his knees.

'You're a tourist then, monsieur?' Savigny asked as he increased speed.

Sean Dillon smiled softly. 'Not really,' he said. 'Just passing through,' and he leaned back in the seat and closed his eyes.

JACK HIGGINS

The world's master thriller writer

THUNDER POINT

St John, the Virgin Islands, 1992…

The lone diver's treasure was priceless: a German U-Boat, sunk in American waters – three weeks after the end of the war. Inside: *the Third Reich's hideous secrets intact…*

Among them: the names of the British Nazi sympathizers – some of them pillars of the Establishment – and the devastating document known as the Windsor Protocol…

Read on for a preview of THUNDER POINT, the brilliant new thriller by Jack Higgins, published by Michael Joseph in hardback.

ONE

J UST BEFORE MIDNIGHT it started to rain as Dillon pulled in
the Mercedes at the side of the road, switched on the interior
light and checked his map. Klagenfurt was twenty miles
behind which meant that the Yugoslavian border must be
very close now. There was a road sign a few yards further on
and he took a torch from the glove compartment, got out of
the car and walked towards it, whistling softly, a small man,
no more than five feet four or five with hair so fair that it
was almost white. He wore an old black leather flying jacket
with a white scarf at his throat and dark blue jeans. The sign
showed Fehring to the right and five kilometres further on.
He showed no emotion, simply took a cigarette from a silver
case, lit it with an old-fashioned Zippo lighter and returned
to the car.

It was raining very heavily now, the road badly surfaced,
mountains rising to his right and he switched on the radio
and listened to a little night music, occasionally whistling the
tune until he came to gates on the left and slowed to read the
sign. It badly needed a fresh coat of paint, but the inscription
was clear enough. Fehring Aero Club. He turned in through
the gates and followed a track, lurching over potholes until
he saw the airfield below.

He switched off his lights and paused. It seemed a poor sort
of place, a couple of hangars, three huts and a rickety excuse
for a control tower, but there was light streaming out from
one of the hangars and from the windows of the end hut. He

moved into neutral, eased off the brake and let the Mercedes run down the hill silently, coming to a halt on the far side of the runway from the hangars. He sat there thinking about things for a moment then took a Walther PPK and black leather gloves from the attaché case on the seat next to him. He checked the Walther, slipped it into his waistband at the rear then pulled on the gloves as he started across the runway in the rain.

The hangar was old and smelled of damp as if not used in years, but the aeroplane that stood there in the dim light looked well enough, a Cessna 441 Conquest with twin turboprop engines. A mechanic in overalls had the cowling on the port engine open and stood on a ladder working on it. The cabin door was open, the stairs down and two men loaded boxes inside.

As they emerged, one of them called in German, 'We're finished, Doctor Wegner.'

A bearded man emerged from the small office in one corner of the hangar. He wore a hunting jacket, the fur collar turned up against the cold.

'All right, you can go.' As they walked away he said to the mechanic, 'Any problems, Tomic?'

'No big deal, Herr Doctor, just fine tuning.'

'Which won't mean a thing unless this damn man Dillon turns up.' As Wegner turned, a young man came in, the woollen cap and reefer coat he wore beaded with rain.

'He'll be here,' Wegner told him. 'I was told he could never resist a challenge, this one.'

'A mercenary,' the young man said. 'That's what we've come down to. The kind of man who kills people for money.'

'There are children dying over there,' Wegner said, 'And they need what's on that plane. To achieve that I'd deal with the Devil himself.'

'Which you'll probably have to.'

'Not kind,' Dillon called in excellent German. 'Not kind at all,' and he stepped out of the darkness at the end of the hangar.

The young man put a hand in his pocket and Dillon's Walther appeared fast. 'Plain view, son, plain view.'

Dillon walked forward, swung the young man round and extracted a Mauser from his right-hand pocket. 'Would you look at that now? You can't trust a soul these days.'

Wegner said in English, 'Mr Dillon? Mr Sean Dillon?'

'So they tell me.' Dillon slipped the Mauser into his hip pocket, took out his silver case one-handed, still holding the Walther and managed to extract a cigarette. 'And who might you be, me old son?' His speech had the hard distinctive edge to it that was found only in Ulster and not in the Republic of Ireland.

'I am Dr Hans Wegner of International Drug Relief and this is Klaus Schmidt from our office in Vienna. He arranged the plane for us.'

'Did he now? That's something to be said in his favour.' Dillon took the Mauser from his hip pocket and handed it back. 'Doing good is all very fine, but playing with guns when you don't know how is a mug's game.'

The young man flushed deeply, took the Mauser and put it in his pocket and Wegner said mildly, 'Herr Schmidt has made the run by road twice with medical supplies.'

'Then why not this time?' Dillon asked, slipping the Walther back in his waistband.

'Because that part of Croatia is disputed territory now,' Schmidt said. 'There's heavy fighting between Serbs and Moslems and Croats.'

'I see,' Dillon said. 'So I'm to manage by air what you can't by road?'

'Mr Dillon, it's a hundred and twenty miles to Sabac from here and the airstrip is still open. Believe it or not, but the phone system still works quite well over there. I'm given to understand that this plane is capable of more than three hundred miles an hour. That means you could be there in twenty minutes or so.'

Dillon laughed out loud 'Would you listen to the man? It's plain to see you don't know the first thing about flying a plane.' He saw that the mechanic high on his ladder was smiling. 'Ah, so you speak English, old son.'

'A little.'

'Tomic is a Croatian,' Dr Wegner said.

Dillon looked up 'What do you think?'

Tomic said, 'I was in the Air Force for seven years. I know Sabac. It's an emergency strip, but a sound asphalt runway.'

'And the flight?'

'Well, if you're just some private pilot out here to do a bit of good in this wicked world you won't last twenty miles.'

Dillon said softly 'Let's just say I've seldom done a good thing in my life and I'm not that kind of pilot. What's the terrain like?'

'Mountainous in parts, heavily forested and the weather forecast stinks, I checked it myself earlier, but it's not only that, it's the Air Force, they still patrol the area regularly.'

'Mig fighters?' Dillon asked.

'That's right.' Tomic slapped the wing of the Conquest with one hand. 'A nice aeroplane, but no match for a Mig.' He shook his head. 'But maybe you've got a death wish.'

'That's enough, Tomic,' Wegner said angrily.

'Oh, it's been said before.' Dillon laughed. 'But let's get on. I'd better look at the charts.'

As they moved towards the office Wegner said, 'Our people in Vienna did make it plain. Your services are purely voluntary We need all the money we can raise for the drugs and medical supplies.'

'Understood,' Dillon said.

They went into the office where a number of charts were spread across the desk. Dillon started to examine them.

'When would you leave?' Wegner asked.

'Just before dawn,' Dillon told him. 'Best time of all and least active. I hope the rain keeps up.'

Schmidt, genuinely curious, said, 'Why would you do this? I don't understand. A man like you.' He seemed suddenly awkward. 'I mean, we know something of your background.'

'Do you now?' Dillon said. 'Well, as the good doctor said, I find it hard to resist a challenge.'

'And for this you would risk your life?'

'Ah, sure and I was forgetting.' Dillon looked up and smiled and an astonishing change came to his face, nothing but warmth and great charm there. 'I should also mention that I'm the last of the World's great adventurers. Now leave me be like a good lad and let me see where I'm going.'

He leaned over the charts and started to examine them intently.

Just before five the rain was as relentless as ever, the darkness as impenetrable as Dillon stood in the entrance of the hangar and peered out. Wegner and Schmidt approached him.

The older man said, 'Can you really take off in weather like this?'

'The problem is landing, not taking off.' Dillon called to Tomic, 'How are things?'

Tomic emerged from the cabin, jumped to the ground and came towards them wiping his hands on a rag. 'Everything in perfect working order.'

Dillon offered him a cigarette and glanced out. 'And this?'

Tomic peered up into the darkness. 'It'll get worse before it gets better and you'll find ground mist over there, especially over the forest, mark my words.'

'Ah, well, better get on with it as the thief said to the hangman.' Dillon crossed to the Conquest.

He went up the steps and examined the interior. All the seats had been removed and it was stacked with long olive green boxes. Each one was stencilled in English: Royal Army Medical Corps.

Schmidt, who had joined him, said, 'As you can see we get our supplies from unusual sources.'

'You can say that again. What's in these?'

'See for yourself.' Schmidt unclipped the nearest one, removed a sheet of oiled paper to reveal box after box of morphine ampoules. 'Over there, Mr Dillon, they sometimes have to hold children down when they operate on them because of the lack of any kind of anaesthetic. These prove a highly satisfactory substitute.'

'Point taken,' Dillon said. 'Now close it up and I'll get moving.'

Schmidt did as he was told, then jumped to the ground. As Dillon pulled up the steps Wegner said, 'God go with you, Mr Dillon.'

'There's always that chance,' Dillon said. 'It's probably the first time I've done anything he'd approve of,' and he closed the door and clamped it in place.

He settled into the left hand pilot's seat, fired the port engine and after that the starboard. The chart was next to him on the other seat, but he had already pretty well committed it to memory. He paused on the apron outside the hangar, rain streaming from his windscreen, did a thorough cockpit check then strapped in and taxied to the end of the runway, turning into the wind. He glanced across to the three men standing in the hangar entrance, raised a thumb then started forward, his engine roar deepening as he boosted power. Within a second or two he had disappeared, the sound of the engines already fading.

Wegner ran a hand over his face. 'God, but I'm tired.' He turned to Tomic. 'Has he a chance?'

Tomic shrugged. 'Quite a man, that one. Who knows?'

Schmidt said, 'Let's get some coffee. We're going to have a long wait.'

Tomic said, 'I'll join you in a minute. I just want to clear my tools away.'

They crossed towards the end hut. He watched them go, waited until they'd gone inside before turning and swiftly crossing to the office. He picked up the telephone and dialled a lengthy series of numbers. As the good doctor had said, the telephone system still worked surprisingly well over there.

When a voice answered he spoke in Serbo-Croat. 'This is Tomic, get me Major Branko.'

There was an instant response. 'Branko here.'

'Tomic. I'm at the airfield at Fehring and I've got traffic for you. Cessna Conquest just left, destination Sabac. Here is his radio frequency.'

'Is the pilot anyone we know?'

'Name of Dillon – Sean Dillon. Irish, I believe. Small man, very fair hair, late thirties I'd say. Doesn't look much. Nice smile, but the eyes tell a different story.'

'I'll have him checked out through Central Intelligence, but you've done well, Tomic We'll give him a warm welcome.'

The phone clicked and Tomic replaced the receiver. He took out a packet of the vile Macedonian cigarettes he affected and lit one. Pity about Dillon. He'd rather liked the Irishman, but that was life and he started to put his tools away methodically.

And Dillon was already in trouble, not only thick cloud and the constant driving rain, but even at a thousand feet a swirling mist that gave only an intermittent view of pine forest below.

'And what in the hell are you doing here, old son?' he asked softly. 'What are you trying to prove?'

He got a cigarette out of his case, lit it and a voice spoke in his earphones in heavily accented English, 'Good morning, Mr Dillon, welcome to Yugoslavia.'

The plane took station to starboard not too far away, the

red stars on its fuselage clear enough, a Mig 21, the old Fishbed, probably the Soviet jet most widely distributed to its allies. Outdated now, but not as far as Dillon was concerned.

The Mig pilot spoke again. 'Course one-two-four, Mr Dillon. We'll come to a rather picturesque castle at the edge of the forest, Kivo it's called, Intelligence Headquarters for this area. There's an airstrip there and they're expecting you. They might even arrange a full English breakfast.'

'Irish,' Dillon said cheerfully. 'A full Irish breakfast and who am I to refuse an offer like that? One-two-four it is.'

He turned on to the new course, climbing to two thousand feet as the weather cleared a little, whistling softly to himself. A Serbian prison did not commend itself, not if the stories reaching Western Europe were even partly true, but in the circumstances, he didn't seem to have any choice and then, a couple of miles away on the edge of the forest beside a river he saw Kivo, a fairytale castle of towers and battlements surrounded by a moat, the airstrip clear beside it.

'What do you think?' the Mig pilot asked. 'Nice, isn't it?'

'Straight out of a story by the Brothers Grimm,' Dillon answered. 'All we need is the ogre.'

'Oh, we have that too, Mr Dillon. Now put down nice and easy and I'll say goodbye.'

Dillon looked down into the interior of the castle, noticed soldiers moving towards the edge of the airstrip preceded by a jeep and sighed. He said into his mike, 'I'd like to say it's been a good life, but then there are those difficult days, like this morning for instance. I mean, why did I even get out of bed?'

He heaved the control column right back and boosted power, climbing fast and the Mig pilot reacted angrily. 'Dillon, do as you're told or I'll blast you out of the sky.'

Dillon ignored him, levelling out at five thousand, searching the sky for any sign and the Mig, already on his tail, came up behind and fired. The Conquest staggered as cannon shell tore through both wings.

'Dillon – don't be a fool!' the pilot cried.

'Ah, but then I always was.'

Dillon went down fast, levelling at two thousand feet over the edge of the forest, aware of vehicles moving from the direction of the castle. The Mig came in again firing his machine guns now and the Conquest's windscreen disintegrated, wind and rain roaring in. Dillon sat there, hands firm on the control column, blood on his face from a glass splinter.

'Now then,' he said into his mike. 'Let's see how good you are.'

He dropped the nose and went straight down, the pine forest waiting for him below and the Mig went after him, firing again. The Conquest bucked, the port engine dying as Dillon levelled out at four hundred feet and behind him the Mig, no time to pull out at the speed it was doing, ploughed into the forest and fireballed.

Dillon, trimming as best he could for flying on one engine, lost power and dropped lower. There was a clearing up ahead and to his left. He tried to bank towards it, was already losing height as he clipped the tops of the pine trees. He cut power instantly and braced himself for the crash. In the end, it was the pine trees which saved him, retarding his progress so much that by the time he hit the clearing for a belly landing, he wasn't actually going all that fast.

The Conquest bounced twice, and came to a shuddering halt. Dillon released his straps, scrambled out of his seat and had the door open in an instant. He was out head first, rolling over in the rain and on his feet and running, his right ankle twisting so that he fell on his face again. He scrambled up and limped away as fast as he could, but the Conquest didn't burst into flame, it simply crouched there in the rain as if tired.

There was thick black smoke above the trees from the burning Mig and then soldiers appeared on the other side of the clearing. A jeep moved out of the trees behind them, top down and Dillon could see an officer standing up in it wearing a winter campaign coat, Russian-style, with a fur collar. More soldiers appeared, some of them with Dobermans, all barking loudly and straining against their leashes.

It was enough. Dillon turned to hobble into the trees and his leg gave out on him. A voice on a loudhailer called in English, 'Oh, come now, Mr Dillon, be sensible, you don't want me to set the dogs on you.'

Dillon paused, balanced on one foot, then he turned and hobbled to the nearest tree and leaned against it. He took a cigarette from his silver case, the last one, and lit it. The smoke tasted good as it bit at the back of his throat and he waited for them.

They stood in a semi-circle, soldiers in baggy tunics, guns covering him, the dogs howling against being restrained. The jeep rolled to a halt and the officer, a major from his shoulder boards, stood up and looked down at him, a good looking man of about thirty with a dark saturnine face.

'So, Mr Dillon, you made it in one piece,' he said in faultless Public School English. 'I congratulate you. My name, by the way, is Branko – John Branko. My mother was English, is, I should say. Lives in Hampstead.'

'Is that a fact.' Dillon smiled. 'A desperate bunch of rascals you've got here, Major, but *Cead mile failte* anyway.'

'And what would that mean, Mr Dillon?'

'Oh, that's Irish for a hundred thousand welcomes.'

'What a charming sentiment.' Branko turned and spoke in Serbo Croat to the large, brutal-looking sergeant who sat behind him clutching an AK assault rifle. The sergeant smiled, jumped to the ground and advanced on Dillon.

Major Branko said, 'Allow me to introduce you to my Sergeant Zekan. I've just told him to offer you a hundred thousand welcomes to Yugoslavia or Serbia as we prefer to say now.'

Dillon knew what was coming, but there wasn't a thing he

could do. The butt of the AK caught him in the left side, driving the wind from him as he keeled over, the sergeant lifted a knee in his face. The last thing Dillon remembered was the dogs barking, the laughter and then there was only darkness.

When Sergeant Zekan took Dillon along the corridor, someone screamed in the distance and there was the sound of heavy blows. Dillon hesitated but the sergeant showed no emotion, simply put a hand between the Irishman's shoulder-blades and pushed him towards a flight of stone steps and urged him up. There was an oaken door at the top banded with iron. Zekan opened it and pushed him through.

The room inside was oak beamed with granite walls, tapestries hanging here and there. A log fire burned in an open hearth and two of the Dobermans sprawled in front of it. Branko sat behind a large desk reading a file and drinking from a crystal glass, a bottle in an ice-bucket beside him. He glanced up and smiled, then took the bottle from the ice-bucket and filled another glass.

'Krug champagne, Mr Dillon, your preferred choice, I understand.'

'Is there anything you don't know about me?' Dillon asked.

'Not much.' Branko lifted the file then dropped it on the desk. 'The Intelligence organizations of most countries have the useful habit of frequently co-operating with each other even when their countries don't. Do sit down and have a drink. You'll feel better.'

Dillon took the chair opposite and accepted the glass that Zekan handed him. He emptied it in one go and Branko smiled, took a cigarette from a packet of Rothmans and tossed it across.

'Help yourself.' He reached out and refilled Dillon's glass. 'I much prefer the non-vintage, don't you?'

'It's the grape mix,' Dillon said and lit the cigarette.

'Sorry about that little touch of violence back there,' Branko told him. 'Just a show for my boys. After all you did cost us that Mig and it takes two years to train the pilots. I should know, I'm one myself.'

'Really?' Dillon said.

'Yes, Cranwell, courtesy of your British Royal Air Force.'

'Not mine,' Dillon told him.

'But you were born in Ulster, I understand. Belfast, is that not so and Belfast, as I understand it, is part of Great Britain and not the Republic of Ireland.'

'A debatable point,' Dillon said. 'Let's say I'm Irish and leave it at that.' He swallowed some more champagne. 'Who dropped me in it? Wegner or Schmidt?' He frowned. 'No, of course not. Just a couple of do-gooders. Tomic. It would be Tomic, am I right?'

'A good Serb.' Branko poured a little more champagne. 'How on earth did you get into this, a man like you?'

'You mean you don't know?'

'I'll be honest, Mr Dillon. I knew you were coming, but no more than that.'

'I was in Vienna for a few days to sample a little opera. I'm partial to Mozart. Bumped into a man I'd had dealings with over the years in the bar during the first interval. Told me he'd been approached by this organization who needed a little help, but were short on money.'

'Ah, I see now.' Branko nodded. 'A good deed in a naughty world as Shakespeare put it? All those poor little children crying out for help? The cruel Serbs.'

'God help me, Major, but you have a way with the words.'

'A sea-change for a man like you I would have thought.' Branko opened the file. 'Sean Dillon, born Belfast, went to live in London when you were a boy, father a widower. A student of the Royal Academy of Dramatic Art at eighteen, even acted with the National Theatre. Your father returned to Belfast in 1971 and was killed by British paratroopers.'

'You *are* well informed.'

'You joined the Provisional IRA, trained in Libya courtesy of Colonel Gadaffi and never looked back.' Branko turned a page. 'You finally broke with the IRA. Some disagreement as to strategy.'

'Bunch of old women.' Dillon reached across and helped himself to more Krug.

'Beirut, the PLO, even the KGB. You really do believe in spreading your services around.' Branko laughed suddenly in a kind of amazement. 'The underwater attack on those two Palestinian gunboats in Beirut in 1990. You were responsible for that? But that was for the Israelis.'

'I charge very reasonable rates,' Dillon said.

'Fluent German, Spanish and French, oh, and Irish.'

'We mustn't forget that.'

'Reasonable Arabic, Italian and Russian.' Branko closed the file. 'Is it true you were responsible for the mortar attack on No. 10 Downing Street during the Gulf War when the British Prime Minister, John Major, was meeting with the War Cabinet?'

'Now do I look as if I'd do a thing like that?'

Branko leaned back and looked at him seriously. 'How do you see yourself, my friend, gun for hire like one of those old Westerns, riding into town to clean things up single-handed?'

'To be honest, Major, I never think about it.'

'And yet you took on a job like this present affair for a bunch of well-meaning amateurs and for no pay?'

'We all make mistakes.'

'You certainly did, my friend. Those boxes on the plane. Morphine ampoules on top, Stinger missiles underneath.'

'Jesus.' Dillon laughed helplessly. 'Now who would have thought it.'

'They say you have a genius for acting, that you can change yourself totally, become another person with a look, a gesture.'

'No, I think that was Laurence Olivier.' Dillon smiled.

'And in twenty years, you've never seen the inside of a cell.'

'True.'

'Not any longer, my friend.' Branko opened a drawer, took out a two hundred pack of Rothmans cigarettes and tossed them across. 'You're going to need those.' He glanced at Zekan and said in Serbo Croat, 'Take him to his cell.'

Dillon felt the sergeant's hand on his shoulder pulling him up and propelling him to the door. As Zekan opened it Branko said, 'One more thing, Mr Dillon. The firing squad operates most mornings here Try not to let it put you off.'

'Ah, yes.' Dillon said. 'Ethnic cleansing, isn't that what you call it?'

'The reason is much simpler than that. We just get short of space. Sleep well.'

They went up a flight of stone steps Zekan pushing Dillon ahead of him He pulled him to a halt outside an oak door on the passageway at the top, took out a key and unlocked it. He inclined his head and stood to one side and Dillon entered. The room was quite large There was an army cot in one corner, a tablet chair, books on a shelf and incredibly, an old toilet in a cubicle in one corner. Dillon went to the window and peered through bars to the courtyard eighty feet below and the pine forest in the near distance.

He turned 'This must be one of your better rooms. What's the catch?' Then realized he was wasting his time for the sergeant had no English

As if perfectly understanding him Zekan smiled. showing bad teeth, took Dillon's silver case and Zippo lighter from a pocket and laid them carefully on the table. He withdrew, closing the door, and the key rattled in the lock

Dillon went to the window and tried the bars, but they seemed firm Too far down anyway. He opened one of the packs of Rothmans and lit one One thing was certain. Branko was being excessively kind and there had to be a reason for that. He went and lay on the bed, smoking his cigarette, staring up at the ceiling and thinking about it.

In 1972, aware of the growing problem of terrorism and its effect on so many aspects of life at both political and national level, the British Prime Minister of the day ordered the setting up of a small elite Intelligence unit, known simply by the code name Group Four. It was to handle all matters concerning terrorism and subversion in the British Isles. Known rather bitterly in more conventional Intelligence circles as the Prime Minister's private army, it owed allegiance to that office alone.

Brigadier Charles Ferguson had headed Group Four since its inception, had served a number of Prime Ministers, both Conservative and Labour, and had no political allegiance whatsoever. He had an office on the third floor of the Ministry of Defence overlooking Horseguards Avenue, and was still working at his desk at nine o'clock that night when there was a knock at the door.

'Come in,' Ferguson said, stood up and walked to the window, a large, rather untidy looking man with a double chin and grey hair who wore a baggy suit and a Guards tie.

As he peered out at the rain towards Victoria Embankment and the Thames the door opened behind him. The man who entered was in his late thirties, wore a tweed suit and glasses. He could have been a clerk, or even a schoolmaster, but Detective Inspector Jack Lane was neither of these things. He was a cop. Not an ordinary one, but a cop all the same and after some negotiating, Ferguson had succeeded in borrowing him from Special Branch at Scotland Yard to act as his personal assistant.

'Got something for me, Jack?' Ferguson's voice was ever so slightly plummy.

'Mainly routine, Brigadier. The word is that the Director General of the Security Services is still unhappy at the Prime

Minister's refusal to do away with Group Four's special status.'

'Good God, don't they ever give up those people? I've agreed to keep them informed on a need-to-know basis and to liaise with Simon Carter, the Deputy Director, and that damned MP, the one with the fancy title. Extra Minister at the Home Office.'

'Sir Francis Pamer, sir.'

'Yes, well that's all the co-operation they're going to get out of me. Anything else?'

Lane smiled. 'Actually, I've saved the best bit till last. Dillon – Sean Dillon?'

Ferguson turned. 'What about him?'

'Had a signal from our contacts in Yugoslavia. Dillon crashed in a light plane this morning, supposedly flying in medical supplies only they turned out to be Stinger missiles. They're holding him in that castle at Kivo. It's all here.'

He passed a sheet of paper across and Ferguson put on half-moon spectacles and studied it. He nodded in satisfaction. 'Twenty years and the bastard never saw the inside of a prison cell.'

'Well he's in one now, sir. I've got his record here. if you want to look at it.'

'And why would I want to do that? No use to anyone now You know what the Serbs are like, Jack. Might as well stick it in the dead letter file. Oh, you can go home now.'

'Good night, sir.'

Lane went out and Ferguson crossed to his drinks cabinet and poured a large Scotch 'Here's to you, Dillon,' he said softly 'And you can chew on that, you bastard.'

He swallowed the whisky down, returned to his desk and started to work again.

LA CINQUIÈME MONTAGNE

Marie, conçue sans péché, Priez pour nous
qui faisons appel à vous, Amen.

PAULO COELHO

La Cinquième Montagne

TRADUIT DU PORTUGAIS (BRÉSIL)
PAR FRANÇOISE MARCHAND-SAUVAGNARGUES

ÉDITIONS ANNE CARRIÈRE

Titre original :

A QUINTA MONTANHA

Cette édition a été publiée avec l'accord de
Sant Jordi Asociados, Barcelone, Espagne.

© 1998 Paulo Coelho
© Editions Anne Carrière, Paris, 1998,
pour la traduction française
ISBN : 978-2-253-14710-7 - 1ʳᵉ publication - LGF

À A. M., guerrier de la lumière

Note de l'auteur

La thèse centrale de mon livre *L'Alchimiste* réside dans une phrase que le roi Melchisédech adresse au berger Santiago : « Quand tu veux quelque chose, tout l'univers conspire à te permettre de réaliser ton désir. »

Je crois entièrement à cette affirmation. Cependant, l'acte de vivre son destin comporte une série d'étapes, bien au-delà de notre compréhension, dont l'objectif est de nous ramener sans cesse sur le chemin de notre Légende Personnelle — ou de nous enseigner les leçons nécessaires à l'accomplissement de ce destin. J'illustrerais mieux ce propos, me semble-t-il, en racontant un épisode de ma propre vie.

Le 12 août 1979, j'allai me coucher avec une seule certitude : à trente ans, j'atteignais le sommet de ma carrière de producteur de disques. Directeur artistique de CBS au Brésil, je venais d'être invité à me rendre aux Etats-Unis pour y rencontrer les patrons de la maison de disques et, assurément, ils allaient m'offrir les meilleures conditions pour réaliser tout ce que je désirais dans ce domaine. Bien sûr, mon grand rêve — être écrivain — avait été mis de côté, mais quelle importance ? En fin de compte, la vie réelle était très différente de celle que j'avais imaginée ; il n'y avait aucun espace pour vivre de littérature au Brésil.

Cette nuit-là, je pris une décision, et j'abandonnai mon rêve : je devais m'adapter aux circonstances et saisir les occasions. Si mon cœur protestait, je pourrais toujours le tromper en composant des textes de chansons chaque fois que je le désirerais et, de temps à autre, en signant un article dans un journal. Du reste, j'étais convaincu que ma vie avait pris une voie différente, mais non moins excitante : un avenir brillant m'attendait dans les multinationales de musique.

A mon réveil, je reçus un appel téléphonique du président : j'étais remercié, sans autre explication. J'eus beau frapper à toutes les portes au cours des deux années qui suivirent, je n'ai jamais retrouvé d'emploi dans ce domaine.

En achevant la rédaction de *La Cinquième Montagne*, je me suis souvenu de cet épisode — et d'autres manifestations de l'inévitable dans ma vie. Chaque fois que je me sentais absolument maître de la situation, un événement se produisait, et me faisait échouer. Je me suis demandé pourquoi. Etais-je condamné à toujours approcher de la ligne d'arrivée, sans jamais la franchir ? Dieu serait-il cruel au point de me faire entrevoir les palmiers à l'horizon uniquement pour me laisser mourir de soif au milieu du désert ?

J'ai mis longtemps à comprendre que l'explication était tout autre. Certains événements sont placés dans nos existences pour nous reconduire vers l'authentique chemin de notre Légende Personnelle. D'autres surgissent pour nous permettre d'appliquer tout ce que nous avons appris. Enfin, quelques-uns se produisent pour nous *enseigner* quelque chose.

Dans *Le Pèlerin de Compostelle*, j'ai tenté de montrer que ces enseignements ne sont pas nécessairement liés à la douleur et à la souffrance ; la discipline et l'attention suffisent. Bien que cette compréhension soit devenue une importante bénédiction dans ma vie, malgré toute ma discipline et toute mon attention, je n'ai pas réussi à comprendre certains moments difficiles par lesquels je suis passé.

L'anecdote que j'ai relatée en est un exemple : j'étais un bon professionnel alors, je m'efforçais de donner ce qu'il y avait de meilleur en moi, et j'avais des idées qu'aujourd'hui encore je considère bonnes. Mais l'inévitable a surgi, au moment précis où je me sentais le plus sûr et le plus confiant. Je pense que cette expérience n'est pas unique ; l'inévitable a frappé la vie de tous les êtres humains à la surface de la Terre. Certains se sont rétablis, d'autres ont cédé — mais nous avons tous été effleurés par l'aile de la tragédie.

Pourquoi ? Pour trouver une réponse à cette question, j'ai laissé Elie me conduire par les jours et les nuits d'Akbar.

PAULO COELHO

« Et il ajouta : "Oui, je vous le déclare, aucun prophète ne trouve accueil dans sa patrie. En toute vérité, je vous le déclare, il y avait beaucoup de veuves en Israël aux jours d'Elie, quand le ciel fut fermé trois ans et six mois et que survint une grande famine sur tout le pays ; pourtant ce ne fut à aucune d'elles qu'Elie fut envoyé, mais bien dans le pays de Sidon, à une veuve de Sarepta." »

Luc, 4, 24-26

Prologue

Au commencement de l'année 870 avant Jésus-Christ, une nation connue sous le nom de Phénicie, que les Israélites appelaient Liban, commémorait presque trois siècles de paix. Ses habitants avaient de bonnes raisons de s'enorgueillir : comme ils n'étaient pas très puissants sur le plan politique, ils avaient dû mettre au point une force de négociation qui faisait des envieux, seul moyen de garantir leur survie dans un monde constamment dévasté par la guerre. Une alliance contractée aux environs de l'an 1000 avant J.-C. avec Salomon, roi d'Israël, avait favorisé la modernisation de la flotte marchande et l'expansion du commerce. Depuis lors, la Phénicie n'avait cessé de se développer.

Ses navigateurs avaient déjà atteint des régions lointaines, comme l'Espagne et les rivages baignés par l'océan Atlantique. Selon certaines théories — qui ne sont pas confirmées —, ils auraient même laissé des inscriptions dans le Nordeste et dans le sud du Brésil. Ils faisaient le négoce du verre, du bois de cèdre, des armes, du fer et de l'ivoire. Les habitants des grandes cités de Sidon, Tyr et Byblos connaissaient les nombres, les calculs astronomiques, la vinification, et ils utilisaient depuis presque deux cents ans un ensemble de caractères pour écrire, que les Grecs dénommaient *alphabet*.

Au commencement de l'année 870 avant J.-C., un conseil de guerre était réuni dans la cité lointaine de Ninive. Un groupe de généraux assyriens avait en

13

effet décidé d'envoyer des troupes conquérir les nations bordant la mer Méditerranée et, en premier lieu, la Phénicie.

Au commencement de l'année 870 avant J.-C., deux hommes, cachés dans une étable de Galaad, en Israël, s'attendaient à mourir dans les prochaines heures.

Première partie

« J'ai servi un Seigneur qui maintenant m'abandonne aux mains de mes ennemis, dit Elie.

— Dieu est Dieu, répondit le lévite. Il n'a pas expliqué à Moïse s'Il était bon ou mauvais, Il a seulement affirmé : *Je suis*. Il est tout ce qui existe sous le soleil — le tonnerre qui détruit la maison, et la main de l'homme qui la reconstruit. »

La conversation était la seule manière d'éloigner la peur ; d'un moment à l'autre, les soldats allaient ouvrir la porte de l'étable, les découvrir et leur proposer le seul choix possible : adorer Baal, le dieu phénicien, ou être exécutés. Ils fouillaient maison après maison, convertissant ou exécutant les prophètes.

Le lévite se convertirait peut-être, échappant ainsi à la mort. Mais Elie n'avait pas le choix : tout arrivait par sa faute, et Jézabel voulait sa tête de toute façon.

« C'est un ange du Seigneur qui m'a envoyé parler au roi Achab et l'avertir qu'il ne pleuvrait pas tant que Baal serait adoré en Israël », expliqua-t-il, en demandant presque pardon pour avoir écouté les paroles de l'ange. « Mais Dieu agit avec lenteur ; quand la sécheresse commencera à produire son effet, la princesse Jézabel aura détruit tous ceux qui sont restés fidèles au Seigneur. »

Le lévite resta silencieux. Il se demandait s'il devait se convertir à Baal ou mourir au nom du Seigneur.

« Qui est Dieu ? poursuivit Elie. Est-ce Lui qui tient l'épée du soldat exécutant les hommes fidèles à la foi de nos patriarches ? Est-ce Lui qui a mis une princesse étrangère sur le trône de notre pays, afin que tous ces malheurs s'abattent sur notre génération ? Est-ce Dieu qui tue les fidèles, les innocents, ceux qui suivent la loi de Moïse ? »

Le lévite prit une décision : il préférait mourir. Alors il se mit à rire, parce que l'idée de la mort ne l'effrayait plus. Il se tourna vers le jeune prophète et s'efforça de le tranquilliser :

« Demande à Dieu qui Il est, puisque tu doutes de Ses décisions. Pour ma part, j'ai déjà accepté mon destin.

— Le Seigneur ne peut pas désirer que nous soyons impitoyablement massacrés, insista Elie.

— Dieu peut tout. S'Il se limitait à faire ce que nous appelons le Bien, nous ne pourrions pas le nommer Tout-Puissant ; Il dominerait seulement une partie de l'univers, et il y aurait quelqu'un de plus puissant que Lui qui surveillerait et jugerait Ses actions. En ce cas, j'adorerais ce quelqu'un plus puissant.

— S'Il peut tout, pourquoi n'épargne-t-Il pas la souffrance à ceux qui L'aiment ? Pourquoi ne nous sauve-t-Il pas, au lieu de donner gloire et pouvoir à Ses ennemis ?

— Je l'ignore, répondit le lévite. Mais il y a à cela une raison, et j'espère la connaître bientôt.

— Tu n'as pas de réponse à cette question.

— Non. »

Ils restèrent tous deux silencieux. Elie avait des sueurs froides.

« Tu as peur, mais moi j'ai accepté mon destin, commenta le lévite. Je vais sortir et mettre fin à cette agonie. Chaque fois que j'entends un cri là-dehors, je souffre en imaginant ce qui se passera lorsque mon heure viendra. Depuis que nous sommes enfermés ici, je suis mort une bonne centaine de fois, et j'aurais pu mourir une seule fois. Puisque je vais être égorgé, que ce soit le plus vite possible. »

Il avait raison. Elie avait entendu les mêmes cris et il avait déjà souffert au-delà de sa capacité de résistance.

« Je t'accompagne. Je suis fatigué de lutter pour quelques heures de vie supplémentaires. »

Il se leva et ouvrit la porte de l'étable, laissant la lumière du soleil révéler la présence des deux hommes qui y étaient cachés.

*

Le lévite le prit par le bras et ils se mirent en marche. A l'exception de quelques cris, on aurait dit un jour normal dans une cité pareille à n'importe quelle autre — un soleil pas trop brûlant, la brise venant de l'océan au loin, rendant la température agréable, les rues poussiéreuses, les maisons faites d'argile mélangée à de la paille.

« Nos âmes sont prisonnières de la terreur de la mort, et c'est une belle journée, dit le lévite. Bien souvent, alors que je me sentais en paix avec Dieu et avec le monde, la chaleur était insupportable, le vent du désert emplissait mes yeux de sable et ne me laissait pas voir à deux pas. Le plan de Dieu ne correspond pas toujours à ce que nous sommes ou sentons ; mais je suis certain qu'Il a une raison pour tout cela.

— J'admire ta foi. »

Le lévite regarda vers le ciel, comme s'il réfléchissait. Puis il se tourna vers Elie :

« N'admire pas, et ne crois pas autant : c'est un pari que j'ai fait avec moi-même. J'ai parié que Dieu existe.

— Tu es un prophète, répliqua Elie. Tu as aussi entendu des voix, et tu sais qu'il existe un monde au-delà de ce monde.

— C'est peut-être le fruit de mon imagination.

— Tu as vu les signes de Dieu », insista Elie, que les commentaires de son compagnon commençaient à rendre anxieux.

« C'est peut-être le fruit de mon imagination, lui fut-il répété. En fait, je n'ai de concret que mon pari : je me suis dit que tout cela venait du Très-Haut. »

*

La rue était déserte. Les gens, dans leurs maisons, attendaient que les soldats d'Achab accomplissent la tâche exigée par la princesse étrangère : l'exécution des prophètes d'Israël. Elie cheminait avec le lévite, et il avait la sensation que, derrière chacune des fenêtres et des portes, quelqu'un l'observait et l'accusait de ce qui était en train de se passer.

« Je n'ai pas demandé à être prophète. Tout cela est peut-être aussi le fruit de mon imagination », se disait Elie.

Mais après ce qui était arrivé dans la charpenterie, il savait qu'il n'en était rien.

*

Depuis son enfance, il entendait des voix et conversait avec les anges. Aussi ses parents insistèrent-ils pour qu'il consultât un prêtre d'Israël. Ce dernier, après nombre de questions, reconnut en lui un *nabi*, un prophète, un « homme de l'esprit », qui « s'exalte à la voix de Dieu ».

Après plusieurs heures d'entretien ininterrompu avec lui, le prêtre expliqua à ses parents que tout ce que cet enfant viendrait à dire devait être pris au sérieux.

Sur le chemin du retour, les parents exigèrent qu'Elie ne racontât jamais à personne ce qu'il voyait ou entendait ; être un prophète impliquait des liens avec le gouvernement, et c'était toujours dangereux.

De toute façon, Elie n'avait jamais rien entendu qui pût intéresser les prêtres ou les rois. Il ne conversait qu'avec son ange gardien et écoutait des conseils concernant sa propre vie. De temps à autre, il avait des visions qu'il ne parvenait pas à comprendre — des océans lointains, des montagnes peuplées d'êtres étranges, des roues avec des ailes et des yeux. Lorsque les visions avaient disparu, obéissant à ses parents, il s'efforçait de les oublier le plus vite possible.

Ainsi les voix et les visions s'étaient-elles faites de

plus en plus rares. Ses parents, satisfaits, n'avaient plus abordé le sujet. Lorsqu'il fut en âge d'assurer sa subsistance, ils lui prêtèrent de l'argent pour qu'il ouvrît une petite charpenterie.

*

Fréquemment, il regardait avec respect les autres prophètes dans les rues de Galaad : ils portaient des manteaux de peau et des ceintures de cuir, et affirmaient que le Seigneur les avait choisis pour guider le peuple élu. Mais en vérité, ce n'était pas son destin. Jamais il ne serait capable de connaître une transe lors d'une danse ou d'une séance d'autoflagellation, une pratique normale chez les « exaltés par la voix de Dieu », parce qu'il avait peur de la douleur. Jamais il ne marcherait dans les rues de Galaad, exhibant fièrement les cicatrices des blessures obtenues au cours de l'extase, parce qu'il était trop timide pour cela.

Elie se considérait comme une personne ordinaire, qui s'habillait comme tout le monde et dont l'âme était torturée des mêmes craintes et tentations que celle des autres mortels. A mesure que progressait son travail dans la charpenterie, les voix cessèrent complètement parce que les adultes et les travailleurs n'ont pas de temps pour cela. Ses parents étaient contents de leur fils, et la vie s'écoulait dans l'harmonie et la paix.

La conversation qu'il avait eue avec le prêtre lorsqu'il était petit devint peu à peu un lointain souvenir. Elie ne pouvait croire que Dieu tout-puissant eût besoin de converser avec les hommes pour faire valoir ses ordres. Ce qui s'était passé dans son enfance n'était que la fantaisie d'un gamin oisif. A Galaad, sa cité natale, il y avait des gens que les habitants considéraient comme fous. Incapables de tenir des propos cohérents, ils ne distinguaient pas la voix du Seigneur des délires de la démence. Ils erraient dans les rues, annonçant la fin du monde et vivant de la charité d'autrui. Pourtant, aucun prêtre ne les considérait comme « exaltés par la voix de Dieu ».

Elie en vint à penser que les prêtres n'avaient jamais la certitude de ce qu'ils affirmaient. Il y avait des « exaltés de Dieu » parce que le pays ne savait pas où il allait, que les frères se querellaient et que le gouvernement était instable. Il n'y avait aucune différence entre les prophètes et les fous.

*

Quand il apprit le mariage de son roi et de Jézabel, princesse de Tyr, Elie n'y accorda pas grande importance. D'autres rois d'Israël avaient agi de même. Il en avait résulté une paix durable dans la région, et le commerce avec le Liban s'était développé. Peu importait à Elie que les habitants du pays voisin croient en des dieux qui n'existaient pas ou se consacrent à des cultes étranges, comme l'adoration des animaux et des montagnes ; ils étaient honnêtes dans les négociations, voilà l'essentiel. Elie continua donc à acheter leur bois de cèdre et à leur vendre les produits de sa charpenterie. Même s'ils se montraient un peu orgueilleux, aucun des commerçants du Liban n'avait jamais cherché à tirer parti de la confusion qui régnait en Israël. Ils payaient les marchandises à leur juste prix et n'émettaient aucun commentaire sur les constantes guerres intestines, ni sur les problèmes politiques auxquels les Israélites étaient sans cesse confrontés.

*

Après son accession au trône, Jézabel avait demandé à Achab de remplacer le culte du Seigneur par celui des dieux du Liban.

Cela aussi était déjà arrivé auparavant. Elie, bien qu'il fût indigné par le consentement d'Achab, continua d'adorer le Dieu d'Israël et d'obéir aux lois de Moïse. « Cela ne durera pas, pensait-il. Jézabel a séduit Achab, mais elle ne parviendra pas à persuader le peuple. »

Mais Jézabel n'était pas une femme comme les autres ; elle avait la conviction que Baal l'avait fait venir au monde pour convertir les peuples et les nations. Subtilement et patiemment, elle se mit à récompenser tous ceux qui se détournaient du Seigneur et acceptaient les nouvelles divinités. Achab ordonna la construction d'un temple pour Baal à Samarie, à l'intérieur duquel il fit bâtir un autel. Les pèlerinages commencèrent, et le culte aux dieux du Liban se répandit de toutes parts.

« Cela passera. Cela durera peut-être une génération, mais ensuite cela passera », pensait toujours Elie.

Alors survint un événement auquel il ne s'attendait pas. Un après-midi, tandis qu'il finissait de fabriquer une table dans sa charpenterie, tout s'obscurcit autour de lui et des milliers de points blancs se mirent à scintiller. Sa tête lui faisait mal comme jamais ; il voulut s'asseoir, mais constata qu'il n'arrivait pas à bouger un seul muscle.

Ce n'était pas le fruit de son imagination.

« Je suis mort, pensa-t-il sur-le-champ. Maintenant, je découvre l'endroit où Dieu nous envoie après notre mort : le milieu du firmament. »

Une des lumières brilla plus fort et soudain, comme si elle venait de partout en même temps, « *la parole du Seigneur lui fut adressée : "Dis à Achab que, par la vie du Seigneur, le Dieu d'Israël au service duquel je suis, il n'y aura ces années-ci ni rosée ni pluie sinon à ma parole."* »

L'instant suivant, tout redevint normal, la charpenterie, la lumière du crépuscule, les voix des enfants jouant dans la rue.

*

Elie ne dormit pas cette nuit-là. Pour la première fois depuis des années, les sensations de son enfance étaient de retour ; et ce n'était pas son ange gardien qui lui parlait, mais « *quelque chose* » de plus puissant. Il redouta, s'il n'obéissait pas à cet ordre, que toutes ses activités ne fussent maudites.

Le lendemain matin, il décida de faire ce qu'on lui avait demandé. En fin de compte, il se contenterait de délivrer un message qui ne le concernait pas ; une fois cette tâche terminée, les voix ne reviendraient plus le déranger.

Il n'eut aucune difficulté à obtenir une audience auprès du roi Achab. Des générations plus tôt, lorsque le roi Saül était monté sur le trône, les prophètes avaient acquis de l'importance dans les affaires et le gouvernement de son pays. Ils pouvaient se marier, avoir des enfants, mais ils devaient rester en permanence à la disposition du Seigneur, afin que les gouvernants ne s'écartent jamais trop du droit chemin. La tradition affirmait que, grâce à ces « exaltés de Dieu », on avait gagné de nombreuses batailles et qu'Israël survivait parce que, quand ses gouvernants se fourvoyaient, il y avait toujours un prophète pour leur faire regagner la voie du Seigneur.

En arrivant, Elie avertit le roi que la sécheresse allait dévaster la région jusqu'à ce que le culte des dieux phéniciens fût abandonné.

Le souverain n'accorda guère d'importance à ces paroles, mais Jézabel, qui se tenait à côté d'Achab et écoutait attentivement, se mit à l'interroger. Elie lui parla alors de la vision, du mal de tête, de la sensation que le temps s'était arrêté quand il écoutait l'ange. Pendant qu'il décrivait ce qui lui était arrivé, il put regarder de près la princesse dont tout le monde parlait. C'était l'une des plus belles femmes qu'il eût jamais vues, avec de longs cheveux noirs descendant jusqu'à sa taille parfaitement tournée. Ses yeux verts, qui brillaient dans son visage brun, restaient fixés sur ceux d'Elie. Il ne parvenait pas à déchiffrer la signification de ce regard, et il ne pouvait pas savoir quel effet lui causaient ses propos.

Il sortit de cette entrevue convaincu qu'il avait accompli sa mission et pouvait désormais retourner à son travail dans la charpenterie. Sur le chemin du retour, il désira Jézabel de toute l'ardeur de ses vingt-trois ans. Et il pria Dieu qu'il lui fût permis de rencontrer plus tard une femme du Liban, parce qu'elles étaient belles, avec leur peau sombre et leurs yeux verts emplis de mystère.

*

Il travailla le reste de la journée et dormit en paix. Le lendemain, il fut réveillé avant l'aurore par le lévite. Jézabel avait persuadé le roi que les prophètes étaient une menace pour la croissance et l'expansion d'Israël. Les soldats d'Achab avaient reçu l'ordre d'exécuter tous ceux qui refuseraient d'abandonner la tâche sacrée que Dieu leur avait confiée. Mais à Elie ils n'avaient pas donné la possibilité de choisir : lui devait être mis à mort.

Elie et le lévite passèrent deux jours cachés dans l'étable au sud de Galaad, tandis que quatre cent cinquante *nabis* étaient exécutés. Cependant, la plupart des prophètes, qui vagabondaient d'ordinaire dans les rues en s'autoflagellant et en prédisant la fin du monde à cause de la corruption et de l'absence de foi, avaient accepté de se convertir à la nouvelle religion.

*

Un bruit sec, suivi d'un cri, interrompit les pensées d'Elie. Alarmé, il se tourna vers son compagnon :

« Que se passe-t-il ? »

Mais il n'obtint pas de réponse : le corps du lévite s'écroula sur le sol, une flèche plantée au milieu de la poitrine.

Devant lui, un soldat mit une nouvelle flèche dans son arc. Elie regarda autour de lui : la rue, les portes et fenêtres fermées, le soleil éblouissant dans le ciel, la brise qui venait d'un océan dont il avait tant entendu parler mais qu'il n'avait jamais vu. Il songea à courir, mais il savait qu'il serait rattrapé avant d'atteindre le coin de la rue.

« Si je dois mourir, que ce ne soit pas d'un coup dans le dos. »

Le soldat banda de nouveau son arc. A sa grande surprise, Elie ne ressentait pas la peur, ni l'instinct de survie, ni rien. C'était comme si toute la scène avait déjà été définie voilà très longtemps, et que l'un et l'autre — lui aussi bien que le soldat — tenaient un rôle dans un drame qui n'avait pas été écrit par eux. Il se rappela son enfance, les matins et les après-midi à Galaad, les ouvrages inachevés qu'il allait laisser dans sa charpenterie. Il songea à sa mère et à son père, qui n'avaient jamais désiré avoir un fils prophète. Il pensa aux yeux de Jézabel et au sourire du roi Achab.

Il pensa qu'il était stupide de mourir à vingt-trois ans, sans avoir jamais connu l'amour d'une femme.

La main lâcha la corde, la flèche fendit l'air, passa en sifflant près de son oreille droite, et se planta derrière lui dans le sol poussiéreux.

Le soldat, encore une fois, arma son arc et le visa. Pourtant, au lieu de tirer, il fixa Elie dans les yeux.

« Je suis le meilleur des archers de toutes les armées d'Achab, dit-il. Cela fait sept ans que je n'ai pas manqué un seul tir. »

Elie se tourna vers le corps du lévite.

« Cette flèche était pour toi. » Le soldat gardait son arc bandé, et ses mains tremblaient. « Elie était le seul prophète qui devait être mis à mort ; les autres pouvaient choisir la foi en Baal.

— Alors, termine ton travail. »

Il était surpris de sa propre tranquillité. Il avait imaginé la mort tant de fois durant les nuits passées dans l'étable, et maintenant il comprenait qu'il avait souffert plus que nécessaire. En quelques secondes, tout serait fini.

« Je n'y arrive pas », dit le soldat, les mains encore tremblantes, et l'arc changeant à chaque instant de direction. « Va-t'en ! Hors de ma présence ! Je pense que Dieu a dévié mes flèches, et qu'il va me maudire si je réussis à te tuer. »

Ce fut alors — à mesure qu'Elie découvrait qu'il avait une chance de survivre — que la peur de mourir afflua de nouveau. Il était encore possible de connaître l'océan, de rencontrer une femme, d'avoir des enfants et d'achever ses ouvrages dans la charpenterie.

« Finis-en vite, dit-il. En ce moment, je suis calme. Si tu attends trop, je vais souffrir pour tout ce que je serai sur le point de perdre. »

Le soldat regarda alentour pour s'assurer que personne n'avait assisté à la scène. Puis il abaissa son arc, remit la flèche dans son carquois, et disparut.

Elie sentit que ses jambes flanchaient ; la terreur revenait dans toute son intensité. Il devait fuir immédiatement, disparaître de Galaad, ne plus jamais avoir à se trouver face à face avec un soldat, l'arc tendu, pointé sur son cœur. Il n'avait pas choisi son destin, et il n'était pas allé voir Achab pour se vanter auprès de ses voisins d'avoir conversé avec le roi. Il n'était pas responsable du massacre des prophètes. Il n'était pas non plus responsable d'avoir vu, un après-midi, le temps s'arrêter et la charpenterie se transformer en un trou noir, empli de points lumineux.

Imitant le soldat, il regarda autour de lui. La rue était déserte. Il songea à vérifier s'il pouvait encore sauver la vie du lévite mais bientôt la terreur revint et, avant que quelqu'un n'apparût, Elie s'enfuit.

Il marcha pendant des heures, s'engageant dans des chemins qui n'étaient plus fréquentés depuis longtemps, et arriva enfin au bord du ruisseau du Kerith. Il avait honte de sa lâcheté, mais il se réjouissait d'être en vie.

Il but un peu d'eau, s'assit, et alors seulement se

rendit compte de la situation dans laquelle il se trouvait : demain, il lui faudrait se nourrir, et il ne trouverait pas de nourriture dans le désert.

Il se rappela la charpenterie, le travail de tant d'années, qu'il avait été contraint de laisser derrière lui. Certains de ses voisins étaient ses amis, mais il ne pouvait pas compter sur eux. L'histoire de sa fuite s'était déjà sans doute répandue dans la cité, et tous le haïraient de s'être échappé, pendant qu'il envoyait au martyre les véritables hommes de foi.

Tout ce qu'il avait fait jusque-là était ruiné uniquement parce qu'il avait cru accomplir la volonté du Seigneur. Demain, et dans les prochains jours, semaines et mois, les commerçants du Liban frapperaient à sa porte, et on les avertirait que le propriétaire s'était enfui, semant derrière lui la mort de prophètes innocents. On ajouterait peut-être qu'il avait tenté de détruire les dieux qui protégeaient la terre et les cieux. L'histoire franchirait bientôt les frontières d'Israël, et il pouvait renoncer pour toujours au mariage avec une femme aussi belle que celles qui vivaient au Liban.

*

« Il y a les navires. »

Oui, il y avait les navires. On avait coutume d'accepter pour marins les criminels, les prisonniers de guerre, les fugitifs, parce que c'était un métier plus dangereux que l'armée. A la guerre, un soldat avait toujours une chance de rester en vie ; mais les mers étaient un territoire inconnu, peuplé de monstres, et, lorsqu'une tragédie survenait, il n'y avait pas de survivant pour raconter ce qui s'était passé.

Certes, il y avait les navires, mais ils étaient contrôlés par les commerçants phéniciens. Elie n'était pas un criminel, un prisonnier ou un fugitif, c'était un homme qui avait osé élever la voix contre le dieu Baal. Lorsqu'on le découvrirait, il serait mis à mort et jeté à la mer, car les marins croyaient fermement que Baal et ses dieux étaient maîtres des tempêtes.

Il ne pouvait pas se diriger vers la mer. Ni continuer vers le nord, car là se trouvait le Liban. Il ne pouvait pas non plus aller vers l'orient, où des tribus israélites menaient une guerre depuis deux générations.

*

Il se souvint de la tranquillité qu'il avait ressentie devant le soldat. En fin de compte, qu'était la mort ? Un instant, rien de plus. Même s'il éprouvait de la douleur, elle passerait rapidement, et le Seigneur des Armées le recevrait en son sein.

Il se coucha sur le sol et resta très longtemps à contempler le ciel. Comme le lévite, il tenta de parier, non sur l'existence de Dieu — il n'avait pas de doutes sur ce point —, mais sur la raison de sa propre vie.

Il vit les montagnes, la terre qu'allait dévaster une longue sécheresse — ainsi l'avait annoncé l'ange du Seigneur — mais qui conservait encore la fraîcheur de nombreuses années de pluies généreuses. Il aperçut le ruisseau du Kerith, dont les eaux se tariraient bientôt. Il fit ses adieux au monde avec ferveur et respect, et pria le Seigneur de l'accueillir quand viendrait son heure.

Il se demanda quel était le motif de son existence, et n'obtint pas de réponse.

Il se demanda où il devait se rendre, et comprit qu'il était cerné.

Le lendemain, il ferait demi-tour et se livrerait, bien que la peur de la mort fût revenue.

Il tenta de se réjouir puisqu'il lui restait quelques heures à vivre. En vain. Il venait de découvrir que l'homme a rarement le pouvoir de prendre une décision.

Lorsque Elie se réveilla le lendemain, il regarda de nouveau le Kerith. Demain, ou dans un an, ce ne serait plus qu'un chemin de sable fin et de galets polis. Les habitants continueraient de le nommer Kerith, et peut-être indiqueraient-ils leur route aux voyageurs en disant : « Tel village se trouve au bord de la rivière qui passe près d'ici. » Les voyageurs marcheraient jusque-là, verraient les galets et le sable fin, et se feraient cette réflexion : « Là, sur cette terre, il y avait une rivière. » Mais la seule chose importante concernant une rivière — son torrent d'eau — ne serait plus là pour étancher leur soif.

Comme les ruisseaux et les plantes, les âmes avaient besoin de la pluie, mais d'une autre sorte : l'espoir, la foi, la raison de vivre. Sinon, même si le corps continuait à vivre, l'âme dépérissait ; et les gens pouvaient dire que « là, dans ce corps, il y avait eu un homme ».

Ce n'était pas le moment de songer à tout cela. Encore une fois il se rappela sa conversation avec le lévite, un peu avant qu'ils ne sortent de l'étable : à quoi bon mourir de tant de morts, s'il suffisait d'une seule ? Tout ce qu'il devait faire, c'était attendre les gardes de Jézabel. Ils arriveraient, sans aucun doute, car les itinéraires n'étaient pas nombreux pour fuir de Galaad. Les malfaiteurs se dirigeaient toujours vers le désert — où on les retrouvait morts au bout de quelques jours —, ou vers le Kerith où ils finissaient par être capturés. Bientôt, donc, les gardes seraient là. Et il se réjouirait en les voyant.

*

Il but un peu de l'eau cristalline, se lava le visage, et chercha un endroit ombragé où attendre ses poursuivants. Un homme ne peut lutter contre son destin — il avait déjà tenté de lutter, et il avait perdu.

Bien qu'il fût considéré par les prêtres comme un prophète, Elie avait décidé de travailler dans une charpenterie, mais le Seigneur l'avait reconduit vers son chemin.

Il n'était pas le seul à avoir essayé d'abandonner la vie que Dieu avait écrite pour chacun sur terre. Il avait eu un ami, doté d'une voix remarquable, dont les parents n'avaient pas non plus accepté qu'il fût chanteur — car c'était un métier qui déshonorait la famille. Une de ses amies d'enfance savait danser comme personne, mais sa famille le lui avait interdit — pour la bonne raison que le roi aurait pu la faire appeler et que nul ne savait combien de temps durerait son règne. En outre, l'atmosphère du palais était dépravée, hostile, écartant à tout jamais l'opportunité d'un bon mariage.

« L'homme est né pour trahir son destin. » Dieu ne mettait dans nos cœurs que des tâches impossibles.

« Pourquoi ? »

Peut-être parce que la tradition devait être maintenue.

Mais ce n'était pas une bonne réponse. « Les habitants du Liban sont plus avancés que nous parce qu'ils n'ont pas suivi la tradition des navigateurs. Alors que tout le monde utilisait le même type de bateau, ils ont décidé de construire un instrument différent. Beaucoup ont perdu la vie en mer, mais leurs navires ont été perfectionnés, et maintenant ils dominent le commerce dans le monde. Ils ont payé un prix élevé pour s'adapter, mais cela en valait la peine. »

L'homme trahissait peut-être son destin parce que Dieu s'était éloigné de lui. Après avoir placé dans les cœurs le rêve d'une époque où tout était possible, Il était allé s'occuper d'autres nouveautés. Le monde s'était transformé, la vie était devenue plus difficile, mais le Seigneur n'était jamais revenu pour modifier les rêves des hommes.

Dieu était loin. Pourtant, s'Il envoyait encore les anges parler aux prophètes, c'est qu'il restait quelque chose à faire ici-bas. Alors, quelle pouvait être la réponse ?

« Peut-être nos parents se sont-ils trompés et ont-ils peur que nous commettions les mêmes erreurs. Ou peut-être qu'ils ne se sont jamais trompés et ne sauront pas comment nous aider si nous avons un problème. »

Il sentait qu'il approchait.

Le ruisseau coulait près de lui, quelques corbeaux tournoyaient dans le ciel, les plantes s'obstinaient à pousser sur le terrain sableux et stérile. S'ils avaient écouté les propos de leurs ancêtres, qu'auraient-ils entendu ?

« Ruisseau, cherche un meilleur endroit pour que tes eaux limpides réfléchissent la clarté du soleil, puisque le désert a fini par t'assécher », aurait dit un dieu des eaux, si par hasard il existait. « Corbeaux, la nourriture est plus abondante en forêt qu'au milieu des rochers et du sable », aurait dit un dieu des oiseaux. « Plantes, jetez vos semences loin d'ici, car le monde est plein de terre fertile et humide, et vous pousserez plus belles », aurait dit un dieu des fleurs.

Mais ni le Kerith, ni les plantes, ni les corbeaux — l'un d'eux s'était posé tout près — n'avaient le courage de faire ce que les autres rivières, oiseaux ou fleurs jugeaient impossible.

Elie fixa le corbeau du regard.

« J'apprends, dit-il à l'oiseau. Même si c'est un apprentissage inutile, parce que je suis condamné à mort.

— Tu as découvert comme tout est simple, sembla répondre le corbeau. Il suffit d'avoir du courage. »

Elie rit, car il plaçait des mots dans la bouche d'un oiseau. C'était un jeu amusant — qu'il avait appris avec une femme qui confectionnait du pain — et il décida de continuer. Il poserait les questions et se donnerait à lui-même une réponse, comme s'il était un véritable sage.

Mais le corbeau s'envola. Elie attendait toujours l'arrivée des soldats de Jézabel, parce qu'il suffisait de mourir une fois.

*

Le jour passa, et rien de nouveau ne se produisit. Avaient-ils oublié que le principal ennemi du dieu Baal était encore en vie ? Pourquoi Jézabel ne le poursuivait-elle pas, puisqu'elle savait probablement où il se trouvait ?

« Parce que j'ai vu ses yeux, et c'est une femme

sage, se dit-il. Si je mourais, je deviendrais un martyr du Seigneur. Considéré comme un fugitif, je ne serai qu'un lâche qui ne croyait pas en ce qu'il disait. »

Oui, c'était cela la stratégie de la princesse.

*

Peu avant la tombée de la nuit, un corbeau — était-ce le même ? — vint se poser sur la branche sur laquelle il l'avait vu ce matin-là. Il tenait dans son bec un petit morceau de viande que par inadvertance il laissa tomber.

Pour Elie, ce fut un miracle. Il courut jusque sous l'arbre, saisit le morceau et le mangea. Il ignorait sa provenance et ne cherchait pas non plus à la connaître ; l'important était d'apaiser sa faim.

Malgré le mouvement brusque, le corbeau ne s'éloigna pas.

« Cet oiseau sait que je vais mourir de faim ici, pensa Elie. Il alimente sa proie pour avoir un meilleur festin. »

Jézabel aussi alimentait la foi en Baal par l'histoire de la fuite d'Elie.

Pendant quelque temps, ils restèrent — l'homme et l'oiseau — à se contempler mutuellement. Elie se rappela son jeu du matin.

« J'aimerais converser avec toi, corbeau. Ce matin, je pensais que les âmes avaient besoin de nourriture. Si mon âme n'est pas encore morte de faim, elle a encore quelque chose à dire. »

L'oiseau restait immobile.

« Et si elle a quelque chose à dire, je dois l'écouter. Puisque je n'ai plus personne à qui parler », continua Elie.

Faisant appel à son imagination, Elie se transforma en corbeau.

« Qu'est-ce que Dieu attend de toi ? se demanda-t-il à lui-même, comme s'il était le corbeau.

— Il attend que je sois un prophète.

— C'est ce qu'ont dit les prêtres. Mais ce n'est peut-être pas ce que désire le Seigneur.

— Si, c'est cela qu'Il veut. Car un ange est apparu dans la charpenterie, et il m'a demandé de parler à Achab. Les voix que j'entendais dans l'enfance...

— ... que tout le monde a entendues dans l'enfance, interrompit le corbeau.

— Mais tout le monde n'a pas vu un ange », remarqua Elie.

Cette fois, le corbeau ne répliqua pas. Au bout d'un moment, l'oiseau — ou, mieux, son âme elle-même, qui délirait sous l'effet du soleil et de la solitude du désert — rompit le silence.

« Te souviens-tu de la femme qui faisait du pain ? » se demanda-t-il à lui-même.

Elie se souvenait. Elle était venue lui demander de fabriquer quelques plateaux. Tandis qu'il s'exécutait, il l'avait entendue dire que son travail était une façon d'exprimer la présence de Dieu.

« A la manière dont tu fabriques ces plateaux, je vois que tu éprouves la même sensation, avait-elle ajouté. Tu souris pendant que tu travailles. »

La femme classait les êtres humains en deux groupes : ceux qui étaient heureux et ceux qui se plaignaient de ce qu'ils faisaient. Ces derniers affirmaient que la malédiction que Dieu lança à Adam : « *Le sol sera maudit à cause de toi. C'est dans la peine que tu t'en nourriras tous les jours de ta vie* » était l'unique vérité. Ils n'avaient pas plaisir à travailler et s'ennuyaient les jours de fête, lorsqu'ils étaient obligés de se reposer. Ils se servaient des paroles du Seigneur comme d'une excuse pour leurs vies inutiles, oubliant qu'Il avait aussi dit à Moïse : « *Le Seigneur ton Dieu te bénira abondamment sur la terre qu'Il te donne en héritage, pour la posséder.* »

« Oui, je me souviens de cette femme, répondit Elie au corbeau. Elle avait raison, j'aimais mon travail dans la charpenterie. » Chaque table qu'il montait, chaque chaise qu'il taillait lui permettaient de comprendre et d'aimer la vie, même s'il ne s'en rendait compte que maintenant. « Elle m'a expliqué que, si je parlais aux objets que je fabriquais, je serais surpris de constater que les tables et les chaises me répondraient, parce que j'y mettrais le meilleur de mon âme, et recevrais en échange la sagesse.

— Si tu n'avais pas été charpentier, tu n'aurais pas su non plus mettre ton âme hors de toi-même, faire semblant d'être un corbeau qui parle, et comprendre que tu es meilleur et plus sage que tu ne le penses. C'est dans la charpenterie que tu as découvert que le sacré est partout.

— J'ai toujours aimé faire semblant de parler aux tables et aux chaises que je fabriquais. N'était-ce pas suffisant ? La femme avait raison. Lorsque je conversais ainsi, il me venait souvent des pensées qui ne m'étaient jamais passées par la tête. Mais au moment où je commençais à comprendre que je pouvais servir Dieu de cette manière, l'ange est apparu et... Eh bien ! tu connais la suite de l'histoire.

— L'ange est apparu parce que tu étais prêt, repartit le corbeau.

— J'étais un bon charpentier.

— Cela faisait partie de ton apprentissage. Quand un homme marche vers son destin, il est bien souvent forcé de changer de direction. Parfois, les circonstances extérieures sont les plus fortes, et il est obligé de se montrer lâche et de céder. Tout cela fait partie de l'apprentissage. »

Elie écoutait avec attention ce que disait son âme.

« Mais personne ne peut perdre de vue ce qu'il désire. Même si, à certains moments, on croit que le monde et les autres sont les plus forts. Le secret est le suivant : ne pas renoncer.

— Je n'ai jamais pensé être un prophète, dit Elie.

— Tu l'as pensé. Mais tu as été convaincu que c'était impossible. Ou que c'était dangereux. Ou que c'était impensable. »

Elie se leva.

« Pourquoi me dis-je des choses que je ne veux pas entendre ? » s'écria-t-il.

Effrayé par ce mouvement, l'oiseau s'enfuit.

*

Le corbeau revint le lendemain matin. Plutôt que de reprendre la conversation, Elie l'observa, car l'animal parvenait toujours à se nourrir et lui apportait même quelques restes.

Une mystérieuse amitié se développa entre eux, et Elie commença à apprendre grâce à l'oiseau. Il vit comment il trouvait sa nourriture dans le désert et découvrit qu'il pourrait survivre quelques jours de plus s'il réussissait à en faire autant. Quand le vol du corbeau devenait circulaire, Elie savait qu'il y avait une proie à proximité ; il courait alors jusqu'à l'endroit et tentait de la capturer. Au début, beaucoup des petits animaux parvenaient à lui échapper, mais peu à peu, à force d'entraînement, il acquit une certaine habileté. Il se servait de branches en guise de lances et creusait des pièges qu'il dissimulait sous une fine couche de cailloux et de sable. Lorsque la proie tombait, Elie partageait sa nourriture avec le corbeau et en gardait une partie pour servir d'appât.

Mais la solitude dans laquelle il se trouvait était terriblement oppressante, si bien qu'il décida de converser de nouveau avec l'oiseau.

« Qui es-tu ? demanda le corbeau.

— Je suis un homme qui a découvert la paix, répondit Elie. Je peux vivre dans le désert, subvenir à mes besoins, et contempler l'infinie beauté de la création divine. J'ai découvert que j'avais en moi une âme meilleure que je ne pensais. »

Ils continuèrent à chasser ensemble au clair de lune. Alors, une nuit que son âme était possédée par la tristesse, il décida de se demander de nouveau :

« Qui es-tu ?

— Je ne sais pas. »

*

Un autre clair de lune mourut et renaquit dans le ciel. Elie sentait que son corps était plus fort, et son esprit plus clair. Cette nuit-là, il se tourna vers le corbeau, toujours posé sur la même branche, et répondit à la question qu'il avait lancée quelque temps auparavant :

36

« Je suis un prophète. J'ai vu un ange pendant que je travaillais, et je ne peux pas douter de ce dont je suis capable, même si tous les hommes du monde m'affirment le contraire. J'ai provoqué un massacre dans mon pays parce que j'ai défié la bien-aimée de mon roi. Je suis dans le désert — comme j'ai été avant dans une charpenterie — parce que mon âme m'a dit qu'un homme devait passer par différentes étapes avant d'accomplir son destin.

— Oui, maintenant tu sais qui tu es », commenta le corbeau.

Cette nuit-là, lorsque Elie rentra de la chasse, il voulut boire un peu d'eau mais le Kerith était asséché. Il était tellement fatigué qu'il décida de dormir.

Dans son rêve, apparut l'ange gardien qu'il ne voyait pas depuis longtemps.

« L'ange du Seigneur a parlé à ton âme, dit celui-ci. Et il a ordonné : *Va-t'en d'ici, dirige-toi vers l'Orient et cache-toi dans le ravin du Kerith, qui est à l'est du Jourdain. Tu boiras au torrent ; et j'ai ordonné aux corbeaux de te ravitailler là-bas.*

— Mon âme a écouté, dit Elie dans son rêve.

— Alors réveille-toi. L'ange du Seigneur me prie de m'éloigner, et il veut parler avec toi. »

Elie se leva d'un bond, effrayé. Que s'était-il passé ?

Malgré la nuit, l'endroit se remplit de lumière, et l'ange du Seigneur apparut.

« Qu'est-ce qui t'a mené ici ? demanda l'ange.

— C'est toi qui m'as mené ici.

— Non. Jézabel et ses soldats t'ont poussé à fuir. Ne l'oublie jamais, car ta mission est de venger le Seigneur ton Dieu.

— Je suis prophète, puisque tu es devant moi et que j'écoute ta voix, dit Elie. J'ai changé maintes fois de direction, tous les hommes font cela. Mais je suis prêt à aller jusqu'à Samarie et à détruire Jézabel.

— Tu as trouvé ton chemin, mais tu ne peux pas détruire sans apprendre à reconstruire. Je t'ordonne : *Lève-toi, et va à Sarepta qui appartient à Sidon, tu y habiteras ; j'ai ordonné là-bas à une femme, une veuve, de te ravitailler.* »

Le lendemain matin, Elie chercha le corbeau pour lui faire ses adieux. Pour la première fois depuis qu'il était arrivé au bord du Kerith, l'oiseau n'apparut pas.

Elie voyagea pendant des jours et atteignit enfin la vallée où se trouvait la cité de Sarepta, à laquelle ses habitants donnaient le nom d'Akbar. Alors qu'il était à bout de forces, il aperçut une femme, vêtue de noir, qui ramassait du bois. La végétation de la vallée était rase, de sorte qu'elle devait se contenter de menu bois sec.

« Qui es-tu ? » demanda-t-il.

La femme regarda l'étranger, sans comprendre ses paroles.

« Donne-moi de l'eau, dit Elie. Je suis seul, j'ai faim et soif, et je n'ai plus assez de forces pour menacer personne.

— Tu n'es pas d'ici, dit-elle enfin. A ta façon de parler, tu viens sans doute du royaume d'Israël. Si tu me connaissais mieux, tu saurais que je n'ai rien.

— Tu es veuve, m'a dit le Seigneur. Et j'ai moins que toi. Si tu ne me donnes pas maintenant de quoi manger et boire, je vais mourir. »

La femme eut peur. Comment cet étranger pouvait-il connaître sa vie ?

« Un homme devrait avoir honte de réclamer de la nourriture à une femme, répliqua-t-elle en se ressaisissant.

— Fais ce que je te demande, je t'en prie », insista Elie, sentant que les forces commençaient à lui manquer. « Dès que j'irai mieux, je travaillerai pour toi. »

La femme rit.

« Il y a un instant, tu m'as dit une vérité : je suis veuve, j'ai perdu mon mari sur l'un des navires de mon pays. Je n'ai jamais vu l'océan, mais je sais que, comme le désert, il tue celui qui le brave. »

38

Et elle poursuivit :

« Maintenant, tu me dis un mensonge. Aussi vrai que Baal vit en haut de la Cinquième Montagne, je n'ai rien à manger. Il y a tout juste une poignée de farine dans une cruche et un peu d'huile dans une jarre. »

Elie sentit que l'horizon vacillait et il comprit qu'il allait bientôt s'évanouir. Rassemblant le peu d'énergie qui lui restait, il implora pour la dernière fois :

« Je ne sais pas si tu crois aux songes, ni si j'y crois moi-même. Pourtant le Seigneur m'a annoncé qu'en arrivant ici, je te rencontrerais. Il a déjà fait des choses qui m'ont fait douter de Sa sagesse, mais jamais de Son existence. Et ainsi, le Dieu d'Israël m'a prié de dire à la femme que je rencontrerais à Sarepta :

Cruche de farine ne se videra,
jarre d'huile ne se désemplira
jusqu'au jour où le Seigneur
donnera la pluie à la surface du sol. »

Sans expliquer comment un tel miracle pouvait se produire, Elie s'évanouit.

La femme demeura immobile à regarder l'homme tombé à ses pieds. Elle savait que le Dieu d'Israël n'était qu'une superstition. Les dieux phéniciens étaient bien plus puissants et ils avaient fait de son pays une des nations les plus respectées du monde. Mais elle était contente ; elle vivait en général en demandant l'aumône, et aujourd'hui, pour la première fois depuis très longtemps, un homme avait besoin d'elle. Elle se sentit plus forte. En fin de compte, il y avait des gens dans une situation pire que la sienne.

« Si quelqu'un me réclame une faveur, c'est que j'ai encore une certaine valeur sur cette terre, pensa-t-elle. Je ferai ce qu'il demande, simplement pour soulager sa souffrance. Moi aussi j'ai connu la faim, et je sais comme elle détruit l'âme. »

Elle retourna jusque chez elle et revint avec un morceau de pain et une cruche d'eau. Elle s'agenouilla, posa contre elle la tête de l'étranger et mouilla ses lèvres. Au bout de quelques minutes, il recouvra les sens.

Elle lui tendit le pain, et Elie mangea en silence, tout en regardant la vallée, les défilés, les montagnes qui pointaient silencieusement vers le ciel. Il apercevait les murailles rouges de la cité de Sarepta, dominant le passage par la vallée.

« Donne-moi l'hospitalité, je suis poursuivi dans mon pays, dit-il.

— Quel crime as-tu commis ?

— Je suis un prophète du Seigneur. Jézabel a ordonné la mort de tous ceux qui refusaient d'adorer les dieux phéniciens.

— Quel âge as-tu ?

— Vingt-trois ans. »

Elle regarda avec compassion le jeune homme qui se tenait devant elle. Il avait les cheveux longs et sales. Il portait la barbe, une barbe encore clairsemée, comme s'il désirait paraître plus vieux qu'il ne l'était réellement. Comment un malheureux pareil pouvait-il braver la princesse la plus puissante du monde ?

« Si tu es ennemi de Jézabel, tu es aussi mon ennemi. Elle est princesse de Tyr et, en épousant son roi, elle a reçu pour mission de convertir son peuple à la foi authentique. C'est ce qu'affirment ceux qui l'ont connue. »

Elle indiqua l'un des pics qui encadraient la vallée.

« Nos dieux habitent au sommet de la Cinquième Montagne depuis des générations. Ils parviennent à maintenir la paix dans notre pays. Mais Israël vit dans la guerre et la souffrance. Comment peut-on continuer à croire au Dieu unique ? Qu'on donne à Jézabel le temps d'accomplir sa tâche et tu verras la paix régner aussi dans vos cités.

— J'ai entendu la voix du Seigneur, répondit Elie. Quant à vous, vous n'êtes jamais montés au sommet de la Cinquième Montagne pour savoir ce qu'il y a là-haut.

— Celui qui gravira ce mont mourra par le feu des cieux. Les dieux n'aiment pas les inconnus. »

Elle se tut. Elle s'était souvenue que, la nuit dernière, elle avait vu en rêve une lumière vive, d'où sortait une voix disant : « Reçois l'étranger qui viendra à ta recherche. »

« Donne-moi l'hospitalité, je n'ai nulle part où dormir, insista Elie.

— Je te l'ai déjà dit, je suis pauvre. J'ai à peine assez pour moi et pour mon fils.

— Le Seigneur t'a priée de me permettre de rester, jamais Il n'abandonne quelqu'un qui aime. Je t'en prie. Je serai ton employé. Je suis charpentier, je sais travailler le cèdre, et j'aurai de quoi faire. Ainsi, le Seigneur se servira de mes mains pour tenir Sa promesse : *"Cruche de farine ne se videra, jarre d'huile ne se désemplira jusqu'au jour où le Seigneur donnera la pluie à la surface du sol."*

— Même si je le voulais, je n'aurais pas de quoi te payer.

— C'est inutile. Le Seigneur y pourvoira. »

Déconcertée par son rêve de la nuit, et bien qu'elle sût que l'étranger était un ennemi de la princesse de Sidon, la femme décida d'obéir.

Les voisins découvrirent bientôt la présence d'Elie. Les gens racontèrent que la veuve avait installé un étranger dans sa demeure, sans respecter la mémoire de son mari — un héros qui avait trouvé la mort alors qu'il cherchait à étendre les routes commerciales de son pays.

Dès qu'elle eut connaissance de ces rumeurs, la veuve expliqua qu'il s'agissait d'un prophète israélite affamé et assoiffé. Et la nouvelle se répandit qu'un prophète israélite, fuyant Jézabel, était caché dans la cité. Une commission alla consulter le grand prêtre.

« Qu'on amène l'étranger devant moi », ordonna-t-il.

Ainsi fut fait. Cet après-midi-là, Elie fut conduit devant l'homme qui, avec le gouverneur et le chef militaire, contrôlait tout ce qui se passait à Akbar.

« Qu'es-tu venu faire ici ? demanda-t-il. Ne vois-tu pas que tu es un ennemi de notre pays ?

— Pendant des années j'ai négocié avec le Liban, et je respecte ton peuple et tes coutumes. Je suis ici parce que je suis persécuté en Israël.

— J'en connais la raison, dit le prêtre. C'est une femme qui t'a fait fuir ?

— Cette femme est la plus belle créature que j'aie rencontrée, quoique je me sois trouvé quelques minutes seulement devant elle. Mais son cœur est de pierre, et derrière ses yeux verts se cache l'ennemi qui entend détruire mon pays. Je n'ai pas fui : j'attends simplement le moment opportun de retourner là-bas. »

Le prêtre rit.

« Alors, prépare-toi à rester à Akbar le reste de ta vie. Nous ne sommes pas en guerre avec ton pays. Tout ce que nous désirons, c'est que la foi authentique se répande — par des moyens pacifiques — à travers le monde entier. Nous ne voulons pas répéter les atrocités que vous avez commises quand vous vous êtes installés en Canaan.

— Assassiner les prophètes est-il un moyen pacifique ?

— Si l'on coupe la tête du monstre, il cesse d'exister. Quelques-uns peuvent mourir, mais les guerres de religion seront évitées pour toujours. Et, d'après ce que m'ont raconté les commerçants, c'est un prophète nommé Elie qui est à l'origine de tout cela et qui ensuite s'est enfui. »

Le prêtre le regarda fixement, avant de poursuivre :

« Un homme qui te ressemblait.

— C'est moi, répondit Elie.

— Parfait. Sois le bienvenu dans la cité d'Akbar. Lorsque nous aurons besoin d'obtenir quelque chose de Jézabel, nous la paierons avec ta tête — la meilleure monnaie d'échange que nous ayons. En attendant, cherche un emploi et apprends à subvenir à tes besoins, ici il n'y a pas de place pour les prophètes. »

Elie se préparait à partir quand le prêtre reprit :

« On dirait qu'une jeune femme de Sidon est plus puissante que ton Dieu unique. Elle a réussi à ériger un autel à Baal, et les anciens prêtres s'agenouillent maintenant devant lui.

— Tout se passera ainsi que le Seigneur l'a écrit, répliqua le prophète. A certains moments, nos vies connaissent des tribulations et nous ne pouvons les éviter. Mais elles ont un motif.

— Lequel ?

— A cette question nous ne pouvons répondre avant, ou pendant, les difficultés. C'est seulement une fois que nous les avons surmontées que nous comprenons pourquoi elles sont survenues. »

*

Sitôt qu'Elie fut parti, le grand prêtre convoqua la commission de citoyens qui était venue le trouver le matin.

« Ne vous en faites pas, dit-il. La tradition nous commande de donner refuge aux étrangers. En outre, ici, il est sous notre contrôle et nous pourrons surveiller ses allées et venues. La meilleure manière de connaître et de détruire un ennemi, c'est de feindre de devenir son ami. Quand arrivera le bon moment, il sera livré à Jézabel, et notre cité recevra de l'or et des récompenses. D'ici là, nous aurons appris comment anéantir ses idées ; pour le moment, nous savons seulement comment détruire son corps. »

Bien qu'Elie fût un adorateur du Dieu unique et un ennemi potentiel de la princesse, le prêtre exigea que le droit d'asile fût respecté. Tous connaissaient la vieille tradition : si une cité refusait d'accueillir un voyageur, les fils de ses habitants connaîtraient semblable malheur. Comme la progéniture de bon nombre des citoyens d'Akbar était dispersée sur la gigantesque flotte marchande du pays, nul n'osa braver la loi de l'hospitalité.

En outre, cela ne coûtait rien d'attendre le jour où la tête du prophète juif serait échangée contre de grandes quantités d'or.

*

Ce soir-là, Elie dîna en compagnie de la veuve et de son fils. Comme le prophète israélite constituait désormais une précieuse monnaie d'échange susceptible d'être négociée plus tard, certains commerçants avaient envoyé suffisamment de nourriture pour permettre à la famille de s'alimenter pendant une semaine.

« On dirait que le Seigneur d'Israël tient sa parole, remarqua la veuve. Depuis que mon mari est mort, jamais ma table n'a été aussi opulente. »

Elie s'intégra peu à peu à la vie de Sarepta. Comme tous ses habitants, il se mit à l'appeler Akbar. Il fit la connaissance du gouverneur, du commandant de la garnison, du grand prêtre, des maîtres artisans qui travaillaient le verre et que l'on admirait dans toute la région. Quand on lui demandait ce qu'il faisait là, il disait la vérité : Jézabel tuait tous les prophètes en Israël.

« Tu es un traître à ton pays, et un ennemi de la Phénicie, rétorquait-on. Mais nous sommes une nation de commerçants, et nous savons que, plus un homme est dangereux, plus élevé est le prix de sa tête. »

Ainsi passèrent quelques mois.

A l'entrée de la vallée, des patrouilles assyriennes avaient installé leur campement et semblaient bien disposées à y rester. C'était un petit groupe de soldats qui ne représentait aucune menace. Néanmoins, le commandant invita le gouverneur à prendre des mesures.

« Ils ne nous ont rien fait, remarqua le gouverneur. Ils sont sans doute en mission commerciale, cherchant un meilleur itinéraire pour acheminer leurs produits. S'ils décident d'utiliser nos routes, ils paieront des impôts, et nous serons encore plus riches. Pourquoi les provoquer ? »

Pour aggraver la situation, le fils de la veuve tomba malade, sans aucune raison apparente. Les voisins attribuèrent l'événement à la présence de l'étranger, et la femme pria Elie de s'en aller. Mais il n'en fit rien — le Seigneur ne l'avait pas encore appelé. Le bruit commença à se répandre que cet étranger avait apporté avec lui la colère des dieux de la Cinquième Montagne.

On pouvait contrôler l'armée et rassurer la population sur l'arrivée des patrouilles assyriennes. Mais lorsque le fils de la veuve tomba malade, le gouverneur eut de plus en plus de mal à apaiser les gens, que la présence d'Elie inquiétait.

Une commission d'habitants vint le trouver pour lui faire une proposition :

« Nous pouvons construire une maison pour l'Israélite de l'autre côté des murailles. Ainsi, nous ne violons pas la loi de l'hospitalité, mais nous nous protégeons contre la colère divine. Les dieux sont mécontents de la présence de cet homme.

— Laissez-le où il est, répondit le gouverneur. Je préfère ne pas créer de problèmes politiques avec Israël.

— Comment ! s'exclamèrent les habitants. Jézabel

45

pourchasse tous les prophètes qui adorent le Dieu unique, elle veut leur mort.

— Notre princesse est une femme courageuse, et fidèle aux dieux de la Cinquième Montagne. Mais, malgré tout son pouvoir actuel, elle n'est pas israélite. Elle peut tomber en disgrâce demain, et il nous faudra affronter la colère de nos voisins. Si nous montrons que nous traitons bien un de leurs prophètes, ils seront complaisants à notre égard. »

Les habitants partirent contrariés, car le grand prêtre avait dit qu'Élie serait un jour échangé contre de l'or et des récompenses. D'ici là, même si le gouverneur faisait erreur, ils ne pouvaient rien faire : selon la tradition, on devait respecter la famille gouvernante.

Au loin, à l'entrée de la vallée, les tentes des guerriers assyriens commencèrent à se multiplier.

Le commandant s'en inquiétait, mais il n'avait le soutien ni du prêtre, ni du gouverneur. Il obligeait ses guerriers à s'entraîner en permanence, tout en sachant qu'aucun d'eux — pas plus que leurs aïeux — n'avait l'expérience du combat. Les guerres appartenaient au passé d'Akbar, et toutes les stratégies qu'il avait apprises étaient rendues obsolètes par les techniques et les armes nouvelles qu'utilisaient les pays étrangers.

« Akbar a toujours négocié sa paix, affirmait le gouverneur. Ce n'est pas cette fois que nous serons envahis. Laisse les pays étrangers se battre entre eux : nous, nous avons une arme beaucoup plus puissante, l'argent. Lorsqu'ils auront fini de se détruire mutuellement, nous entrerons dans leurs cités — et nous vendrons nos produits. »

Le gouverneur réussit à tranquilliser la population

au sujet des Assyriens. Mais le bruit courait toujours que l'Israélite avait attiré la malédiction des dieux sur Akbar. Elie représentait un problème qui s'aggravait chaque jour.

*

Un après-midi, l'état du petit garçon empira. Il ne parvenait déjà plus à se tenir debout, ni à reconnaître les gens qui venaient lui rendre visite. Avant que le soleil ne descendît sur l'horizon, Elie et la femme s'agenouillèrent près du lit de l'enfant.

« Seigneur tout-puissant, Toi qui as dévié les flèches du soldat et m'as mené jusqu'ici, fais que cet enfant soit sauf. Il est innocent de mes péchés et des péchés de ses parents. Sauve-le, Seigneur. »

L'enfant ne bougeait presque plus ; ses lèvres étaient blanches, ses yeux perdaient rapidement leur éclat.

« Adresse une prière à ton Dieu unique, demanda la femme. Parce que seule une mère est capable de reconnaître le moment où l'âme de son fils est en train de s'en aller. »

Elie eut envie de lui prendre la main, de lui dire qu'elle n'était pas seule, et que le Dieu tout-puissant devrait exaucer son souhait. Il était prophète, il avait accepté cette mission sur les rives du Kerith, et désormais les anges se tenaient à ses côtés.

« Je n'ai plus de larmes, continua-t-elle. S'Il n'a pas de compassion, s'Il a besoin d'une vie, alors prie-Le de m'emporter et de laisser mon fils se promener dans la vallée et par les rues d'Akbar. »

Elie fit son possible pour se concentrer sur son oraison ; mais la souffrance de cette mère était si intense qu'elle semblait emplir la chambre et pénétrer partout, dans les murs et les portes.

Il toucha le corps du gamin. Sa température n'était plus aussi élevée que les jours précédents, et c'était mauvais signe.

*

Le prêtre était passé à la maison le matin et, comme il l'avait fait durant deux semaines, il avait appliqué des cataplasmes d'herbes sur le visage et la poitrine de l'enfant. Ces jours derniers, les femmes d'Akbar avait apporté des remèdes dont les recettes s'étaient transmises de génération en génération au fil des siècles et dont le pouvoir de guérison avait été démontré en maintes occasions. Tous les après-midi, elles se réunissaient au pied de la Cinquième Montagne et faisaient des sacrifices pour que l'âme du petit ne quittât pas son corps.

Emu par tous ces événements, un marchand égyptien de passage dans la cité remit sans se faire payer une poudre rouge, très onéreuse, qui devait être mélangée à la nourriture de l'enfant. Selon la légende, le secret de fabrication de cette poudre avait été confié aux médecins égyptiens par les dieux eux-mêmes.

Elie avait prié sans arrêt tout ce temps.

Mais rien, absolument rien, aucun progrès.

*

« Je sais pourquoi ils t'ont permis de rester ici », dit la femme, d'une voix de plus en plus éteinte parce qu'elle avait passé plusieurs jours sans dormir. « Je sais que ta tête est mise à prix et qu'un jour tu seras envoyé en Israël, où on t'échangera contre de l'or. Si tu sauves mon fils, je jure par Baal et par les dieux de la Cinquième Montagne que tu ne seras jamais capturé. Je connais des chemins que cette génération a oubliés, et je t'apprendrai comment t'enfuir d'Akbar sans que l'on te voie. »

Elie resta silencieux.

« Adresse une prière à ton Dieu unique, supplia de nouveau la femme. S'Il sauve mon fils, je jure que je renierai Baal et que je croirai en Lui. Explique à ton Seigneur que je t'ai donné refuge quand tu en as eu besoin, que j'ai fait exactement ce qu'Il avait ordonné. »

Elie pria encore, et il implora de toutes ses forces. A ce moment précis, l'enfant bougea.

« Je veux sortir d'ici », dit l'enfant d'une voix faible.

Les yeux de la mère brillaient de contentement, et ses larmes coulaient.

« Viens, mon fils. Allons où tu veux, fais ce que tu désires. »

Elie tenta de prendre l'enfant dans ses bras, mais le petit écarta sa main.

« Je veux sortir seul. »

Il se leva lentement et se dirigea vers la salle. Au bout de quelques pas, il tomba sur le sol, comme foudroyé.

Elie et la veuve s'approchèrent. Le gamin était mort.

Il y eut un instant pendant lequel ni l'un ni l'autre ne parlèrent. Tout à coup, la femme se mit à hurler.

« Maudits soient les dieux, maudits soient ceux qui ont emporté l'âme de mon fils ! Maudit soit l'homme qui a porté le malheur sur ma maison ! Mon fils unique ! criait-elle. J'ai respecté la volonté des cieux, j'ai été généreuse avec un étranger, et finalement mon fils est mort ! »

Les voisins écoutèrent les lamentations de la veuve et virent son fils étendu sur le sol. Elle continuait à crier, donnant des coups de poing au prophète israélite qui se tenait debout à côté d'elle — il semblait avoir perdu toute capacité de réaction et ne faisait rien pour se défendre. Pendant que les femmes essayaient de la calmer, les hommes saisirent Elie par le bras et l'emmenèrent devant le gouverneur.

« Cet homme a rétribué la générosité par la haine. Il a jeté un sortilège sur la maison de la veuve dont le fils est mort. Nous donnons refuge à un individu maudit par les dieux. »

L'Israélite pleurait : « Seigneur, mon Dieu, même à cette veuve qui a été généreuse avec moi Tu veux du mal ? songeait-il. Si Tu as fait mourir son fils, c'est parce que je n'accomplis pas la mission qui m'a été confiée, et je mérite la mort. »

*

Dans la soirée, le conseil de la cité d'Akbar fut réuni, sous la présidence du prêtre et du gouverneur. Elie fut traduit en jugement.

« Tu as décidé de rétribuer l'amour par la haine. Pour cela, je te condamne à mort, décréta le gouverneur.

— Même si ta tête vaut un sac d'or, nous ne pouvons pas réveiller la colère des dieux de la Cinquième Montagne. Sinon, après cela, plus personne en ce monde ne sera capable de rendre la paix à cette cité », ajouta le prêtre.

Elie baissa la tête. Il méritait toute la souffrance qu'il pourrait supporter, parce que le Seigneur l'avait abandonné.

« Tu partiras gravir la Cinquième Montagne, ordonna le prêtre. Tu demanderas pardon aux dieux offensés. Ils feront descendre le feu des cieux pour te tuer. S'ils s'en abstiennent, c'est qu'ils désirent que la justice soit accomplie par nos mains ; nous attendrons ton retour, et demain tu seras exécuté, selon le rituel. »

Elie connaissait bien les exécutions sacrées : on arrachait le cœur de la victime et on lui coupait la tête. Selon la coutume, un homme qui n'avait plus de cœur ne pouvait entrer au Paradis.

« Pourquoi m'as-Tu choisi pour cela, Seigneur ? » s'écria-t-il à voix haute, sachant que les hommes qui l'entouraient ne comprendraient pas le choix que le Seigneur avait fait pour lui. « Ne vois-tu pas que je suis incapable d'accomplir ce que tu exiges ? »

Il n'entendit pas de réponse.

Les hommes et les femmes d'Akbar suivirent en procession le groupe de gardes qui emmenait l'Israélite jusqu'au pied de la Cinquième Montagne. Ils criaient des insultes et lui jetaient des pierres. Les soldats parvinrent à grand-peine à contenir la fureur de la foule. Au bout d'une demi-heure de marche, ils atteignirent la montagne sacrée.

Le groupe s'arrêta devant les autels de pierre sur lesquels le peuple avait coutume de déposer les offrandes, de consommer les sacrifices, de prononcer vœux et prières. Tous connaissaient la légende des géants qui vivaient là et se souvenaient des individus qui, bravant l'interdit, avaient été frappés par le feu du ciel. Les voyageurs qui empruntaient de nuit le chemin de la vallée assuraient avoir entendu les rires des dieux et des déesses. Bien que l'on n'eût aucune certitude de tout cela, personne ne se risquait à défier les dieux.

« Allons-y, dit un soldat, en poussant Elie de la pointe de sa lance. Celui qui a tué un enfant mérite le pire des châtiments. »

*

Elie foula le sol interdit et commença à gravir la pente. Quand il eut marché assez longtemps pour ne plus percevoir les cris des habitants d'Akbar, il s'assit sur un rocher et pleura : depuis cet après-midi, dans la charpenterie, où il avait vu des lumières scintiller dans l'obscurité, il n'avait réussi qu'à porter malheur aux autres. Le Seigneur avait perdu ses porte-parole en Israël et le culte des dieux phéniciens s'était renforcé. La première nuit qu'il avait passée près du ruisseau du Kerith, Elie avait cru que Dieu l'avait choisi pour qu'il devînt un martyr, comme cela s'était produit pour tant d'autres.

Bien au contraire, le Seigneur avait envoyé un corbeau — un oiseau de mauvais augure —, qui l'avait nourri jusqu'à ce que le Kerith fût asséché. Pourquoi un corbeau, et pas une colombe, ou un ange ? Tout cela n'avait-il été que le délire d'un homme désireux de cacher sa peur, ou dont la tête était restée trop longtemps exposée au soleil ? Elie n'était maintenant plus sûr de rien : peut-être le Mal avait-il trouvé son instrument et était-il, lui, cet instrument. Pourquoi, au lieu de s'en retourner et d'en finir avec la princesse qui causait tellement de tort à son peuple, Dieu lui avait-il ordonné de se rendre à Akbar ?

Il s'était senti lâche mais il avait obéi. Il avait lutté pour s'adapter à ce peuple inconnu, gentil, mais dont la culture lui était complètement étrangère. Au moment où il croyait accomplir son destin, le fils de la veuve était mort.

« Pourquoi moi ? » se demandait-il.

*

Il se leva, se remit en marche et pénétra dans le brouillard qui enveloppait le sommet de la montagne. Il pouvait profiter de l'absence de visibilité pour échapper à ses poursuivants, mais à quoi bon ? Il était fatigué de fuir, il savait que jamais il ne réussirait à trouver sa place dans ce monde. Même s'il parvenait à se sauver maintenant, la malédiction l'accompagnerait dans une autre cité, et de nouvelles tragédies se produiraient. Il emporterait avec lui, où qu'il allât, l'ombre de ces morts. Il valait mieux qu'on lui arrache le cœur de la poitrine et qu'on lui coupe la tête.

Il s'assit de nouveau, cette fois au beau milieu du brouillard. Il était décidé à attendre un peu, de façon à laisser croire aux hommes en bas qu'il était monté jusqu'au sommet du mont. Ensuite il retournerait à Akbar et se laisserait capturer.

« Le feu du ciel. » Beaucoup en étaient morts, bien qu'Elie doutât qu'il fût envoyé par le Seigneur. Les nuits sans lune, son éclat traversait le firmament, apparaissant puis disparaissant brusquement. Peut-être brûlait-il. Peut-être tuait-il instantanément, sans souffrance.

*

La nuit tomba et le brouillard se dissipa. Il aperçut la vallée, en bas, les lumières d'Akbar et les feux du campement assyrien. Il écouta l'aboiement des chiens et le chant de guerre des guerriers.

« Je suis prêt, se dit-il. J'ai accepté d'être un prophète, et j'ai fait de mon mieux. Mais j'ai échoué, et maintenant Dieu a besoin de quelqu'un d'autre. »

A ce moment, une lumière descendit jusqu'à lui.

« Le feu du ciel ! »

La lumière, cependant, ne le toucha pas et demeura devant lui. Une voix dit :

« Je suis un ange du Seigneur. »

Elie s'agenouilla, le visage contre terre.

« Je t'ai déjà vu plusieurs fois, et j'ai obéi à l'ange du Seigneur qui me fait semer le malheur partout où je passe », répliqua Elie, toujours prosterné.

Mais l'ange reprit :

« Lorsque tu regagneras la cité, prie trois fois pour que l'enfant revienne à la vie. Le Seigneur t'entendra la troisième fois.

— Pour quoi ferais-je cela ?

— Pour la grandeur de Dieu.

— Quoi qu'il advienne, j'ai douté de moi-même. Je ne suis plus digne de ma tâche, rétorqua Elie.

— Tout homme a le droit de douter de sa tâche et d'y faillir de temps en temps. La seule chose qu'il ne puisse faire, c'est l'oublier. Celui qui ne doute pas de soi est indigne — car il a une confiance aveugle dans sa valeur et pèche par orgueil. Béni soit celui qui traverse des moments d'indécision.

— Il y a un instant, tu as pu voir que je n'étais même plus sûr que tu sois un émissaire de Dieu.

— Va, et fais ce que je dis. »

*

Un long moment s'écoula, puis Elie redescendit de la montagne. Les gardes l'attendaient près des autels de sacrifice, mais la foule s'en était déjà retournée à Akbar.

« Je suis prêt à mourir, déclara-t-il. J'ai imploré le pardon des dieux de la Cinquième Montagne, et ils exigent, avant que mon âme ne quitte mon corps, que je passe chez la veuve qui m'a accueilli et que je lui demande d'avoir pitié de mon âme. »

Les soldats le ramenèrent devant le prêtre. Là, ils transmirent sa requête.

« Je te l'accorde, dit le prêtre au prisonnier. Puisque tu as sollicité le pardon des dieux, tu dois aussi implorer celui de la veuve. Pour que tu ne t'enfuies pas, quatre soldats en armes t'accompagneront. Mais ne crois pas que tu réussiras à la convaincre de réclamer la clémence pour ta vie. Au lever du jour, nous t'exécuterons au centre de la place. »

Le prêtre voulut l'interroger sur ce qu'il avait vu là-haut. Mais, en présence des soldats, la réponse risquait de le mettre dans l'embarras. Il décida donc de ne rien dire. Il songeait toutefois que c'était une bonne idée qu'Elie demandât pardon publiquement ; plus personne ne mettrait en doute le pouvoir des dieux de la Cinquième Montagne.

Elie et les soldats s'engagèrent dans la ruelle misérable où il avait habité pendant quelques mois. La porte et les fenêtres de la maison de la veuve étaient grandes ouvertes, afin que — selon la coutume — l'âme de son fils pût s'en aller rejoindre le séjour des dieux. Le corps était placé au centre de la petite salle, veillé par tous les voisins.

Quand ils virent apparaître l'Israélite, hommes et femmes furent horrifiés.

« Faites-le sortir d'ici ! crièrent-ils aux gardes. Le mal qu'il a déjà causé ne suffit-il pas ? Cet homme est tellement mauvais que les dieux de la Cinquième Montagne n'ont pas voulu souiller leurs mains de son sang !

— Laissez-nous la tâche de le tuer ! cria un autre. Nous allons le faire sur-le-champ, sans attendre l'exécution rituelle ! »

Affrontant les bourrades et les gifles, Elie se libéra des mains qui le retenaient, et il courut jusqu'à la veuve qui pleurait dans un coin.

« Je peux faire revenir ton fils d'entre les morts. Laisse-moi le toucher. Juste un instant. »

La veuve ne releva même pas la tête.

« Je t'en prie, insista-t-il. Même si c'est la dernière chose que tu fais pour moi dans cette vie, donne-moi une chance de te récompenser pour ta générosité. »

Des hommes s'emparèrent de lui, voulant l'éloigner. Mais Elie se débattait et luttait de toutes ses forces, implorant qu'on le laissât toucher l'enfant mort.

Malgré sa vigueur, on parvint à le repousser sur le seuil. « Ange du Seigneur, où es-tu ? » s'écria-t-il à l'adresse des cieux.

Tous s'arrêtèrent. La veuve s'était levée et elle se dirigeait vers lui. Elle le prit par la main, le conduisit jusqu'à la dépouille de son fils et retira le drap qui la recouvrait.

« Voici le sang de mon sang, dit-elle. Qu'il descende sur la tête de tes parents si tu ne réussis pas ce que tu désires. »

Il s'approcha pour le toucher.

« Un instant, dit la veuve. Prie ton Dieu que ma malédiction s'accomplisse. »

Le cœur d'Elie battait la chamade. Mais il croyait aux paroles de l'ange.

« Que le sang de cet enfant descende sur mes parents, sur mes frères et sur les fils et les filles de mes frères si j'échoue. »

Alors, malgré tous ses doutes, sa culpabilité et ses craintes,

il le prit des bras de la femme, et le porta dans la chambre haute où il logeait. Puis il invoqua les cieux en disant :

"Veux-tu du mal, Seigneur, même à cette veuve qui m'a donné l'hospitalité, au point que tu fasses mourir son fils ?"

Il s'étendit trois fois sur l'enfant et invoqua le Seigneur en disant : "Seigneur mon Dieu, que le souffle de cet enfant revienne en lui !"

Pendant quelques instants, rien ne se passa. Elie se vit de nouveau à Galaad, devant le soldat, la flèche pointée sur son cœur. Il savait que très souvent le destin d'un homme n'a rien à voir avec ce qu'il croit ou redoute. Il se sentait tranquille et confiant comme cet après-midi-là, car il savait que, quelle que fût l'issue, il y avait une raison à tout cela. Au sommet de la Cinquième Montagne, l'ange avait appelé cette raison « la grandeur de Dieu ». Il espérait comprendre un jour pourquoi le Créateur avait besoin de Ses créatures pour montrer cette gloire.

C'est alors que l'enfant ouvrit les yeux.

« Où est ma mère ? demanda-t-il.

— Là en bas, elle t'attend, répondit Elie en souriant.

— J'ai fait un rêve étrange. Je voyageais dans un tunnel noir, à une vitesse bien plus grande que le cheval de course le plus rapide d'Akbar. J'ai vu un homme, dont je sais qu'il était mon père, bien que je ne l'aie jamais connu. Alors je suis arrivé dans un endroit magnifique, où j'aurais beaucoup aimé rester. Mais un autre homme — je ne le connais pas, mais il m'a paru très bon et très brave — m'a demandé doucement de revenir. J'aurais voulu aller plus loin, mais tu m'as réveillé. »

L'enfant semblait triste. Ce lieu dans lequel il était presque entré devait être fort beau.

« Ne me laisse pas seul, car tu m'as fait revenir d'un endroit où je savais que j'étais protégé.

— Descendons, dit Elie. Ta mère veut te voir. »

L'enfant essaya de se lever, mais il était trop faible pour marcher. Elie le prit contre lui, et ils descendirent.

*

En bas, dans la salle, les gens semblaient saisis d'une profonde terreur.

« Pourquoi y a-t-il tant de monde ici ? » demanda l'enfant.

Avant qu'Elie ait pu répondre, la veuve prit son fils dans ses bras et l'embrassa en pleurant.

« Qu'est-ce qu'ils t'ont fait, maman ? Pourquoi es-tu triste ?

— Je ne suis pas triste, mon fils, répondit-elle en séchant ses larmes. Je n'ai jamais été aussi heureuse de ma vie. »

La veuve se jeta à genoux et se mit à crier :

« Je sais maintenant que tu es un homme de Dieu ! La vérité du Seigneur sort de tes paroles ! »

Elie la serra dans ses bras et lui demanda de se relever.

« Libérez cet homme ! dit-elle aux soldats. Il a combattu le mal qui s'était abattu sur ma maison ! »

Les gens réunis là ne pouvaient en croire leurs yeux. Une jeune fille de vingt ans, qui était peintre, s'agenouilla près de la veuve. Peu à peu, tous l'imitèrent — même les soldats qui étaient chargés de conduire Elie en captivité.

« Levez-vous, pria-t-il. Et adorez le Seigneur. Je ne suis qu'un de Ses serviteurs, peut-être le plus mal préparé. »

Mais tous restaient à genoux, tête baissée.

Il entendit quelqu'un qui disait : « Tu as conversé avec les dieux de la Cinquième Montagne. Et maintenant tu peux faire des miracles.

— Il n'y a pas de dieux là-bas, répliqua-t-il. J'ai vu un ange du Seigneur, qui m'a ordonné de faire cela.

— Tu as rencontré Baal et ses frères », renchérit un autre.

Elie se fraya un chemin parmi les gens à genoux et sortit dans la rue. Son cœur cognait toujours dans sa poitrine, comme s'il n'avait pas correctement accompli la tâche que l'ange lui avait assignée. « A quoi bon ressusciter un mort, si personne ne comprend d'où vient tant de pouvoir ? » L'ange lui avait demandé de crier trois fois le nom du Seigneur mais il ne lui avait rien dit sur la façon d'expliquer le miracle à la foule amassée en bas. « Serait-ce que, comme les anciens prophètes, je me suis contenté de faire preuve de vanité ? » se demandait-il.

Il entendit la voix de son ange gardien, avec lequel il conversait depuis son enfance :

« Tu as rencontré aujourd'hui un ange du Seigneur.

— Oui, répondit Elie. Mais les anges du Seigneur ne conversent pas avec les hommes. Ils ne font que transmettre les ordres de Dieu.

— Sers-toi de ton pouvoir », commanda l'ange gardien.

Elie ne comprit pas ce qu'il entendait par là. « Je n'ai pas de pouvoir qui ne vienne du Seigneur.

— Personne n'en a. Tout le monde possède le pouvoir du Seigneur, mais personne ne s'en sert. »

Et l'ange ajouta :

« Désormais, et jusqu'à ce que tu retournes dans le pays que tu as quitté, aucun autre miracle ne te sera accordé.

— Et quand y retournerai-je ?

— Le Seigneur a besoin de toi pour reconstruire Israël. Tu fouleras de nouveau son sol lorsque tu auras appris à reconstruire. »

Et il n'en dit pas plus.

Seconde partie

Le grand prêtre adressa ses prières au soleil qui se levait et demanda au dieu de la tempête, ainsi qu'à la déesse des animaux, d'avoir pitié des fous. On lui avait raconté, ce matin-là, qu'Elie avait ramené le fils de la veuve du royaume des morts.

La cité en était effrayée et excitée tout à la fois. Ils croyaient tous que l'Israélite avait reçu son pouvoir des dieux sur la Cinquième Montagne, si bien que désormais il était beaucoup plus difficile d'en finir avec lui. « Mais l'heure viendra », se dit le prêtre.

Les dieux lui donneraient l'occasion de tuer cet homme. Pourtant, la colère divine avait un autre motif, et la présence des Assyriens à l'entrée de la vallée était un signe. Pourquoi des siècles de paix prendraient-ils fin ainsi ? Il connaissait la réponse à cette question : à cause de l'invention de Byblos. Son pays avait développé une forme d'écriture accessible à tous — même à ceux qui n'étaient pas préparés à l'utiliser. N'importe qui pouvait l'apprendre en peu de temps, et ce serait la fin de la civilisation.

Le prêtre savait que, de toutes les armes de destruction inventées par l'homme, la plus terrible — et la plus puissante — était la parole. Poignards et lances laissaient des traces de sang ; les flèches se voyaient de loin ; on finissait par détecter les poisons et par les éviter. Mais la parole parvenait à détruire sans laisser de traces. Si les rituels sacrés pouvaient être diffusés, bien des gens s'en serviraient pour tenter de transformer l'univers, et les dieux en seraient perturbés. Jusque-là, seule la caste sacerdotale détenait la mémoire des ancêtres — que l'on se transmettait oralement, sous le serment que les informations seraient maintenues secrètes. Ou alors, il fallait des années d'étude pour arriver à déchiffrer les caractères que les Egyptiens avaient répandus de par le monde ; ainsi, seuls ceux qui étaient très préparés, scribes et prêtres, étaient en mesure d'échanger des informations.

D'autres cultures avaient leurs méthodes pour enregistrer l'Histoire, mais elles étaient tellement compliquées que nul ne s'était préoccupé de les apprendre hors des régions où elles étaient en usage. L'invention de Byblos, elle, risquait d'avoir des effets considérables : n'importe quel pays pouvait l'utiliser, quelle que soit sa langue. Même les Grecs, qui en général rejetaient tout ce qui n'était pas originaire de leurs cités, avaient déjà adopté l'écriture de Byblos et la pratiquaient couramment dans leurs transactions commerciales. Comme ils étaient spécialistes dans l'art de s'approprier tout ce qui avait un caractère novateur, ils l'avaient baptisée du nom grec d'*alphabet*.

Les secrets gardés pendant des siècles de civilisation couraient le risque d'être exposés au grand jour. En comparaison, le sacrilège d'Elie — qui avait ramené un être de l'autre rive du fleuve de la Mort, comme les Egyptiens avaient coutume de le faire — était insignifiant.

« Nous sommes punis parce que nous sommes incapables de protéger soigneusement ce qui est sacré, pensa-t-il. Les Assyriens sont à nos portes, ils traverseront la vallée et ils détruiront la civilisation de nos ancêtres. »

Et ils mettraient fin à l'écriture. Le prêtre savait que la présence de l'ennemi n'était pas fortuite. C'était le prix à payer. Les dieux avaient organisé les choses afin que personne ne devinât qu'ils étaient les véritables responsables ; ils avaient placé au pouvoir un gouverneur qui s'inquiétait davantage des affaires que de l'armée, excité la convoitise des Assyriens, fait en sorte que la pluie se raréfiât, et envoyé un infidèle pour diviser la cité. Bientôt, le combat final s'engagerait. Akbar continuerait d'exister, mais la menace que représentaient les caractères de Byblos serait à tout jamais rayée de la surface de la terre.

Le prêtre nettoya avec soin la pierre qui signalait l'endroit où, des générations plus tôt, un pèlerin étranger avait trouvé le lieu indiqué par les cieux et fondé la cité. « Comme elle est belle ! » pensa-t-il. Les pierres étaient une image des dieux — dures, résistantes, survivant à toutes les situations, et n'ayant nul besoin d'expliquer la raison de leur présence. La tradition orale rapportait que le centre du monde était marqué d'une pierre et, dans son enfance, il avait parfois pensé à en chercher l'emplacement. Il avait nourri ce projet jusqu'à cette année. Mais quand il avait constaté la présence des Assyriens au fond de la vallée, il avait compris que jamais il ne réaliserait son rêve.

« Cela n'a pas d'importance. Le sort a voulu que ma génération fût offerte en sacrifice pour avoir offensé les dieux. Il y a des choses inévitables dans l'histoire du monde, il nous faut les accepter. »

Il se promit d'obéir aux dieux : il ne chercherait pas à empêcher la guerre.

« Peut-être sommes-nous arrivés à la fin des temps. Il n'y a pas moyen de contourner les crises qui sont de plus en plus nombreuses. »

Le prêtre prit son bâton et sortit du petit temple ; il avait rendez-vous avec le commandant de la garnison d'Akbar.

Il avait presque atteint le rempart sud quand Elie l'aborda.

« Le Seigneur a fait revenir un enfant d'entre les morts, dit l'Israélite. La cité croit en mon pouvoir.

— L'enfant n'était sans doute pas mort, répliqua le grand prêtre. Cela s'est déjà produit d'autres fois ; le cœur s'arrête, et bientôt se remet à battre. Aujourd'hui, toute la cité en parle. Demain, les gens se souviendront que les dieux sont proches et qu'ils peuvent écouter leurs paroles. Alors, leurs bouches redeviendront muettes. Je dois y aller, parce que les Assyriens se préparent au combat.

— Ecoute ce que j'ai à te dire : après le miracle de la nuit dernière, je suis allé dormir à l'extérieur des murailles, parce que j'avais besoin d'un peu de tranquillité. Alors l'ange que j'avais vu en haut de la Cinquième Montagne m'est apparu de nouveau. Et il m'a dit : "Akbar sera détruite par la guerre."

— Les cités ne peuvent pas être détruites. Elles seront reconstruites soixante-dix-sept fois, parce que les dieux savent où ils les ont placées, et ils ont besoin qu'elles soient là. »

Le gouverneur s'approcha, accompagné d'un groupe de courtisans :

« Qu'est-ce que tu dis ? demanda-t-il.

— Recherchez la paix, reprit Elie.

— Si tu as peur, retourne d'où tu viens, rétorqua sèchement le prêtre.

— Jézabel et son roi attendent les prophètes fugitifs pour les mettre à mort, dit le gouverneur. Mais j'aimerais que tu m'expliques comment tu as pu gravir la Cinquième Montagne sans être détruit par le feu du ciel ? »

Le prêtre devait absolument interrompre cette conversation : le gouverneur avait l'intention de négocier avec les Assyriens et peut-être chercherait-il à se servir d'Elie pour parvenir à ses fins.

« Ne l'écoute pas, dit le prêtre au gouverneur. Hier, quand on l'a amené devant moi pour qu'il soit jugé, je l'ai vu pleurer de peur.

— Je pleurais pour le mal que je pensais avoir causé. Car je n'ai peur que du Seigneur et de moi-même. Je n'ai pas fui Israël et je suis prêt à y retourner dès que le Seigneur le permettra. Je détruirai sa belle princesse et la foi d'Israël survivra à cette nouvelle menace.

— Il faut avoir le cœur très dur pour résister aux charmes de Jézabel, ironisa le gouverneur. Mais en ce cas nous enverrions une autre femme encore plus belle, comme nous l'avons déjà fait avant Jézabel. »

64

Le prêtre disait vrai. Deux cents ans auparavant, une princesse de Sidon avait séduit le plus sage de tous les gouvernants d'Israël, le roi Salomon. Elle lui avait demandé de construire un autel en hommage à la déesse Astarté, et Salomon avait obéi. A cause de ce sacrilège, le Seigneur avait levé les armées voisines contre son pays et Salomon avait été maudit par Dieu.

« La même chose arrivera à Achab, le mari de Jézabel », songea Elie. Le Seigneur lui ferait accomplir sa tâche quand l'heure serait venue. Mais à quoi bon tenter de convaincre ces hommes ? Ils étaient comme ceux qu'il avait vus la nuit précédente, agenouillés sur le sol dans la maison de la veuve, priant les dieux de la Cinquième Montagne. Jamais la tradition ne leur permettrait de penser autrement.

« Il est regrettable que nous devions respecter la loi de l'hospitalité », remarqua le gouverneur qui, apparemment, avait déjà oublié les commentaires d'Elie sur la paix. « Sinon, nous aiderions Jézabel dans sa tâche de destruction des prophètes.

— Ce n'est pas pour cela que vous épargnez ma vie. Vous savez que je représente une précieuse monnaie d'échange, et vous voulez donner à Jézabel le plaisir de me tuer de ses propres mains. Mais — depuis hier — le peuple m'a attribué des pouvoirs miraculeux. Les gens pensent que j'ai rencontré les dieux au sommet de la Cinquième Montagne ; quant à vous, cela ne vous dérangerait pas d'offenser les dieux, mais vous ne voulez pas irriter les habitants de la cité. »

Le gouverneur et le prêtre laissèrent Elie monologuer et se dirigèrent vers les murailles. A ce moment précis, le prêtre décida qu'il tuerait le prophète israélite à la première occasion ; celui qui jusque-là ne représentait qu'une monnaie d'échange était devenu une menace.

*

En les voyant s'éloigner, Elie se désespéra. Que pouvait-il faire pour aider le Seigneur ? Alors il se mit à crier au milieu de la place :

« Peuple d'Akbar ! Hier soir, j'ai gravi la Cinquième

Montagne et j'ai conversé avec les dieux qui habitent là-haut. A mon retour, j'ai pu ramener un enfant du royaume des morts ! »

Les gens se groupèrent autour de lui. L'histoire était déjà connue dans toute la cité. Le gouverneur et le grand prêtre s'arrêtèrent en chemin et firent demi-tour pour voir ce qui se passait : le prophète israélite racontait qu'il avait vu les dieux de la Cinquième Montagne adorer un Dieu supérieur.

« Je le ferai tuer, déclara le prêtre.

— Et la population se rebellera contre nous », répliqua le gouverneur, qui s'intéressait aux propos de l'étranger. « Mieux vaut attendre qu'il commette une erreur.

— Avant que je ne descende de la montagne, les dieux m'ont chargé de venir en aide au gouverneur contre la menace des Assyriens, poursuivait Elie. Je sais que c'est un homme d'honneur et qu'il veut bien m'entendre. Mais il y a des gens qui ont tout intérêt à ce que la guerre se produise, et ils ne me laissent pas l'approcher.

— L'Israélite est un homme saint, dit un vieillard au gouverneur. Personne ne peut monter sur la Cinquième Montagne sans être foudroyé par le feu du ciel, mais cet homme a réussi, et maintenant il ressuscite les morts.

— Tyr, Sidon et toutes les cités phéniciennes ont une tradition de paix, dit un autre vieillard. Nous avons connu de pires menaces, et nous les avons surmontées. »

Des malades et des estropiés s'approchèrent, se frayant un passage dans la foule, touchant les vêtements d'Elie et lui demandant de guérir leurs maux.

« Avant de conseiller le gouverneur, guéris les malades, ordonna le prêtre. Alors nous croirons que les dieux de la Cinquième Montagne sont avec toi. »

Elie se souvint de ce que lui avait dit l'ange la nuit précédente : seule la force des personnes ordinaires lui serait accordée.

« Les malades appellent à l'aide, insista le prêtre. Nous attendons.

— Nous veillerons d'abord à éviter la guerre. Il y

aura beaucoup d'autres malades et d'autres infirmes si nous n'y parvenons pas. »

Le gouverneur interrompit la discussion :

« Elie viendra avec nous. Il a été touché par l'inspiration divine. »

Bien qu'il ne crût pas qu'il existât des dieux sur la Cinquième Montagne, il avait besoin d'un allié pour convaincre le peuple que la paix avec les Assyriens était la seule issue.

Tandis qu'ils allaient à la rencontre du commandant, le prêtre s'expliqua avec Elie.

« Tu ne crois en rien de ce que tu affirmes.

— Je crois que la paix est la seule issue. Mais je ne crois pas que les hauteurs de cette montagne soient habitées par des dieux. J'y suis allé.

— Et qu'as-tu vu ?

— Un ange du Seigneur. Je l'avais déjà vu auparavant, dans plusieurs lieux où je suis passé. Et il n'existe qu'un seul Dieu. »

Le prêtre rit.

« Tu veux dire que, selon toi, le dieu qui a fait la tempête a fait aussi le blé, même si ce sont des choses complètement différentes ?

— Tu vois la Cinquième Montagne ? demanda Elie. De quelque côté que tu regardes, elle te semble différente, pourtant c'est la même montagne. Il en est ainsi de tout ce qui a été créé : ce sont les nombreuses faces du même Dieu. »

Ils arrivèrent au sommet de la muraille, d'où l'on apercevait au loin le campement de l'ennemi. Dans la vallée désertique, la blancheur des tentes sautait aux yeux.

Quelque temps auparavant, lorsque des sentinelles avaient remarqué la présence des Assyriens à une extrémité de la vallée, les espions avaient affirmé qu'ils étaient là en mission de reconnaissance ; le commandant avait suggéré qu'on les fît prisonniers et qu'on les vendît comme esclaves. Le gouverneur avait opté pour une autre stratégie : ne rien faire. Il misait sur le fait qu'en établissant de bonnes relations avec les Assyriens, il pourrait ouvrir un nouveau marché pour le commerce du verre fabriqué à Akbar. En outre, même s'ils étaient là pour préparer une guerre, les Assyriens savaient bien que les petites cités se rangent toujours du côté des vainqueurs. Les généraux assyriens désiraient simplement traverser ces villes, sans qu'elles opposent de résistance, pour atteindre Tyr et Sidon où l'on conservait le trésor et le savoir de leur peuple.

La patrouille campait à l'entrée de la vallée et, peu à peu, des renforts étaient arrivés. Le prêtre affirmait en connaître la raison : la cité possédait un puits, le seul à plusieurs jours de marche dans le désert. Si les Assyriens voulaient conquérir Tyr ou Sidon, ils avaient besoin de cette eau pour approvisionner leurs armées.

Au bout d'un mois, ils pouvaient encore les chasser. Au bout de deux, ils pouvaient encore les vaincre facilement et négocier une retraite honorable des soldats assyriens.

Ils étaient prêts au combat, mais ils n'attaquaient pas. Au bout de cinq mois, ils pouvaient encore gagner la bataille. « Les Assyriens vont bientôt attaquer, parce qu'ils doivent souffrir de la soif », se disait le gouverneur. Il demanda au commandant d'élaborer des stratégies de défense et d'entraîner constamment ses hommes pour réagir à une attaque surprise.

Mais il ne se concentrait que sur la préparation de la paix.

*

Six mois avaient passé et l'armée assyrienne ne bougeait toujours pas. La tension à Akbar, croissante durant les premières semaines d'occupation, avait totalement disparu ; les gens s'étaient remis à vivre, les agriculteurs retournaient aux champs, les artisans fabriquaient le vin, le verre et le savon, les commerçants continuaient à vendre et à acheter leurs marchandises. Tous croyaient que, comme Akbar n'avait pas attaqué l'ennemi, la crise serait rapidement résolue par des négociations. Tous savaient que le gouverneur était conseillé par les dieux et connaissait toujours la meilleure décision à prendre.

Lorsque Elie était arrivé dans la cité, le gouverneur avait fait répandre des rumeurs sur la malédiction que l'étranger apportait avec lui ; de cette manière, si la menace de guerre devenait insupportable, il pourrait l'accuser d'être la cause principale du désastre. Les habitants d'Akbar seraient convaincus qu'avec la mort de l'Israélite tout rentrerait dans l'ordre. Le gouverneur expliquerait alors qu'il était désormais trop tard pour exiger le départ des Assyriens ; il ferait tuer Elie, et il expliquerait à son peuple que la paix constituait la meilleure solution. A son avis, les marchands — qui désiraient eux aussi la paix — forceraient les autres à admettre cette idée.

Pendant tous ces mois, il avait lutté contre la pression du prêtre et du commandant, exigeant une attaque rapide. Mais les dieux de la Cinquième Montagne ne l'avaient jamais abandonné. Après la miraculeuse résurrection de l'autre nuit, la vie d'Elie était plus importante que son exécution.

*

« Que fait cet étranger avec vous ? demanda le commandant.

— Il est inspiré par les dieux, répondit le gouverneur. Et il va nous aider à trouver la meilleure issue. »

Il changea rapidement de sujet de conversation.

« On dirait que le nombre de tentes a augmenté aujourd'hui.

— Et il augmentera encore demain, dit le commandant. Si nous avions attaqué alors qu'ils n'étaient qu'une patrouille, ils ne seraient probablement pas revenus.

— Tu te trompes. L'un d'eux aurait fini par s'échapper, et ils seraient revenus pour se venger.

— Lorsque l'on tarde pour la cueillette, les fruits pourrissent, insista le commandant. Mais quand on repousse les problèmes, ils ne cessent de croître. »

Le gouverneur expliqua que la paix régnait en Phénicie depuis presque trois siècles et que c'était la grande fierté de son peuple. Que diraient les générations futures s'il interrompait cette ère de prospérité ?

« Envoie un émissaire négocier avec eux, conseilla Elie. Le meilleur guerrier est celui qui parvient à faire de l'ennemi un ami.

— Nous ne savons pas exactement ce qu'ils veulent. Nous ne savons même pas s'ils désirent conquérir notre cité. Comment pouvons-nous négocier ?

— Il y a des signes de menace. Une armée ne perd pas son temps à faire des exercices militaires loin de son pays. »

Chaque jour arrivaient de nouveaux soldats — et le gouverneur imaginait la quantité d'eau qui serait nécessaire à tous ces hommes. En peu de temps, la cité serait sans défense devant l'armée ennemie.

« Pouvons-nous attaquer maintenant ? demanda le prêtre au commandant.

— Oui, nous le pouvons. Nous allons perdre beaucoup d'hommes mais la cité sera sauve. Cependant, il nous faut prendre rapidement une décision.

— Nous ne devons pas faire cela, gouverneur. Les dieux de la Cinquième Montagne m'ont affirmé que nous avions encore le temps de trouver une solution pacifique », dit Elie.

Bien qu'il eût écouté la conversation entre le prêtre et l'Israélite, le gouverneur feignit de l'approuver. Pour lui, peu importait que Sidon et Tyr fussent gouvernées par les Phéniciens, par les Cananéens ou par les Assyriens. L'essentiel était que la cité pût continuer à faire le commerce de ses produits.

« Attaquons, insista le prêtre.

— Encore un jour, pria le gouverneur. La situation va peut-être se résoudre. »

Il lui fallait décider rapidement de la meilleure façon d'affronter la menace des Assyriens. Il descendit de la muraille, se dirigea vers le palais et demanda à l'Israélite de l'accompagner.

En chemin, il observa le peuple autour de lui : les bergers menant les brebis aux pâturages, les agriculteurs allant aux champs, essayant d'arracher à la terre desséchée un peu de nourriture pour eux et leur famille. Les soldats faisaient des exercices avec leurs lances et des marchands arrivés récemment exposaient leurs produits sur la place. Aussi incroyable que cela pût paraître, les Assyriens n'avaient pas fermé la route qui traversait la vallée dans toute sa longueur ; les commerçants continuaient à circuler avec leurs marchandises, payant à la cité l'impôt sur le transport.

« Maintenant qu'ils ont réussi à rassembler une force puissante, pourquoi ne ferment-ils pas la route ? s'enquit Elie.

— L'empire assyrien a besoin des produits qui arrivent aux ports de Sidon et de Tyr, répondit le gouverneur. Si les commerçants étaient menacés, le flux de ravitaillement se tarirait. Et les conséquences seraient plus graves qu'une défaite militaire. Il doit y avoir un moyen d'éviter la guerre.

— Oui, renchérit Elie. S'ils désirent de l'eau, nous pouvons la vendre. »

Le gouverneur resta silencieux. Mais il comprit qu'il pouvait faire de l'Israélite une arme contre ceux qui désiraient la guerre. Il avait gravi la Cinquième Montagne, il avait défié les dieux et, au cas où le prêtre persisterait dans l'idée de faire la guerre aux Assyriens, seul Elie pourrait lui tenir tête. Il lui proposa de sortir faire un tour avec lui, pour discuter un peu.

Le prêtre resta immobile à observer l'ennemi du haut de la muraille.

« Que peuvent faire les dieux pour arrêter les envahisseurs ? demanda le commandant.

— J'ai accompli les sacrifices devant la Cinquième Montagne. J'ai prié pour qu'on nous envoie un chef plus courageux.

— Nous aurions dû agir comme Jézabel et tuer les prophètes. Cet Israélite qui hier était condamné à mort, le gouverneur se sert aujourd'hui de lui pour convaincre la population de choisir la paix. »

Le commandant regarda en direction de la montagne.

« Nous pouvons faire assassiner Elie. Et recourir à mes guerriers pour éloigner le gouverneur de ses fonctions.

— Je donnerai l'ordre de mettre à mort Elie, répliqua le prêtre. Quant au gouverneur, nous ne pouvons rien faire : ses ancêtres sont au pouvoir depuis plusieurs générations. Son grand-père a été notre chef, il a donné le pouvoir des dieux à son père, qui le lui a transmis à son tour.

— Pourquoi la tradition nous empêche-t-elle de placer au gouvernement un personnage plus efficace ?

— La tradition existe pour maintenir le monde en ordre. Si nous nous en mêlons, le monde prend fin. »

Le prêtre regarda autour de lui, le ciel et la terre, les montagnes et la vallée, chaque élément accomplissant ce qui avait été écrit pour lui. Parfois la terre tremblait, d'autres fois — comme à présent — il ne pleuvait pas pendant très longtemps. Mais les étoiles restaient à leur place et le soleil n'était pas tombé sur la tête des hommes. Tout cela parce que, depuis le Déluge, les hommes avaient appris qu'il était impossible de modifier l'ordre de la Création.

Autrefois, il n'y avait que la Cinquième Montagne. Hommes et dieux vivaient ensemble, se promenaient dans les jardins du Paradis, conversaient et riaient. Mais les êtres humains avaient péché et les dieux les en avaient chassés ; comme ils n'avaient nulle part où les envoyer, ils avaient finalement créé la terre autour de la montagne, pour pouvoir les y précipiter, les garder sous surveillance et faire en sorte qu'ils se souviennent toujours de se trouver sur un plan bien inférieur à celui des occupants de la Cinquième Montagne.

Mais ils avaient pris soin de laisser entrouverte une porte de retour. Si l'humanité suivait le bon chemin, elle finirait par revenir au sommet de la montagne. Et, pour que cette idée ne fût pas oubliée, les dieux avaient chargé les prêtres et les gouvernants de la maintenir vivante dans l'imagination du monde.

Tous les peuples partageaient la même croyance : si les familles ointes par les dieux s'éloignaient du pouvoir, les conséquences seraient graves. Nul ne se rappelait pourquoi ces familles avaient été choisies, mais tous savaient qu'elles avaient un lien de parenté avec les familles divines. Akbar existait depuis des centaines d'années, et elle avait toujours été administrée par les ancêtres de l'actuel gouverneur. Envahie plusieurs fois, elle était tombée aux mains d'oppresseurs et de barbares, mais avec le temps les envahisseurs s'en allaient ou ils étaient chassés. Alors, l'ordre ancien se rétablissait et les hommes reprenaient leur vie d'antan.

Les prêtres étaient tenus de préserver cet ordre : le monde avait un destin et il était régi par des lois. Il n'était plus temps de chercher à comprendre les dieux. Il fallait désormais les respecter et faire tout ce qu'ils voulaient. Ils étaient capricieux et s'irritaient facilement.

Sans les rituels de la récolte, la terre ne donnerait pas de fruits. Si certains sacrifices étaient oubliés, la cité serait infestée par des maladies mortelles. Si le dieu du Temps était de nouveau provoqué, il pourrait mettre fin à la croissance du blé et des hommes.

« Regarde la Cinquième Montagne, dit le grand prêtre au commandant. De son sommet, les dieux gouvernent la vallée et nous protègent. Ils ont de toute éternité un plan pour Akbar. L'étranger sera mis à mort, ou bien il retournera dans son pays, le gouverneur disparaîtra un jour, et son fils sera plus sage que lui. Ce que nous vivons maintenant est passager.

— Il nous faut un nouveau chef, déclara le commandant. Si nous restons aux mains de ce gouverneur, nous serons détruits. »

Le prêtre savait que c'était ce que voulaient les dieux, pour mettre fin à la menace de l'écriture de Byblos. Mais il ne dit rien. Il se réjouit de constater une fois de plus que les gouvernants accomplissent toujours — qu'ils le veuillent ou non — le destin de l'univers.

Elie se promena dans la cité, expliqua ses plans de paix au gouverneur et fut nommé son auxiliaire. Quand ils arrivèrent au milieu de la place, de nouveaux malades s'approchèrent — mais il déclara que les dieux de la Cinquième Montagne lui avaient interdit d'accomplir des guérisons. A la fin de l'après-midi, il retourna chez la veuve. L'enfant jouait au milieu de la rue et il le remercia d'avoir été l'instrument d'un miracle du Seigneur.

La femme l'attendait pour dîner. A sa surprise, il y avait une carafe de vin sur la table.

« Les gens ont apporté des présents pour te remercier, dit-elle. Et je veux te demander pardon pour mon injustice.

— Quelle injustice ? s'étonna Elie. Ne vois-tu pas que tout fait partie des desseins de Dieu ? »

La veuve sourit, ses yeux brillèrent, et il put constater à quel point elle était belle. Elle avait au moins dix ans de plus que lui, mais il éprouvait pour elle une profonde tendresse. Ce n'était pas son habitude et il eut peur ; il se rappela les yeux de Jézabel, et la prière qu'il avait faite en sortant du palais d'Achab — il aurait aimé se marier avec une femme du Liban.

« Même si ma vie a été inutile, au moins j'ai eu mon fils. Et l'on se souviendra de son histoire parce qu'il est revenu du royaume des morts, dit-elle.

— Ta vie n'est pas inutile. Je suis venu à Akbar sur ordre du Seigneur et tu m'as accueilli. Si l'on se souvient un jour de l'histoire de ton fils, sois certaine que l'on n'oubliera pas la tienne. »

La femme remplit les deux coupes. Ils burent tous deux au soleil qui se cachait et aux étoiles dans le ciel.

« Tu es venu d'un pays lointain en suivant les signes d'un Dieu que je ne connaissais pas, mais qui est désormais mon Seigneur. Mon fils aussi est revenu d'une contrée lointaine et il aura une belle histoire à raconter à ses petits-enfants. Les prêtres recueilleront ses paroles et les transmettront aux générations à venir. »

C'était grâce à la mémoire des prêtres que les cités avaient connaissance de leur passé, de leurs conquêtes, de leurs dieux anciens, des guerriers qui avaient défendu la terre de leur sang. Même s'il existait désormais de nouvelles méthodes pour enregistrer le passé, les habitants d'Akbar n'avaient confiance qu'en la mémoire des prêtres. Tout le monde peut écrire ce qu'il veut ; mais personne ne parvient à se souvenir de choses qui n'ont jamais existé.

« Et moi, qu'ai-je à raconter ? » continua la femme en remplissant la coupe qu'Elie avait vidée rapidement. « Je n'ai pas la force ni la beauté de Jézabel. Ma vie ressemble à toutes les autres : le mariage arrangé par les parents lorsque j'étais encore enfant, les tâches domestiques quand je suis devenue adulte, le culte, les jours sacrés, le mari toujours occupé à autre chose. De son vivant, nous n'avons jamais eu de conversation sur un sujet important. Lui était tout le temps préoccupé par ses affaires, moi, je prenais soin de la maison, et nous avons passé ainsi les meilleures années de notre vie.

« Après sa mort, il ne m'est resté que la misère et l'éducation de mon fils. Quand il sera grand, il ira traverser les mers, et je ne compterai plus pour personne. Je n'ai pas de haine, ni de ressentiment, seulement la conscience de mon inutilité. »

Elie remplit encore un verre. Son cœur commençait à donner des signaux d'alarme. Il aimait la compagnie de cette femme. L'amour pouvait être une expérience plus redoutable que lorsqu'il s'était trouvé devant un soldat d'Achab, une flèche pointée vers son cœur ; si la flèche l'avait atteint, il serait mort — et Dieu se serait chargé du reste. Mais si l'amour l'atteignait, il devrait lui-même en assumer les conséquences.

« J'ai tant désiré l'amour dans ma vie », pensa-t-il. Et pourtant, maintenant qu'il l'avait devant lui — aucun doute, il était là, il suffisait de ne pas le fuir —, il n'avait qu'une idée, l'oublier le plus vite possible.

Sa pensée revint au jour où il était arrivé à Akbar, après son exil dans la région du Kerith. Il était tellement fatigué et assoiffé qu'il ne se souvenait de rien, sauf du moment où il s'était remis de son évanouissement et où il avait vu la femme lui verser un peu d'eau entre les lèvres. Son visage était proche du sien, plus proche que ne l'avait jamais été celui d'une autre femme. Il avait remarqué qu'elle avait les yeux du même vert que ceux de Jézabel, mais d'un éclat différent, comme s'ils pouvaient refléter les cèdres, l'océan dont il avait tant rêvé sans le connaître, et même — comment était-ce possible ? — son âme.

« J'aimerais tant le lui dire, pensa-t-il. Mais je ne sais comment m'y prendre. Il est plus facile de parler de l'amour de Dieu. »

*

Elie but encore un peu. Elle devina qu'elle avait dit quelque chose qui lui avait déplu, et elle décida de changer de sujet.

« Tu as gravi la Cinquième Montagne ? » demanda-t-elle.

Il acquiesça.

Elle aurait aimé lui demander ce qu'il avait vu

là-haut, et comment il avait réussi à échapper au feu des cieux. Mais il semblait mal à l'aise.

« C'est un prophète. Il lit dans mon cœur », pensa-t-elle.

Depuis que l'Israélite était entré dans sa vie, tout avait changé. Même la pauvreté était plus facile à supporter — parce que cet étranger avait éveillé un sentiment qu'elle n'avait jamais connu : l'amour. Lorsque son fils était tombé malade, elle avait lutté contre tous les voisins pour qu'il restât chez elle.

Elle savait que, pour lui, le Seigneur comptait plus que tout ce qui advenait sous les cieux. Elle avait conscience que c'était un rêve impossible, car cet homme pouvait s'en aller à tout moment, faire couler le sang de Jézabel et ne jamais revenir pour lui raconter ce qui s'était passé.

Pourtant, elle continuerait de l'aimer car, pour la première fois de sa vie, elle avait conscience de ce qu'était la liberté. Elle pouvait l'aimer — quand bien même il ne le saurait jamais. Elle n'avait pas besoin de sa permission pour sentir qu'il lui manquait, penser à lui à longueur de journée, l'attendre pour dîner, et s'inquiéter de ce que les gens pouvaient comploter contre un étranger. C'était cela la liberté : sentir ce que son cœur désirait, indépendamment de l'opinion des autres. Elle s'était opposée à ses amis et à ses voisins au sujet de la présence de l'étranger dans sa maison. Elle n'avait pas besoin de lutter contre elle-même.

Elie but un peu de vin, prit congé et gagna sa chambre. Elle sortit, se réjouit de voir son fils jouer devant la maison et décida d'aller faire une courte promenade.

Elle était libre, car l'amour libère.

*

Elie demeura très longtemps à regarder le mur de sa chambre. Finalement, il décida d'invoquer son ange.

« Mon âme est en danger », dit-il.

L'ange resta silencieux. Elie hésita à poursuivre,

77

mais il était maintenant trop tard : il ne pouvait pas l'invoquer sans motif.

« Quand je suis devant cette femme, je ne me sens pas bien.

— Au contraire, répliqua l'ange. Et cela te dérange. Parce que tu es peut-être sur le point de l'aimer. »

Elie eut honte, parce que l'ange connaissait son âme.

« L'amour est dangereux, dit-il.

— Très, renchérit l'ange. Et alors ? »

Puis il disparut.

*

Son ange n'éprouvait pas les doutes qui le tourmentaient. Oui, il connaissait l'amour ; il avait vu le roi d'Israël abandonner le Seigneur parce que Jézabel, une princesse de Sidon, avait conquis son cœur. La tradition racontait que le roi Salomon avait perdu son trône à cause d'une étrangère. Le roi David avait envoyé l'un de ses meilleurs amis à la mort parce qu'il était tombé amoureux de son épouse. A cause de Dalila, Samson avait été fait prisonnier et les Philistins lui avaient crevé les yeux.

Comment, il ne connaissait pas l'amour ? L'Histoire abondait en exemples tragiques. Et même s'il n'avait pas connu les Ecritures saintes, il avait l'exemple d'amis — et d'amis de ses amis — perdus dans de longues nuits d'attente et de souffrance. S'il avait eu une femme en Israël, il aurait difficilement pu quitter sa cité quand le Seigneur l'avait ordonné, et maintenant il serait mort.

« Je mène un combat inutile, pensa-t-il. L'amour va gagner cette bataille, et je l'aimerai pour le reste de mes jours. Seigneur, renvoie-moi en Israël pour que jamais il ne me faille dire à cette femme ce que je ressens. Elle ne m'aime pas, et elle va me rétorquer que son cœur a été enterré avec le corps de son mari, ce héros. »

Le lendemain, Elie retourna voir le commandant. Il apprit que de nouvelles tentes avaient été installées.

« Quelle est actuellement la proportion des guerriers ? demanda-t-il.

— Je ne donne pas d'informations à un ennemi de Jézabel.

— Je suis conseiller du gouverneur. Il m'a nommé son auxiliaire hier soir, tu en as été informé et tu me dois une réponse. »

Le commandant eut envie de mettre fin à la vie de l'étranger.

« Les Assyriens ont deux soldats pour un des nôtres », répondit-il enfin.

Elie savait que l'ennemi avait besoin d'une force très supérieure.

« Nous approchons du moment idéal pour entreprendre les négociations de paix, dit-il. Ils comprendront que nous sommes généreux et nous obtiendrons de meilleures conditions. N'importe quel général sait que, pour conquérir une cité, il faut cinq envahisseurs pour un défenseur.

— Ils atteindront ce nombre si nous n'attaquons pas maintenant.

— Malgré toutes les mesures d'approvisionnement, ils n'auront pas assez d'eau pour ravitailler tous ces hommes. Et ce sera le moment d'envoyer nos ambassadeurs.

— Quand cela ?

— Laissons le nombre de guerriers assyriens augmenter encore un peu. Lorsque la situation sera insupportable, ils seront forcés d'attaquer mais, dans la proportion de trois ou quatre pour un des nôtres, ils savent qu'ils seront mis en déroute. C'est alors que nos émissaires leur proposeront la paix, la liberté de passage et la vente d'eau. Telle est l'idée du gouverneur. »

Le commandant resta silencieux et laissa partir l'étranger. Même si Elie mourait, le gouverneur pouvait s'accrocher à cette idée. Il se jura que si la situation en arrivait à ce point, il tuerait le gouverneur ; puis il se suiciderait pour ne pas assister à la fureur des dieux. Cependant, en aucune manière il ne permettrait que son peuple fût trahi par l'argent.

*

« Renvoie-moi en terre d'Israël, Seigneur ! criait Elie tous les soirs en marchant dans la vallée. Ne laisse pas mon cœur devenir prisonnier à Akbar ! »

Selon une coutume des prophètes qu'il avait connue enfant, il se donnait des coups de fouet chaque fois qu'il pensait à la veuve. Son dos était à vif et, pendant deux jours, il délira de fièvre. A son réveil, la première chose qu'il vit fut le visage de la femme ; elle soignait ses blessures à l'aide d'onguent et d'huile d'olive. Comme il était trop faible pour descendre jusqu'à la salle, elle montait ses aliments à la chambre.

*

Dès qu'il se sentit bien, il reprit ses marches dans la vallée.

« Renvoie-moi en terre d'Israël, Seigneur ! disait-il. Mon cœur est prisonnier à Akbar, mais mon corps peut encore poursuivre le voyage. »

L'ange apparut. Ce n'était pas l'ange du Seigneur qu'il avait vu au sommet de la montagne, mais celui qui le protégeait et dont la voix lui était familière.

« Le Seigneur écoute les prières de ceux qui prient pour oublier la haine. Mais il est sourd à ceux qui veulent échapper à l'amour. »

*

Tous les trois, ils dînaient ensemble chaque soir. Ainsi que le Seigneur l'avait promis, jamais la farine n'avait manqué dans la cruche, ni l'huile dans la jarre.

Ils conversaient rarement pendant les repas. Mais un soir, l'enfant demanda :

« Qu'est-ce qu'un prophète ?

— C'est un homme qui écoute encore les voix qu'il entendait lorsqu'il était enfant et qui croit toujours en elles. Ainsi, il peut savoir ce que pensent les anges.

— Oui, je sais de quoi tu parles, dit le gamin. J'ai des amis que personne d'autre ne voit.

— Ne les oublie jamais, même si les adultes te disent que c'est une sottise. Ainsi, tu sauras toujours ce que Dieu veut.

— Je connaîtrai l'avenir, comme les devins de Babylone, affirma le gamin.

— Les prophètes ne connaissent pas l'avenir. Ils ne font que transmettre les paroles que le Seigneur leur inspire dans le présent. C'est pourquoi je suis ici, sans savoir quand je retournerai vers mon pays. Il ne me le dira pas avant que cela ne soit nécessaire. »

Les yeux de la femme s'emplirent de tristesse. Oui, un jour il partirait.

*

Elie n'implorait plus le Seigneur. Il avait décidé que, lorsque ce serait le moment de quitter Akbar, il emmènerait la veuve et son fils. Il n'en dirait rien jusqu'à ce que l'heure fût venue.

Peut-être ne désirait-elle pas s'en aller. Peut-être n'avait-elle pas deviné ce qu'il ressentait pour elle — car il avait lui-même tardé à le comprendre. Dans ce cas, et cela vaudrait mieux, il pourrait se consacrer entièrement à l'expulsion de Jézabel et à la reconstruction d'Israël. Son esprit serait trop occupé pour penser à l'amour.

« *Le Seigneur est mon berger*, dit-il, se rappelant une vieille prière du roi David. *Apaise mon âme, et mène-moi auprès des eaux reposantes.* Et tu ne me laisseras pas perdre le sens de ma vie », conclut-il avec ses mots à lui.

*

81

Un après-midi, il revint à la maison plus tôt que d'habitude et il trouva la veuve assise sur le seuil.

« Que fais-tu ?

— Je n'ai rien à faire.

— Alors apprends quelque chose. En ce moment, beaucoup de gens ont renoncé à vivre. Ils ne s'ennuient pas, ils ne pleurent pas, ils se contentent d'attendre que le temps passe. Ils n'ont pas accepté les défis de la vie et elle ne les défie plus. Tu cours ce risque. Réagis, affronte la vie, mais ne renonce pas.

— Ma vie a retrouvé un sens, dit-elle en baissant les yeux. Depuis que tu es arrivé. »

Pendant une fraction de seconde, il sentit qu'il pouvait lui ouvrir son cœur. Mais il n'osa pas — elle faisait certainement allusion à autre chose.

« Trouve une occupation, dit-il pour changer de sujet. Ainsi, le temps sera un allié, non un ennemi.

— Que puis-je apprendre ? »

Elie réfléchit.

« L'écriture de Byblos. Elle te sera utile si tu dois voyager un jour. »

La femme décida de se consacrer corps et âme à cet apprentissage. Jamais elle n'avait songé à quitter Akbar mais, à la manière dont il en parlait, peut-être pensait-il l'emmener avec lui.

De nouveau elle se sentit libre. De nouveau elle se réveilla tôt le matin et marcha en souriant dans les rues de la cité.

« Elie est toujours en vie, dit le commandant au prêtre, deux mois plus tard. Tu n'as pas réussi à le faire assassiner.

— Il n'y a pas, dans tout Akbar, un seul homme qui veuille accomplir cette mission. L'Israélite a consolé les malades, rendu visite aux prisonniers, nourri les affamés. Quand quelqu'un a une querelle à résoudre avec son voisin, il a recours à lui, et tous acceptent ses jugements — parce qu'ils sont justes. Le gouverneur se sert de lui pour accroître sa popularité, mais personne ne s'en rend compte.

— Les marchands ne désirent pas la guerre. Si le gouverneur est populaire au point de convaincre la population que la paix est préférable, nous ne parviendrons jamais à chasser les Assyriens d'ici. Il faut qu'Elie soit mis à mort sans tarder. »

Le prêtre indiqua la Cinquième Montagne, son sommet toujours dissimulé par les nuages.

« Les dieux ne permettront pas que leur pays soit humilié par une puissance étrangère. Ils vont trouver une astuce : un incident se produira, et nous saurons profiter de l'occasion.

— Laquelle ?

— Je l'ignore. Mais je serai attentif aux signes. Abstiens-toi de fournir les chiffres exacts concernant les forces assyriennes. Si l'on t'interroge, dis que la proportion des guerriers envahisseurs est encore de quatre pour un. Et continue à entraîner tes troupes.

— Pourquoi dois-je faire cela ? S'ils atteignent la proportion de cinq pour un, nous sommes perdus.

— Non : nous serons en situation d'égalité. Lorsque le combat aura lieu, tu ne lutteras pas contre un ennemi inférieur, et on ne pourra pas te considérer comme un lâche qui abuse des faibles. L'armée d'Akbar affrontera un adversaire aussi puissant qu'elle et elle gagnera la bataille — parce que son commandant a mis au point la meilleure stratégie. »

Piqué par la vanité, le commandant accepta cette proposition. Et dès lors il commença à dissimuler des informations au gouverneur et à Elie.

Deux mois encore avaient passé et, ce matin-là, l'armée assyrienne avait atteint la proportion de cinq soldats pour un défenseur d'Akbar. A tout moment elle pouvait attaquer.

Depuis quelque temps, Elie soupçonnait le commandant de mentir à propos des forces ennemies, mais cela finirait par se retourner à son avantage : quand la proportion atteindrait le point critique, il serait facile de convaincre la population que la paix était la seule issue.

Il songeait à cela en se dirigeant vers la place où, tous les sept jours, il aidait les habitants à résoudre leurs différends. En général il s'agissait de problèmes sans importance : des querelles de voisinage, des vieux qui ne voulaient plus payer d'impôts, des commerçants qui se jugeaient victimes de préjudices dans leurs affaires.

Le gouverneur était là ; il faisait une apparition de temps en temps, pour le voir en action. L'antipathie qu'Elie ressentait pour lui avait complètement disparu ; il découvrait en lui un homme sage, désireux de régler les difficultés avant qu'elles ne surviennent — même s'il ne croyait pas dans le monde spirituel et avait très peur de mourir. A plusieurs reprises il avait usé de son autorité pour donner à une décision d'Elie valeur de loi. D'autres fois, il s'était opposé à une sentence et, avec le temps, Elie avait compris qu'il avait raison.

Akbar devenait un modèle de cité phénicienne. Le gouverneur avait créé un système d'impôts plus juste, il avait rénové les rues, et il savait administrer avec intelligence les profits provenant des taxes sur les marchandises. A une certaine époque Elie avait réclamé l'interdiction de la consommation de vin et de bière, parce que la majorité des affaires qu'il avait à résoudre concernait des agressions commises par des individus ivres. Mais le gouverneur avait fait valoir que c'était ce genre de choses qui faisait une grande cité. Selon la tradition, les dieux se réjouissaient quand les hommes se divertissaient à la fin d'une journée de travail, et ils protégeaient les ivrognes. De plus, la région avait la réputation de produire un des meilleurs vins du monde, et les étrangers se méfieraient si ses propres habitants ne le consommaient plus. Elie respecta la décision du gouverneur et, finalement, il dut admettre que, joyeux, les gens produisaient mieux.

« Tu n'as pas besoin de faire tant d'efforts », dit le gouverneur, avant qu'Elie entreprît le travail de la journée. « Un auxiliaire aide le gouvernement simplement en lui faisant part de ses opinions.

— J'ai la nostalgie de mon pays et je veux y retourner. Occupé à ces activités, j'arrive à me sentir utile et j'oublie que je suis un étranger », répondit-il.

« Et je réussis mieux à contrôler mon amour pour elle », pensa-t-il en lui-même.

*

Le tribunal populaire était désormais suivi par une assistance toujours très attentive. Petit à petit, les gens arrivèrent : les uns étaient des vieillards qui n'avaient plus la force de travailler aux champs et venaient applaudir, ou huer, les décisions d'Elie ; d'autres avaient un intérêt direct dans les affaires qui seraient traitées — soit parce qu'ils avaient été victimes, soit parce qu'ils pourraient tirer profit du jugement. Il y avait aussi des femmes et des enfants qui, faute de travail, devaient occuper leur temps libre.

Elie présenta les affaires de la matinée. Le premier cas était celui d'un berger qui avait rêvé d'un trésor caché en Egypte près des pyramides et qui avait besoin d'argent pour s'y rendre. Elie n'était jamais allé en Egypte mais il savait que c'était loin. Il expliqua au berger qu'il lui serait difficile de trouver les moyens nécessaires auprès d'autrui, mais que, s'il se décidait à vendre ses brebis et à payer le prix de son rêve, il trouverait assurément ce qu'il cherchait.

Ensuite vint une femme qui désirait apprendre l'art de la magie d'Israël. Elie rappela qu'il n'était pas un maître, seulement un prophète.

Alors qu'il se préparait à trouver une solution à l'amiable dans l'affaire d'un agriculteur qui avait maudit la femme d'un autre, un soldat ruisselant de sueur s'avança, écartant la foule, et s'adressa au gouverneur :

« Une patrouille a réussi à capturer un espion. On le conduit ici ! »

Un frisson parcourut l'assemblée ; c'était la première fois qu'on allait assister à un jugement de ce genre.

« A mort ! cria quelqu'un. Mort aux ennemis ! »

Tous les participants semblaient d'accord, à en croire leurs mugissements. En un clin d'œil, la nouvelle se répandit dans toute la cité et la place se remplit encore. Les autres affaires furent jugées à grand-peine. A tout instant on interrompait Elie, en demandant que l'étranger fût présenté sur-le-champ.

« Je ne peux pas juger ce genre d'affaire, expliquait-il. Cela relève des autorités d'Akbar.

— Qu'est-ce que les Assyriens sont venus faire ici ? s'exclamait l'un. Ils ne voient pas que nous sommes en paix depuis des générations ?

— Pourquoi veulent-ils notre eau ? criait un autre. Pourquoi menacent-ils notre cité ? »

Depuis des mois personne n'osait évoquer en public la présence de l'ennemi. Tout le monde voyait un nombre croissant de tentes se dresser à l'horizon, les marchands affirmaient qu'il fallait entreprendre aussitôt les négociations de paix, pourtant le peuple d'Akbar se refusait à croire qu'il vivait sous la menace d'une invasion. Excepté l'incursion ponctuelle d'une tribu insignifiante, dont on venait à bout rapidement, les guerres n'existaient que dans la mémoire des prêtres. Ceux-ci évoquaient un pays nommé Egypte, ses chevaux, ses chars de guerre et ses dieux aux formes d'animaux. Mais cela s'était passé voilà fort longtemps, l'Egypte n'était plus une nation puissante, et les guerriers à la peau sombre qui parlaient une langue inconnue avaient regagné leurs terres. Maintenant les habitants de Tyr et de Sidon dominaient les mers, étendant un nouvel empire sur le monde, et, bien qu'ils fussent des guerriers expérimentés, ils avaient découvert une nouvelle façon de lutter : le commerce.

« Pourquoi sont-ils nerveux ? demanda le gouverneur à Elie.

— Parce qu'ils sentent que quelque chose a changé. Tu sais comme moi que désormais les Assyriens peuvent attaquer à tout moment. Et que le commandant ment sur le nombre des troupes ennemies.

— Mais il ne peut pas être assez fou pour dire la vérité ! Il sèmerait la panique.

— Les gens devinent lorsqu'ils sont en danger ; ils ont des réactions étranges, des pressentiments, ils sentent quelque chose dans l'air. Ils essaient de se cacher la réalité, se croyant incapables de faire face à la situation. Jusqu'à maintenant, eux se sont raconté des histoires ; mais le moment approche où il leur faudra affronter la vérité. »

Le prêtre arriva.

« Allons au palais réunir le Conseil d'Akbar. Le commandant est en route.

— Ne fais pas cela, dit Elie à voix basse au gouverneur. Ils te forceront à faire ce que tu ne veux pas faire.

— Allons-y, insista le prêtre. Un espion a été arrêté et il faut prendre des mesures d'urgence.

— Rends le jugement au milieu du peuple, chuchota Elie. Le peuple t'aidera, parce qu'il désire la paix — même s'il réclame la guerre.

— Qu'on amène cet homme ici ! » ordonna le gouverneur.

La foule poussa des cris de joie. Pour la première fois, elle allait assister à une réunion du Conseil.

« Nous ne pouvons pas faire cela ! s'exclama le prêtre. C'est une affaire délicate, qui doit être résolue dans le calme ! »

Quelques huées. De nombreuses protestations.

« Qu'on l'amène ici, répéta le gouverneur. Il sera jugé sur cette place, au milieu du peuple. Nous travaillons ensemble à transformer Akbar en une cité prospère, et ensemble nous jugerons tout ce qui la menace. »

La décision fut accueillie par une salve d'applaudissements. Un groupe de soldats apparut, traînant un homme à demi nu, couvert de sang. Il avait sans doute été frappé abondamment avant d'arriver jusque-là.

Les bruits cessèrent. Un silence pesant s'abattit sur l'assistance, et l'on entendait le grognement des porcs et le bruit des enfants qui jouaient dans le coin opposé de la place.

« Pourquoi avez-vous fait cela au prisonnier ? s'écria le gouverneur.

— Il s'est débattu, répondit un garde. Il a déclaré qu'il n'était pas un espion. Qu'il était venu jusqu'ici pour vous parler. »

Le gouverneur envoya chercher trois sièges. Ses domestiques apportèrent également le manteau de la justice, qu'il portait chaque fois que devait se réunir le Conseil d'Akbar.

Le gouverneur et le grand prêtre prirent place. Le troisième siège était réservé au commandant, qui n'était pas encore arrivé.

« Je déclare solennellement ouvert le tribunal de la cité d'Akbar. Que les anciens s'approchent. »

Un groupe de vieillards se présenta et se plaça en demi-cercle derrière les sièges. Ils formaient le Conseil des anciens ; autrefois, leurs opinions étaient respectées et suivies d'effet, mais aujourd'hui ce groupe n'avait plus qu'un rôle décoratif : ils étaient là pour entériner toutes les décisions du gouvernement.

Une fois accomplies certaines formalités — une prière aux dieux de la Cinquième Montagne et la déclamation des noms de quelques héros du passé —, le gouverneur s'adressa au prisonnier :

« Que veux-tu ? »

L'homme ne répondit pas. Il le dévisageait d'une manière étrange, comme s'il était son égal.

« Que veux-tu ? » insista le gouverneur.

Le prêtre lui toucha le bras.

« Nous avons besoin d'un interprète. Il ne parle pas notre langue. »

L'ordre fut donné et un garde partit à la recherche

88

d'un commerçant qui pût servir d'interprète. Toujours très occupés par leurs affaires et leurs profits, les marchands n'allaient jamais assister aux séances qu'organisait Elie.

Tandis qu'ils attendaient, le prêtre murmura :

« Ils ont frappé le prisonnier parce qu'ils ont peur. Laisse-moi conduire ce procès et ne dis rien : la panique les rend tous agressifs et, si nous ne faisons pas preuve d'autorité, nous risquons de perdre le contrôle de la situation. »

Le gouverneur ne répondit pas. Lui aussi avait peur. Il chercha Elie des yeux mais, de l'endroit où il était assis, il ne le voyait pas.

*

Un commerçant arriva, amené de force par le garde. Il protesta contre le tribunal parce qu'il perdait son temps et qu'il avait beaucoup d'affaires à régler. Mais le prêtre, d'un regard sévère, lui intima l'ordre de se tenir tranquille et de traduire la conversation.

« Que viens-tu faire ici ? interrogea le gouverneur.

— Je ne suis pas un espion, répondit l'homme. Je suis un général de l'armée. Je suis venu discuter avec vous. »

L'assistance, qui était totalement silencieuse, se mit à crier à peine la phrase traduite. Le public affirmait que c'était un mensonge et exigeait la peine de mort immédiate.

Le prêtre réclama le silence et se tourna de nouveau vers le prisonnier :

« De quoi veux-tu discuter ?

— Le gouverneur a la réputation d'être un homme sage, répondit l'Assyrien. Nous ne voulons pas détruire cette cité : ce qui nous intéresse, c'est Tyr et Sidon. Mais Akbar se trouve au milieu du chemin et contrôle cette vallée. Si nous sommes obligés de combattre, nous perdrons du temps et des hommes. Je viens proposer un règlement. »

« Cet homme dit la vérité », songea Elie. Il avait remarqué qu'il était entouré par un groupe de soldats qui l'empêchaient de voir l'endroit où le gouverneur était assis. « Il pense comme nous. Le Seigneur a réalisé un miracle, et il va mettre un point final à cette situation périlleuse. »

Le prêtre se leva et cria au peuple :

« Vous voyez ? Ils veulent nous détruire sans combat !

— Continue ! » reprit le gouverneur.

Mais le prêtre s'interposa une fois de plus :

« Notre gouverneur est un homme bon, qui refuse de faire couler le sang. Mais nous sommes dans une situation de guerre et le prévenu qui se tient devant vous est un ennemi !

— Il a raison ! » s'écria quelqu'un dans l'assistance.

Elie comprit son erreur. Le prêtre jouait avec l'auditoire tandis que le gouverneur ne cherchait qu'à faire justice. Il tenta de s'approcher mais on le bouscula. Un soldat le saisit par le bras.

« Attends ici. En fin de compte, l'idée était de toi. »

Elie se retourna : c'était le commandant, et il souriait.

« Nous ne pouvons écouter aucune proposition, poursuivit le prêtre, laissant l'émotion émaner de ses gestes et de ses propos. Si nous montrons que nous voulons négocier, ce sera la preuve que nous avons peur. Et le peuple d'Akbar est courageux. Il est en mesure de résister à n'importe quelle invasion.

— Cet homme recherche la paix », dit le gouverneur, en s'adressant à la foule.

Une voix s'éleva :

« Les marchands recherchent la paix. Les prêtres désirent la paix. Les gouverneurs administrent la paix. Mais une armée ne souhaite qu'une chose : la guerre !

— Ne voyez-vous pas que nous parvenons à faire face à la menace religieuse d'Israël sans mener aucune guerre ? hurla le gouverneur. Nous n'avons pas envoyé d'armées, ni de navires, mais Jézabel. Maintenant ils adorent Baal sans que nous ayons eu besoin de sacrifier un seul homme au front.

— Eux, ils n'ont pas envoyé une belle femme, mais leurs guerriers ! » cria le prêtre encore plus fort.

Le peuple exigeait la mort de l'Assyrien. Le gouverneur retint le prêtre par le bras.

« Assieds-toi, ordonna-t-il. Tu vas trop loin.

— C'est toi qui as eu l'idée d'un procès public. Ou, mieux, c'est le traître israélite, qui semble dicter les actes du gouverneur d'Akbar.

— Je m'expliquerai plus tard avec lui. Maintenant nous devons apprendre ce que veut l'Assyrien. Pendant des générations, les hommes ont cherché à imposer leur volonté par la force ; ils disaient ce qu'ils voulaient, mais ils ne tenaient aucun compte de ce que pensait le peuple, et tous ces empires ont finalement été détruits. Notre peuple est devenu grand parce qu'il a appris à écouter. Ainsi, nous avons développé le commerce, en écoutant ce que l'autre désire et en faisant notre possible pour l'obtenir. Le résultat est le profit. »

Le prêtre hocha la tête.

« Tes propos semblent sages, et c'est le pire de tous les dangers. Si tu disais des sottises, il serait facile de prouver que tu te trompes. Mais ce que tu viens d'affirmer nous conduit tout droit à un piège. »

Les gens qui se trouvaient au premier rang intervenaient dans la discussion. Jusque-là, le gouverneur s'était toujours efforcé de tenir compte de l'opinion du Conseil, et Akbar avait une excellente réputation ; Tyr et Sidon avaient envoyé des émissaires pour observer comment elle était administrée ; le nom du gouverneur était parvenu aux oreilles de l'empereur et, avec un peu de chance, il pourrait terminer ses jours comme ministre de la Cour. Mais aujourd'hui, on avait bravé publiquement son autorité. S'il ne prenait pas rapidement des mesures, il perdrait le respect du peuple — et il ne pourrait plus prendre de décisions capitales parce que personne ne lui obéirait.

« Continue », lança-t-il au prisonnier, ignorant le regard furieux du prêtre et exigeant que l'interprète traduisît sa question.

« Je suis venu proposer un arrangement, dit l'Assyrien. Vous nous laissez passer, et nous marcherons contre Tyr et Sidon. Une fois que ces cités seront vaincues — elles le seront certainement, car une grande partie de leurs guerriers sont sur les navires pour surveiller le commerce —, nous serons généreux avec Akbar. Et nous te garderons comme gouverneur.

— Vous voyez ? s'exclama le prêtre en se relevant. Ils pensent que notre gouverneur est capable d'échanger l'honneur d'Akbar contre un poste élevé ! »

La foule en colère se mit à gronder. Ce prisonnier blessé, à moitié nu, voulait imposer ses conditions ! Un homme vaincu qui proposait la reddition de la cité ! Certains se levèrent et s'apprêtèrent à l'agresser. Les gardes eurent bien du mal à maîtriser la situation.

« Attendez ! reprit le gouverneur, qui tentait de parler plus fort que tous. Nous avons devant nous un homme sans défense, il ne peut donc pas nous faire peur. Nous savons que notre armée est la mieux préparée et que nos guerriers sont les plus vaillants. Nous n'avons rien à prouver à personne. Si nous décidons de combattre, nous vaincrons, mais les pertes seront énormes. »

Elie ferma les yeux et pria pour que le gouverneur parvînt à convaincre le peuple.

« Nos ancêtres nous parlaient de l'empire égyptien, mais ce temps est révolu, continua-t-il. Maintenant nous revenons à l'âge d'or, nos pères et nos grands-pères ont vécu en paix. Pourquoi devrionsnous rompre cette tradition ? Les guerres modernes se font dans le commerce, non sur les champs de bataille. »

Peu à peu, la foule redevint silencieuse. Le gouverneur était sur le point de réussir.

Quand le bruit cessa, il s'adressa à l'Assyrien.

« Ce que tu proposes ne suffit pas. Vous devrez payer les taxes dont les marchands s'acquittent pour traverser nos territoires.

— Crois-moi, gouverneur, vous n'avez pas le choix, répliqua le prisonnier. Nous avons suffisamment d'hommes pour raser cette cité et tuer tous ses habitants. Vous êtes en paix depuis très longtemps et vous ne savez plus lutter, alors que, nous, nous sommes en train de conquérir le monde. »

Les murmures reprirent dans l'assistance. Elie pensait : « Il ne peut pas flancher maintenant. » Mais il devenait difficile d'affronter le prisonnier assyrien qui, même dominé, imposait ses conditions. A chaque minute, la foule augmentait — Elie remarqua que les commerçants avaient abandonné leur travail et s'étaient mêlés aux spectateurs, inquiets du déroulement des événements. Le jugement revêtait une importance considérable ; il n'y avait plus moyen de reculer, la décision fût-elle la négociation ou la mort.

*

Les spectateurs commencèrent à se diviser ; les uns défendaient la paix, les autres exigeaient la résistance d'Akbar. Le gouverneur dit tout bas au prêtre :

« Cet homme m'a défié publiquement. Mais toi aussi. »

Le prêtre se tourna vers lui. Et, parlant de manière que personne ne pût l'entendre, il lui ordonna de condamner immédiatement l'Assyrien à mort.

« Je ne demande pas, j'exige. C'est moi qui te maintiens au pouvoir et je peux mettre fin quand je veux à cette situation, tu comprends ? Je connais des sacrifices qui peuvent apaiser la colère des dieux lorsque nous sommes contraints de remplacer la famille gouvernante. Ce ne sera pas la première fois : même en Egypte, un empire qui a duré des milliers d'années, de nombreuses dynasties ont été remplacées. Et pourtant l'univers est resté en ordre et le ciel ne nous est pas tombé sur la tête. »

Le gouverneur pâlit.

« Le commandant se trouve dans l'assistance, avec une partie de ses soldats. Si tu persistes à négocier avec cet homme, je dirai à tout le monde que les dieux t'ont abandonné. Et tu seras déposé. Nous allons poursuivre le procès. Et tu vas faire exactement ce que je t'ordonnerai. »

Si Elie avait été en vue, le gouverneur aurait encore eu une solution : il aurait demandé au prophète israélite d'affirmer qu'il avait vu un ange au sommet de la Cinquième Montagne, ainsi qu'il le lui avait raconté. Il aurait rappelé l'histoire de la résurrection du fils de la veuve. Et cela aurait été la parole d'Elie, un homme qui s'était déjà montré capable de faire des miracles, contre la parole d'un homme qui jamais n'avait fait la preuve d'aucune sorte de pouvoir surnaturel.

Mais Elie l'avait abandonné, et il n'avait plus le choix. En outre, ce n'était qu'un prisonnier — et aucune armée au monde n'entreprend une guerre parce qu'elle a perdu un soldat.

« Tu gagnes cette partie », dit-il au prêtre. Un jour, il négocierait une contrepartie.

Le prêtre hocha la tête. Le verdict fut rendu peu après.

« Personne ne défie Akbar, proclama le gouverneur. Et personne n'entre dans notre cité sans la permission de son peuple. Tu as tenté de le faire et tu es condamné à mort. »

Là où il se trouvait, Elie baissa les yeux. Le commandant souriait.

On conduisit le prisonnier, accompagné d'une foule de plus en plus nombreuse, jusqu'à un terrain non loin des remparts. Là, on lui arracha ce qui lui restait de vêtements et on le laissa nu. Un soldat le poussa au fond d'une fosse. Les gens, agglutinés tout autour, se bousculaient à celui qui le verrait le mieux.

« Un soldat porte avec fierté son uniforme de guerre et se rend visible à l'ennemi parce qu'il a du courage. Un espion s'habille en femme, car il est lâche ! cria le gouverneur, pour être entendu de tous. C'est pourquoi je te condamne à quitter cette vie sans la dignité des braves. »

Le peuple hua le prisonnier et applaudit le gouverneur.

Le prisonnier parlait, mais l'interprète n'était plus là et personne ne le comprenait. Elie parvint à se frayer un chemin pour rejoindre le gouverneur, mais il était trop tard. Quand il toucha son manteau, il fut violemment repoussé.

« C'est ta faute. Tu as voulu un procès public.

— C'est *ta* faute, rétorqua Elie. Même si le Conseil d'Akbar s'était réuni en secret, le commandant et le prêtre auraient obtenu ce qu'ils désiraient. J'étais entouré de gardes pendant tout le procès. Ils avaient tout arrangé. »

La coutume voulait qu'il revînt au prêtre de déterminer la durée du supplice. Celui-ci se baissa, ramassa une pierre et la tendit au gouverneur : elle n'était pas assez grosse pour entraîner une mort rapide, ni assez petite pour prolonger la souffrance très longtemps.

« A toi l'honneur.

— J'y suis obligé, murmura le gouverneur afin que seul le prêtre l'entendît. Mais tu sais que ce n'est pas la bonne voie.

— Pendant toutes ces années, tu m'as forcé à adopter les positions les plus dures, tandis que tu tirais profit des décisions qui faisaient plaisir au peuple, répliqua le prêtre, lui aussi à voix basse. J'ai dû affronter le doute et la culpabilité, et j'ai passé des nuits d'insomnie, poursuivi par le fantôme des erreurs que j'aurais pu commettre. Mais comme je ne suis pas un lâche, Akbar est aujourd'hui une cité enviée du monde entier. »

Les gens étaient allés chercher des pierres de la taille requise. Pendant quelque temps, on n'entendit plus que le bruit des cailloux qui s'entrechoquaient. Le prêtre poursuivit :

« Je peux me tromper en condamnant à mort cet homme. Mais je suis sûr de l'honneur de notre cité ; nous ne sommes pas des traîtres. »

*

Le gouverneur leva la main et jeta la première pierre ; le prisonnier l'esquiva. Mais aussitôt, la foule, au milieu des cris et des huées, se mit à le lapider.

L'homme tentait de protéger son visage de ses bras, et les pierres atteignaient sa poitrine, son dos, son ventre. Le gouverneur voulut s'en aller ; il avait tant de fois vu ce spectacle, il savait que la mort était lente et douloureuse, que le visage deviendrait une bouillie d'os, de cheveux et de sang, que les gens continueraient à jeter des pierres bien après que la vie aurait abandonné ce corps. Dans quelques minutes, le prisonnier cesserait de se défendre et baisserait les bras. S'il avait été un homme bon dans cette vie, les dieux guideraient l'une des pierres, qui atteindrait le devant du crâne, provoquant l'évanouissement. En revanche, s'il avait commis des cruautés, il resterait conscient jusqu'à la dernière minute.

La foule criait, lançait des pierres avec une férocité croissante, et le condamné cherchait à se défendre de son mieux. Soudain, l'homme écarta les bras et parla dans une langue que tous pouvaient comprendre. Surprise, la foule s'interrompit.

« Vive l'Assyrie ! s'exclama-t-il. En ce moment, je contemple l'image de mon peuple et je meurs heureux, car je meurs comme un général qui a tenté de sauver la vie de ses guerriers. Je vais rejoindre la compagnie des dieux et je suis content car je sais que nous conquerrons cette terre !

— Tu as entendu ? dit le prêtre. Il a écouté et compris toute notre conversation au cours du procès ! »

Le gouverneur l'admit. L'homme parlait leur langue, et maintenant il savait que le Conseil d'Akbar était divisé.

« Je ne suis pas en enfer, parce que la vision de mon pays me donne dignité et force. La vision de mon pays me donne la joie ! Vive l'Assyrie ! » cria l'homme de nouveau.

Revenue de sa stupeur, la foule se remit à le lapider. L'homme gardait les bras écartés sans chercher à se protéger — c'était un guerrier vaillant. Quelques secondes plus tard, la miséricorde des dieux se manifesta : une pierre le frappa au front et il s'évanouit.

« Nous pouvons nous en aller maintenant, déclara le prêtre. Le peuple d'Akbar se chargera d'achever la tâche. »

*

Elie ne retourna pas chez la veuve. Il se promena sans but dans le désert.

« Le Seigneur n'a rien fait, disait-il aux plantes et aux rochers. Et Il aurait pu intervenir. »

Il regrettait sa décision, il se jugeait encore une fois coupable de la mort d'un homme. S'il avait accepté l'idée d'une réunion secrète du Conseil d'Akbar, le gouverneur aurait pu l'emmener avec lui ; ils auraient été deux face au prêtre et au commandant. Leurs chances auraient été minces mais tout de même plus sérieuses que dans un procès public.

Pire encore : il avait été impressionné par la manière dont le prêtre s'était adressé à la foule ; même s'il n'était pas d'accord avec tous ses propos, il était bien obligé de reconnaître que cet homme avait une profonde connaissance du commandement. Il tâcherait de se rappeler chaque détail de cette scène pour le jour où — en Israël — il devrait affronter le roi et la princesse de Tyr.

Il marcha sans but, regardant les montagnes, la cité et le campement assyrien au loin. Il n'était qu'un point dans cette vallée et un monde immense l'entourait — un monde si vaste que, même s'il voyageait sa vie entière, il n'en atteindrait pas le bout. Ses amis, et ses ennemis, avaient peut-être mieux compris que lui la terre où ils vivaient : ils pouvaient voyager vers des pays lointains, naviguer sur des mers inconnues, aimer une femme sans se sentir coupables. Aucun d'eux n'écoutait plus les anges de l'enfance, ni ne se proposait de lutter au nom du Seigneur. Ils vivaient dans le présent et ils étaient heureux. Elie était une personne comme les autres, et, à ce moment, alors qu'il se promenait dans la vallée, il désirait n'avoir jamais entendu la voix du Seigneur et de Ses anges.

Mais la vie n'est pas faite de désirs, elle est faite des actes de chacun. Il se souvint qu'il avait déjà tenté à plusieurs reprises de renoncer à sa mission, et pourtant il était là, au milieu de cette vallée, parce que le Seigneur l'avait exigé ainsi.

« J'aurais pu n'être qu'un charpentier, mon Dieu, et j'aurais été encore utile à Ton entreprise. »

Mais Elie accomplissait ce qu'on avait exigé de lui, portant le poids de la guerre à venir, le massacre des prophètes par Jézabel, la lapidation du général assyrien, la peur de son amour pour une femme d'Akbar. Le Seigneur lui avait fait un cadeau, et il ne savait qu'en faire.

Au milieu de la vallée surgit la lumière. Ce n'était pas son ange gardien — celui qu'il écoutait toujours, mais voyait rarement. C'était un ange du Seigneur, qui venait le consoler.

« Je ne peux rien faire de plus ici, dit Elie. Quand retournerai-je en Israël ?

— Quand tu auras appris à reconstruire, répondit l'ange. Rappelle-toi ce que Dieu a enseigné à Moïse avant un combat. Profite de chaque moment, si tu ne veux pas plus tard avoir des regrets, et te dire que tu as perdu ta jeunesse. A chaque âge, le Seigneur donne à l'homme ses inquiétudes particulières. »

« *Le Seigneur dit à Moïse :*
"N'aie pas peur, ne laisse pas ton cœur faiblir avant le combat, ne sois pas terrifié devant tes ennemis. L'homme qui a planté une vigne et n'en a pas encore profité, qu'il le fasse vite, afin que, s'il meurt dans la lutte, ce ne soit pas un autre qui en profite. L'homme

*qui aime une femme, et ne l'a pas encore reçue, qu'il
retourne chez elle, afin que, s'il meurt dans la lutte, ce
ne soit pas un autre homme qui la reçoive." »*

Elie marcha encore quelque temps, cherchant à
comprendre ce qu'il venait d'entendre. Alors qu'il se
préparait à retourner à Akbar, il aperçut la femme
qu'il aimait assise sur un rocher au pied de la Cinquième Montagne — à quelques minutes de l'endroit
où il se trouvait.

« Que fait-elle ici ? Serait-elle au courant du procès, de la condamnation à mort, et des risques que
nous courons désormais ? »

Il devait l'avertir immédiatement. Il décida de la
rejoindre.

Elle remarqua sa présence et lui fit signe. Elie semblait avoir oublié les paroles de l'ange, car d'un seul
coup son inquiétude revint. Il feignit d'être préoccupé par les problèmes de la cité, afin qu'elle ne devinât pas la confusion qui régnait dans son cœur et
dans son esprit.

« Que fais-tu ici ? demanda-t-il en arrivant près
d'elle.

— Je suis venue chercher un peu d'inspiration.
L'écriture que j'apprends me fait penser à la Main qui
a dessiné les vallées, les monts, la cité d'Akbar. Des
commerçants m'ont donné des encres de toutes les
couleurs car ils désirent que j'écrive pour eux. J'ai
songé à les utiliser pour décrire le monde qui
m'entoure mais je sais que c'est difficile : même si je
dispose des couleurs, seul le Seigneur parvient à les
mélanger avec une telle harmonie. »

Elle gardait les yeux fixés sur la Cinquième Montagne. Elle était devenue complètement différente de
la personne qu'il avait rencontrée quelques mois
auparavant, ramassant du bois à la porte de la cité.

Sa présence solitaire, au milieu du désert, lui inspirait confiance et respect.

« Pourquoi toutes les montagnes ont-elles un nom, sauf la Cinquième Montagne, que l'on désigne par un nombre ? demanda Elie.

— Pour ne pas susciter de querelle entre les dieux, répondit-elle. La tradition raconte que si l'homme avait donné à cette montagne le nom d'un dieu particulier, les autres, furieux, auraient détruit la terre. C'est pour cela qu'elle s'appelle le Mont Cinq. Parce que c'est le cinquième mont que nous apercevons au-delà des murailles. Ainsi, nous n'offensons personne, et l'Univers reste en ordre. »

Ils se turent quelque temps. Puis la femme rompit le silence :

« Je réfléchis sur les couleurs, mais je pense aussi au danger que représente l'écriture de Byblos. Elle peut offenser les dieux phéniciens et le Seigneur notre Dieu.

— Seul existe le Seigneur, l'interrompit Elie. Et tous les pays civilisés ont leur écriture.

— Mais celle-ci est différente. Quand j'étais enfant, j'allais souvent sur la place assister au travail que le peintre de mots réalisait pour les marchands. Ses dessins, fondés sur l'écriture égyptienne, exigeaient adresse et savoir. Maintenant, l'antique et puissante Egypte est décadente, elle n'a plus d'argent pour acheter quoi que ce soit, et personne n'utilise plus son langage. Les navigateurs de Tyr et de Sidon répandent l'écriture de Byblos dans le monde entier. On peut inscrire les mots et les cérémonies sacrées sur les tablettes d'argile et les transmettre d'un peuple à l'autre. Qu'adviendra-t-il du monde si des gens sans scrupules se mettent à utiliser les rituels pour intervenir dans l'univers ? »

Elie comprenait ce que la femme voulait dire. L'écriture de Byblos était fondée sur un système très simple : il suffisait de transformer les dessins égyptiens en sons, puis de désigner une lettre pour chaque son. Selon l'ordre dans lequel on plaçait ces lettres, on pouvait créer tous les sons possibles et décrire tout ce qui existait dans l'univers. Certains sons étant malaisés à prononcer, les Grecs avaient résolu la difficulté en ajoutant cinq lettres — appelées *voyelles* — aux vingt et quelques caractères de Byblos. Ils avaient baptisé cette innovation *alphabet*, nom qui maintenant servait à désigner la nouvelle forme d'écriture.

Les relations commerciales entre les différentes cultures en avaient été grandement facilitées. Avec l'écriture égyptienne, il fallait beaucoup d'espace et d'habileté pour parvenir à exprimer ses idées, et une profonde connaissance pour les interpréter ; elle avait été imposée aux peuples conquis, mais n'avait pas survécu à la décadence de l'empire. Le système de Byblos, pendant ce temps, se répandait rapidement à travers le monde, et son adoption ne dépendait plus de la puissance économique de la Phénicie.

La méthode de Byblos, avec son adaptation grecque, avait plu aux marchands de diverses nations ; depuis les temps anciens, c'étaient eux qui décidaient de ce qui devait demeurer dans l'Histoire, et de ce qui disparaîtrait à la mort de tel roi ou de tel haut personnage. Tout indiquait que l'invention phénicienne était destinée à devenir le langage courant des affaires, survivant à ses navigateurs, ses rois, ses princesses séductrices, ses producteurs de vin, ses maîtres verriers.

« Dieu disparaîtra des mots ? s'enquit la femme.

— Il sera toujours en eux, répondit Elie. Mais chacun sera responsable devant Lui de tout ce qu'il écrira. »

Elle retira de la manche de son vêtement une tablette d'argile portant une inscription.

« Qu'est-ce que cela signifie ? demanda Elie.

— C'est le mot *amour*. »

Elie prit la tablette, mais il n'eut pas le courage de demander pourquoi elle la lui avait tendue. Sur ce morceau d'argile, quelques traits griffonnés résumaient pourquoi les étoiles restaient suspendues dans les cieux et pourquoi les hommes marchaient sur la terre.

Il voulut la lui rendre mais elle refusa.

« J'ai écrit cela pour toi. Je connais ta responsabilité, je sais qu'un jour il te faudra partir, et que tu te transformeras en ennemi de mon pays car tu désires anéantir Jézabel. Ce jour-là, je serai peut-être à ton côté, t'apportant mon soutien pour que tu accomplisses ta tâche. Ou peut-être lutterai-je contre toi, parce que le sang de Jézabel est celui de mon pays ; ce mot, que tu tiens dans tes mains, est empli de mystères. Personne ne peut savoir ce qu'il éveille dans le cœur d'une femme — pas même les prophètes qui conversent avec Dieu.

— Je connais ce mot, dit Elie en rangeant la tablette dans son manteau. J'ai lutté jour et nuit contre lui, car si j'ignore ce qu'il éveille dans le cœur d'une femme, je sais ce qu'il peut faire d'un homme. J'ai suffisamment de courage pour affronter le roi d'Israël, la princesse de Sidon, le Conseil d'Akbar, mais ce seul mot, *amour*, me cause une terreur profonde. Avant que tu ne le dessines sur la tablette, tes yeux l'avaient déjà écrit dans mon cœur. »

Ils restèrent tous deux silencieux. Il y avait la mort de l'Assyrien, le climat de tension dans la cité, l'appel du Seigneur qui pouvait survenir à tout moment ; mais le mot qu'elle avait inscrit était plus puissant que tout cela.

Elie tendit la main, et elle la prit. Ils restèrent ainsi jusqu'à ce que le soleil se cache derrière la Cinquième Montagne.

« Merci, dit-elle sur le chemin du retour. Il y a longtemps que je désirais passer une fin d'après-midi avec toi. »

Quand ils arrivèrent à la maison, un émissaire du gouverneur attendait : il demandait à Elie d'aller le retrouver immédiatement.

« Je t'ai soutenu, et pour me remercier tu t'es montré lâche, dit le gouverneur. Que dois-je faire de ta vie ?

— Je ne vivrai pas une seconde de plus que le Seigneur ne le désire, répondit Elie. C'est Lui qui décide, pas toi. »

Le gouverneur s'étonna du courage d'Elie.

« Je peux te faire décapiter sur-le-champ. Ou te traîner par les rues de la cité, en disant que tu as porté malheur à notre peuple, répliqua-t-il. Et ce ne sera pas une décision de ton Dieu unique.

— Quel que soit mon destin, il se réalisera. Mais je veux que tu saches que je n'ai pas fui ; les soldats du commandant m'ont empêché d'arriver jusqu'à toi. Il voulait la guerre, et il a tout fait pour y parvenir. »

Le gouverneur décida de mettre un terme à cette discussion stérile. Il lui fallait expliquer son plan au prophète israélite.

« Ce n'est pas le commandant qui désire la guerre ; en bon militaire, il a conscience que son armée est inférieure, qu'elle manque d'expérience et sera décimée par l'ennemi. En homme d'honneur, il sait que cela risque d'être un motif de honte pour ses descendants. Mais l'orgueil et la vanité ont endurci son cœur.

— Il pense que l'ennemi a peur. Il ne sait pas que les guerriers assyriens sont bien entraînés : dès qu'ils entrent dans l'armée, ils plantent un arbre, et chaque jour ils sautent par-dessus l'endroit où la graine est enfouie. La graine se transforme en pousse et ils sautent toujours par-dessus. La pousse devient plante et ils continuent de sauter. Ils ne s'ennuient pas, ils ne trouvent pas que ce soit une perte de temps. Peu à peu, l'arbre grandit — et les guerriers sautent de plus en plus haut. Ils se préparent ainsi aux obstacles avec patience et dévouement.

— Ils sont habitués à reconnaître un défi. Ils nous observent depuis des mois. »

Elie interrompit le gouverneur :

« Qui a intérêt à cette guerre ?

— Le prêtre. Je l'ai compris pendant le procès du prisonnier assyrien.

— Pour quelle raison ?

— Je l'ignore. Mais il a été suffisamment habile pour persuader le commandant et le peuple. Maintenant, la cité entière est de son côté, et je ne vois qu'une issue à la difficile situation dans laquelle nous nous trouvons. »

Il fit une longue pause et fixa l'Israélite dans les yeux :

« Toi. »

Le gouverneur se mit à marcher de long en large, parlant vite et laissant paraître sa nervosité.

« Les commerçants aussi désirent la paix, mais ils ne peuvent rien faire. En outre, ils sont assez riches pour s'installer dans une autre cité ou attendre que les conquérants commencent à acheter leurs produits. Le reste de la population a perdu la raison et exige que nous attaquions un ennemi infiniment supérieur. La seule chose qui puisse les convaincre de changer d'avis, c'est un miracle. »

Elie était tendu.

« Un miracle ?

— Tu as ressuscité un enfant que la mort avait déjà emporté. Tu as aidé le peuple à trouver son chemin et, bien qu'étant étranger, tu es aimé de presque tout le monde.

— La situation était celle-là jusqu'à ce matin, dit Elie. Mais maintenant elle est différente : dans le contexte que tu viens de décrire, quiconque défendra la paix sera considéré comme un traître.

— Il ne s'agit pas de défendre quoi que ce soit. Je veux que tu fasses un miracle aussi grand que la résurrection de l'enfant. Alors, tu diras au peuple que la paix est la seule issue et il t'écoutera. Le prêtre perdra complètement son pouvoir. »

Il y eut un moment de silence. Le gouverneur reprit :

« Je suis prêt à passer un accord : si tu fais ce que je te demande, la religion du Dieu unique sera obligatoire à Akbar. Tu plairas à Celui que tu sers, et moi je parviendrai à négocier les conditions de paix. »

Elie monta à l'étage de la maison, où se trouvait sa chambre. Il avait, à ce moment-là, une opportunité qu'aucun prophète n'avait eue auparavant : convertir une cité phénicienne. Ce serait la manière la plus cuisante de montrer à Jézabel qu'il y avait un prix à payer pour ce qu'elle avait fait dans son pays.

Il était excité par la proposition du gouverneur. Il pensa même réveiller la femme, qui dormait en bas, mais il changea d'avis ; elle devait rêver du bel après-midi qu'ils avaient passé ensemble.

Il invoqua son ange. Et celui-ci apparut.

« Tu as entendu la proposition du gouverneur, dit Elie. C'est une chance unique.

— Aucune chance n'est unique, répondit l'ange. Le Seigneur offre aux hommes de nombreuses occasions. En outre, rappelle-toi ce qui a été annoncé : aucun autre miracle ne te sera permis jusqu'à ce que tu sois retourné au sein de ta patrie. »

Elie baissa la tête. A ce moment, l'ange du Seigneur surgit et fit taire son ange gardien. Et il déclara :

« Voici ton prochain miracle :

« Tu iras réunir tout le peuple devant la montagne. D'un côté, tu ordonneras que soit élevé un autel à Baal, et un bouvillon lui sera présenté. De l'autre côté, tu élèveras un autel au Seigneur ton Dieu, et sur lui aussi tu placeras un bouvillon.

« Et tu diras aux adorateurs de Baal : "Invoquez le nom de votre dieu, tandis que j'invoquerai le nom du Seigneur." Laisse-les faire d'abord ; qu'ils passent toute la matinée à prier et à crier, demandant à Baal de descendre pour recevoir ce qui lui est offert.

« Ils crieront à haute voix et ils se tailladeront avec leurs poignards et ils prieront que le bouvillon soit reçu par le dieu, mais il ne se passera rien.

« Quand ils seront fatigués, tu empliras quatre jarres d'eau et tu les verseras sur ton bouvillon. Tu feras une seconde fois. Et tu le feras encore une troisième fois. Alors tu imploreras le Dieu d'Abraham, d'Isaac et d'Israël de montrer à tous Son pouvoir.

« A ce moment, le Seigneur enverra le feu du ciel et il dévorera ton sacrifice. »

Elie s'agenouilla et rendit grâces.

« Cependant, poursuivit l'ange, ce miracle ne peut avoir lieu qu'une seule fois dans ta vie. Choisis si tu désires le réaliser ici, pour empêcher une bataille, ou si tu préfères le réaliser dans ton pays, pour délivrer les tiens de la menace de Jézabel. »

Et l'ange du Seigneur s'en fut.

La femme se réveilla tôt et vit Elie assis sur le seuil. Il avait les yeux cernés de quelqu'un qui n'a pas dormi.

Elle aurait aimé lui demander ce qui s'était passé la nuit précédente, mais elle redoutait sa réponse. Son insomnie pouvait avoir été causée par sa conversation avec le gouverneur, et par la menace de guerre ; mais il y avait peut-être un autre motif, la tablette d'argile qu'elle lui avait offerte. Alors, si elle soulevait la question, elle risquait d'entendre que l'amour d'une femme ne convenait pas aux desseins de Dieu.

« Viens manger quelque chose », fut son seul commentaire.

Son fils se réveilla à son tour. Ils se mirent tous les trois à table et mangèrent.

« J'aurais aimé rester avec toi hier, dit Elie. Mais le gouverneur avait besoin de moi.

— Ne t'en fais pas pour lui, dit-elle, sentant que son

cœur se calmait. Sa famille gouverne Akbar depuis des générations, et il saura quoi faire devant la menace.

— J'ai aussi conversé avec un ange. Et il a exigé de moi une décision très difficile.

— Tu ne dois pas non plus t'inquiéter à cause des anges. Peut-être vaut-il mieux croire que les dieux changent avec le temps. Mes ancêtres adoraient les dieux égyptiens qui avaient forme d'animaux. Ces dieux sont partis et, jusqu'à ton arrivée, on m'a appris à faire des sacrifices à Astarté, à El, à Baal et à tous les habitants de la Cinquième Montagne. Maintenant j'ai connaissance du Seigneur mais il se peut que lui aussi nous quitte un jour, et que les prochains dieux soient moins exigeants. »

L'enfant réclama un peu d'eau. Il n'y en avait pas.

« Je vais en chercher, dit Elie.

— Je viens avec toi », proposa l'enfant.

*

Ils prirent ensemble la direction du puits. En chemin, ils passèrent là où, tôt le matin, le commandant entraînait ses soldats.

« Allons jeter un coup d'œil, dit le gamin. Je serai soldat quand je serai grand. »

Elie acquiesça.

« Lequel d'entre nous est le meilleur au maniement de l'épée ? demandait un guerrier.

— Va jusqu'à l'endroit où l'espion a été lapidé hier, dit le commandant. Ramasse une grosse pierre et insulte-la.

— Pourquoi cela ? La pierre ne me répondra pas.

— Alors attaque-la avec ton épée.

— Mon épée se brisera, dit le soldat. Et ce n'était pas ma question ; je veux savoir qui est le meilleur au maniement de l'épée.

— Le meilleur est celui qui ressemble à une pierre, répondit le commandant. Sans sortir la lame du fourreau, il réussit à prouver que personne ne pourra le vaincre. »

« Le gouverneur a raison : le commandant est un

sage, pensa Elie. Mais même la plus grande sagesse peut être occultée par l'éclat de la vanité. »

*

Ils poursuivirent leur chemin. L'enfant lui demanda pourquoi les soldats s'entraînaient autant.

« Pas seulement les soldats, mais ta mère aussi, et moi, et ceux qui suivent leur cœur. Tout, dans la vie, exige de l'entraînement.

— Même pour être prophète ?

— Même pour comprendre les anges. Nous voulons tellement leur parler que nous n'écoutons pas ce qu'ils disent. Il n'est pas facile d'écouter : dans nos prières, nous cherchons toujours à expliquer en quoi nous nous sommes trompés et ce que nous aimerions qu'il nous arrive. Mais le Seigneur sait déjà tout cela, et parfois Il nous demande seulement d'entendre ce que nous dit l'univers. Et d'avoir de la patience. »

Le gamin le regardait, surpris. Il ne devait rien comprendre, et pourtant Elie éprouvait le besoin de poursuivre la conversation. Peut-être — quand il serait grand — ces propos l'aideraient-ils dans une situation difficile.

« Toutes les batailles de la vie nous enseignent quelque chose, même celles que nous perdons. Lorsque tu seras grand, tu découvriras que tu as soutenu des mensonges, que tu t'es menti à toi-même, ou que tu as souffert pour des bêtises. Si tu es un bon guerrier, tu ne te sentiras pas coupable, mais tu ne laisseras pas non plus tes erreurs se répéter. »

Il décida de se taire ; un enfant de cet âge ne pouvait pas comprendre ce qu'il disait. Ils marchaient lentement, et Elie regardait les rues de la cité qui un jour l'avait accueilli et qui, maintenant, était près de disparaître. Tout dépendait de la décision qu'il prendrait.

Akbar était plus silencieuse que de coutume. Sur la place centrale, les gens discutaient à voix basse — comme s'ils redoutaient que le vent ne transportât leurs propos jusqu'au campement assyrien. Les plus vieux affirmaient qu'il n'arriverait rien, les jeunes étaient excités par l'éventualité de la lutte, les marchands et les artisans projetaient d'aller à Tyr et à Sidon en attendant que les choses se calment.

« Pour eux il est facile de partir, pensa-t-il. Les marchands peuvent transporter leurs biens dans n'importe quelle partie du monde. Les artisans peuvent travailler même là où l'on parle une langue étrangère. Mais moi, il me faut la permission du Seigneur. »

*

Ils arrivèrent au puits et remplirent deux jarres d'eau. En général, cet endroit était plein de monde ; les femmes se réunissaient pour laver, teindre les étoffes et épiloguaient sur tout ce qui se passait dans la cité. Aucun secret n'existait plus quand il parvenait près du puits ; les nouvelles concernant le commerce, les trahisons familiales, les problèmes de voisinage, la vie intime des gouvernants, tous les sujets — sérieux ou superficiels — y étaient débattus, commentés, critiqués ou applaudis. Même durant les mois où la force ennemie n'avait cessé de croître, Jézabel — la princesse qui avait conquis le roi d'Israël — restait le sujet préféré. Les femmes faisaient l'éloge de son audace, de sa bravoure, certaines que, si un malheur arrivait à la cité, elle reviendrait dans son pays pour les venger.

Mais, ce matin-là, il n'y avait presque personne. Les rares femmes présentes disaient qu'il fallait aller chercher à la campagne le plus de céréales possible parce que les Assyriens allaient bientôt fermer les portes de la cité. Deux d'entre elles projetaient de se rendre jusqu'à la Cinquième Montagne pour offrir un sacrifice aux dieux — elles ne voulaient pas que leurs fils meurent au combat.

« Le prêtre a dit que nous pouvions résister plusieurs mois, expliqua l'une d'elles à Elie. Il suffit que nous ayons le courage nécessaire pour défendre l'honneur d'Akbar, et les dieux nous aideront. »

L'enfant était effrayé.

« L'ennemi va attaquer ? » demanda-t-il.

Elie ne répondit pas ; cela dépendait du choix que l'ange lui avait proposé la nuit précédente.

« J'ai peur, insista le gamin.

— Cela prouve que tu aimes la vie. C'est normal d'avoir peur, aux bons moments. »

*

Elie et l'enfant revinrent à la maison avant la fin de la matinée. La femme avait disposé autour d'elle de petits récipients, contenant des encres de différentes couleurs.

« Je dois travailler, dit-elle en regardant les lettres et les phrases inachevées. A cause de la sécheresse, la cité est envahie par la poussière. Les pinceaux sont toujours sales, et l'encre impure, et tout est plus difficile. »

Elie demeura silencieux : il ne voulait pas lui faire partager ses préoccupations. Il s'assit dans un coin de la salle et resta absorbé dans ses pensées. L'enfant sortit jouer avec ses amis.

« Il a besoin de silence », songea la femme, et elle s'efforça de se concentrer sur son travail.

Elle passa le reste de la matinée à achever quelques mots qui auraient pu être écrits en deux fois moins de temps, et elle se sentit coupable de ne pas faire ce que l'on attendait d'elle ; en fin de compte, pour la première fois de sa vie, elle avait la chance de subvenir aux besoins de sa famille.

Elle se remit au travail ; elle utilisait du papyrus, un matériau qu'un marchand venu d'Egypte lui avait récemment apporté — lui demandant de noter quelques messages commerciaux qu'il devait expédier à Damas. La feuille n'était pas de la meilleure qualité et l'encre débordait sans cesse. « Malgré toutes ces difficultés, c'est mieux que de dessiner sur l'argile. »

Les pays voisins avaient coutume d'envoyer leurs messages sur des plaques d'argile ou sur du parchemin. L'Egypte était peut-être un pays décadent, et son écriture dépassée, mais au moins y avait-on découvert un moyen pratique et léger d'enregistrer le commerce et l'Histoire : on découpait en plusieurs épaisseurs la tige d'une plante qui poussait sur les rives du Nil, et, selon un processus simple, on collait ces couches l'une à côté de l'autre pour former une feuille jaunâtre. Akbar devait importer le papyrus car il était impossible de le cultiver dans la vallée. Même s'il coûtait cher, les marchands le préféraient car ils pouvaient transporter les feuilles écrites dans leur sac — ce qui se révélait impossible avec les tablettes d'argile et les parchemins.

« Tout devient plus simple », pensa-t-elle. Dommage qu'il fallût l'autorisation du gouvernement pour employer l'alphabet de Byblos sur le papyrus. Une loi dépassée soumettait encore les textes écrits au contrôle du Conseil d'Akbar.

Son travail terminé, elle le montra à Elie, qui avait passé tout ce temps à la regarder faire, sans le moindre commentaire.

« Que penses-tu du résultat ? » demanda-t-elle.

Il parut sortir d'une transe.

« Oui, c'est joli », répondit-il sans prêter attention à ce qu'elle disait.

Il devait converser avec le Seigneur. Et elle ne voulait pas l'interrompre. Elle sortit et alla chercher le prêtre.

*

A son retour, Elie était toujours assis au même endroit. Les deux hommes se dévisagèrent. Tous deux restèrent silencieux pendant un long moment. Ce fut le prêtre qui rompit le silence. « Tu es un prophète, et tu parles avec les anges. Je ne fais qu'interpréter les lois anciennes, exécuter des rituels, et tenter de protéger mon peuple des erreurs qu'il commet. C'est pourquoi je sais que ce combat n'oppose pas des hommes. C'est une bataille des dieux, et je ne dois pas l'empêcher.

— J'admire ta foi, même si tu adores des dieux qui n'existent pas, répondit Elie. Si la situation présente est, comme tu l'affirmes, digne d'une bataille céleste, le Seigneur fera de moi Son instrument pour détruire Baal et ses compagnons de la Cinquième Montagne. Il aurait mieux valu que tu ordonnes mon assassinat.

— J'y ai songé. Mais ce n'était pas nécessaire ; au moment opportun, les dieux m'ont été favorables. »

Elie ne répliqua pas. Le prêtre se retourna et prit le papyrus sur lequel la femme venait d'écrire un texte.

« C'est du bon travail », commenta-t-il. Après l'avoir lu soigneusement, il retira sa bague de son doigt, la trempa dans l'encre et appliqua son sceau dans le coin gauche. Quiconque se faisait prendre avec un papyrus dépourvu du sceau du prêtre pouvait être condamné à mort.

« Pourquoi devez-vous toujours faire cela ? demanda-t-elle.

— Parce que ces papyrus colportent des idées, répondit-il. Et les idées ont un pouvoir.

— Ce ne sont que des transactions commerciales.

— Mais ce pourrait être des plans de bataille. Ou un rapport sur nos richesses. Ou nos prières secrètes. De nos jours, au moyen des lettres et des papyrus, on peut sans peine voler l'inspiration d'un peuple. Il est plus difficile de cacher des tablettes d'argile ou des parchemins ; mais la combinaison du papyrus et de l'alphabet de Byblos peut mettre fin à la culture de chaque pays et détruire le monde. »

Une femme entra.

« Prêtre ! Prêtre ! Viens voir ce qui se passe ! »

Elie et la veuve le suivirent. Des gens affluaient de toutes les directions au même endroit ; la poussière qu'ils soulevaient rendait l'air pratiquement irrespirable. Les enfants couraient en tête, riant et faisant du vacarme. Les adultes avançaient lentement, en silence.

Quand ils atteignirent la porte Sud de la cité, une petite foule s'y trouvait déjà réunie. Le prêtre se fraya un chemin et s'enquit du motif de toute cette confusion.

Une sentinelle d'Akbar se tenait à genoux, les bras écartés, les mains clouées sur un morceau de bois placé en travers de ses épaules. Ses vêtements étaient déchirés et un morceau de bois lui avait crevé l'œil gauche.

Sur sa poitrine, quelques caractères assyriens

avaient été tracés avec la lame d'un poignard. Le prêtre comprenait l'égyptien mais la langue assyrienne n'était pas encore assez répandue pour être enseignée et sue par cœur ; il dut faire appel à un commerçant qui assistait à la scène.

« *Nous déclarons la guerre*, voilà ce qui est écrit », traduisit l'homme.

Les gens tout autour n'avaient dit mot. Elie pouvait lire la panique sur leurs visages.

« Donne-moi ton épée », dit le prêtre à un soldat.

Le soldat obéit. Le prêtre demanda qu'on avertît le gouverneur et le commandant de ce qui était arrivé. Puis, d'un geste rapide, il enfila la lame dans le cœur de la sentinelle agenouillée.

L'homme poussa un gémissement et tomba à terre, mort, libéré de la douleur et de la honte de s'être laissé capturer.

« Demain je me rendrai sur la Cinquième Montagne pour offrir des sacrifices, dit-il au peuple effrayé. Et les dieux de nouveau se souviendront de nous. »

Avant de partir, il se tourna vers Elie :

« Tu le vois de tes propres yeux : les cieux continuent de nous venir en aide.

— Une seule question, dit Elie. Pourquoi veux-tu voir sacrifier ton peuple ?

— Parce qu'il faut en passer par là pour tuer une idée. »

Lorsqu'il l'avait entendu converser avec la femme ce matin-là, Elie avait déjà compris de quelle idée il s'agissait : l'alphabet.

« Il est trop tard. Il est déjà répandu de par le monde, et les Assyriens ne peuvent pas conquérir la terre entière.

— Qui t'a dit cela ? En fin de compte, les dieux de la Cinquième Montagne sont du côté de leurs armées. »

*

Pendant des heures, il marcha dans la vallée, comme il l'avait fait l'après-midi précédent. Il savait

113

qu'il y aurait encore au moins une soirée et une nuit de paix : on ne fait pas la guerre dans l'obscurité, car les guerriers ne peuvent y distinguer l'ennemi. Cette nuit-là, le Seigneur lui laissait une chance de changer le destin de la cité qui l'avait accueilli.

« Salomon saurait quoi faire maintenant, expliqua-t-il à son ange. Et David, et Moïse, et Isaac. Ils étaient des hommes de confiance du Seigneur, mais moi, je ne suis qu'un serviteur indécis. Le Seigneur me donne un choix qui aurait dû être le Sien.

— L'histoire de nos ancêtres abonde apparemment en hommes qui étaient la bonne personne au bon endroit, répliqua l'ange. Ne crois pas cela : le Seigneur n'exige de chacun que ce qui est du domaine de ses possibilités.

— Alors, Il s'est trompé avec moi.

— Tous les malheurs ont une fin. Ainsi en est-il aussi des gloires et des tragédies du monde.

— Je ne l'oublierai pas, dit Elie. Mais, quand elles se retirent, les tragédies laissent des marques éternelles, et les gloires laissent de vains souvenirs. »

L'ange ne répondit pas.

« Pourquoi, pendant tout le temps que j'ai passé à Akbar, ai-je été incapable de trouver des alliés pour lutter en faveur de la paix ? Quelle importance a un prophète solitaire ?

— Quelle importance a le soleil qui poursuit sa course dans le ciel ? Quelle importance a une montagne qui surgit au milieu d'une vallée ? Quelle importance a un puits isolé ? Ce sont pourtant eux qui indiquent le chemin que doit suivre la caravane.

— Mon cœur suffoque de tristesse, dit Elie en s'agenouillant et en tendant les bras vers le ciel. Si seulement je pouvais mourir ici et ne jamais avoir les mains tachées du sang de mon peuple, ou d'un peuple étranger. Regarde là-derrière : que vois-tu ?

— Tu sais bien que je suis aveugle, dit l'ange. Mes yeux gardent encore la lumière de la gloire du Seigneur, et je ne peux rien voir d'autre. Tout ce que je perçois, c'est ce que ton cœur me raconte. Tout ce que je peux entrevoir, ce sont les vibrations des dangers qui te menacent. Je ne peux pas savoir ce qui se trouve derrière toi.

— Eh bien, je vais te le dire : il y a Akbar. A cette heure, le soleil de l'après-midi illuminant son profil, elle est belle. Je me suis habitué à ses rues et à ses murailles, à son peuple généreux et accueillant. Même si les habitants de la cité sont encore prisonniers du commerce et des superstitions, ils ont le cœur aussi pur que celui de n'importe quelle autre nation du monde. J'ai appris grâce à eux beaucoup de choses que j'ignorais ; en échange, j'ai écouté leurs plaintes et, inspiré par Dieu, j'ai réussi à résoudre leurs conflits internes. Souvent j'ai été en danger, et toujours quelqu'un m'a aidé. Pourquoi dois-je choisir entre sauver cette cité ou racheter mon peuple ?

— Parce qu'un homme doit choisir, répondit l'ange. En cela réside sa force : le pouvoir de ses décisions.

— C'est un choix difficile : il exige d'accepter la mort d'un peuple pour en sauver un autre.

— Il est encore plus difficile de définir sa propre voie. Celui qui ne fait pas de choix meurt aux yeux du Seigneur, même s'il continue à respirer et à marcher dans les rues. En outre, personne ne meurt. L'Eternité accueille toutes les âmes et chacune poursuivra sa tâche. Il y a une raison pour tout ce qui se trouve sous le soleil. »

Elie leva de nouveau les bras vers les cieux :

« Mon peuple s'est éloigné du Seigneur à cause de la beauté d'une femme. La Phénicie peut être détruite parce qu'un prêtre pense que l'écriture constitue une menace pour les dieux. Pourquoi Celui qui a créé le monde préfère-t-Il se servir de la tragédie pour écrire le livre du destin ? »

Les cris d'Elie résonnèrent dans la vallée et l'écho revint à ses oreilles.

« Tu ne sais pas ce que tu dis, rétorqua l'ange. Il n'y a pas de tragédie, il y a seulement l'inévitable. Tout a sa raison d'être : c'est à toi de savoir distinguer ce qui est passager de ce qui est définitif.

— Qu'est-ce qui est passager ? demanda Elie.

— L'inévitable.
— Et qu'est-ce qui est définitif ?
— Les leçons de l'inévitable. »
Sur ces mots, l'ange s'éloigna.

Cette nuit-là, au cours du dîner, Elie dit à la femme et à l'enfant :
« Préparez vos affaires. Nous pouvons partir à tout moment.
— Voilà deux jours que tu ne dors pas, remarqua la femme. Un émissaire du gouverneur est venu cet après-midi ; il demandait que tu te rendes au palais. J'ai dit que tu étais parti dans la vallée et que tu y dormirais.
— Tu as bien fait », répliqua-t-il. Puis il gagna directement sa chambre et sombra dans un profond sommeil.

Il fut réveillé le lendemain matin par le son d'instruments de musique. Quand il descendit voir ce qui se passait, l'enfant était déjà sur le seuil.
« Regarde ! disait-il, les yeux brillants d'excitation. C'est la guerre ! »
Un bataillon de soldats, imposants avec leurs uniformes de guerre et leur armement, se dirigeait vers la porte Sud d'Akbar. Un groupe de musiciens les suivait, marquant le pas au rythme des tambours.
« Hier tu avais peur, dit Elie au gamin.
— Je ne savais pas que nous avions tant de soldats. Nos guerriers sont les meilleurs ! »
Elie quitta l'enfant et sortit dans la rue ; il lui fallait à tout prix rencontrer le gouverneur. Les habitants de la cité, réveillés au son des hymnes de guerre, étaient hypnotisés ; pour la première fois de leur vie, ils assistaient au défilé d'un bataillon organisé, en uniforme militaire, lances et boucliers reflé-

tant les premiers rayons du soleil. Le commandant avait réussi un tour de force ; il avait préparé son armée à l'insu de tous, et maintenant — Elie le redoutait — il pouvait laisser croire que la victoire sur les Assyriens était possible.

Il se fraya un chemin parmi les soldats et parvint jusqu'au devant de la colonne. Là, montés sur leurs chevaux, le commandant et le gouverneur ouvraient la marche.

« Nous avons passé un accord, lança Elie tout en courant à côté du gouverneur. Je peux faire un miracle ! »

Le gouverneur ne lui répondit pas. La garnison franchit les remparts de la cité et sortit en direction de la vallée.

« Tu sais que cette armée est une chimère, insista-t-il. Les Assyriens sont cinq fois plus nombreux, et ils ont l'expérience de la guerre ! Ne laisse pas détruire Akbar !

— Qu'attends-tu de moi ? demanda le gouverneur, sans arrêter sa monture. Hier soir, j'ai envoyé un émissaire te chercher pour que nous discutions, et on m'a fait dire que tu étais absent de la cité. Que pouvais-je faire de plus ?

— Affronter les Assyriens en terrain ouvert est un suicide ! Vous le savez bien ! »

Le commandant écoutait la conversation sans faire le moindre commentaire. Il avait déjà discuté de sa stratégie avec le gouverneur ; le prophète israélite serait surpris.

Elie courait à côté des chevaux, sans savoir exactement ce qu'il devait faire. La colonne de soldats s'éloignait de la cité et se dirigeait vers le centre de la vallée.

« Aide-moi, Seigneur, pensait-il. De même que tu as caché le soleil pour aider Josué au combat, arrête le temps et fais que je réussisse à persuader le gouverneur de son erreur. »

A peine avait-il eu cette pensée que le commandant cria : « Halte ! »

« C'est peut-être un signal, se dit Elie. Je dois en profiter. »

Les soldats formèrent deux lignes, semblables à des murs d'hommes, les boucliers prenant solidement appui sur le sol et les armes pointées en avant.

« Tu crois voir les guerriers d'Akbar, dit le gouverneur à Elie.

— Je vois des jeunes gens qui rient devant la mort.

— Mais sache qu'ici il n'y a qu'un seul bataillon. La plupart de nos hommes sont restés dans la cité, en haut des murailles. Nous avons disposé des chaudrons d'huile bouillante prêts à être versés sur la tête de quiconque tenterait de les escalader. Nous avons réparti des réserves dans différentes maisons pour éviter que des flèches incendiaires ne détruisent nos provisions. Selon les calculs du commandant, nous pouvons résister presque deux mois au siège de la cité. Pendant que les Assyriens se préparaient, nous faisions la même chose.

— On ne m'a jamais raconté cela, dit Elie.

— Rappelle-toi : même si tu as aidé le peuple d'Akbar, tu restes un étranger, et certains militaires pouvaient te prendre pour un espion.

— Mais toi, tu désires la paix !

— La paix reste possible, même après le commencement d'un combat. Seulement, nous négocierons en position d'égalité. »

Le gouverneur raconta que des messagers avaient été envoyés à Tyr et à Sidon pour rendre compte de la gravité de la situation. Il lui en coûtait de réclamer du secours : on pouvait le croire incapable de maîtriser la situation. Mais il était parvenu à la conclusion que c'était la seule solution.

Le commandant avait mis au point un plan ingénieux ; dès que le combat s'engagerait, il retournerait dans la cité pour organiser la résistance. De son côté, la troupe qui se trouvait maintenant sur le terrain devait tuer le plus d'ennemis possible, puis se retirer dans les montagnes. Les soldats connaissaient cette vallée mieux que personne et ils pouvaient attaquer les Assyriens par de petites escarmouches, diminuant ainsi la pression du siège.

Les secours arriveraient rapidement, et l'armée assyrienne serait écrasée.

« Nous pouvons résister soixante jours, mais ce ne sera pas nécessaire, dit le gouverneur à Elie.

— Mais il y aura beaucoup de morts.

— Nous sommes tous en présence de la mort. Et personne n'a peur, pas même moi. »

Le gouverneur était étonné de son propre courage. Il ne s'était jamais trouvé à la veille d'une bataille et, à mesure que le combat approchait, il avait dressé des plans pour fuir la cité. Ce matin-là, il avait combiné avec les plus fidèles de ses hommes la meilleure manière de battre en retraite. Il ne pourrait pas aller à Tyr ou à Sidon, parce qu'il serait considéré comme un traître, mais Jézabel l'accueillerait puisqu'elle avait besoin d'hommes de confiance à ses côtés.

Cependant, en foulant le champ de bataille, il percevait dans les yeux des soldats une joie immense — comme s'ils s'étaient entraînés leur vie entière pour un objectif et qu'enfin ce grand moment était arrivé.

« La peur existe jusqu'au moment où survient l'inévitable, dit-il à Elie. Après, nous ne devons plus perdre notre énergie à cause d'elle. »

Elie était troublé. Il ressentait la même chose, bien qu'il eût honte de le reconnaître ; il se souvint de l'excitation de l'enfant au passage de la troupe.

« Va-t'en, ordonna le gouverneur. Tu es un étranger, désarmé, et tu n'as pas besoin de combattre pour une idée à laquelle tu ne crois pas. »

Elie demeura immobile.

« Ils vont venir, insista le commandant. Tu n'en reviens pas, mais nous sommes prêts. »

Mais Elie resta là.

Ils regardèrent l'horizon ; pas la moindre poussière, l'armée assyrienne ne bougeait pas.

Les soldats du premier rang tenaient fermement leurs lances pointées en avant, les archers avaient déjà tendu la corde de leurs arcs pour décocher leurs flèches dès que le commandant en donnerait l'ordre. Des hommes qui s'entraînaient fendaient l'air de leurs épées, pour garder leurs muscles échauffés.

« Tout est prêt, répéta le commandant. Ils vont attaquer. »

Elie nota l'euphorie dans sa voix. Il était sans doute impatient que la bataille commençât ; il voulait lutter et montrer sa bravoure. Assurément, il imaginait les guerriers assyriens, les coups d'épée, les cris et la confusion, il se figurait que les prêtres phéniciens le citeraient en exemple pour son efficacité et son courage.

Le gouverneur interrompit ses pensées :

« Ils ne bougent pas. »

Elie se rappela ce qu'il avait demandé au Seigneur : que le soleil s'arrêtât dans les cieux, comme il l'avait fait pour Josué. Il tenta de converser avec son ange, mais il n'entendit pas sa voix.

Peu à peu, les lanciers baissèrent leurs armes, les archers relâchèrent la tension de leurs arcs, les hommes remirent leurs épées au fourreau. Ce fut le soleil brûlant de midi, et des guerriers s'évanouirent sous l'effet de la chaleur ; pourtant, le détachement se tint prêt jusqu'à la fin de l'après-midi.

Quand le soleil se cacha, les guerriers retournèrent à Akbar. Ils semblaient désappointés d'avoir survécu un jour de plus.

Seul Elie resta au cœur de la vallée. Il marcha sans but quelque temps ; soudain il vit la lumière. L'ange du Seigneur apparut devant lui.

« Dieu a entendu tes prières. Et Il a vu le tourment de ton âme. »

Elie se tourna vers les cieux et remercia des bénédictions.

« Le Seigneur est la source de la gloire et du pouvoir. Il a retenu l'armée assyrienne.

— Non, répliqua l'ange. Tu as dit que le choix devait être le Sien. Et Il a fait le choix pour toi. »

« Partons, dit-il à la femme et à son fils.

— Je ne veux pas m'en aller, répliqua l'enfant. Je suis fier des soldats d'Akbar. »

Sa mère l'obligea à rassembler ses affaires : « Emporte seulement ce que tu peux porter.

— Tu oublies, ma mère, que nous sommes pauvres et que je n'ai pas grand-chose. »

Elie monta à sa chambre. Il en fit le tour du regard, comme si c'était la première et la dernière fois qu'il la voyait ; puis il redescendit et observa la veuve qui rangeait ses encres.

« Merci de m'emmener avec toi, dit-elle. Quand je me suis mariée, j'avais à peine quinze ans, et je ne savais rien de la vie. Nos familles avaient tout arrangé, j'avais été élevée dès l'enfance pour ce moment et soigneusement préparée à assister mon mari en toute circonstance.

— Tu l'aimais ?

— J'ai éduqué mon cœur pour cela. Puisque je n'avais pas le choix, je me suis convaincue que c'était la meilleure voie. Quand j'ai perdu mon mari, je me suis habituée aux jours et aux nuits identiques, et j'ai demandé aux dieux de la Cinquième Montagne — à cette époque je croyais encore en eux — de m'emporter lorsque mon fils serait en âge de vivre seul.

« C'est alors que tu es venu. Je te l'ai déjà dit, et je le répète : à partir de ce jour-là, j'ai découvert la beauté de la vallée, la sombre silhouette des montagnes se projetant sur le ciel, la lune qui change de forme pour que le blé puisse pousser. Souvent, la nuit, pendant que tu dormais, je me promenais dans Akbar, j'écoutais les pleurs des nouveau-nés, les chansons des hommes qui avaient bu après le travail, les pas fermes des sentinelles en haut de la muraille. Combien de fois avais-je vu ce paysage sans remarquer comme il était beau ? Combien de fois avais-je regardé le ciel sans voir sa profondeur ? Combien de fois avais-je entendu les bruits d'Akbar autour de moi sans comprendre qu'ils faisaient partie de ma vie ? J'ai retrouvé une

121

immense envie de vivre. Tu m'as conseillé d'étudier les caractères de Byblos, et je l'ai fait. Je pensais seulement te faire plaisir mais je me suis enthousiasmée pour ce que je faisais et j'ai découvert ceci : *le sens de ma vie était celui que je voulais lui donner.* »

Elie lui caressa les cheveux. C'était la première fois.

« Pourquoi n'as-tu pas toujours été ainsi ? demanda-t-elle.

— Parce que j'avais peur. Mais aujourd'hui, en attendant la bataille, j'ai entendu les paroles du gouverneur et j'ai pensé à toi. La peur va jusqu'où commence l'inévitable ; dès lors, elle n'a plus de sens. Et il ne nous reste que l'espoir de prendre la bonne décision.

— Je suis prête, dit-elle.

— Nous retournerons en Israël. Le Seigneur m'a indiqué ce que je dois faire, et je le ferai. Jézabel sera écartée du pouvoir. »

Elle resta silencieuse. Comme toutes les femmes de Phénicie, elle était fière de sa princesse. Quand ils arriveraient à destination, elle tenterait de le convaincre de changer d'avis.

« Ce sera un long voyage et nous n'aurons pas de repos jusqu'à ce que j'aie fait ce qu'Il m'a demandé, dit Elie, comme s'il devinait sa pensée. Cependant, ton amour sera mon soutien, et aux moments où je serai fatigué des batailles en Son nom, je pourrai me reposer entre tes bras. »

L'enfant s'approcha, un petit sac sur l'épaule. Elie le prit et dit à la femme :

« L'heure est venue. Quand tu traverseras les rues d'Akbar, grave en toi le souvenir de chaque maison, de chaque bruit. Parce que tu ne la reverras jamais.

— Je suis née à Akbar, dit-elle. Et la cité restera toujours dans mon cœur. »

L'enfant entendit, et il se promit que jamais il n'oublierait les paroles de sa mère. Si un jour il pouvait revenir, il verrait la cité comme s'il voyait son visage.

Il faisait nuit lorsque le prêtre arriva au pied de la Cinquième Montagne. Il tenait dans la main droite un bâton et portait un sac dans la gauche.

Il sortit du sac l'huile sacrée et s'en frotta le front et les poignets. Puis, avec le bâton, il dessina sur le sable le taureau et la panthère, symboles du dieu de la Tempête et de la Grande Déesse. Il récita les prières rituelles ; enfin il leva ses bras écartés vers le ciel pour recevoir la révélation divine.

Les dieux se taisaient. Ils avaient dit tout ce qu'ils avaient à dire et maintenant ils n'exigeaient plus que l'accomplissement des rituels. Les prophètes avaient disparu partout dans le monde — sauf en Israël, un pays arriéré, superstitieux, où l'on croyait encore que les hommes peuvent communiquer avec les créateurs de l'Univers.

Il se rappela que, deux générations auparavant, Tyr et Sidon avaient fait du négoce avec un roi de Jérusalem appelé Salomon. Il faisait construire un grand temple et voulait l'orner de ce que le monde offrait de meilleur ; aussi avait-il fait acheter des cèdres de la Phénicie, qu'on appelait Liban. Le roi de Tyr avait fourni le matériau nécessaire et reçu en échange vingt cités de Galilée, mais celles-ci ne lui avaient pas plu. Salomon, alors, l'avait aidé à construire ses premiers navires, et désormais la Phénicie possédait la plus grande flotte commerciale du monde.

A cette époque, Israël était encore une grande nation — bien qu'elle rendît un culte à un dieu unique, dont on ne connaissait même pas le nom et qu'on appelait seulement le « Seigneur ». Une princesse de Sidon avait réussi à faire revenir Salomon à la foi authentique, et il avait édifié un autel aux dieux de la Cinquième Montagne. Les Israélites persistaient à affirmer que le « Seigneur » avait puni le plus sage de leurs rois en faisant en sorte que les guerres l'éloignent du pouvoir.

Mais Jéroboam, qui régna après lui, poursuivit le culte que Salomon avait initié. Il fit faire deux veaux d'or que le peuple d'Israël adorait. C'est alors que les prophètes entrèrent en scène et entreprirent une lutte sans trêve contre le souverain.

Jézabel avait raison : la seule manière de maintenir vivante la foi authentique était de tuer les prophètes. Cette femme douce, élevée dans la tolérance et l'horreur de la guerre, savait qu'il y a un moment où la violence est la seule issue. Le sang qui lui salissait maintenant les mains serait pardonné par les dieux qu'elle servait.

« Bientôt, moi aussi j'aurai du sang sur les mains, dit le prêtre à la montagne silencieuse devant lui. De même que les prophètes sont la malédiction d'Israël, l'écriture est la malédiction de la Phénicie. Elle peut comme eux causer un mal irrémédiable et il faut les arrêter tant que c'est encore possible. Le dieu du Temps ne peut pas nous abandonner maintenant. »

Il était inquiet de ce qui s'était produit le matin ; l'armée ennemie n'avait pas attaqué. Par le passé, le dieu du Temps s'était déjà détourné de la Phénicie, irrité contre ses habitants. En conséquence, le feu des lampes s'était éteint, les brebis et les vaches avaient délaissé leurs petits, le blé et l'orge étaient restés verts. Le dieu Soleil avait envoyé à sa recherche des personnages importants — l'aigle et le dieu de la Tempête — mais en vain. Finalement, la Grande Déesse dépêcha une abeille, qui le découvrit endormi dans un bois et le piqua. Il se réveilla, furieux, et se mit à tout détruire autour de lui. Il fallut s'en emparer et extraire de son âme la haine qui s'y trouvait, puis tout redevint normal.

S'il décidait de se retirer de nouveau, la bataille n'aurait pas lieu. Les Assyriens resteraient à tout jamais à l'entrée de la vallée, et Akbar continuerait d'exister.

« Le courage est la peur qui fait ses prières, dit-il. C'est pour cela que je suis ici ; parce que je ne peux pas fléchir au moment du combat. Je dois montrer aux guerriers d'Akbar qu'il y a une raison de défendre la cité. Ce n'est pas le puits, ce n'est pas le marché, ce n'est pas le palais du gouverneur. Nous allons affronter l'armée assyrienne parce que nous devons donner l'exemple. »

La victoire des Assyriens mettrait fin à tout jamais à la menace de l'alphabet. Les conquérants imposeraient leur langue et leurs coutumes, tout en continuant d'adorer les mêmes dieux sur la Cinquième Montagne ; voilà ce qui importait.

« Plus tard, nos navigateurs emporteront dans d'autres pays les exploits de nos guerriers. Les prêtres se rappelleront leurs noms et le jour où Akbar tenta de résister à l'invasion assyrienne. Les peintres dessineront des caractères égyptiens sur les papyrus, les écrits de Byblos seront morts. Les textes sacrés resteront au seul pouvoir de ceux qui sont nés pour les apprendre. Alors, les générations futures tenteront d'imiter ce que nous avons fait et nous construirons un monde meilleur.

« Mais aujourd'hui, poursuivit-il, nous devons perdre cette bataille. Nous lutterons avec bravoure, mais nous sommes en situation d'infériorité ; et nous mourrons glorieusement. »

A ce moment le prêtre écouta la nuit et comprit qu'il avait raison. Ce silence précédait l'instant d'un combat décisif, mais les habitants d'Akbar l'interprétaient de manière erronée ; ils avaient abaissé leurs lances et se divertissaient au lieu de monter la garde. Ils ne prêtaient pas attention à l'exemple de la nature : les animaux sont silencieux à l'approche du danger.

« Que s'accomplissent les desseins des dieux. Que les cieux ne tombent pas sur la terre, car nous avons fait tout ce qu'il fallait et nous avons obéi à la tradition », ajouta-t-il.

Elie, la femme et l'enfant marchaient sur le chemin qui menait vers Israël ; il n'était pas nécessaire de passer par le campement assyrien, situé au sud.

La pleine lune facilitait leur progression mais, en même temps, elle projetait des ombres étranges et des formes sinistres sur les rochers et les chemins pierreux de la vallée.

Du fond de l'obscurité surgit l'ange du Seigneur. Il tenait une épée de feu dans la main droite.

« Où vas-tu ? demanda-t-il.

— En Israël, répondit Elie.

— Le Seigneur t'a appelé ?

— Je connais déjà le miracle que Dieu attend de moi. Et maintenant je sais où je dois le réaliser.

— Le Seigneur t'a appelé ? » répéta l'ange.

Elie resta silencieux.

« Le Seigneur t'a appelé ? reprit l'ange pour la troisième fois.

— Non.

— Alors retourne d'où tu viens, car tu n'as pas encore accompli ton destin. Le Seigneur ne t'a pas encore appelé.

— Laisse-les au moins partir, ils n'ont rien à faire ici », implora Elie.

Mais l'ange n'était déjà plus là. Elie jeta par terre le sac qu'il portait. Il s'assit au milieu de la route et pleura amèrement.

« Que s'est-il passé ? demandèrent la femme et l'enfant, qui n'avaient rien vu.

— Nous allons retourner, dit-il. Ainsi le veut le Seigneur. »

*

Il ne réussit pas à dormir. Il se réveilla en pleine nuit et sentit une tension dans l'air autour de lui ; un vent méchant soufflait dans les rues, semant la peur et la méfiance.

« Dans l'amour d'une femme j'ai découvert l'amour pour toutes les créatures, priait-il en silence. J'ai besoin d'elle. Je sais que le Seigneur n'oubliera pas que je suis un de Ses instruments, peut-être le plus faible qu'Il ait choisi. Aide-moi, Seigneur, car je dois me reposer tranquille au milieu des batailles. »

Il se rappela le commentaire du gouverneur sur

l'inutilité de la peur. Malgré cela, il ne pouvait trouver le sommeil. « J'ai besoin d'énergie et de calme ; donne-moi le repos tant que c'est possible. »

Il songea à appeler son ange, pour converser un peu avec lui ; mais il risquait d'entendre des choses qu'il ne désirait pas et il changea d'avis. Pour se détendre, il descendit dans la salle ; les sacs que la femme avait préparés pour leur fuite n'étaient même pas défaits.

Il pensa aller jusqu'à la chambre de celle-ci. Il se rappela que le Seigneur avait dit à Moïse avant une bataille : « *L'homme qui aime une femme et ne l'a pas encore reçue, qu'il retourne chez elle, afin que, s'il meurt dans la lutte, ce ne soit pas un autre homme qui la reçoive.* »

Ils n'avaient pas encore cohabité. Mais la nuit avait été épuisante et ce n'était pas le moment.

Il décida de vider les sacs et de ranger chaque chose à sa place. Il découvrit qu'elle avait emporté avec elle, outre les quelques vêtements qu'elle possédait, les instruments dont elle se servait pour dessiner les caractères de Byblos.

Il prit un stylet, mouilla une tablette d'argile et commença à griffonner quelques lettres ; il avait appris à écrire en regardant la femme travailler.

« Que c'est simple et ingénieux ! » pensa-t-il, en essayant de distraire son esprit. Souvent, quand il allait au puits chercher de l'eau, il écoutait les commentaires des femmes : « Les Grecs ont volé notre plus importante invention. » Elie savait que ce n'était pas exact : l'adaptation qu'ils en avaient faite, en introduisant les voyelles, avait transformé l'alphabet en un instrument que les peuples de toutes les nations pourraient utiliser. De surcroît, ils avaient donné à leurs collections de parchemins le nom de *biblia*, en hommage à la cité où était née cette invention.

Les livres grecs étaient rédigés sur des peaux d'animaux. C'était un support bien fragile pour conserver les mots, pensait Elie ; le cuir était moins résistant que les tablettes d'argile, et facile à voler. Quant aux papyrus, ils s'abîmaient au bout d'un certain temps de manipulation, et pouvaient être détruits par l'eau. « Les parchemins et les papyrus sont périssables ; seules les tablettes d'argile sont destinées à durer toujours », songea-t-il.

Si Akbar survivait, il recommanderait au gouverneur de faire consigner l'histoire de son pays et de conserver les tablettes d'argile dans une salle spéciale, afin que les générations futures puissent les consulter. Si jamais les prêtres phéniciens — qui gardaient en mémoire l'histoire de leur peuple — venaient à disparaître un jour, les faits des guerriers et des poètes ne tomberaient pas dans l'oubli.

Il joua ainsi un moment, dessinant les mêmes lettres dans un ordre différent et formant des mots distincts. Il fut émerveillé du résultat. Cette occupation le détendit et il retourna se coucher.

*

Un grand fracas le réveilla peu après ; la porte de sa chambre fut projetée par terre.

« Ce n'est pas un rêve. Ce ne sont pas les armées du Seigneur au combat. »

Des ombres surgissaient de toute part, poussant des cris de déments dans une langue qu'il ne comprenait pas.

« Les Assyriens. »

D'autres portes tombaient, des murs étaient abattus sous de puissants coups de masse, les hurlements des envahisseurs se mêlaient aux appels au secours qui montaient de la place. Il tenta de se lever, mais une ombre le renversa à terre. Un bruit sourd secoua l'étage au-dessous.

« Le feu, pensa Elie. Ils ont mis le feu à la maison. »

« C'est toi ! s'exclama quelqu'un en phénicien. Tu es le chef ! Caché comme un lâche dans la maison d'une femme. »

Elie regarda le visage de celui qui venait de parler ; les flammes illuminaient la pièce, et il put voir un homme avec une longue barbe, en uniforme militaire. Oui, les Assyriens étaient arrivés.

« Vous avez attaqué de nuit ? » demanda-t-il, désorienté.

Mais l'homme ne répondit pas. Elie vit l'éclat des épées sorties de leur fourreau et un guerrier le blessa au bras droit.

Il ferma les yeux ; toute sa vie défila devant lui en une fraction de seconde. Il retourna jouer dans les rues de la cité où il était né, il se rendit pour la première fois à Jérusalem, il sentit l'odeur du bois coupé dans la charpenterie, il fut de nouveau ébloui par l'étendue de la mer et les vêtements que l'on portait dans les cités prospères de la côte. Il se revit parcourant les vallées et les montagnes de la Terre promise, il se rappela qu'il avait connu Jézabel, elle semblait encore une petite fille et elle enchantait tous ceux qui l'approchaient. Il assista de nouveau au massacre des prophètes et entendit la voix du Seigneur qui lui ordonnait de se rendre au désert. Il revit les yeux de la femme qui l'attendait à l'entrée de Sarepta — que ses habitants appelaient Akbar — et comprit qu'il l'avait aimée dès le premier instant. Il gravit encore la Cinquième Montagne, ressuscita un enfant et fut accueilli par le peuple comme un sage et un juste. Il regarda le ciel où les constellations se mouvaient rapidement, s'émerveilla de la lune qui montrait ses quatre phases en même temps, sentit le froid, le chaud, l'automne et le printemps, éprouva encore une fois la pluie et l'éclair de la foudre. Les nuages prirent mille formes différentes et les eaux des rivières coulèrent pour la seconde fois dans le même lit. Il revécut le jour où il avait vu s'installer la première tente assyrienne, puis la deuxième, et d'autres encore, de plus en plus nombreuses, les anges qui allaient et venaient, l'épée de feu sur le chemin d'Israël, les nuits d'insomnie, les dessins sur les tablettes, et...

Il était revenu au présent. Il pensa à ce qui se passait à l'étage au-dessous, il fallait à tout prix sauver la veuve et son fils.

« Au feu ! dit-il aux soldats ennemis. La maison prend feu ! »

Il n'avait pas peur ; son seul souci était pour la

veuve et son fils. Quelqu'un lui poussa la tête contre le sol, et il sentit le goût de la terre dans sa bouche. Il l'embrassa, lui dit combien il l'aimait et expliqua qu'il avait fait son possible pour empêcher cela. Il voulut se libérer de ses assaillants, mais quelqu'un lui maintenait un pied sur la poitrine.

« Elle a dû s'enfuir, pensa-t-il. Ils ne feraient pas de mal à une femme sans défense. »

Un calme profond envahit son cœur. Peut-être le Seigneur s'était-Il rendu compte qu'il n'était pas l'homme de la situation et avait-Il découvert un autre prophète pour sauver Israël du péché. La mort était enfin venue, comme il l'espérait, par le martyre. Il accepta son destin et attendit le coup fatal.

Quelques secondes passèrent ; les guerriers continuaient à vociférer, le sang jaillissait de sa blessure, mais le coup mortel ne venait pas.

« Je vous en prie, tuez-moi vite ! » cria-t-il, convaincu qu'au moins l'un d'eux parlait sa langue.

Personne ne prêta attention à ses paroles. Ils discutaient vivement, comme si une erreur avait été commise. Des soldats se mirent à le frapper et, pour la première fois, Elie constata que l'instinct de survie revenait. Il en fut paniqué.

« Je ne peux pas désirer la vie plus longtemps, pensa-t-il, désespéré. Parce que je ne sortirai pas vivant de cette pièce. »

Mais rien ne se passait. Le monde paraissait s'éterniser dans cette confusion de cris, de bruits et de poussière. Le Seigneur avait peut-être agi comme Il l'avait fait avec Josué, arrêtant le temps en plein milieu du combat.

C'est alors qu'il entendit les cris de la femme en dessous. Dans un effort surhumain, il parvint à repousser un garde et à se lever, mais il fut aussitôt rejeté à terre. Un soldat lui frappa la tête et il s'évanouit.

*

Quelques minutes plus tard, il recouvra ses esprits. Les Assyriens l'avaient traîné dans la rue.

Encore étourdi, il leva la tête : toutes les maisons du quartier étaient en flammes.

« Une femme innocente et sans défense est prisonnière là-dedans ! Sauvez-la ! »

Cris, course, confusion de toutes parts. Il tenta de se redresser mais on le renversa de nouveau.

« Seigneur, Tu peux faire ce que Tu veux de moi, parce que j'ai consacré ma vie et ma mort à Ta cause, pria Elie. Mais sauve celle qui m'a accueilli ! »

Quelqu'un le tira par le bras.

« Viens voir, dit l'officier assyrien qui connaissait sa langue. Tu l'as bien mérité. »

Deux gardes le saisirent et le poussèrent vers la porte. La maison était dévorée par les flammes et le feu illuminait tout alentour. Des cris montaient de tous côtés : un enfant en pleurs, des vieux implorant pardon, des femmes désespérées qui cherchaient leurs enfants. Mais il n'entendait que les appels au secours de celle qui l'avait accueilli.

« Que se passe-t-il ? Il y a une femme et un enfant là-dedans ! Pourquoi leur faites-vous cela ?

— Elle a tenté de cacher le gouverneur d'Akbar.

— Je ne suis pas le gouverneur d'Akbar ! Vous commettez une terrible erreur ! »

L'officier assyrien le poussa sur le seuil. Le toit s'était effondré dans l'incendie, et la femme était à demi ensevelie sous les ruines. Elie n'apercevait que son bras qui s'agitait désespérément. Elle appelait au secours, suppliant qu'on ne la laissât pas brûler vive.

« Pourquoi m'épargner et lui faire cela ? implora-t-il.

— Nous ne t'épargnons pas, nous voulons que tu souffres le plus possible. Notre général est mort lapidé et sans honneur, devant les murailles de la cité. Il venait chercher la vie et il a été condamné à mort. Tu vas connaître le même destin. »

Elie luttait désespérément pour se libérer. Les gardes l'emmenèrent. Ils parcoururent les rues d'Akbar dans une chaleur infernale — les soldats ruisselaient de sueur, et certains semblaient choqués par la scène qu'ils venaient de voir. Elie se débattait et implorait les cieux à grands cris, mais les Assyriens, comme le Seigneur, étaient muets.

Ils allèrent jusqu'au centre de la place. La plupart des édifices de la cité étaient en feu, et le grondement de l'incendie se mêlait aux cris des habitants d'Akbar.

« Heureusement, il y a la mort. »

Combien de fois avait-il pensé cela, depuis ce jour dans l'étable !

Des cadavres — des guerriers d'Akbar, pour la plupart sans uniforme — jonchaient le sol. Des gens couraient dans toutes les directions, ne sachant où ils allaient, ne sachant ce qu'ils cherchaient, poussés par la nécessité de faire semblant d'agir, et de lutter contre la mort et la destruction.

« Où courent-ils ainsi ? pensait-il. Ne voient-ils pas que la cité est aux mains de l'ennemi et qu'ils n'ont nulle part où fuir ? » Tout s'était passé très vite. Les Assyriens avaient profité de leur énorme avantage numérique, et ils avaient réussi à épargner le combat à leurs guerriers. Les soldats d'Akbar avaient été exterminés presque sans lutter.

Au centre de la place, on fit mettre Elie à genoux et on lui attacha les mains. Il n'entendait plus les cris de la femme ; peut-être était-elle morte rapidement, sans connaître la lente torture d'être brûlée vive. Elle était dans les bras du Seigneur. Et elle tenait son fils contre elle.

Un autre groupe de soldats assyriens amenait un prisonnier dont le visage était défiguré par les coups. Elie reconnut pourtant le commandant.

« Vive Akbar ! criait-il. Longue vie à la Phénicie et à ses guerriers qui se battent contre l'ennemi durant le jour ! Mort aux lâches qui attaquent dans l'obscurité ! »

Le commandant eut à peine le temps de terminer sa phrase, l'épée d'un général assyrien s'abattit et sa tête roula à terre.

« Cette fois c'est mon tour, se dit Elie. Je la retrouverai au Paradis, et nous nous promènerons main dans la main. »

132

C'est alors qu'un homme s'approcha et se mit à discuter avec les officiers. C'était un habitant d'Akbar, un habitué des réunions sur la place. Elie se souvenait qu'il l'avait aidé à résoudre un grave problème avec un voisin.

Les Assyriens discutaient de plus en plus fort, et le montraient du doigt. L'homme s'agenouilla, baisa les pieds de l'un d'entre eux, tendit les mains en direction de la Cinquième Montagne et pleura comme un enfant. La fureur des Assyriens sembla diminuer.

La conversation paraissait interminable. L'homme implorait et ne cessait de pleurer, désignant Elie et la maison où vivait le gouverneur. Les soldats ne semblaient pas satisfaits.

Finalement, l'officier qui parlait sa langue s'approcha :

« Notre espion, dit-il en montrant l'homme, affirme que nous nous trompons. C'est lui qui nous a donné les plans de la cité, et nous pouvons lui faire confiance. Tu n'es pas celui que nous voulions tuer. »

Il poussa Elie du pied et ce dernier tomba à terre.

« Il prétend que tu vas partir en Israël pour renverser la princesse qui a usurpé le trône. C'est vrai ? »

Elie ne répondit pas.

« Dis-moi si c'est vrai, insista l'officier. Et tu pourras t'en aller et retourner chez toi, à temps pour sauver cette femme et son fils.

— Oui, c'est la vérité. »

Peut-être le Seigneur l'avait-Il entendu et l'aiderait-Il à les sauver.

« Nous pourrions t'emmener en captivité à Tyr et à Sidon, poursuivit l'officier. Mais nous avons encore beaucoup de batailles à mener, et tu serais un fardeau. Nous pourrions exiger une rançon, mais à qui ? Tu es un étranger, même dans ton pays. »

De son pied, l'officier lui écrasa le visage.

« Tu n'es d'aucune utilité. Tu ne sers ni aux ennemis, ni aux amis. Tu es comme ta cité ; ce n'est pas la peine de laisser une partie de notre armée ici, pour la maintenir sous notre domination. Quand nous aurons conquis la côte, Akbar sera à nous, de toute façon.

— J'ai une question, dit Elie. Une seule question. » L'officier le regarda, méfiant.

« Pourquoi avez-vous attaqué de nuit ? Ne savez-vous pas que les guerres se font durant le jour ?

— Nous n'avons pas transgressé la loi. Aucune tradition ne l'interdit, répliqua l'officier. Et nous avons largement eu le temps de reconnaître le terrain. Vous vous souciez tellement de respecter les coutumes que vous avez oublié que les temps changent. »

Sans plus un mot, le groupe le laissa. L'espion s'approcha et lui détacha les mains.

« Je me suis promis qu'un jour je te rendrais ta générosité ; j'ai tenu parole. Quand les Assyriens sont entrés dans le palais, un serviteur les a informés que celui qu'ils cherchaient s'était réfugié dans la maison de la veuve. Le temps qu'ils aillent jusque-là, le véritable gouverneur avait réussi à s'enfuir. »

Elie ne l'écoutait pas. Le feu crépitait de toute part, et les cris s'élevaient toujours.

Au milieu de la confusion, on pouvait remarquer qu'un groupe maintenait la discipline ; obéissant à un ordre invisible, les Assyriens se retiraient en silence.

La bataille d'Akbar était terminée.

*

« Elle est morte, se dit-il. Je ne veux pas y retourner, elle est déjà morte. Ou bien un miracle l'a sauvée, et elle viendra me retrouver. »

Son cœur, cependant, lui commandait de se lever et d'aller jusqu'à la maison où ils habitaient. Elie luttait contre lui-même ; ce n'était pas seulement l'amour d'une femme qui était en jeu à ce moment-là, mais toute sa vie, sa foi dans les desseins du Seigneur, le départ de sa cité natale, l'idée qu'il avait une mission et qu'il était capable de l'accomplir.

Il regarda autour de lui, cherchant une épée pour mettre fin à ses jours, mais les Assyriens avaient emporté toutes les armes d'Akbar. Il pensa se jeter dans les flammes, mais il eut peur de la douleur.

Il resta quelques instants complètement figé. Peu à peu, il retrouva son discernement et put réfléchir à la situation dans laquelle il se trouvait. La femme et son fils avaient sans doute déjà quitté cette terre, mais il devait les enterrer selon la coutume. Œuvrer pour le Seigneur — qu'Il existât ou non — était son seul réconfort en ce moment. Une fois son devoir religieux accompli, il se laisserait aller à la souffrance et au doute.

En outre, il restait une possibilité qu'ils fussent encore en vie. Il ne pouvait pas rester là sans rien faire.

« Je ne veux pas les voir le visage brûlé, la peau détachée de la chair. Leurs âmes se promènent librement dans les cieux. »

Pourtant, il se dirigea vers la maison en suffoquant, aveuglé par la fumée qui l'empêchait de distinguer le chemin. Il put constater peu à peu la situation dans la cité. Bien que les ennemis se fussent déjà retirés, la panique augmentait d'une manière effrayante. Les gens continuaient à errer sans but, pleurant, réclamant aux dieux leurs morts.

Alors qu'il cherchait quelqu'un pour lui demander de l'aide, il ne vit qu'un homme à l'air égaré, en état de choc.

« Mieux vaut y aller directement et ne plus demander d'aide. » Il connaissait Akbar aussi bien que sa ville natale et il réussit à s'orienter, même s'il ne reconnaissait pas la plupart des lieux où il passait d'habitude. Les cris qu'il entendait étaient maintenant plus cohérents. Le peuple commençait à comprendre qu'une tragédie avait eu lieu et qu'il fallait réagir.

« Il y a un blessé ici !

— Nous avons encore besoin d'eau ! Nous n'allons pas pouvoir maîtriser le feu !

— Aidez-moi ! Mon mari est enfermé à l'intérieur ! »

Il atteignit l'endroit où, des mois plus tôt, il avait été reçu et hébergé comme un ami. Une vieille était assise au milieu de la rue, non loin de la maison, complètement nue. Elie voulut lui venir en aide, mais elle le repoussa :

« Elle est en train de mourir, s'écria la vieille. Fais quelque chose ! Ote ce mur qui l'écrase ! » Et elle se mit à pousser des cris hystériques. Elie l'attrapa par les bras et la repoussa, car ses hurlements l'empêchaient d'entendre les gémissements de la femme. Autour de lui tout n'était que désolation — toit et murs s'étant effondrés, il lui était difficile de savoir où exactement il l'avait aperçue pour la dernière fois. Les flammes avaient diminué mais la chaleur était encore insupportable ; il franchit les décombres qui couvraient le sol et gagna l'endroit où auparavant se trouvait la chambre de la femme.

Malgré la confusion au-dehors, il put distinguer un gémissement. C'était sa voix.

Instinctivement, il secoua la poussière de ses vêtements, comme pour arranger son apparence. Il resta silencieux, cherchant à se concentrer. Il entendait le crépitement du feu, les appels au secours de gens enterrés dans les maisons voisines — et il avait envie de leur dire de se taire, car il avait besoin de savoir où se trouvaient la femme et son fils. Très longtemps après, il entendit de nouveau du bruit ; quelqu'un grattait le bois qui se trouvait sous ses pieds.

Il s'agenouilla et commença à creuser comme un fou. Il retourna la terre, les pierres et le bois. Finalement, sa main toucha quelque chose de chaud : c'était du sang.

« Ne meurs pas, je t'en prie, supplia-t-il.

— Laisse les débris sur moi, dit la voix. Je ne veux pas que tu voies mon visage. Va secourir mon fils. »

Il continua à creuser, et la voix répéta :

« Va chercher le corps de mon fils. S'il te plaît, fais ce que je te demande. »

Elie laissa sa tête retomber sur sa poitrine et se mit à pleurer tout bas.

« J'ignore où il est enseveli. Je t'en prie, ne t'en va pas ; je voudrais tant que tu restes avec moi. J'ai besoin que tu m'apprennes à aimer, mon cœur est prêt.

« Avant ton arrivée, j'ai désiré la mort pendant des années. Elle a dû m'entendre et elle est venue me chercher. »

Elle poussa un gémissement. Elie se mordit les lèvres en silence. Quelqu'un lui toucha l'épaule.

Effrayé, il se retourna et vit le gamin. Il était couvert de poussière et de suie, mais il ne semblait pas blessé.

« Où est ma mère ? demanda-t-il.

— Je suis là, mon fils, répondit la voix de sous les ruines. Tu es blessé ? »

L'enfant se mit à pleurer. Elie le prit dans ses bras.

« Tu pleures, mon fils, reprit la voix, plus faiblement. Cesse de pleurer. Ta mère a mis si longtemps à comprendre que la vie a un sens ; j'espère avoir réussi à t'enseigner cela. Dans quel état est la cité où tu es né ? »

Elie et l'enfant étaient calmes, serrés l'un contre l'autre.

« Elle va bien, mentit Elie. Des guerriers sont morts, mais les Assyriens se sont retirés. Ils cherchaient le gouverneur pour venger la mort d'un de leurs généraux. »

De nouveau le silence. Et de nouveau la voix, de plus en plus faible.

« Dis-moi que ma cité est sauve. »

Elie devina qu'elle allait passer d'un instant à l'autre.

« La cité est intacte. Et ton fils va bien.

— Et toi ?

— J'ai survécu. »

Il savait que, par ses mots, il libérait son âme et lui permettait de mourir en paix.

« Dis à mon fils de se mettre à genoux, reprit la femme au bout d'un certain temps. Et je veux que tu me fasses un serment, au nom du Seigneur ton Dieu.

— Ce que tu voudras. Tout ce que tu voudras.

— Un jour, tu m'as dit que le Seigneur était partout, et je l'ai cru. Tu as dit que les âmes n'allaient pas en haut de la Cinquième Montagne, et je l'ai cru aussi. Mais tu ne m'as pas expliqué où elles allaient.

« Voici le serment que je te demande : vous n'allez

pas me pleurer, et vous veillerez l'un sur l'autre
— jusqu'à ce que le Seigneur permette à chacun de
suivre sa route. A partir de maintenant, mon âme se
mêle à tout ce que j'ai connu sur cette terre : je suis
la vallée, les montagnes tout autour, la cité, les gens
qui marchent dans ses rues. Je suis ses blessés et ses
mendiants, ses soldats, ses prêtres, ses commerçants, ses nobles. Je suis le sol que tu foules, et le
puits qui étanche la soif de tous. Ne pleurez pas pour
moi, car vous n'avez pas de raison d'être tristes.
Désormais, je suis Akbar, et la cité est belle. »

Vint le silence de la mort, et le vent cessa de souf-
fler. Elie n'entendait pas les cris au-dehors, ni les
flammes qui craquaient dans les maisons voisines ;
il n'entendait que le silence, presque palpable tant il
était intense.

Alors Elie éloigna l'enfant, déchira ses vêtements
et, se tournant vers les cieux, il hurla à pleins pou-
mons :

« Seigneur mon Dieu ! Pour Toi j'ai quitté Israël,
et je n'ai pu T'offrir mon sang comme l'ont fait les
prophètes restés là-bas. Mes amis m'ont traité de
lâche, et mes ennemis, de traître.

« Pour Toi, je n'ai mangé que ce que les corbeaux
m'apportaient, et j'ai traversé le désert jusqu'à
Sarepta, que ses habitants appellent Akbar. Guidé
par Tes mains, j'ai rencontré une femme ; guidé par
Toi, mon cœur a appris à l'aimer. Mais à aucun
moment je n'ai oublié ma vraie mission ; tous les
jours que j'ai passés ici, j'ai toujours été prêt à partir.

« La belle Akbar n'est plus que ruines, et la femme
que Tu m'as confiée gît au-dessous. En quoi ai-je
péché, Seigneur ? A quel moment me suis-je éloigné
de ce que Tu désirais de moi ? Si Tu n'étais pas
content de moi, pourquoi ne m'as-Tu pas enlevé à ce
monde ? Au contraire, Tu as causé encore une fois
le malheur de ceux qui m'avaient aidé et aimé.

« Je ne comprends pas Tes desseins. Je ne vois pas
de justice dans Tes actes. Je ne suis pas capable de
supporter la souffrance que Tu m'as imposée.

Eloigne-Toi de ma vie, car moi aussi je suis ruines, feu et poussière. »

Au milieu du feu et de la désolation, Elie vit la lumière. Et l'ange du Seigneur apparut.

« Que viens-tu faire ici ? demanda Elie. Ne vois-tu pas qu'il est trop tard ?

— Je suis venu te dire qu'une fois encore le Seigneur a entendu ta prière, et ce que tu demandes te sera accordé. Tu n'écouteras plus ton ange et je ne reviendrai pas te voir tant que tes jours d'épreuves ne seront pas accomplis. »

*

Elie prit l'enfant par la main et ils se mirent à marcher sans but. La fumée, jusque-là dispersée par le vent, se concentrait maintenant dans les rues, rendant l'air irrespirable. « C'est peut-être un rêve, pensa-t-il. C'est peut-être un cauchemar. »

« Tu as menti à ma mère, dit l'enfant. La cité est détruite.

— Quelle importance ? Si elle ne voyait pas ce qui se passait autour d'elle, pourquoi ne pas la laisser mourir heureuse ?

— Parce qu'elle a eu confiance en toi, et elle a dit qu'elle était Akbar. »

Il se blessa le pied dans les débris de verre et de céramique répandus sur le sol ; la douleur lui prouva qu'il n'était pas dans un rêve, que tout, autour de lui, était terriblement réel. Ils parvinrent à gagner la place où — voilà combien de temps ? — le peuple se réunissait et où il aidait les gens à résoudre leurs querelles ; le ciel était doré de la lumière des incendies.

« Je ne veux pas que ma mère soit ce que je vois, insista l'enfant. Tu lui as menti. »

Le gamin parvenait à tenir son serment ; pas une larme ne coulait sur son visage.

« Que puis-je faire ? » se demanda Elie. Son pied saignait, et il décida de se concentrer sur la douleur ; elle l'éloignerait du désespoir.

Il regarda la coupure que l'épée de l'Assyrien avait

faite sur son corps ; elle n'était pas aussi profonde qu'il avait imaginé. Il s'assit avec l'enfant à l'endroit même où il avait été attaché par les ennemis et sauvé par un traître. Les gens ne couraient plus ; ils marchaient lentement au milieu de la fumée, de la poussière et des ruines, tels des morts vivants. On aurait dit des âmes oubliées par les cieux, désormais condamnées à errer éternellement sur la terre. Rien n'avait de sens.

Quelques-uns réagissaient ; on continuait d'entendre les voix de femmes et les ordres contradictoires de soldats qui avaient survécu au massacre. Mais ils étaient peu nombreux et n'obtenaient aucun résultat.

Le grand prêtre avait dit une fois que le monde était le rêve collectif des dieux. Et si, au fond, il avait raison ? Pourrait-il maintenant aider les dieux à se réveiller de ce cauchemar et les endormir de nouveau avec un rêve plus doux ? Quand il avait des visions nocturnes, il se réveillait toujours et se rendormait ; pourquoi la même chose n'arriverait-elle pas aux créateurs de l'univers ?

Il butait sur les morts. Aucun d'eux n'avait plus à se soucier des impôts à payer, des Assyriens qui campaient dans la vallée, des rituels religieux ou de l'existence d'un prophète errant qui, un jour peut-être, leur avait adressé la parole.

« Je ne peux pas rester ici. L'héritage qu'elle m'a laissé est cet enfant, et j'en serai digne, même si c'est la dernière chose que je ferai sur cette terre. »

Péniblement, il se leva, reprit le garçon par la main, et ils se remirent en marche. Des gens pillaient les magasins et les boutiques qui avaient été saccagés. Pour la première fois, Elie tenta de réagir aux événements et leur demanda de ne pas agir ainsi.

Mais ils le bousculaient en disant : « Nous mangeons les restes de ce que le gouverneur a dévoré tout seul. Laisse-nous donc. »

Elie n'avait pas la force de discuter ; il emmena l'enfant hors de la cité et ils avancèrent dans la vallée. Les anges ne reviendraient pas avec leurs épées de feu.

« La pleine lune. »

Loin de la fumée et de la poussière, le clair de lune illuminait la nuit. Quelques heures plus tôt, lorsque Elie avait tenté de quitter la cité en direction de Jérusalem, il avait trouvé son chemin sans difficulté ; la même chose était arrivée aux Assyriens.

L'enfant trébucha sur un corps et poussa un cri. C'était celui du grand prêtre ; il avait les bras et les jambes mutilés mais il était encore vivant et gardait les yeux fixés sur le sommet de la Cinquième Montagne.

« Tu vois, les dieux phéniciens ont remporté la bataille céleste », dit-il avec difficulté mais d'une voix calme. Le sang coulait de sa bouche.

« Laisse-moi mettre fin à ta souffrance, répondit Elie.

— La douleur ne signifie rien auprès de la joie d'avoir accompli mon devoir.

— Ton devoir était-il de détruire une cité d'hommes justes ?

— Une cité ne meurt pas ; seuls meurent ses habitants et les idées qu'ils portaient avec eux. Un jour, d'autres viendront à Akbar, ils boiront son eau, et la pierre de son fondateur sera polie et gardée par de nouveaux prêtres. Va-t'en, ma douleur prendra fin bientôt, tandis que ton désespoir durera le reste de ta vie. »

Le corps mutilé respirait avec difficulté, et Elie le laissa. A cet instant, un groupe de gens — hommes, femmes et enfants — accourut vers lui et l'entoura.

« C'est toi ! criaient-ils. Tu as déshonoré ton pays, et tu as apporté la malédiction sur notre cité !

— Que les dieux en soient témoins ! Qu'ils sachent qui est le coupable ! »

Les hommes le bousculaient et le secouaient par les épaules. L'enfant se protégea de ses mains et disparut. Les gens frappaient Elie au visage, sur la poitrine, dans le dos, mais lui ne pensait qu'à l'enfant ; il n'avait même pas réussi à le garder près de lui.

La correction ne dura pas très longtemps ; peut-être étaient-ils tous fatigués de tant de violence. Elie tomba à terre.

« Va-t'en d'ici ! lança quelqu'un. Tu as rétribué notre amour de ta haine ! »

Le groupe s'éloigna. Il n'avait pas la force de se relever. Quand il parvint à se remettre de la honte éprouvée, il n'était plus le même homme. Il ne voulait ni mourir, ni continuer à vivre. Il ne voulait rien : il n'avait ni amour, ni haine, ni foi.

*

Il fut réveillé par le contact d'une main sur son visage. Il faisait encore nuit mais la lune n'était plus dans le ciel.

« J'ai promis à ma mère que je veillerais sur toi, dit le gamin. Mais je ne sais pas quoi faire.

— Retourne dans la cité. Les gens sont bons et quelqu'un t'accueillera.

— Tu es blessé. Je dois soigner ton bras. Peut-être qu'un ange apparaîtra et me dira quoi faire.

— Tu es ignorant, tu ne sais rien de ce qui se passe ! s'écria Elie. Les anges ne reviendront plus, parce que nous sommes des gens ordinaires, et tout le monde est faible devant la souffrance. Quand surviennent les tragédies, les gens ordinaires doivent se débrouiller par leurs propres moyens ! »

Il respira profondément et tenta de se calmer ; cela n'avançait à rien de discuter.

« Comment es-tu arrivé jusqu'ici ?

— Je ne suis pas parti.

— Alors tu as vu ma honte. Tu as vu que je n'avais plus rien à faire à Akbar.

— Tu m'as dit que toutes les batailles servaient à quelque chose, même celles que nous perdons. »

Il se souvenait de la promenade au puits, le matin précédent. Mais il lui semblait que des années s'étaient écoulées depuis, et il avait envie de rétorquer que les belles paroles ne signifient rien lorsqu'on est confronté à la souffrance ; pourtant il préféra ne pas effrayer le gamin par ces paroles.

« Comment as-tu échappé à l'incendie ? »

L'enfant baissa la tête.

« Je ne dormais pas. J'avais décidé de passer la

nuit éveillé pour savoir si tu irais retrouver ma mère dans sa chambre. J'ai vu quand les premiers soldats sont entrés. »

Elie se leva et se mit en marche. Il cherchait le rocher, devant la Cinquième Montagne, où, un après-midi, il avait assisté au coucher du soleil avec la femme.

« Je ne dois pas y aller, pensa-t-il. Je serai encore plus désespéré. »

Mais une force l'attirait dans cette direction. Une fois arrivé, il pleura amèrement ; comme la cité d'Akbar, l'endroit était marqué par une pierre — mais il était le seul, dans toute cette vallée, à en comprendre la signification ; elle ne serait pas honorée par de nouveaux habitants, ni polie par des couples découvrant le sens de leur amour.

Il prit l'enfant dans ses bras et s'endormit.

« J'ai soif et j'ai faim, dit l'enfant à Elie, à peine éveillé.

— Nous pouvons aller chez des bergers qui vivent près d'ici. Rien n'a dû leur arriver parce qu'ils n'habitaient pas à Akbar.

— Nous devons restaurer la cité. Ma mère a dit qu'elle était Akbar. »

Quelle cité ? Il n'y avait plus de palais, ni de marché, ni de murailles. Les gens de bien s'étaient transformés en brigands, et les jeunes soldats avaient été massacrés. Les anges ne reviendraient plus — mais c'était le cadet de ses soucis.

« Tu trouves que la destruction, la douleur, les morts de la nuit dernière ont un sens ? Tu penses qu'il faut anéantir des milliers de vies pour enseigner à quelqu'un ta façon de voir les choses ? »

Le gamin le regarda d'un air épouvanté.

« Oublie ce que je viens de dire, dit Elie. Allons trouver le berger.

— Et allons restaurer la cité », insista l'enfant.

lie ne répondit pas. Il savait qu'il ne parviendrait plus à imposer son autorité au peuple qui l'accusait d'avoir apporté le malheur. Le gouverneur s'était enfui, le commandant était mort, Tyr et Sidon tomberaient probablement bientôt sous la domination étrangère. La femme avait peut-être raison ; les dieux changeaient toujours — et cette fois c'était le Seigneur qui était parti.

« Quand retournerons-nous là-bas ? » interrogea de nouveau l'enfant.

Elie le prit par les épaules et se mit à le secouer violemment.

« Regarde derrière toi ! Tu n'es pas un ange aveugle, mais un gamin désireux de surveiller ce que faisait sa mère. Qu'est-ce que tu vois ? Tu as remarqué les colonnes de fumée qui montent dans le ciel ? Tu sais ce que cela signifie ?

— Tu me fais mal ! Je veux partir d'ici, je veux m'en aller ! »

Elie s'arrêta, effrayé par sa propre attitude : jamais il n'avait agi de la sorte. L'enfant s'écarta et se mit à courir en direction de la cité. Il parvint à le rattraper et s'agenouilla devant lui.

« Pardonne-moi. Je ne sais pas ce que je fais. »

Le gamin sanglotait, mais pas une larme ne coulait sur son visage. Il s'assit près de lui, en attendant qu'il se calme.

« Ne pars pas, demanda-t-il. Avant que ta mère ne s'en aille, je lui ai promis de rester avec toi jusqu'à ce que tu puisses suivre ton propre chemin.

— Tu as promis aussi que la cité était intacte. Et elle a dit...

— Inutile de le répéter. Je suis honteux, perdu dans ma propre faute. Laisse-moi me retrouver. Excuse-moi, je ne voulais pas te blesser. »

Le gamin le serra dans ses bras. Mais pas une larme ne roula de ses yeux.

*

144

Ils atteignirent la maison au cœur de la vallée ; une femme se tenait près de la porte et deux petits enfants jouaient devant. Le troupeau était dans l'enclos — ce qui signifiait que le berger n'était pas parti dans les montagnes ce matin-là.

La femme regarda d'un air effrayé l'homme et l'enfant qui marchaient à sa rencontre. Elle eut instinctivement envie de les chasser, mais la tradition — et les dieux — exigeaient qu'elle obéît à la loi universelle de l'hospitalité. Si elle ne les accueillait pas maintenant, un malheur semblable pourrait arriver plus tard à ses enfants.

« Je n'ai pas d'argent, dit-elle. Mais je peux vous donner un peu d'eau et de nourriture. »

Ils s'assirent sur la petite terrasse ombragée par un toit de paille, et elle apporta des fruits secs accompagnés d'un broc d'eau. Ils mangèrent en silence, retrouvant un peu, pour la première fois depuis la nuit précédente, leurs gestes quotidiens. Les enfants, épouvantés par l'aspect des nouveaux venus, s'étaient réfugiés à l'intérieur de la maison.

Son repas terminé, Elie s'enquit du berger.

« Il ne va pas tarder, répondit-elle. Nous avons entendu un grand vacarme, et ce matin quelqu'un est venu nous dire qu'Akbar avait été détruite. Il est parti voir ce qui s'était passé. »

Les enfants l'appelèrent et elle rentra.

« Inutile de chercher à convaincre le gamin, pensa Elie. Tant que je n'aurai pas fait ce qu'il demande, il ne me laissera pas en paix. C'est à moi de lui montrer que c'est impossible. »

La nourriture et l'eau faisaient des miracles ; il se sentait de nouveau faire partie du monde. Ses pensées coulaient avec une incroyable rapidité, cherchant des solutions plutôt que des réponses.

*

Quelque temps après, le berger arriva. Inquiet pour la sécurité de sa famille, il considéra avec crainte l'homme et l'enfant. Mais il comprit bien vite la situation.

« Vous êtes sans doute des réfugiés d'Akbar, dit-il. J'en reviens.

— Que se passe-t-il ? demanda le gamin.

— La cité a été détruite et le gouverneur est en fuite. Les dieux ont désorganisé le monde.

— Nous avons tout perdu, expliqua Elie. Nous aimerions que vous nous accueilliez.

— Ma femme vous a déjà accueillis et nourris. Maintenant, vous devez partir et affronter l'inévitable.

— Je ne sais pas quoi faire de l'enfant. J'ai besoin d'aide.

— Mais si, tu sais. Il est jeune, il a l'air intelligent et il est plein d'énergie. Et toi, tu as l'expérience d'un homme qui a connu beaucoup de victoires et de défaites dans cette vie. C'est une combinaison parfaite car elle peut t'aider à trouver la sagesse. »

Regardant la blessure au bras d'Elie, le berger affirma qu'elle n'était pas grave ; il alla chercher dans la maison des herbes et un morceau de tissu. Le gamin l'aida à maintenir en place le cataplasme. Quand le berger lui fit remarquer qu'il pouvait y arriver tout seul, l'enfant rétorqua qu'il avait promis à sa mère de veiller sur cet homme.

Le berger rit.

« Ton fils est un homme de parole.

— Je ne suis pas son fils. Et lui aussi est un homme de parole. Il va reconstruire la cité parce qu'il doit faire revenir ma mère, tout comme il l'a fait avec moi. »

Elie comprit soudain ce qui préoccupait l'enfant, mais avant qu'il ait pu dire un mot, le berger cria à sa femme qui, à ce moment précis, sortait de la maison, qu'il allait repartir. « Mieux vaut reconstruire la vie sans attendre, déclara-t-il. Cela prendra longtemps pour que tout redevienne comme avant.

— Rien ne sera jamais comme avant.

— Tu sembles être un jeune homme sage, et tu peux comprendre bien des choses que je ne comprends pas. Mais la nature m'a enseigné une leçon que je n'oublierai jamais : un homme qui dépend du temps et des saisons, comme seul en dépend un berger, peut survivre aux événements inévitables. Il soigne son troupeau, traite chaque animal comme s'il était unique, cherche à aider les mères et les petits, ne s'éloigne jamais trop d'un endroit où les bêtes peuvent boire. Cependant, une fois de temps en temps, une brebis à laquelle il a consacré tant d'efforts finit par mourir dans un accident, causé par un serpent, un animal sauvage, ou même une chute dans un précipice. L'inévitable se produit toujours. »

Elie regarda en direction d'Akbar et se rappela la conversation avec l'ange. L'inévitable survient toujours.

« Il faut de la discipline et de la patience pour le surmonter, ajouta le berger.

— Et de l'espoir. Quand l'espoir n'existe plus, il ne faut pas gâcher son énergie à lutter contre l'impossible.

— Ce n'est pas une question d'espoir dans l'avenir. Il s'agit de recréer le passé lui-même. »

Le berger n'était plus pressé, son cœur s'était empli de pitié pour ces réfugiés. Puisque lui et sa famille avaient été épargnés par la tragédie, ça ne lui coûtait rien de leur venir en aide — et de plaire ainsi aux dieux. En outre, il avait entendu parler du prophète israélite qui avait gravi la Cinquième Montagne sans être atteint par le feu du ciel ; tout indiquait que c'était cet homme qui se tenait devant lui.

« Vous pouvez rester un jour de plus, si vous voulez.

— Je n'ai pas compris ce que tu viens de dire, remarqua Elie. A propos de recréer le passé lui-même.

— J'ai toujours vu les gens qui passaient par ici pour aller à Tyr et à Sidon. Certains se plaignaient de n'avoir rien réussi à Akbar, et ils étaient à la recherche d'une nouvelle destinée. Un jour, ces gens revenaient. Ils n'avaient pas trouvé ce qu'ils cherchaient, parce qu'ils avaient emporté avec eux, outre leurs bagages, le poids de leur échec passé. L'un ou l'autre rentrait avec un emploi au gouvernement, ou la joie d'avoir donné une meilleure éducation à ses enfants — mais rien de plus, parce que le passé à

147

Akbar les avait rendus craintifs, et ils n'avaient pas suffisamment confiance en eux pour prendre des risques.

« Et puis, sont passés aussi devant ma porte des gens pleins d'enthousiasme. Ils avaient profité de chaque minute de leur existence à Akbar et gagné — avec beaucoup d'efforts — l'argent nécessaire au voyage qu'ils voulaient entreprendre. Pour eux, la vie était une victoire permanente, et elle continuerait de l'être. Eux aussi revenaient, mais avec des histoires merveilleuses. Ils avaient conquis tout ce qu'ils désiraient parce qu'ils n'étaient pas limités par les frustrations du passé. »

*

Les propos du berger touchaient le cœur d'Elie.

« Il n'est pas difficile de reconstruire une vie, de même qu'il n'est pas impossible de relever Akbar de ses ruines, poursuivit le berger. Il suffit pour cela d'avoir conscience que nous avons la même force qu'auparavant, et de nous en servir à notre avantage. »

L'homme le regarda dans les yeux.

« Si tu as un passé dont tu n'es pas satisfait, oublie-le maintenant. Imagine une nouvelle histoire pour ta vie et crois en elle. Concentre-toi seulement sur les moments où tu as réussi ce que tu désirais — et cette force t'aidera à obtenir ce que tu veux. »

« A une époque j'ai désiré être charpentier, ensuite j'ai voulu être un prophète envoyé pour le salut d'Israël, pensa Elie. Les anges descendaient des cieux, et le Seigneur me parlait. Et puis j'ai compris qu'Il n'était pas juste et que Ses motifs seraient toujours au-delà de mon entendement. »

Le berger cria à sa femme qu'il n'allait pas repartir — tout compte fait, il était déjà allé à pied jusqu'à Akbar et il n'avait pas le courage de refaire le chemin.

« Merci de nous accueillir, dit Elie.

— Ça ne coûte rien de vous abriter pour une nuit. »

L'enfant intervint dans la conversation :
« Nous voulons retourner à Akbar.

— Attendez jusqu'à demain. Les habitants de la cité sont en train de la saccager, et il n'y a nulle part où dormir. »

Le gamin regarda le sol, se mordit les lèvres et, une fois de plus, se retint de pleurer. Le berger les conduisit à l'intérieur, rassura sa femme et ses enfants et passa le reste de la journée à parler du temps pour les distraire tous les deux.

Le lendemain, ils se réveillèrent tôt, prirent un repas que leur avait préparé la femme du berger et allèrent jusqu'à la porte de la maison.

« Je te souhaite longue vie et prospérité à ton troupeau, dit Elie. J'ai mangé ce dont mon corps avait besoin, et mon âme a appris ce que j'ignorais encore. Que Dieu n'oublie jamais ce que vous avez fait pour nous, et que vos enfants ne soient jamais des étrangers sur une terre étrangère.

— Je ne sais à quel Dieu tu fais allusion ; ils sont nombreux, les habitants de la Cinquième Montagne », dit le berger durement. Puis aussitôt, changeant de ton : « Rappelle-toi les bonnes choses que tu as réalisées. Elles te donneront du courage.

— J'en ai fait bien peu, et aucune grâce à mes qualités.

— Alors il est temps de faire davantage.

— J'aurais peut-être pu éviter l'invasion. »

Le berger rit :

« Même si tu avais été le gouverneur d'Akbar, tu n'aurais pas pu empêcher l'inévitable.

— Le gouverneur aurait peut-être dû attaquer les Assyriens quand ils sont arrivés dans la vallée avec quelques troupes. Ou négocier la paix avant que la guerre n'éclate.

— Tout ce qui aurait pu arriver mais n'est pas arrivé, le vent l'emporte et il n'en reste nulle trace, dit le berger. La vie est faite de nos attitudes. *Et il est des choses que les dieux nous obligent à vivre.* Peu importe la raison qui est la leur, et faire tout notre possible pour les éviter ne sert à rien.

— Pourquoi ?

— Demande à un prophète israélite qui vivait à Akbar. Il paraît qu'il a réponse à tout. »

L'homme se dirigea vers l'enclos. « Je dois mener mon troupeau au pâturage. Hier, les bêtes ne sont pas sorties et elles sont impatientes. »

Il prit congé d'un signe de tête et s'éloigna avec ses brebis.

L'enfant et l'homme avançaient dans la vallée.

« Tu marches lentement, disait le gamin. Tu as peur de ce qui pourra t'arriver.

— Je n'ai peur que de moi, répondit Elie. Ils ne peuvent rien me faire, car mon cœur n'existe plus.

— Le Dieu qui m'a fait revenir de la mort est encore vivant. Il peut ramener ma mère, si tu accomplis la même chose pour la cité.

— Oublie ce Dieu. Il est loin, et Il ne réalise plus les miracles que nous attendons de Lui. »

Le berger avait raison. Désormais, il fallait reconstruire son propre passé, oublier qu'un jour on jugerait un prophète qui devait libérer Israël mais qui avait échoué dans sa mission de sauver une simple cité.

Cette pensée lui procura un étrange sentiment d'euphorie. Pour la première fois de sa vie, il se sentit libre, prêt à faire ce qu'il voulait, quand il voulait. Il n'entendrait plus les anges, mais en contrepartie il était libre de retourner en Israël, de reprendre son travail de charpentier, de voyager jusqu'en Grèce pour y suivre l'enseignement des sages, ou de gagner avec les navigateurs phéniciens les contrées de l'autre côté de la mer.

Mais auparavant, il devait se venger. Il avait consacré les meilleures années de sa jeunesse à un Dieu sourd qui lui donnait sans cesse des ordres tout en faisant toujours les choses à Sa manière. Il avait appris à accepter Ses décisions et à respecter Ses desseins. Mais sa fidélité avait été récompensée par l'abandon, son dévouement ignoré, ses efforts pour accomplir la Volonté suprême avaient abouti à la mort de la seule femme qu'il avait aimée dans sa vie.

« Tu as toute la force du monde et des étoiles », dit Elie dans sa langue natale, afin que l'enfant ne comprît pas le sens de ses paroles. « Tu peux détruire une cité, un pays, comme nous détruisons les insectes. Alors, envoie le feu du ciel et mets fin à mes jours tout de suite, sinon j'irai contre Ton œuvre. »

Akbar apparut au loin. Il prit la main du gamin et la serra de toutes ses forces.

« Désormais, jusqu'à ce que nous franchissions les portes de la cité, je marcherai les yeux fermés ; il faut que tu me guides, dit-il à l'enfant. Si je meurs en cours de route, fais ce que tu m'as demandé de faire : reconstruis Akbar, même si pour cela il te faut d'abord grandir, puis apprendre à couper le bois ou à tailler la pierre. »

L'enfant resta silencieux. Elie ferma les yeux et se laissa guider. Il écoutait le bruit du vent et le son de ses pas sur le sable.

Il se rappela Moïse. Après qu'il eut libéré et conduit le peuple élu dans le désert, surmontant d'énormes difficultés, Dieu l'avait empêché d'entrer en Canaan. Alors, Moïse avait dit : « *Permets que je passe de l'autre côté, et que je voie le bon pays qui est au-delà du Jourdain.* »

Mais le Seigneur s'était indigné de sa requête. Et il avait répondu : « *Assez. Cesse de me parler de cela. Lève les yeux vers l'ouest et vers le nord, vers le sud et vers l'est ; regarde de tous tes yeux car tu ne passeras pas le Jourdain que voici.* »

Ainsi le Seigneur avait-il récompensé Moïse pour

sa longue et rude tâche : il ne lui avait pas permis de poser le pied en Terre promise. Que serait-il arrivé s'il avait désobéi ?

Elie tourna de nouveau sa pensée vers les cieux.

« Seigneur, cette bataille n'a pas eu lieu entre les Assyriens et les Phéniciens, mais entre Toi et moi. Tu ne m'as pas averti de notre guerre singulière et — comme toujours — Tu as gagné et fait accomplir Ta volonté. Tu as détruit la femme que j'ai aimée et la cité qui m'a accueilli quand j'étais loin de ma patrie. »

Le vent souffla plus fort à ses oreilles. Elie eut peur, mais il continua :

« Il m'est impossible de faire revenir la femme, mais je peux changer le destin de Ton œuvre de destruction. Moïse a accepté Ta volonté, et il n'a pas franchi le fleuve. Moi, je poursuivrai : tue-moi sur-le-champ, car, si Tu me laisses arriver jusqu'aux portes de la cité, je reconstruirai ce que Tu as voulu faire disparaître de la surface de la terre. Et j'irai contre Ta décision. »

Il se tut. Il fit le vide dans son esprit et attendit la mort. Pendant très longtemps, il se concentra seulement sur le son des pas dans le sable ; il ne voulait pas entendre la voix des anges ou les menaces du Ciel. Son cœur était libre et il n'avait plus peur de ce qui pourrait lui arriver. Cependant, dans les profondeurs de son âme, quelque chose commença à le perturber — comme s'il avait oublié un élément d'importance.

Longtemps après, l'enfant s'arrêta et secoua le bras d'Elie.

« Nous sommes arrivés », dit-il.

Il ouvrit les yeux. Le feu du ciel n'était pas descendu sur lui et les murailles en ruine d'Akbar l'entouraient.

*

Il regarda l'enfant qui lui tenait les mains comme s'il craignait qu'il ne s'échappât. L'aimait-il ? Il l'ignorait. Mais ces réflexions pouvaient être remises à plus tard ; il avait maintenant une tâche à accomplir — la première depuis des années qui ne lui fût pas imposée par Dieu.

De là où ils se tenaient, ils pouvaient sentir l'odeur de brûlé. Des charognards tournoyaient dans le ciel, attendant le moment propice pour dévorer les cadavres de sentinelles qui pourrissaient sur le sol. Elie prit l'épée à la ceinture d'un soldat mort. Dans la confusion de la nuit précédente, les Assyriens avaient oublié de ramasser les armes qui se trouvaient hors de la cité.

« Pourquoi prends-tu cette épée ? demanda l'enfant.

— Pour me défendre.

— Les Assyriens sont partis.

— Il est tout de même bon d'en avoir une sur moi. Nous devons nous tenir prêts. »

Sa voix tremblait. Il était impossible de savoir ce qui se passerait lorsqu'ils franchiraient la muraille à moitié démolie, mais il était prêt à tuer quiconque tenterait de l'humilier.

« J'ai été détruit comme cette cité, dit-il à l'enfant. Mais, de même que cette cité, je n'ai pas encore terminé ma mission. »

Le gamin sourit.

« Tu parles comme autrefois, dit-il.

— Ne te laisse pas abuser par les mots. Avant, j'avais l'objectif de chasser du trône Jézabel et de rendre Israël au Seigneur, mais maintenant qu'Il nous a oubliés, nous aussi nous devons L'oublier. Ma mission consiste à accomplir ce que tu me demandes. »

L'enfant le regarda, méfiant :

« Sans Dieu, ma mère ne reviendra pas d'entre les morts. »

Elie lui caressa la tête.

« Seul le corps de ta mère s'en est allé. Elle est toujours parmi nous et, comme elle nous l'a dit, elle est Akbar. Nous devons l'aider à retrouver sa beauté. »

*

La cité était quasi déserte. Des vieux, des femmes et des enfants erraient dans les rues — répétant la scène qu'il avait vue durant la nuit de l'invasion. Ils semblaient ne pas savoir quoi faire, quoi décider.

Chaque fois qu'ils croisaient quelqu'un, l'enfant remarquait qu'Elie serrait de toutes ses forces la poignée de l'épée. Mais les gens leur manifestaient de l'indifférence : la plupart reconnaissaient le prophète d'Israël, certains le saluaient de la tête, et personne ne lui adressait la moindre parole — même de haine.

« Ils ont perdu jusqu'au sentiment de la colère », pensa-t-il, regardant vers la Cinquième Montagne, dont le sommet restait couvert de ses éternels nuages. Alors il se rappela les paroles du Seigneur :

« Je jetterai vos cadavres sur les cadavres de vos dieux ; mon âme se lassera de vous. Votre pays sera dévasté et vos cités seront désertées.

Et ceux d'entre vous qui resteront, je leur mettrai dans le cœur une telle anxiété que le bruit d'une feuille qui bouge les poursuivra.

Et ils tomberont sans que personne ne les poursuive. »

« Voilà ce que Tu as fait, Seigneur : Tu as tenu Ta parole, et les morts vivants continuent d'errer sur la terre. Et Akbar est la cité choisie pour les abriter. »

Ils gagnèrent tous deux la place principale, s'assirent sur des décombres et regardèrent alentour. La destruction semblait avoir été plus rigoureuse et implacable qu'il ne l'avait pensé ; la plupart des toits s'étaient écroulés, la saleté et les insectes prenaient possession de tout.

« Il faut enlever les morts, dit-il. Ou bien la peste entrera dans la cité par la grande porte. »

L'enfant gardait les yeux baissés.

« Lève la tête, dit Elie. Nous devons beaucoup travailler pour que ta mère soit contente. »

Mais le gamin n'obéit pas ; il commençait à comprendre que, quelque part dans ces ruines, se trouvait le corps qui lui avait donné la vie, et que ce corps était dans le même état que tous les autres épars autour de lui.

Elie n'insista pas. Il se leva, prit un cadavre sur ses épaules et le porta au centre de la place. Il ne parvenait pas à se rappeler les recommandations du Seigneur sur l'enterrement des morts ; tout ce qu'il devait faire, c'était empêcher que ne survînt la peste, et la seule solution était de les incinérer.

Il travailla ainsi toute la matinée. L'enfant ne quitta pas cet endroit et ne leva pas les yeux un instant, mais il tint la promesse qu'il avait faite à sa mère : pas une larme ne tomba sur le sol d'Akbar.

Une femme s'arrêta et resta un moment à observer l'activité d'Elie.

« L'homme qui résolvait les problèmes des vivants débarrasse les corps des morts, remarqua-t-elle.

— Où sont donc les hommes d'Akbar ? demanda Elie.

— Ils sont partis et ont emporté le peu qui restait. Il n'y a plus rien qui vaille la peine de s'attarder ici. Les seuls à n'avoir pas quitté la cité sont ceux qui étaient incapables de le faire : les vieux, les veuves et les orphelins.

— Mais ils étaient ici depuis des générations ! On ne peut pas renoncer aussi facilement.

— Essaie d'expliquer cela à quelqu'un qui a tout perdu.

— Aide-moi, dit Elie tout en prenant un des corps sur son dos puis en le mettant sur le tas. Nous allons les incinérer pour que le dieu de la peste ne vienne pas nous rendre visite. Il a horreur de l'odeur de la chair qui brûle.

— Que vienne le dieu de la peste, répliqua la femme. Et qu'il nous emporte tous, le plus vite possible. »

Elie continua son travail. La femme s'assit à côté

de l'enfant et le regarda faire. Quelque temps après, elle s'approcha de nouveau.

« Pourquoi désires-tu sauver une cité condamnée ?

— Si je m'arrête pour réfléchir, je me retrouverai incapable d'agir comme je le veux », répondit-il.

Le vieux berger avait raison : oublier son passé d'incertitudes et se créer une nouvelle histoire était la seule issue. L'ancien prophète était mort avec la femme dans l'incendie de sa maison ; maintenant, il était un homme sans foi en Dieu, habité de nombreux doutes. Mais il était en vie, même après avoir bravé la malédiction divine. S'il voulait poursuivre sa route, il devait suivre ses conseils.

La femme choisit un corps plus léger et le traîna par les pieds jusqu'au tas qu'Elie avait commencé.

« Ce n'est pas par peur du dieu de la peste, dit-elle. Ni pour Akbar, puisque les Assyriens reviendront bientôt. C'est pour le gamin assis là, tête basse ; il doit comprendre qu'il a encore la vie devant lui.

— Merci, dit Elie.

— Ne me remercie pas. Quelque part dans ces ruines, nous trouverons le corps de mon fils. Il avait à peu près le même âge que ce gamin. »

Elle mit sa main sur son visage et pleura abondamment. Elie la prit délicatement par le bras.

« La douleur que toi et moi ressentons ne passera jamais, mais le travail nous aidera à la supporter. La souffrance n'a pas la force de meurtrir un corps fatigué. »

Ils consacrèrent la journée entière à cette tâche macabre, ramasser et empiler les morts ; la plupart étaient des jeunes gens que les Assyriens avaient pris pour des membres de l'armée d'Akbar. Mais plus d'une fois il reconnut des amis, et il pleura, sans toutefois interrompre sa besogne.

*

A la fin de l'après-midi, ils étaient épuisés. Pourtant, le travail réalisé était loin de suffire ; et aucun autre habitant d'Akbar ne leur avait prêté main-forte.

Ils revinrent tous les deux près de l'enfant. Pour la première fois, il leva la tête.

« J'ai faim, dit-il.

— Je vais chercher quelque chose, répondit la femme. Il y a suffisamment de nourriture cachée dans les habitations d'Akbar : les gens s'étaient préparés à un siège prolongé.

— Apporte de la nourriture pour toi et moi, parce que nous prenons soin de la cité à la sueur de notre front, répliqua Elie. Mais si ce petit veut manger, il devra se débrouiller tout seul. »

La femme comprit ; elle aurait agi de la même manière avec son fils. Elle se rendit jusqu'à l'endroit où auparavant s'élevait sa maison ; les pillards avaient quasiment tout retourné à la recherche d'objets de valeur, et sa collection de vases, créés par les grands maîtres verriers d'Akbar, gisait en morceaux sur le sol. Mais elle trouva les fruits secs et la farine qu'elle avait stockés.

Elle retourna sur la place et partagea sa nourriture avec Elie. L'enfant ne dit rien.

Un vieux s'approcha :

« J'ai vu que vous aviez passé la journée entière à ramasser les corps. Vous perdez votre temps. Ne savez-vous pas que les Assyriens reviendront, une fois Tyr et Sidon conquises ? Que le dieu de la peste vienne donc s'installer ici, pour les détruire aussi.

— Nous ne faisons pas cela pour eux, ni pour nous-mêmes, répliqua Elie. Elle travaille dans le but d'enseigner à un enfant qu'il existe un avenir. Et moi, je le fais pour montrer qu'un passé n'est plus.

— Ainsi, le prophète n'est plus une menace pour la grande princesse de Tyr : quelle surprise ! Jézabel gouvernera Israël jusqu'à la fin de ses jours, et nous aurons toujours un endroit où nous réfugier, si les Assyriens ne sont pas généreux avec les vaincus. »

Elie resta silencieux. Le nom qui autrefois lui inspirait tant de haine sonnait maintenant d'une manière étrangement lointaine.

« Akbar sera reconstruite, de toute façon, insista le vieillard. Ce sont les dieux qui choisissent les lieux où l'on élève les cités, et ils ne vont pas l'abandon-

157

ner ; mais nous pouvons laisser ce travail aux générations futures.

— Nous pouvons. Mais nous n'allons pas le faire. »

Elie tourna le dos au vieil homme, mettant fin à la conversation.

*

Ils dormirent tous les trois à la belle étoile. La femme prit l'enfant dans ses bras et remarqua que la faim faisait gronder son estomac. Elle pensa lui donner un peu de nourriture ; mais elle changea aussitôt d'avis : la fatigue physique diminuait réellement la douleur, et cet enfant, qui paraissait souffrir beaucoup, devait s'occuper à quelque chose. La faim le persuaderait peut-être de travailler.

Le lendemain, Elie et la femme reprirent leur ouvrage. Le vieillard qui s'était approché la veille revint les voir.

« Je n'ai rien à faire et je pourrais vous aider, dit-il. Mais je suis trop faible pour porter les corps.

— Alors, rassemble le petit bois et les briques. Tu nettoieras les cendres. »

Le vieux se mit au travail.

*

Quand le soleil atteignit le zénith, Elie s'assit par terre, épuisé. Il savait que son ange était à ses côtés mais il ne pouvait plus l'entendre. « A quoi bon ? Il a été incapable de m'aider quand j'en avais besoin, maintenant je ne veux pas de ses conseils ; tout ce que je dois faire, c'est laisser cette cité en ordre, montrer à Dieu que je suis capable de L'affronter, et ensuite partir où je le désirerai. »

Jérusalem n'était pas loin, à sept jours de marche seulement, sans passages difficiles, mais là-bas il était recherché comme traître. Il valait peut-être mieux aller à Damas, ou trouver un emploi de scribe dans une cité grecque.

Il sentit qu'on le touchait. Il se retourna et vit l'enfant, un petit vase à la main.

« Je l'ai trouvé dans une maison », dit le gamin, et il le lui tendit.

Il était plein d'eau. Elie but jusqu'à la dernière goutte.

« Mange quelque chose, dit-il. Tu travailles, tu mérites ta récompense. »

Pour la première fois depuis la nuit de l'invasion, un sourire apparut sur les lèvres du gamin, qui se précipita vers l'endroit où la femme avait laissé les fruits et la farine.

Elie se remit au travail ; il entrait dans les maisons en ruine, écartait les décombres, prenait les corps et les portait jusqu'au tas amoncelé au centre de la place. Le pansement que le berger lui avait fait au bras était tombé, mais cela n'avait pas d'importance ; il devait se prouver à lui-même qu'il était assez fort pour reconquérir sa dignité.

Le vieux, qui maintenant rassemblait les ordures répandues sur la place, avait raison ; d'ici peu, les ennemis seraient de retour, récoltant les fruits de ce qu'ils n'avaient pas semé. Elie épargnait du travail aux assassins de la seule femme qu'il avait aimée de toute sa vie, puisque les Assyriens, étant superstitieux, reconstruiraient Akbar de toute manière. D'après leurs croyances, les dieux avaient disposé les cités selon un ordre bien précis, en harmonie avec les vallées, les animaux, les fleuves, les mers. Dans chacune d'elles, ils avaient conservé un lieu sacré où se reposer durant leurs longs voyages de par le monde. Lorsqu'une cité était détruite, il y avait toujours un grand risque que les cieux ne tombent sur la terre.

La légende racontait que le fondateur d'Akbar,

venant du nord, était passé par là, voilà des siècles. Il décida de dormir sur place et, pour marquer l'endroit où il avait laissé ses affaires, il enfonça une baguette de bois dans le sol. Le lendemain, comme il ne réussissait pas à l'arracher, il comprit la volonté de l'univers ; il marqua d'une pierre l'endroit où le miracle s'était produit et découvrit une source non loin de là. Peu à peu, des tribus s'installèrent à proximité de la pierre et du puits : Akbar était née.

Le gouverneur avait expliqué une fois à Elie que, selon la tradition phénicienne, toute cité était le *troisième point*, l'élément de liaison entre la volonté des cieux et celle de la terre. L'univers faisait que la semence se transformât en plante, le sol lui permettait de se développer, les hommes la cueillaient et la portaient à la cité, où ils consacraient aux dieux les offrandes avant de les abandonner sur les montagnes sacrées. Même s'il n'avait pas beaucoup voyagé, Elie savait que de nombreuses nations dans le monde partageaient cette vision.

Les Assyriens avaient peur de priver de nourriture les dieux de la Cinquième Montagne ; ils ne désiraient pas mettre fin à l'équilibre de l'univers.

« Pourquoi pensé-je tout cela si cette lutte est une lutte entre ma volonté et celle du Seigneur qui m'a laissé seul au beau milieu de mes tribulations ? »

L'impression qu'il avait eue la veille au moment où il bravait Dieu revint. Il oubliait un élément important, et il avait beau chercher dans sa mémoire, il ne parvenait pas à s'en souvenir.

Un autre jour passa. ils avaient déjà rassemblé la plupart des corps, quand une femme inconnue s'approcha.

« Je n'ai rien à manger, dit-elle.

— Nous non plus, répliqua Elie. Hier et aujourd'hui nous avons partagé en trois la part destinée à une personne. Va voir où l'on peut trouver des aliments et tiens-moi au courant.

— Comment le découvrir ?

— Demande aux enfants. Ils savent tout. »

Depuis qu'il lui avait offert de l'eau, le gamin paraissait reprendre un peu goût à la vie. Elie l'avait envoyé ramasser les ordures et les débris avec le vieux, mais il n'avait pas réussi à le faire travailler très longtemps ; maintenant il jouait en compagnie d'autres enfants dans un coin de la place.

« Cela vaut mieux. Il aura bien le temps de suer, une fois adulte. » Mais il ne regrettait pas de lui avoir fait endurer la faim une nuit entière, sous prétexte qu'il devait travailler ; s'il l'avait traité en pauvre orphelin, victime de la méchanceté des guerriers assyriens, jamais il ne serait sorti de la dépression dans laquelle il était plongé lorsqu'ils étaient revenus dans la cité. Dorénavant il avait l'intention de le laisser quelques jours tout seul trouver ses propres réponses à ce qui s'était passé.

« Comment les enfants peuvent-ils savoir quelque chose ? insista la femme qui lui avait demandé à manger.

— Vois par toi-même. »

La femme et le vieux qui aidaient Elie la virent discuter avec les enfants qui jouaient dans la rue. Ils lui dirent quelques mots, elle se retourna, sourit et disparut au coin de la place.

« Comment as-tu découvert que les enfants savaient ? demanda le vieux.

— Parce que j'ai été gamin, et je sais que les enfants n'ont pas de passé, répondit-il, se rappelant de nouveau la conversation avec le berger. Ils ont été horrifiés par la nuit de l'invasion mais ils ne s'en soucient déjà plus ; la cité est transformée en un immense parc où ils peuvent aller et venir sans être dérangés. Tôt ou tard, ils devaient bien tomber sur la nourriture stockée par les habitants d'Akbar pour soutenir le siège.

« Un enfant peut toujours enseigner trois choses à un adulte : être content sans raison, s'occuper tou-

jours à quelque chose, et savoir exiger — de toutes
ses forces — ce qu'il désire. C'est à cause de ce gosse
que je suis revenu à Akbar. »

*

Cet après-midi-là, d'autres vieillards et d'autres
femmes participèrent au ramassage des morts. Les
enfants éloignaient les charognards et apportaient
des morceaux de bois et de tissu. Quand la nuit
tomba, Elie mit feu à la montagne de corps. Les survivants d'Akbar contemplèrent en silence la fumée
qui s'élevait vers les cieux.

Sa tâche terminée, Elie s'effondra de fatigue. Mais
avant de dormir, il éprouva de nouveau la sensation
qu'il avait eue le matin même : un élément capital
luttait désespérément pour lui revenir en mémoire.
Ce n'était rien qu'il eût appris pendant le temps qu'il
avait passé à Akbar, mais une histoire ancienne, qui
semblait donner sens à tout ce qui était en train de
se produire.

« *Cette nuit-là, un homme lutta avec Jacob jusqu'au
lever du jour. Voyant qu'il ne pouvait l'emporter sur
lui, il lui dit : "Laisse-moi partir."*

*Jacob répondit : "Je ne te laisserai pas, que tu ne
m'aies béni."*

*Alors l'homme lui dit : « Comme un prince, tu as
lutté avec Dieu. Comment t'appelles-tu ? "*

*Jacob dit son nom, et l'homme répondit : "Désor-
mais, tu t'appelleras Israël."* »

Elie se réveilla d'un bond et regarda le firmament. Voilà l'histoire qui manquait !

Longtemps auparavant, alors que le patriarche Jacob avait installé son camp, quelqu'un entra dans sa tente au cours de la nuit et lutta avec lui jusqu'au lever du soleil. Jacob accepta le combat, bien qu'il sût que son adversaire était le Seigneur. A l'aube, il n'était toujours pas vaincu, et le combat ne prit fin que lorsque Dieu accepta de le bénir.

L'histoire s'était transmise de génération en génération afin que personne ne l'oubliât jamais : *quelquefois il était nécessaire de lutter avec Dieu*. Tout être humain, à un moment donné, voyait une tragédie traverser sa vie ; ce pouvait être la destruction d'une cité, la mort d'un enfant, une accusation sans preuve, une maladie qui le laissait invalide à tout jamais. A cet instant, Dieu le mettait au défi de L'affronter et de répondre à Sa question : « Pourquoi t'accrocher autant à une existence si courte et si pleine de souffrances ? Quel est le sens de ta lutte ? »

L'homme qui ne savait répondre se résignait. Mais celui qui cherchait un sens à l'existence trouvait que Dieu avait été injuste, et il bravait le destin. C'est alors qu'un autre feu descendait des cieux, non pas celui qui tue, mais celui qui détruit les antiques murailles et donne à chaque être humain ses véritables possibilités. Les lâches ne laissent jamais cette flamme embraser leur cœur — tout ce qu'ils désirent, c'est que la situation redevienne vite ce qu'elle était auparavant, afin qu'ils puissent continuer de vivre et de penser comme ils y étaient accoutumés. En revanche, les courageux mettent le feu à ce qui était vieux, dépassé, et, même au prix d'une grande souffrance intérieure, ils abandonnent tout, y compris Dieu, et vont de l'avant.

« Les courageux sont toujours têtus. »

Du ciel, le Seigneur sourit de contentement : c'était cela qu'Il voulait, que chacun prît en main la responsabilité de sa propre vie. Finalement, il avait donné à ses enfants le plus grand de tous les dons : la capacité de choisir et de décider de leurs actes.

Seuls les hommes et les femmes ayant le feu sacré avaient le courage de L'affronter. Et eux seuls connaissaient la voie du retour vers Son amour, car ils comprenaient enfin que la tragédie n'était pas une punition, mais un défi.

Elie revit chacun de ses pas ; depuis qu'il avait quitté la charpenterie, il avait accepté sa mission sans discuter. Même si elle était juste — et il pensait qu'elle l'était —, il n'avait jamais eu l'occasion de regarder ce qui se passait sur les chemins qu'il s'était refusé à parcourir par peur de perdre sa foi, son dévouement, sa volonté. Il considérait qu'il était très risqué de prendre le chemin des gens ordinaires — il pouvait finir par s'y habituer et aimer ce qu'il voyait. Il ne comprenait pas qu'il était lui aussi comme tout le monde, même s'il entendait des anges et recevait de temps en temps des ordres de Dieu ; il était tellement convaincu de savoir ce qu'il voulait qu'il s'était comporté de la même manière que ceux qui n'avaient jamais pris une décision importante de leur vie.

Il avait échappé au doute, à la défaite, aux moments d'indécision. Mais le Seigneur était généreux, et Il l'avait conduit à l'abîme de l'inévitable pour lui montrer que l'homme a besoin de *choisir* — et non d'*accepter* — son destin.

Bien des années auparavant, par une nuit semblable à celle-ci, Jacob n'avait pas laissé Dieu partir avant qu'Il ne l'ait béni. C'est alors que le Seigneur lui avait demandé : « *Comment t'appelles-tu ?* »

Telle était la question : avoir un nom. Une fois que Jacob eut répondu, Dieu l'avait baptisé *Israël*. Chacun a un nom au berceau, mais il doit apprendre à baptiser sa vie du mot qu'il a choisi pour lui donner un sens.

« Je suis *Akbar* », avait-elle dit.

Il avait fallu la destruction de la cité et la perte de la femme aimée pour qu'Elie comprît qu'il avait besoin d'un nom. Et, à l'instant même, il donna à sa vie le nom de *Libération*.

Il se leva et regarda la place devant lui : la fumée montait encore des cendres de ceux qui avaient perdu la vie. En mettant le feu à ces corps, il avait bravé une coutume très ancienne de son pays qui exigeait que les gens fussent enterrés selon les rites. Il avait lutté avec Dieu et la tradition en décidant l'incinération, mais il sentait qu'il n'avait pas péché, car il fallait une solution nouvelle à un problème nouveau. Dieu était infini dans Sa miséricorde, et implacable dans Sa rigueur à l'égard de ceux qui n'ont pas le courage d'oser.

Il parcourut de nouveau la place du regard : quelques survivants n'étaient pas encore allés se coucher et ils gardaient les yeux fixés sur les flammes, comme si ce feu avait consumé aussi leurs souvenirs, leur passé, les deux cents ans de paix et d'inertie d'Akbar. L'époque de la peur et de l'attente était révolue : il ne restait désormais que la reconstruction ou la défaite.

Comme Elie, eux aussi pouvaient se choisir un nom. *Réconciliation, Sagesse, Amant, Pèlerin*, il y avait autant de choix que d'étoiles dans le ciel, mais chacun devait donner un nom à sa vie.

Elie se leva et pria :

« J'ai lutté contre Toi, Seigneur, et je n'ai pas honte. Ainsi, j'ai découvert que je suis sur mon chemin parce que je le désire, non parce que cela m'a été imposé par mes parents, par les traditions de mon pays, ou par Toi-même.

« Vers Toi, Seigneur, j'aimerais revenir en cet instant. Je veux T'offrir toute la force de ma volonté, et non la lâcheté de celui qui n'a pas su choisir un chemin différent. Cependant, pour que Tu me confies Ton importante mission, je dois poursuivre cette bataille contre Toi, jusqu'à ce que Tu me bénisses. »

Reconstruire Akbar. Ce qu'Elie prenait pour un défi à Dieu était, en vérité, ses retrouvailles avec Lui.

La femme qui avait réclamé de la nourriture reparut le lendemain matin. Elle était accompagnée d'autres femmes.

« Nous avons découvert plusieurs dépôts, dit-elle. Comme beaucoup de gens sont morts et que beaucoup d'autres ont fui avec le gouverneur, nous avons des réserves pour un an.

— Trouve de vieilles personnes pour superviser la distribution des aliments, ordonna Elie. Elles ont l'expérience de l'organisation.

— Les vieux n'ont pas envie de vivre.

— Prie-les de venir de toute façon. »

La femme se préparait à partir quand Elie la retint :

« Tu sais écrire en te servant des lettres ?

— Non.

— J'ai appris, et je peux t'enseigner. Cela te sera utile pour m'aider à administrer la cité.

— Mais les Assyriens vont revenir.

— Quand ils arriveront, ils auront besoin de notre aide pour gérer les affaires de la cité.

— Pourquoi faire cela pour l'ennemi ?

— Fais-le pour que chacun puisse donner un nom à sa vie. L'ennemi n'est qu'un prétexte pour mettre à l'épreuve notre force. »

Les vieux vinrent, ainsi qu'il l'avait prévu.

« Akbar a besoin de votre aide, leur dit Elie. Et devant cela, vous ne pouvez pas vous offrir le luxe d'être vieux ; nous avons besoin de la jeunesse que vous aviez jadis et que vous avez perdue.

— Nous ne savons pas où la retrouver, répondit l'un d'eux. Elle a disparu avec les rides et les désillusions.

— Ce n'est pas vrai. Vous n'avez jamais eu d'illusions, et c'est pour cette raison que la jeunesse se cache. Il est temps de la retrouver, puisque nous avons un rêve commun : reconstruire Akbar.

— Comment pouvons-nous réaliser quelque chose d'impossible ?

166

— Avec enthousiasme. »

Les yeux voilés par la tristesse et le découragement voulaient briller de nouveau. Ce n'étaient plus les habitants bons à rien qui allaient assister aux jugements en quête d'un sujet de conversation pour la fin de l'après-midi ; ils avaient maintenant devant eux une mission importante, ils étaient nécessaires.

Les plus résistants séparèrent les matériaux encore utilisables des maisons qui avaient été très endommagées et s'en servirent pour remettre en état celles qui tenaient encore debout. Les plus âgés aidèrent à disperser dans les champs les cendres des cadavres incinérés, afin qu'on se rappelât les morts de la cité lors de la prochaine récolte ; d'autres se chargèrent de séparer les grains emmagasinés dans toute la cité dans le plus grand désordre, de fabriquer le pain et de tirer l'eau du puits.

Deux nuits plus tard, Elie réunit tous les habitants sur la place, nettoyée maintenant de la plus grande partie des décombres. On alluma des torches et il prit la parole :

« Nous n'avons pas le choix. Nous pouvons laisser l'étranger faire ce travail, mais alors cela signifie que nous renonçons à la seule chance que nous offre une tragédie : celle de reconstruire notre vie.

« Les cendres des morts que nous avons incinérés il y a quelques jours vont nourrir des plantes qui naîtront au printemps. Le fils perdu la nuit de l'invasion s'est changé en de nombreux enfants qui courent librement dans les rues détruites et s'amusent à envahir des lieux interdits et des maisons qu'ils n'avaient jamais connues. Jusqu'à présent, seuls les enfants ont été capables de surmonter les événements parce qu'ils n'ont pas de passé — pour eux, tout ce qui compte est le moment présent. Alors, essayons d'agir comme eux.

— Un homme peut-il éteindre dans son cœur la douleur d'une perte ? demanda une femme.

— Non. Mais il peut se réjouir d'avoir gagné quelque chose. »

Elie se retourna et montra la cime de la Cinquième Montagne, toujours couverte de nuages. La destruction des murailles la rendait visible du centre de la place.

« Je crois en un Seigneur unique, mais vous, vous pensez que les dieux habitent dans ces nuages, au sommet de la Cinquième Montagne. Je ne veux pas discuter maintenant pour savoir si mon Dieu est plus fort ou plus puissant que les vôtres ; je ne veux pas évoquer nos différences, mais nos ressemblances. La tragédie nous a réunis en un sentiment commun : le désespoir. Pourquoi est-ce arrivé ? Parce que nous pensions que tout avait trouvé une réponse et une solution dans nos âmes, et nous ne pouvions accepter le moindre changement.

« Vous et moi, nous appartenons à des nations commerçantes, mais nous savons aussi nous comporter en guerriers, poursuivit-il. Et un guerrier est toujours conscient du motif pour lequel cela vaut la peine de lutter. Il n'entreprend pas des combats dénués d'intérêt, et il ne perd jamais son temps en provocations.

« Un guerrier accepte la défaite. Il ne la traite pas comme un événement indifférent, ni ne tente de la transformer en victoire. La douleur de la perte le rend amer, il souffre de la froideur et la solitude le désespère. Une fois qu'il est passé par tout cela, il lèche ses blessures et prend un nouveau départ. Un guerrier sait que la guerre est faite de nombreuses batailles ; il va de l'avant.

« Des tragédies surviennent. Nous pouvons en découvrir la raison, en rendre les autres coupables, imaginer combien nos vies auraient été différentes sans elles. Mais rien de tout cela n'a d'importance : elles sont arrivées, point. Dès lors, nous devons oublier la peur qu'elles ont suscitée et entreprendre la reconstruction.

« Chacun de vous se donnera désormais un nom nouveau. Ce sera un nom sacré, qui synthétise tout ce pour quoi vous avez rêvé de vous battre. Je me suis choisi le nom de *Libération*. »

La place resta silencieuse un certain temps. Alors, la femme qui la première avait aidé Elie se leva.

« Mon nom est *Retrouvailles*, dit-elle.

— Je m'appelle *Sagesse* », déclara un vieux.

Le fils de la veuve qu'Elie avait tant aimée s'écria : « Mon nom est *Alphabet*. »

Les gens éclatèrent de rire. Honteux, l'enfant se rassit.

« Comment peut-on s'appeler *Alphabet* ? » cria un autre enfant.

Elie aurait pu intervenir mais il était bon que le garçon apprît à se défendre tout seul.

« Parce que c'est ce que faisait ma mère, dit le gamin. Chaque fois que je regarderai les lettres dessinées, je penserai à elle. »

Cette fois, personne ne rit. Un à un, les orphelins, les veuves et les vieillards d'Akbar annoncèrent leur nom et leur nouvelle identité. La cérémonie terminée, Elie conseilla à tout le monde de se coucher tôt : ils devaient se remettre au travail le lendemain matin.

Il prit l'enfant par la main et ils regagnèrent l'endroit de la place où ils avaient étendu quelques tissus en forme de tente.

A partir de cette nuit-là, il lui enseigna l'écriture de Byblos.

Les jours devinrent des semaines, et Akbar changeait de visage. L'enfant avait rapidement appris à dessiner les lettres et il parvenait désormais à créer des mots qui avaient un sens. Elie le chargea d'écrire sur des tablettes d'argile l'histoire de la reconstruction de la cité.

Les plaques d'argile étaient cuites dans un four improvisé, transformées en céramique et soigneusement archivées par un couple de vieillards. Lors des réunions qui se tenaient chaque soir, Elie demandait aux vieux de raconter ce qu'ils avaient vu dans leur enfance et il enregistrait le plus grand nombre d'histoires possible.

« Nous conserverons la mémoire d'Akbar dans un matériau que le feu ne peut détruire, expliquait-il. Un jour, nos enfants et petits-enfants sauront que la défaite n'a pas été acceptée et que l'inévitable a été surmonté. Cela peut leur servir d'exemple. »

Toutes les nuits, après l'étude avec le gamin, Elie marchait dans la cité déserte, il allait jusqu'au début de la route menant à Jérusalem, songeait à partir, puis y renonçait.

Le poids de sa tâche l'obligeait à se concentrer sur le présent. Il savait que les habitants d'Akbar comptaient sur lui pour la reconstruction ; il les avait déçus une fois, le jour où il s'était montré incapable d'empêcher la mort de l'espion, et d'éviter la guerre. Pourtant, Dieu offre toujours une seconde chance à ses enfants, et il devait saisir l'opportunité nouvelle. En outre, il s'attachait de plus en plus à l'enfant ; il voulait lui enseigner non seulement les caractères de Byblos, mais la foi dans le Seigneur et la sagesse de ses ancêtres.

Cependant, il n'oubliait pas que, dans son pays, régnaient une princesse et un dieu étranger. Il n'y avait plus d'anges tenant des épées de feu ; il était libre de partir quand il voulait et de faire ce que bon lui semblait.

Toutes les nuits, il songeait à s'en aller. Et toutes les nuits, il levait les mains vers le ciel et priait :

« Jacob a lutté la nuit entière et il a été béni à l'aurore. J'ai lutté contre Toi pendant des jours, des mois, et Tu refuses de m'écouter. Mais si Tu regardes autour de Toi, Tu sauras que je suis en train de vaincre : Akbar se relève de ses ruines et je vais reconstruire ce que Toi, en te servant des épées des Assyriens, Tu as transformé en cendres et en poussière.

« Je lutterai avec Toi jusqu'à ce que Tu me bénisses, et que Tu bénisses les fruits de mon travail. Un jour, Tu devras me répondre. »

*

Femmes et enfants apportaient l'eau dans les champs et luttaient contre la sécheresse qui paraissait sans fin. Un jour que le soleil implacable brillait de toute sa force, Elie entendit ce commentaire :

« Nous travaillons sans arrêt, nous ne pensons plus aux douleurs de cette nuit-là, et nous oublions même que les Assyriens reviendront dès qu'ils auront fini de mettre à sac Tyr, Sidon, Byblos et toute la Phénicie. Cela nous a fait du bien.

« Cependant, parce que nous sommes très concentrés sur la reconstruction de la cité, rien ne semble changer ; nous ne voyons pas le résultat de notre effort. »

Elie médita quelque temps sur ces paroles. Il exigea désormais que, au terme de chaque journée de travail, les gens se réunissent au pied de la Cinquième Montagne pour contempler ensemble le coucher du soleil.

Ils étaient en général tellement fatigués qu'ils échangeaient à peine un mot, mais ils découvraient combien il était important de laisser sa pensée errer sans but, comme les nuages dans le ciel. Ainsi, l'anxiété abandonnait leur cœur et tous retrouvaient la force et l'inspiration nécessaires pour le lendemain.

A son réveil, Elie annonça qu'il n'irait pas travailler.

« Aujourd'hui, dans mon pays, on célèbre le jour du Pardon.

— Il n'y a pas de péché dans ton âme, remarqua une femme. Tu as fait de ton mieux.

— Mais la tradition doit être maintenue. Et je la respecterai. »

Les femmes allèrent porter l'eau dans les champs, les vieux retournèrent à leur tâche, élever des murs et façonner des portes et des fenêtres en bois. Les enfants aidaient à mouler les petites briques d'argile qui, plus tard, seraient cuites dans le feu. Elie les contempla, une joie immense dans le cœur. Ensuite, il quitta Akbar et se rendit dans la vallée.

Il marcha sans but, faisant les prières qu'il avait apprises enfant. Le soleil n'était pas encore complètement levé et, de là où il se trouvait, il voyait l'ombre gigantesque de la Cinquième Montagne recouvrir une partie de la vallée. Il eut un horrible pressentiment : cette lutte entre le Dieu d'Israël et les dieux des Phéniciens allait se prolonger durant des générations et des millénaires.

*

Il se rappela qu'un soir il était monté jusqu'au sommet de la montagne et qu'il avait conversé avec un ange ; mais, depuis qu'Akbar avait été détruite, plus jamais il n'avait entendu les voix venant du ciel.

« Seigneur, aujourd'hui c'est le jour du Pardon, et la liste des péchés que j'ai commis envers Toi est longue », dit-il en se tournant en direction de Jérusalem. « J'ai été faible, parce que j'ai oublié ma propre force. J'ai été compatissant quand j'aurais dû être dur. Je n'ai pas choisi, de crainte de prendre de mauvaises décisions. J'ai renoncé avant l'heure, et j'ai blasphémé lorsque j'aurais dû remercier.

« Cependant, Seigneur, Tes péchés envers moi

forment aussi une longue liste. Tu m'as fait souffrir plus que nécessaire, emportant de ce monde quelqu'un que j'aimais. Tu as détruit la cité qui m'a accueilli, Tu as fait échouer ma quête, Ta dureté m'a presque fait oublier l'amour que j'ai pour Toi. Pendant tout ce temps, j'ai lutté avec Toi, et Tu n'admets pas la dignité de mon combat.

« Si nous comparons la liste de mes péchés et la liste des Tiens, Tu verras que Tu as une dette envers moi. Mais, comme aujourd'hui c'est le jour du Pardon, Tu me pardonnes et je Te pardonne, pour que nous puissions continuer à marcher ensemble. »

A ce moment le vent souffla, et il sentit que son ange lui parlait : « Tu as bien fait, Elie. Dieu a accepté ton combat. »

Des larmes coulèrent de ses yeux. Il s'agenouilla et embrassa le sol aride de la vallée.

« Merci d'être venu, parce que j'ai encore un doute : n'est-ce pas un péché d'agir ainsi ? »

L'ange répondit :

« Quand un guerrier lutte avec son instructeur, l'offense-t-il ?

— Non, c'est la seule manière d'apprendre la technique dont il a besoin.

— Alors continue jusqu'à ce que le Seigneur t'appelle et te renvoie en Israël, reprit l'ange. Lève-toi et continue à prouver que ta lutte a un sens, parce que tu as su traverser le courant de l'Inévitable. Beaucoup y naviguent et font naufrage ; d'autres sont rejetés vers des lieux qui ne leur étaient pas destinés. Mais toi, tu affrontes la traversée avec dignité, tu sais contrôler la direction de ton bateau et tu t'efforces de transformer la douleur en action.

— Dommage que tu sois aveugle, dit Elie. Sinon tu verrais comme les orphelins, les veuves et les vieillards ont été capables de reconstruire une cité. Bientôt, tout redeviendra comme avant.

— J'espère que non, répliqua l'ange. Finalement, ils ont payé le prix fort pour que leurs vies changent. »

Elie sourit. L'ange avait raison.

« J'espère que tu te comporteras comme les

hommes à qui l'on offre une seconde chance : ne commets pas deux fois la même erreur. N'oublie jamais la raison de ta vie.

— Je n'oublierai pas », répondit-il, content que l'ange fût revenu.

Les caravanes n'empruntaient plus le chemin de la vallée ; les Assyriens avaient dû détruire les routes et modifier les voies commerciales. Chaque jour, des enfants montaient dans la seule tour des remparts qui avait échappé à la destruction ; ils étaient chargés de surveiller l'horizon et d'avertir au cas où les guerriers ennemis reviendraient.

Elie projetait de les recevoir avec dignité et de leur remettre le commandement. Alors, il pourrait partir.

Mais, chaque jour qui passait, il sentait qu'Akbar faisait partie de sa vie. Sa mission n'était peut-être pas de chasser Jézabel du trône, mais de rester là, avec ces gens, jusqu'à sa mort, jouant l'humble rôle de serviteur du conquérant assyrien. Il aiderait à rétablir les voies commerciales, il apprendrait la langue de l'ennemi et, dans ses moments de repos, il pourrait s'occuper de la bibliothèque qui s'enrichissait de plus en plus.

Ce que l'on avait pris, une certaine nuit perdue dans le temps, pour la fin d'une cité signifiait maintenant la possibilité de la rendre encore plus belle. Les travaux de reconstruction comprenaient l'élargissement des rues, l'installation de toits plus résistants, et un ingénieux système pour porter l'eau du puits jusqu'aux endroits les plus éloignés. Son âme aussi se renouvelait ; chaque jour, il apprenait, des vieux, des enfants, des femmes, quelque chose de nouveau. Ce groupe — qui n'avait pas abandonné Akbar en raison de l'impossibilité absolue où il était de le faire — formait maintenant une équipe disciplinée et compétente.

« Si le gouverneur avait su qu'ils étaient aussi utiles, il aurait inventé un autre type de défense, et Akbar n'aurait pas été détruite. »

Elie réfléchit un peu et comprit qu'il se trompait. Akbar devait être détruite, pour que tous puissent réveiller en eux les forces qui dormaient.

Des mois passèrent, et les assyriens ne donnaient pas signe de vie. Akbar était maintenant quasi prête et Elie pouvait songer à l'avenir ; les femmes récupéraient les morceaux d'étoffe et en confectionnaient des vêtements. Les vieux réorganisaient les demeures et s'occupaient de l'hygiène de la cité. Les enfants aidaient quand on les sollicitait mais, en général, ils passaient la journée à jouer : c'est la principale obligation des enfants.

Elie vivait avec le gamin dans une petite maison en pierre, reconstruite sur le terrain de ce qui avait été autrefois un dépôt de marchandises. Chaque soir, les habitants d'Akbar s'asseyaient autour d'un feu sur la place principale et racontaient des histoires qu'ils avaient entendues au cours de leur vie ; avec l'enfant, il notait tout sur les tablettes qu'ils faisaient cuire le lendemain. La bibliothèque grossissait à vue d'œil.

La femme qui avait perdu son fils apprenait elle aussi les caractères de Byblos. Quand il vit qu'elle savait créer des mots et des phrases, il la chargea d'enseigner l'alphabet au reste de la population ; ainsi, lorsque les Assyriens reviendraient, ils pourraient servir d'interprètes ou de professeurs.

« C'était justement cela que le prêtre voulait éviter », dit un après-midi un vieux qui s'était appelé *Océan*, car il désirait avoir l'âme aussi vaste que la mer. « Que l'écriture de Byblos survécût et menaçât les dieux de la Cinquième Montagne.

— Qui peut éviter l'inévitable ? » rétorqua-t-il.

Les gens travaillaient le jour, assistaient ensemble au coucher du soleil et contaient des histoires à la veillée.

Elie était fier de son œuvre. Et il l'aimait de plus en plus.

*

Un enfant chargé de la surveillance descendit en courant.

« J'ai vu de la poussière à l'horizon ! dit-il, excité. L'ennemi est de retour ! »

Elie monta dans la tour et constata que l'information était exacte. Il calcula qu'ils arriveraient aux portes d'Akbar le lendemain.

L'après-midi, il prévint les habitants qu'ils ne devraient pas assister au coucher du soleil mais se retrouver sur la place. La journée de travail terminée, il rejoignit l'assemblée et remarqua que les gens avaient peur.

« Aujourd'hui nous ne raconterons pas des histoires du passé, et nous n'évoquerons pas les projets d'Akbar, dit-il. Nous allons parler de nous-mêmes. »

Personne ne dit mot.

*

« Il y a quelque temps, la pleine lune a brillé dans le ciel. Ce jour-là, il est arrivé ce que tous nous pressentions, mais que nous ne voulions pas accepter : Akbar a été détruite. Lorsque l'armée assyrienne s'est retirée, nos meilleurs hommes étaient morts. Les rescapés ont vu qu'il ne valait pas la peine de rester ici et ils ont décidé de s'en aller. Seuls sont restés les vieillards, les veuves et les orphelins, c'est-à-dire les bons à rien.

« Regardez autour de vous ; la place est plus belle que jamais, les bâtiments sont plus solides, la nourriture est partagée, et tous apprennent l'écriture inventée à Byblos. Quelque part dans cette cité se trouve une collection de tablettes sur lesquelles nous avons inscrit nos histoires, et les générations futures se rappelleront ce que nous avons fait.

« Aujourd'hui, nous savons que les vieux, les orphelins et les veuves sont partis aussi. Ils ont laissé place à une bande de jeunes gens de tous âges, pleins d'enthousiasme, qui ont donné un nom et un sens à leur vie.

« A chaque moment de la reconstruction, nous savions que les Assyriens allaient revenir. Nous savions qu'un jour il nous faudrait leur livrer notre cité et, avec elle, nos efforts, notre sueur, notre joie de la voir plus belle qu'avant. »

La lumière du feu illumina les larmes qui coulaient des visages. Même les enfants, qui d'habitude jouaient pendant les réunions nocturnes, étaient attentifs à ses paroles. Elie poursuivit :

« Cela n'a pas d'importance. Nous avons accompli notre devoir envers le Seigneur, car nous avons accepté Son défi et l'honneur de Sa lutte. Avant cette nuit-là, Il insistait auprès de nous, disant : "Marche !" Mais nous ne l'écoutions pas. Pourquoi ?

« Parce que chacun de nous avait déjà décidé de son propre avenir : je pensais chasser Jézabel du trône, la femme qui maintenant s'appelle *Retrouvailles* voulait que son fils fût navigateur, l'homme qui aujourd'hui porte le nom de *Sagesse* désirait simplement passer le reste de ses jours à boire du vin sur la place. Nous étions habitués au mystère sacré de la vie et nous ne lui accordions plus d'importance.

« Alors le Seigneur s'est dit : "Ils ne veulent pas marcher ? Alors ils vont rester arrêtés très longtemps !"

« Et là, seulement, nous avons compris Son message. L'acier de l'épée assyrienne a emporté nos jeunes gens, et la lâcheté s'est emparée des adultes. Où qu'ils soient à cette heure, ils sont encore arrêtés ; ils ont accepté la malédiction de Dieu.

« Mais nous, nous avons lutté contre le Seigneur. Comme nous avons lutté avec les hommes et les femmes que nous aimions durant notre vie, parce que c'est le combat qui nous bénit et qui nous fait grandir. Nous avons saisi l'opportunité de la tragédie et nous avons accompli notre devoir envers Lui, prouvant que nous étions capables d'obéir à l'ordre de *marcher*. Même dans les pires circonstances, nous sommes allés de l'avant.

« Il y a des moments où Dieu exige obéissance. Mais il y a des moments où Il désire tester notre volonté et nous met au défi de comprendre Son amour. Nous avons compris cette volonté quand les murailles d'Akbar se sont écroulées : elles ont ouvert notre horizon et laissé chacun de nous voir de quoi il était capable. Nous avons cessé de réfléchir à la vie, et nous avons décidé de la vivre. Le résultat a été bon. »

Elie remarqua que les yeux se mettaient à briller. Les gens avaient compris.

« Demain, je livrerai Akbar sans lutte ; je suis libre de partir quand je veux, car j'ai accompli ce que le Seigneur attendait de moi. Cependant, mon sang, ma sueur et mon unique amour sont dans le sol de cette cité, et j'ai décidé de passer ici le reste de mes jours, pour empêcher qu'elle ne soit de nouveau détruite. Que chacun prenne la décision qu'il voudra, mais n'oubliez jamais ceci : vous êtes bien meilleurs que vous ne le pensiez.

« Vous avez saisi la chance que la tragédie vous a donnée ; tout le monde n'en est pas capable. »

Elie se leva et annonça que la réunion était close. Il avertit l'enfant qu'il allait rentrer tard et lui conseilla de se coucher sans l'attendre.

*

Il alla jusqu'au temple, le seul monument ayant échappé à la destruction ; ils n'avaient pas eu besoin de le reconstruire, bien que les statues des dieux aient été emportées par les Assyriens. Respectueusement, il toucha la pierre qui marquait l'endroit où, selon la tradition, un ancêtre avait enfoncé une baguette dans le sol et n'était pas parvenu à la retirer.

Il songea que, dans son pays, Jézabel avait édifié des monuments comme celui-ci et qu'une partie de son peuple se prosternait pour adorer Baal et ses divinités. De nouveau, le pressentiment traversa son âme : la guerre entre le Seigneur d'Israël et les dieux des Phéniciens durerait très longtemps, bien au-delà de ce que son imagination pouvait atteindre. Comme dans une vision, il entrevit les étoiles qui croisaient le soleil et répandaient dans les deux pays la destruction et la mort. Des hommes qui parlaient des langues inconnues chevauchaient des animaux d'acier et s'affrontaient en duel au milieu des nuages.

« Ce n'est pas cela que tu dois voir maintenant, car le temps n'est pas encore venu, lui dit son ange. Regarde par la fenêtre. »

Elie obéit. Dehors, la pleine lune illuminait les maisons et les rues d'Akbar, et, bien qu'il fût tard, il pouvait entendre les conversations et les rires de ses habitants. Malgré le retour des Assyriens, ce peuple avait encore envie de vivre, il était prêt à affronter une nouvelle étape de son existence.

Alors, il aperçut une silhouette et il sut que c'était la femme qu'il avait tant aimée et qui maintenant marchait de nouveau orgueilleusement dans la cité. Il sourit et sentit qu'elle touchait son visage.

« Je suis fière, semblait-elle dire. Akbar demeure vraiment belle. »

Il eut envie de pleurer mais il se rappela l'enfant qui jamais n'avait laissé couler une larme pour sa mère. Il contrôla ses pleurs et se remémora les plus beaux moments de l'histoire qu'ils avaient vécue ensemble — depuis la rencontre aux portes de la cité jusqu'à l'instant où elle avait écrit le mot « amour » sur une tablette d'argile. Il revit sa robe, ses cheveux, l'arête fine de son nez.

« Tu m'as dit que tu étais Akbar. Alors j'ai pris soin de toi, je t'ai guérie de tes blessures, et maintenant je te rends à la vie. Sois heureuse avec tes nouveaux compagnons. Et je voudrais te dire une chose : moi aussi j'étais Akbar, et je ne le savais pas. »

Il avait la certitude qu'elle souriait.

« Le vent du désert, il y a très longtemps, a effacé nos pas sur le sable. Mais, à chaque seconde de mon existence, je pense à ce qui s'est passé, et tu marches encore dans mes rêves et dans ma réalité. Merci d'avoir croisé mon chemin. »

Il s'endormit là, dans le temple, sentant que la femme lui caressait les cheveux.

Le chef des marchands aperçut un groupe de gens en guenilles au milieu de la route. Il crut que c'étaient des brigands et demanda à tous les membres de la caravane de s'emparer de leurs armes.

« Qui êtes-vous ? interrogea-t-il.

— Nous sommes le peuple d'Akbar », répondit un barbu, les yeux brillants. Le chef de la caravane remarqua qu'il parlait avec un accent étranger.

« Akbar a été détruite. Nous sommes chargés par le gouvernement de Tyr et de Sidon de localiser son puits, afin que les caravanes puissent de nouveau emprunter cette vallée. Les communications avec le reste du pays ne peuvent rester interrompues pour toujours.

— Akbar existe encore, répliqua l'homme. Où sont les Assyriens ?

— Le monde entier sait où ils sont, répondit en riant le chef de la caravane. Ils rendent plus fertile le sol de notre pays et il y a longtemps qu'ils nourrissent nos oiseaux et nos bêtes sauvages.

— Mais c'était une armée puissante.

— Une armée n'a aucun pouvoir, si l'on sait quand elle va attaquer. Akbar a fait prévenir qu'ils approchaient et Tyr et Sidon ont organisé une embuscade à l'autre bout de la vallée. Ceux qui ne sont pas morts au combat ont été vendus comme esclaves par nos navigateurs. »

Les gens en haillons applaudissaient et s'embrassaient, pleurant et riant en même temps.

« Qui êtes-vous ? répéta le marchand. Qui es-tu ? demanda-t-il en indiquant le chef.

— Nous sommes les jeunes guerriers d'Akbar »,
lui fut-il répondu.

La troisième récolte avait commencé, et Elie était
le gouverneur d'Akbar. Il y avait eu beaucoup de
résistance au début — l'ancien gouverneur voulait
revenir occuper son poste, ainsi que l'ordonnait la
tradition. Mais les habitants de la cité avaient refusé
de le recevoir et menacé pendant des jours d'empoi-
sonner l'eau du puits. L'autorité phénicienne avait
finalement cédé à leurs requêtes — au bout du
compte, Akbar n'avait pas tant d'importance, sinon
pour l'eau qu'elle procurait aux voyageurs, et le gouvernement d'Israël était aux mains d'une princesse
de Tyr. En concédant le poste de gouverneur à un
Israélite, les gouvernants phéniciens pouvaient bâtir
une alliance commerciale plus solide.

La nouvelle parcourut toute la région, portée par
les caravanes de marchands qui s'étaient remises à
circuler. Une minorité en Israël considérait Elie
comme le pire des traîtres, mais Jézabel se charge-
rait en temps voulu d'éliminer cette résistance, et la
paix reviendrait dans la région. La princesse était
satisfaite parce que l'un de ses pires ennemis était
devenu son meilleur allié.

*

La rumeur d'une nouvelle invasion assyrienne se
répandit et on releva les murailles d'Akbar. On mit
au point un nouveau système de défense, avec des
sentinelles et des garnisons disséminées entre Tyr et
Akbar ; de cette manière, si l'une des cités était assié-
gée, l'autre pourrait dépêcher des troupes par terre
et assurer le ravitaillement par mer.

La région prospérait à vue d'œil : le nouveau gouverneur israélite avait instauré un rigoureux contrôle des taxes et des marchandises, fondé sur l'écriture. Les vieux d'Akbar s'occupaient de tout, utilisaient les nouvelles techniques et résolvaient patiemment les problèmes qui surgissaient.

Les femmes partageaient leur temps entre leur labeur et le tissage. Pendant la période d'isolement de la cité, pour remettre en état le peu de tissus qui leur restaient, elles avaient été obligées d'inventer de nouveaux motifs de broderie ; lorsque les premiers marchands arrivèrent, ils furent enchantés par les dessins et passèrent de nombreuses commandes.

Les enfants avaient appris l'écriture de Byblos ; Elie était certain que cela leur serait utile un jour.

Comme toujours avant la récolte, il se promenait dans la campagne et il remerciait le Seigneur cet après-midi-là des innombrables bénédictions qu'il avait reçues pendant toutes ces années. Il vit les gens tenant les paniers chargés de grain, les enfants jouant tout autour. Il leur fit signe et ils lui répondirent.

Un sourire sur le visage, il se dirigea vers la pierre où, très longtemps auparavant, il avait reçu une tablette d'argile portant le mot « amour ». Il venait tous les jours visiter cet endroit, pour assister au coucher du soleil et se rappeler chaque instant qu'ils avaient passé ensemble.

« *La parole du Seigneur fut adressée à Elie, la troisième année :*

"Va, montre-toi à Achab, je vais donner de la pluie sur la surface du sol." »

De la pierre sur laquelle il était assis, Elie vit le monde trembler autour de lui. Le ciel devint noir pendant un moment, puis très vite le soleil se remit à briller.

Il vit la lumière. Un ange du Seigneur se tenait devant lui.

« Que s'est-il passé ? demanda Elie, effrayé. Dieu a-t-Il pardonné à Israël ?

— Non, répondit l'ange. Il veut que tu retournes libérer ton peuple. Ton combat avec Lui est terminé et, à cet instant, Il t'a béni. Il t'a donné la permission de poursuivre Son travail sur cette terre. »

Elie était abasourdi.

« Maintenant, justement quand mon cœur vient de retrouver la paix ?

— Rappelle-toi la leçon qui t'a été enseignée une fois. Et rappelle-toi les paroles que le Seigneur adressa à Moïse :

"Souviens-toi du chemin sur lequel le Seigneur t'a guidé, pour t'humilier, pour te mettre à l'épreuve, pour savoir ce qui était dans ton cœur.

Quand tu auras mangé à satiété, quand tu auras construit de belles maisons pour y habiter, quand ton troupeau et ton bétail se seront multipliés, garde-toi de devenir orgueilleux et d'oublier le Seigneur ton Dieu." »

Elie se tourna vers l'ange.

« Et Akbar ? demanda-t-il.

— Elle peut vivre sans toi, car tu as laissé un héritier. Elle survivra de nombreuses années. »

L'ange du Seigneur disparut.

Elie et l'enfant arrivèrent au pied de la Cinquième Montagne. Les broussailles avaient poussé entre les pierres des autels ; depuis la mort du grand prêtre, plus personne ne venait ici.

« Nous allons monter, dit-il.

— C'est interdit.

— Oui, c'est interdit. Mais ce n'est pas dangereux pour autant. »

Il le prit par la main, et ils commencèrent à monter en direction du sommet. Ils s'arrêtaient de temps en temps et regardaient la vallée en contrebas ; la sécheresse avait marqué le paysage et, à l'exception des champs cultivés autour d'Akbar, le reste semblait un désert aussi rude que les terres d'Egypte.

« J'ai entendu mes amis dire que les Assyriens allaient revenir, dit le gamin.

— Peut-être, mais ce que nous avons fait valait la peine ; c'est la manière que Dieu a choisie pour que nous apprenions.

— Je ne sais pas s'Il se donne beaucoup de mal pour nous, remarqua l'enfant. Il n'avait pas besoin d'être aussi sévère.

— Il a dû essayer par d'autres moyens, jusqu'à ce qu'Il découvre que nous ne L'écoutions pas. Nous étions trop habitués à nos existences, et nous ne lisions plus Ses paroles.

— Où sont-elles écrites ?

— Dans le monde autour de toi. Il suffit de faire attention à ce qui se passe dans ta vie, et tu vas découvrir où, à chaque moment du jour, Il cache Ses paroles et Sa volonté. Essaie d'accomplir ce qu'Il demande : c'est ta seule raison d'être en ce monde.

— Si je les découvre, je les écrirai sur les tablettes d'argile.

— Fais-le. Mais écris-les surtout dans ton cœur ; là, elles ne pourront pas être brûlées ou détruites, et tu les emporteras où que tu ailles. »

Ils marchèrent encore un moment. Les nuages étaient maintenant tout proches.

« Je ne veux pas entrer là-dedans, dit l'enfant en les montrant du doigt.

— Ils ne te causeront aucun mal : ce ne sont que des nuages. Viens avec moi. »

Il le prit par la main, et ils montèrent. Peu à peu, ils pénétrèrent dans le brouillard ; l'enfant se serra contre lui sans mot dire, même si, de temps en temps, Elie tentait d'engager la conversation. Ils marchèrent parmi les rochers nus du sommet.

« Retournons », pria l'enfant.

Elie décida de ne pas insister, cet enfant avait déjà rencontré beaucoup de difficultés dans sa brève existence et connu la peur. Il fit ce qu'il demandait ; ils sortirent de la brume et de nouveau distinguèrent la vallée en bas.

« Un jour, cherche dans la bibliothèque d'Akbar ce que j'ai laissé écrit pour toi. Cela s'appelle *Le Manuel du guerrier de la lumière*.

— Je suis un guerrier de la lumière, répliqua l'enfant.

— Tu sais comment je m'appelle ? demanda Elie.

— *Libération*, répondit le gamin.

— Assieds-toi là près de moi, dit Elie en indiquant un rocher. Il m'est impossible d'oublier mon nom. Je dois poursuivre ma mission, même si, en ce moment, tout ce que je désire est rester avec toi. C'est pour cela qu'Akbar a été reconstruite ; pour nous enseigner qu'il faut aller de l'avant, aussi difficile que cela puisse paraître.

— Tu t'en vas.

— Comment le sais-tu ? demanda-t-il, surpris.

— Je l'ai écrit sur une tablette, hier soir. Quelque chose me l'a dit ; peut-être ma mère, ou bien un ange. Mais je le sentais déjà dans mon cœur. »

Elie caressa la tête de l'enfant.

« Tu as su lire la volonté de Dieu, dit-il, content. Alors je n'ai rien à t'expliquer.

— Ce que j'ai lu, c'était la tristesse dans tes yeux. Je n'ai pas eu de mal, certains de mes amis l'ont perçue aussi.

— Cette tristesse que vous avez lue dans mon regard est une partie de mon histoire. Mais une petite partie, qui ne va durer que quelques jours. Demain, quand je prendrai la direction de Jérusalem, elle aura perdu de sa force, et peu à peu elle disparaîtra. Les tristesses ne durent pas éternellement, lorsque nous marchons vers ce que nous avons toujours désiré.

— Faut-il toujours partir ?

— Il faut toujours savoir quand finit une étape de la vie. Si tu persistes à y demeurer au-delà du temps nécessaire, tu perds la joie et le sens du repos. Et tu risques d'être rappelé à l'ordre par Dieu.

— Le Seigneur est dur.

— Seulement avec Ses élus. »

*

Elie regarda Akbar tout en bas. Oui, Dieu pouvait parfois se montrer très dur, mais jamais au-delà de ce que chacun pouvait endurer : l'enfant ignorait que, à l'endroit où ils étaient assis, Elie avait reçu la visite d'un ange du Seigneur et qu'il avait appris comment le ramener d'entre les morts.

« Je vais te manquer ? demanda-t-il.

— Tu m'as dit que la tristesse disparaissait si nous allions de l'avant, répondit le gamin. Il reste beaucoup à faire pour rendre Akbar aussi belle que ma mère le mérite. Elle se promène dans ses rues.

— Reviens ici lorsque tu auras besoin de moi. Et regarde en direction de Jérusalem : j'y serai, cherchant à donner un sens à mon nom, *Libération*. Nos cœurs sont liés à tout jamais.

— C'est pour cela que tu m'as amené en haut de la Cinquième Montagne ? Pour que je puisse voir Israël ?

— Pour que tu voies la vallée, la cité, les autres montagnes, les rochers et les nuages. Le Seigneur avait coutume d'ordonner à Ses prophètes de se rendre sur les montagnes pour converser avec Lui. Je me suis toujours demandé pourquoi, et maintenant je comprends la réponse : du sommet, nous sommes capables de voir tout petit. Nos gloires et nos chagrins perdent leur importance. Ce que nous avons gagné ou perdu est resté là en bas. Du haut de la montagne, tu peux voir comme le monde est vaste et comme l'horizon s'étend loin. »

L'enfant regarda tout autour. Du haut de la Cinquième Montagne, il percevait l'odeur de la mer qui baignait les plages de Tyr. Il entendait le vent du désert qui soufflait d'Egypte.

« Un jour, je gouvernerai Akbar, dit-il à Elie. Je connais ce qui est grand, mais je connais aussi chaque recoin de la cité. Je sais ce qu'il faut transformer.

— Alors, transforme-le. Ne laisse pas les choses se figer.

— Dieu ne pouvait-Il pas choisir une meilleure manière de nous montrer tout cela ? A un moment, j'ai pensé qu'Il était mauvais. »

Elie resta silencieux. Il se rappelait une conversation qu'il avait eue, des années auparavant, avec un prophète lévite, alors qu'ils attendaient que les soldats de Jézabel viennent les mettre à mort.

« Dieu peut-Il être mauvais ? insista l'enfant.

— Dieu est tout-puissant, répondit Elie. Il peut tout, et rien ne Lui est interdit ; sinon, cela signifierait qu'il existe quelqu'un de plus puissant et de plus grand que Lui pour l'empêcher de faire certaines choses. En ce cas, je préférerais adorer et révérer ce quelqu'un plus puissant. »

Il s'interrompit quelques instants, pour que le gamin pénètre bien le sens de ses propos. Puis il reprit :

« Cependant, dans Son infini pouvoir, Il a choisi de faire seulement le Bien. Si nous parvenons jusqu'à la fin de notre histoire, nous verrons que très souvent le Bien a l'apparence du Mal mais qu'il reste le Bien et fait partie du plan qu'Il a créé pour l'humanité. »

Il prit le garçon par la main et ils s'en retournèrent en silence.

*

Cette nuit-là, l'enfant dormit serré contre lui. Dès que le jour commença à poindre, Elie l'écarta délicatement de sa poitrine pour ne pas le réveiller.

Ensuite, il s'habilla du seul vêtement qu'il possédait et sortit. Sur le chemin, il ramassa un morceau
de bois et s'en fit un bâton. Il avait l'intention de ne
jamais s'en séparer : c'était le souvenir de son combat avec Dieu, de la destruction et de la reconstruction d'Akbar.

Sans regarder en arrière, il prit la direction
d'Israël.

Epilogue

Cinq ans plus tard, l'Assyrie envahit de nouveau le pays, cette fois avec une armée plus professionnelle et des généraux plus compétents. Toute la Phénicie tomba sous la domination du conquérant étranger, à l'exception de Tyr et de Sarepta, que ses habitants dénommaient Akbar.

L'enfant se fit homme, gouverna la cité et fut considéré comme un sage par ses contemporains. Il mourut âgé, entouré des êtres qu'il chérissait, et disant toujours qu'« il fallait garder la cité belle et forte, parce que sa mère se promenait encore dans ces rues ». Grâce à un système de défense développé conjointement, Tyr et Sarepta ne furent occupées par le roi assyrien Sennachérib qu'en 701 avant Jésus-Christ, presque cent soixante ans après les faits relatés dans ce livre.

Mais les cités phéniciennes ne retrouvèrent jamais leur importance ; elles subirent dès lors une succession d'invasions — par les néo-Babyloniens, les Perses, les Macédoniens, les Séleucides, et enfin les Romains. Pourtant elles ont continué d'exister jusqu'à nos jours, parce que, selon la tradition antique, le Seigneur ne choisissait jamais par hasard les lieux qu'Il désirait voir habités. Tyr, Sidon et Byblos font toujours partie du Liban, qui est aujourd'hui encore un champ de bataille.

Elie retourna en Israël et réunit les prophètes sur le mont Carmel. Là, il leur demanda de se séparer en deux groupes : ceux qui adoraient Baal, et ceux qui croyaient dans le Seigneur. Suivant les instructions de l'ange, il offrit un bouvillon aux premiers et leur enjoignit de prier à grands cris leur dieu de recevoir le sacrifice. La Bible raconte :

« A midi, Elie se moqua d'eux et dit : "Criez plus fort, c'est un dieu ; peut-être qu'il médite, ou qu'il est en voyage, ou qu'il dort."

Ils crièrent plus fort et, selon leur coutume, se tailladèrent à coups de couteaux et de lances, mais il n'y eut ni voix, ni personne qui répondît, ni aucune réaction. »

Alors Elie saisit l'animal et l'offrit selon les instructions de l'ange du Seigneur. A ce moment, le feu du ciel descendit et *« dévora l'holocauste, le bois, les pierres »*. Quelques minutes plus tard, une pluie abondante tomba, mettant fin à quatre années de sécheresse.

A partir de cet instant, une guerre civile éclata. Elie fit exécuter les prophètes qui avaient trahi le Seigneur, et Jézabel le recherchait partout pour le faire mettre à mort. Mais il se réfugia sur le flanc ouest de la Cinquième Montagne, qui donnait vers Israël.

Des gens venus de Syrie envahirent le pays et tuèrent le roi Achab, époux de la princesse de Tyr, d'une flèche qui pénétra accidentellement par une ouverture de son armure. Jézabel se réfugia dans son palais et, après quelques soulèvements populaires, après l'ascension et la chute de plusieurs gouvernants, elle finit par être capturée. Elle préféra se jeter par la fenêtre plutôt que de se livrer aux hommes envoyés pour l'arrêter.

Elie demeura dans la montagne jusqu'à la fin de ses jours. La Bible raconte qu'un certain soir, tandis qu'il conversait avec Elisée, le prophète qu'il avait désigné comme son successeur, « *un char de feu et des chevaux de feu les séparèrent l'un de l'autre ; et Elie monta au ciel dans la tempête* ».

Quelque huit cents ans plus tard, Jésus invite Pierre, Jacques et Jean à gravir une montagne. L'évangéliste Matthieu raconte que « [Jésus] *fut transfiguré devant eux ; son visage resplendit comme le soleil et ses habits devinrent blancs comme la lumière. Et voici que leur apparurent Moïse et Elie qui s'entretenaient avec lui* ».

Jésus demande aux apôtres de ne pas raconter cette vision tant que le Fils de l'homme ne sera pas ressuscité des morts, mais ils rétorquent que cela ne se produira que lorsque Elie reviendra.

Matthieu (17, 10-13) relata la suite de l'histoire :

« *Et les disciples l'interrogèrent : "Pourquoi donc les scribes disent-ils qu'Elie doit venir d'abord ?"*

Jésus répondit alors : "Certes, Elie va venir et il rétablira tout ; mais, je vous le déclare, Elie est déjà venu et, au lieu de le reconnaître, ils ont fait de lui tout ce qu'ils ont voulu."

Alors les disciples comprirent qu'il leur parlait de Jean le Baptiste. »

Composition réalisée par JOUVE

Achevé d'imprimer en juillet 2007 en France sur Presse Offset par

CPI

Brodard & Taupin

La Flèche (Sarthe).
N° d'imprimeur : 40211 – N° d'éditeur : 85291
Dépôt légal 1ʳᵉ publication : octobre 1999
Édition 11 – juillet 2007
LIBRAIRIE GÉNÉRALE FRANÇAISE – 31, rue de Fleurus – 75278 Paris cedex 06.

31/4710/5